JESSAMINE

ALSO BY SHANI STRUTHERS

EVE: A CHRISTMAS GHOST STORY
(PSYCHIC SURVEYS PREQUEL)

PSYCHIC SURVEYS BOOK ONE:
THE HAUNTING OF HIGHDOWN HALL

PSYCHIC SURVEYS BOOK TWO:
RISE TO ME

PSYCHIC SURVEYS BOOK THREE:
44 GILMORE STREET

BLAKEMORT
(A PSYCHIC SURVEYS COMPANION NOVEL BOOK ONE)

THIRTEEN
(A PSYCHIC SURVEYS COMPANION NOVEL BOOK TWO)

THIS HAUNTED WORLD BOOK ONE:
THE VENETIAN

THIS HAUNTED WORLD BOOK TWO:
THE ELEVENTH FLOOR

JESSAMINE

SHANI STRUTHERS

Jessamine
Copyright © Shani Struthers 2018

Authors Reach
www.authorsreach.co.uk

ISBN: 978-1-9999137-4-8

For Lesley – because it's your favourite.

Acknowledgements

First of all thanks to Patrice Brown for coming up with the title. I remember we were driving in my car and I said I wanted to write a book based in Scotland and give it a woman's name as a title. Immediately she came up with Jessamin. Jessamin became *Jessamine* and an idea was born...

Thanks also to my trusty band of beta readers – Robert Struthers, Lesley Hughes, Louisa Taylor, Margaret Johnson, Gail Keene and Jane Tyrrell – your feedback was invaluable (as ever!). Thanks also to Jeff Gardiner for first edits, V K McGivney for second edits and Gina Dickerson for a cover that perfectly captures the mood of the book. Last but by no means least, thanks to Scotland for being such a beautiful country to write about. Of all the places I've travelled, it's my favourite, and I hope to set many more books there.

Prologue

THE road is empty – three lanes coming out of nowhere and leading nowhere – an endless stretch of motorway. As always she is helpless, a wraith, unable to do anything more constructive than stand by and watch as a car speeds out of the darkness and breaks the stillness of the night. She holds her breath. The car is unmistakable. It's his car, his toy – a beautiful plaything driven way too fast.

Is anger the fuel propelling him forwards? They'd argued the last time they'd spoken. He was tired; she was tired; everyday stress building up until it reached boiling point, overflowing – overwhelming them both. She shouldn't have insisted or accused him as she'd done. Of course he's angry; he has every right to be.

In the distance an owl hoots – the sound a welcome distraction from the roar of the engine, from the accelerator being floored. It's clear ahead, so why not? If he has to come home, at least he can have a little fun on the way.

This scene, where the car whizzes by, replays over and over, the breeze in its wake causing her hair to ripple. Other than that the night is perfect – no rain, although it had rained earlier, with stars as bright as beacons. A clement October night, there's only a slight chill in the air; a chill that causes her to shiver.

Here he comes again. This time she strains to look inside

the car, to catch a glimpse of the man driving. There he is! His eyes are intent, staring straight ahead, his blonde hair falling forward slightly and covering his forehead. She can imagine the music on the CD player. Either Feeder or Biosphere, the latter ambient but still played at ear-splitting level.

Does the music distract him? Perhaps the owl swoops low. Or is he so tired – as tired as he professed to be – that his eyes close for a moment? One fateful moment.

She steels herself. This is when it happens. The car swerves – gracefully at first like a ballet dancer, but then more dramatically, spinning from lane to lane, crashing into the steel barrier before being shunted forwards. This is when she prays the car will stop, come to a grinding halt, the driver shaken but not hurt, his breath coming in short, sharp gasps – a lesson learnt. But the car doesn't stop and there's an embankment and trees. So many trees, waiting, like her, for impact.

She spins around too. The car – where's it gone? As though it were a hungry mouth, the night has devoured it. All she can hear is noise: the squeal of brakes – useless brakes – and then a thunderclap that rents the world in two. *Her* world. Finally, there is screaming, confusing her until she realises who's responsible. It's *her* voice, full of terror and disbelief. But as wretched as it is, she is thankful for it – it relieves the otherwise ominous silence, which is far, far worse. She screams and then she runs towards where the car has veered; where smoke is forming thick clouds of mist. At the edge of the precipice, she looks down. No one is crawling from the wreckage, looking up at her, an arm outstretched, bloodied and beseeching. There's just one unholy, tangled mess. She reaches up and tears at her hair, not screaming now but wailing, her heart on the point of exploding.

"James!" she cries. "James! James! JAMES!"

The realisation she must exist without him is too sudden; it's too much to bear. She yearns to be in that car also, her body smashed alongside his.

Her breath catching in her throat, it threatens to choke her. If only it would. Throwing her arms wide in supplication she is ready – waiting, *praying* – to be delivered.

She waits and then she wakes. Every morning Jessamin wakes.

Chapter One

EYES wide open, Jessamin stared at the ceiling. Her heaving chest would take a while to calm. At last, able to breathe a little easier, she pushed herself off the bed and walked over to the bay window, the bright morning sunlight forcing her to squint as she opened the curtains. Before her, in all its glory, lay Brighton, her hometown. From her south-facing hilltop position she could see rows and rows of terraced houses sandwiched together; the grey outline of Bedford Tower and the roof of St Bartholomew church - the tallest in Europe apparently. Beyond them only the sea.

For a few moments she stood and stared, committing to memory every colour, every contour, every haphazard detail; then she turned and walked away.

On the bedside table her phone rang.

"Hey, it's me, you up yet?"

"Hi, Sarah. Yeah, I'm up. I just need to shower and dress, then I'm good to go."

"Don't leave before I get there," Sarah replied, a dire warning in her voice.

"I won't," Jessamin promised, although if she were honest, she'd prefer to just slip away.

"See you soon," said Sarah, ending the call.

Stifling a yawn, Jessamin swapped the bedroom for the bathroom, ran the shower and stood beneath it, keeping the water cold initially to blast her awake. Sleep, as usual, had played hard to get. Most of the night she'd lain with her eyes stubbornly shut, willing oblivion to wrap its arms around her. It was only in the early hours she'd found such comfort; scant comfort as it turned out, with the nightmare quickly descending.

Increasing the water temperature, she allowed herself to wallow for a few moments in its steamy warmth, one finger idly tracing patterns on the glass door. What had once been a sensuous pleasure, often shared with James, was now a mere necessity best to get over and done with. Lingering no longer, she finished, grabbed her towel and packed away shampoo and conditioner. Pausing at the door, Jessamin glanced around. It was just another anonymous room – all signs she'd been there successfully erased.

The bedroom too was bereft of everything except her bed, a wardrobe and a Lloyd Loom chair – furniture the new owners wanted to keep. The only remaining personal items were her clothes, neatly laid out, and a holdall waiting beside them. Dropping the towel, Jessamin pulled on jeans, tee shirt and a jumper, securing her damp brown hair in a bun. She then turned to strip the bed – the bed she'd slept in for over a decade, her husband beside her. Pausing briefly, she ran her hand over the memory foam mattress, the cruel irony of its name not lost on her. She was leaving other items for Jane and Luke: the dining table, dining chairs, the sofa, and a coffee table. The rest of her furniture was in storage – and could stay there for all she cared.

Finally, slipping on socks and boots, Jessamin picked up her holdall, left the room without so much as a cursory glance backwards, and went to wait for Sarah downstairs.

She didn't have to wait long.

"Oh, Jess," said Sarah, entering the hallway. "I can't believe you're doing this." Following Jessamin through to the kitchen, she looked around in obvious dismay.

"The house looks so… sad."

"It won't be for long," Jessamin tried her best to reassure her. "Jane and Luke have got two young children. There'll be laughter here again soon."

"But this is your home, not theirs," Sarah protested, pushing strands of blonde hair out of her eyes. "I don't know how I'm ever going to pass it without crying, I'm just going to have to avoid this road I think. And not just this road, the entire area."

"Don't be silly," Jessamin smiled at her friend. "You'll get used to it… in time."

Sarah shook her head in denial. "I'll never get used to you not being here."

"In that case, you should understand why I'm doing this. I'll never get used to being here either – not without James."

Sarah gazed at her for a few moments and then stepped forward to hug her tightly. "I'm going to miss you so much."

"I'm going to miss you too," replied Jessamin, her voice muffled against Sarah's shoulder.

She was surprised to find tears pricking at her eyes; surprised because she didn't think she had any more to shed. But then Sarah was her rock – more so than ever recently; at her side day and night in those first days, despite the fact she had a husband of her own, one who was living and breathing, waiting for her at home.

"You're all that matters," Sarah had told her. "You'd do the same for me."

Jessamin couldn't resist following Sarah's eyes as they continued to sweep the room.

She'd been twenty, James thirty-two when they – or rather he – had bought the house. By then earning a fortune as a director in a multi-media company, he had thought it time to buy instead of rent. She was fresh out of college and temping, her earnings a pittance by comparison. He wanted Jessamin to move in straightaway, and she had, on condition that she'd pay the bills.

"Oh God," he'd teased. "We're gonna freeze."

But quickly she'd gone from temping to landing a job at a travel company in nearby Crawley, rising to Marketing Manager by the end of her second year, and earning a decent wage, enough to pay for heating and more besides.

She and James lived well – both busy with their careers but coming together during the evening to spend time with each other. Although they had many friends, it was their nights in alone, cooking dinner (or rather James cooking, as he had a real flair for it) and cuddling up on the sofa afterwards to watch a movie, that she loved the most. Jessamin never tired of those evenings; had looked forward to them, feeling ridiculously excited to see her husband, night after night, year after year.

The last time she spoke to James she'd been angry. It had been a crap day at work, her boss giving her hell because a major brochure – their main money-spinner – had missed its print deadline. It hadn't strictly been her fault, more a succession of mistakes from her team, some beyond her control, but she'd had to 'shut up and put up' because she was the manager. The last thing she needed was James calling to say he couldn't be bothered to drive home from London.

"No," she'd said. "I want you here, with me."

"But I won't have this report done until nine at least. It makes sense to stay."

"You've got your car and rush hour will be long over. You'll be home by eleven."

"Eleven? That's pushing it."

"Look, it doesn't matter. You'll be home that's the main thing."

"But I'm already exhausted. By the time I've finished I'll be on my knees."

His company kept a certain amount of rooms in a hotel close by if staff needed them. James knew he could get a bed there, a good night's rest, and return the next day refreshed. But it was Friday; she wanted to wake up with him on Saturday, spend the morning in bed together.

"Just come home," she'd repeated. "I feel like we never see each other any more."

"Oh, don't exaggerate," he'd said, amusement vying with the tiredness in his voice.

"But we don't. You're always working late and I'm home alone most of the time…" and then she'd added, "You're not having an affair, are you?"

She knew how ridiculous she sounded, petulant even, but she couldn't help it. She was fed up and getting more fed up by the minute. It really had been a rubbish day and now she had a rubbish evening ahead of her. She hated being on her own overnight, he knew that – every strange noise, every creak of Victorian floorboards, causing her imagination to run riot. Just as he laughed at her fear of being home alone, he now laughed at her accusation.

"An affair? Chance would be a fine thing."

Incensed at being mocked, particularly as she knew she deserved it, Jessamin started shouting. "You are, aren't you? That's why you won't come home. It's got nothing to do with work at all."

8

"Jess," he'd said eventually, finally giving in to annoyance, "you know as well as I do I am not having an affair but, if it means that much to you, I'll come home. Feeling like this, I don't fancy the drive in the dark, that's all. I wish I'd caught the bloody train now."

"Why didn't you then?"

"You know why, because I had to see some clients in Surrey first. It just seemed easier to go by car."

"Leave it there, get the train back."

"I can't leave it here all weekend, can I? The cost will be astronomical."

"Stop making excuses and come home."

"Okay, okay, you win," he'd conceded. "Give me an hour or so to finish and then I'll be on my way. I'm starving, though. Can you rustle up something to eat?"

"I'll do pasta," she'd replied, still grumpy even though she'd got her way; perhaps because she *had* got her way. "Something quick and easy."

"See you around eleven."

"Just hurry," she'd said, ending the call.

Two words; such simple words, but how she wished she could snatch them back.

It was well beyond midnight when there'd been a knock on the door. Fed up of waiting for James, she'd dozed off, Friday night TV unable to keep her rapt.

The late hour had barely registered. Instead, she flew to the door and yanked it open, not worried, angry still.

"James!" she'd yelled.

Two strangers stood there: a man, too young to be taken seriously as an officer of the law, and a shorter woman with concern etched all over her face. Concern for whom?

"Mrs Wade?" the female police officer enquired.

"Yes," she replied warily.

"Can we come in?"

From thereon memory faded, minutiae lost forever. She must have told them Sarah's telephone number because the next thing she knew Sarah was on her doorstep too, thanking the man and woman in uniform and telling them not to worry; that of course she would stay with Jessamin that night; that no way would she be left alone.

It took hours but gradually what the police had been trying to tell her; what Sarah had continued to impress on her; sank in, but only in snatches. Motorway crash. Speeding perhaps. Nobody else involved. He's dead. He's dead. He's dead.

"HE IS NOT DEAD!" she'd shouted at last. He couldn't be. Not James. He was warm and vital still, wholly alive. But the empty days that followed, the weeks and the months, proved otherwise. Her husband, her soul mate, her *raison d'être* was gone.

The world simply ceased to exist as she locked herself away. Self-loathing kicked in immediately. She couldn't bear her reflection in the mirror; wouldn't wash, wouldn't eat and sipped only infrequently at water, wanting her traitorous body to fade away, to disappear too. Friends and family all expressed concern, visited regularly, but ultimately were unable to help her; unable, in the end, to bear her grief. All except Sarah, who stayed, who cried and who finally demanded she damn well pull herself together, insisting that James would hate to see her this way; that he'd be heartbroken if he could.

And that did it. That's what got through.

Could James still see her? Was such a thing possible? What a comfort if it was. She imagined him close; talked to him, at first in her mind but gradually out loud. She'd tell him how much she loved him, how she missed him. 'Jessa*mine*' he used to call her, because she was his and he was hers. She reminded him of this as though it were a pact.

After months and months of talking to him – spending whole evenings doing so, even laughing on occasion when she recalled a joke or a funny incident they'd shared – there'd been so many – she had heard a voice.

Leave this place. Go.

She was startled at first; had looked wildly about her. Who did the voice belong to?

"James? Are you there?"

There was only silence.

Even so, a seed had been planted. The more she thought about leaving, the more attractive the prospect became. James wasn't in these four walls; James was in her heart. It was getting harder to bear the empty space beside her in bed. She couldn't stand eating alone at the breakfast bar either, or sitting on their sofa, curled up in one corner. The house, far from being a comfort, only served as a stark reminder that he was gone.

Sarah had been livid when she'd put it on the market.

"And where do you think you're going?" she'd asked. "What are you going to do?"

"I don't know yet," Jessamin replied. "Let's wait and see."

With property much sought after in Brighton, the house sold straightaway to a couple in a hurry to get their young daughters settled into one of three schools nearby – schools Jessamin had envisaged *her* children going to one day; the children she and James had talked about, and had decided to start trying for.

A cash deal, the sale had been straightforward, finalised in weeks. Where to go indeed? It took Jessamin only a few days to decide – she'd go to Scotland, the Lochalsh region as depicted in a painting that had hung in the living room of her family home. As a child the picture had fascinated her with its lowering sky and unconquerable mountains rising out of a depthless loch. Although crudely executed, passion was evident in every brushstroke; the artist had clearly found drama and excitement in that view, capturing the timeless essence of its beauty. She'd often find herself staring at it instead of at the TV. It was infinitely more interesting. Who lived in such a landscape, amidst such loneliness and desolation? She'd resolved to visit one day, to find out, but had taken her travels abroad instead; she barely knew her own country, let alone Scotland.

The painting – a modestly sized watercolour – was by an S McCabe, his or her signature a black scrawl. It was Jessamin's mother who had revealed it was the Lochalsh region.

"It's where your grandfather came from," she'd elaborated.

Jessamin knew that – his accent had always sounded heavy to her, exotic even.

"I liberated it from behind the sofa, that's where he kept it, shoved against the wall."

"Why did he keep it there?"

Her mother had shrugged. "I don't know, he never said. I liked it though."

She clearly liked it enough to hang it on the living room wall at least. "Did you spend time in Scotland too?" Jessamin asked.

"No. Dad moved down here long before I was born. He always said there was no point in going back; there's nothing much there, certainly no employment. It's bleak apparently."

If that were the case, it would suit her perfectly. What had happened to that painting? Her mother was dead; she died when Jessamin was in her mid-twenties. Her father had since re-married and lived in the south of France. His wife, much younger than him, was pregnant with their second child – a brand new family in the making. All the possessions furnishing the modest terraced home where Jessamin grew up had been divided between her, her father, her elder brother, Dane, and her Mum's sister, Lara. One of them must have the painting. She certainly hoped so – it would be awful to think of it no longer being in the family. Why she hadn't taken it, she couldn't fathom. Then again, when someone close to you dies, it's impossible to think straight – she knew that well enough by now. Instead, she'd focussed on other mementoes: jewellery – her mother's wedding ring in particular and a pearl choker she loved to wear; her wedding dress, and family photos, copious amounts of them. The picture that had registered so prominently in childhood had been forgotten – until now.

If Sarah had been livid when Jessamin put the house on the market, it was nothing compared to her reaction when she found out where she was planning to go.

"What?" she screamed. "It's the arse end of nowhere!"

"It's where I want to be," Jessamin coolly replied. And it was.

Scouring the Internet, she found a fully furnished cottage for rent – Skye Croft – on the edge of a small village called Glenelk, promising 'sublime views of the Isle of Skye from the warm and cosy living room.' Clicking on images of the interior, it did indeed look cosy with a real log fire, something she'd always coveted. The cottage also had a slate roof, a bright red door and land all around it. As she continued to stare at it, she suddenly heard the voice again.

13

That's it! That's the one!

It had to be James! Although his tone was much gruffer than she was used to. He was answering her, filling the void, guiding her. And whatever he wanted, she would do.

Sarah continued to make a fuss.

"I'm just going to rent," Jessamin assured her, "and only for six months. If I don't like it, I'll come back early. As long as I'm fully paid up, no-one will mind."

"And then what?" Sarah quizzed further.

"Then I'll buy a flat or something with the profit from the house.'

"A flat? First of all, you're giving up a lovely house for a miniscule, no doubt damp-ridden crofter's cottage in bloody Scotland of all places, and if that doesn't work out – which of course it won't – not to worry because you'll come back and buy a flat?" Sarah practically spat the last word at her. "It's wrong, Jess, all wrong."

Whether it was wrong or not, it was done. She was leaving, in a few minutes, in fact. Doing as the 'voice' had instructed: going away, to recuperate, to be closer to James, although in what way exactly, she wasn't yet sure. As far as she knew, he'd never been north of the border either; hadn't even mentioned wanting to go there. But the feeling it was the right place to be, persisted. That particular region of Scotland was not just the subject of a much-loved painting from childhood; it was also part of her heritage. It may not have impressed her grandfather but right now, in her blood, the call of the wild was strong.

Looking at her watch, she said, "It's time, Sarah. I have to go."

"Don't," Sarah pleaded. "Stay with me. I'll look after you."

"I can't stay, not here," Jessamin whispered back, biting down hard on her lip. And then looking firmly into Sarah's eyes, she added, "Not after what I've done."

"What you've done?" Sarah was incredulous – incredulous and angry too. "How many times do I have to tell you, what happened wasn't your fault."

It was! A voice raged inside her – not James's this time; it was very much her own. *It was!*

Chapter Two

"SO," Jessamin asked James, "how come we never visited Scotland?"

"I don't know, too busy going abroad I suppose."

"Yeah," she conceded, quickly checking the traffic behind her in the rear-view mirror before pulling into the middle lane. "I suppose we were."

"And it's cold, arctic on occasion."

Jessamin pulled a face. "Don't remind me. I've seen the weather forecasts."

"Did you remember to pack thermals?"

"I did. The boot's full of them."

"So, come on, run it by me one more time: why are we doing this?" James continued – the James in her head; the James she had breathed life back into.

"Doing what?" Deliberately she played dumb, intent on keeping the conversation flowing.

"You know what." His tone was playful rather than annoyed. "I mean, I know what you said about that painting in your mum's house; how much you liked it; how it used to make you dream of hunky Highlanders coming down from the mountains to sweep you off your feet; but Sarah was right. Glenelk really is the arse end of nowhere."

"I thought you liked the cottage I chose!"

"To be honest, I wasn't taking much notice."

"Oh." That was a surprise, especially as she thought she had his seal of approval. Answering his original question, she said, "To be closer to you."

James seemed to consider this. She could imagine his look exactly – his brow slightly furrowed; his head tilted to one side; his blue eyes preoccupied – allowing her the opportunity to gaze at him unreservedly. She'd always loved his face: he was gently handsome, a bit like the actor, Robert Redford. She'd once watched a film he'd starred in alongside Paul Newman: *Butch Cassidy and the Sundance Kid*. Her mum preferred Newman, had swooned over him, but Redford was the one who appealed to her. As soon as she saw James, she was struck by the likeness. He in turn compared her to Rachel Weisz. 'It's your eyes,' he'd said. 'They're green like hers; feline.'

"Christ," Jessamin cried out, only just managing to avoid a white saloon car as it swerved in front of her.

"Bloody Volvo drivers," James cursed also. "They think they own the road."

"He must be on drugs or something the way he's driving." Jessamin tried to control her trembling. "Shame I didn't manage to get his number plate, I could have reported him."

"He's gone – that's all that matters. Just keep your eyes peeled and drive safely. I want you to arrive in one piece at least."

Jessamin had only just started driving again. For so long – since his accident – she couldn't even contemplate it. But James had finally persuaded her.

"You've *got* to drive, Jess. How are you going to get around?"

"By bus?" she'd offered.

"That's still a form of driving."

"But it's less risky."

"How?"

"I don't know," she'd struggled with that one. "Buses can't go as fast."

Aware of her true meaning, James replied, "Jess, I *wasn't* going fast."

"You were going fast enough," she mumbled back.

"Accidents happen." He'd sighed heavily as he said it. "You know my theory: we've all got a sell by date and mine just happened to be up. All this refusing to drive business, it's ridiculous. You've got to take control and it's not just the car I'm talking about."

He was right and she knew it. Six weeks ago she'd had some refresher lessons and attended a road safety programme. And now here she was, driving hundreds of miles and feeling really quite confident about it, despite the stupid Volvo driver – confident because she wasn't alone, even though all passenger seats were empty.

"That's it, cruise nice and steady: keep your distance and just focus on the road ahead," James told her and that's exactly what she did. Heading onto the M1, she drove further and further north, leaving behind the only home she'd ever known.

"I'm still confused," James said after a few moments of companionable silence.

"What about?"

"Why you're moving to Scotland to be closer to me. We're close enough already, aren't we?"

"Yeah... but..."

"But what?"

"There's so much noise in Brighton, so much jingle jangle."

"Jingle, jangle?" He was amused again, she could tell.

"I just think if I go somewhere quieter, less polluted, I'll be able to hear you better."

"Liar."

Jessamin's mouth dropped open. "James, what the—"

"Relax, relax." He was laughing outright now. "You can hear me perfectly well, Jessamin Wade, I know you can. What you're hoping is that you'll be able to see me as well."

"I'm not," she protested.

"Do you really want me to repeat myself?"

Jessamin sighed heavily, deliberately so. "You know what your trouble is, don't you? You think you know everything."

Again she heard that laugh – like quicksilver – far too fleeting.

Bypassing Northampton, she couldn't resist asking. "But will I? See you again I mean?"

"Concentrate on driving," was his teasing reply.

* * *

Jessamin stopped overnight in York at a Premier Inn – the hotel chain that promised you a good night's sleep or your money back. *We'll see about that*, she thought, checking into a room just like every other room in the building, and therefore soulless. It was comfortable though, she had to admit, and spacious. Kicking off her boots, she lay down, right in the middle of the double bed.

"Another long day tomorrow," James whispered as her eyes began to flutter, the exhaustion of driving such a long distance on virtually no sleep catching up with her. "Sleep well, my love, and dream of sweet things."

"Stay with me?" she murmured.

19

"Always. Now hush, darling, my Jess, Jessa*mine*; drift away."

And she did – not stirring, not dreaming either, until the room was light again. Pushing herself up on to one elbow, she squinted at the clock. It was seven thirty – later than she'd intended to wake. Quickly, she calculated how long the day's journey was likely to take. From York to the North West Highlands it would be another seven hours at least, with the lack of motorways beyond Glasgow the main reason. If she left within the hour, she'd be at Glenelk by late afternoon. Being early March, that would give her plenty of time to get her bearings and settle in before the night took hold again.

She hadn't really fancied breakfast, but James insisted.

"It's not just the car that needs fuel; you do too. Go and eat."

In the adjoining restaurant, empty but for two elderly couples and a group of four friends, all female, Jessamin helped herself to coffee, a croissant and a pat of butter – rock hard she noted, and therefore of very little use. Still, she was glad James had insisted – she *was* hungry. She devoured the croissant and then went back for a second one.

As she returned, a waiter appeared at the side of her table, a bored young man with acne-pitted cheeks. "Any hot items for you?"

"Hot items?" she queried, temporarily nonplussed.

"Bacon, sausage, eggs and tomatoes" he reeled off. "You can have them boiled, scrambled or fried, the eggs I mean."

She'd gathered he meant that. God, he looked bored. As bored as she had become in her own job – able to do it on autopilot with no engagement of the brain at all. Since James's accident, she hadn't stepped foot over the threshold of *First Resort*. Her boss understood at first but his understanding had quickly worn thin, and he demanded she return to work with what could only be described as thinly disguised menace. Refusing to be bullied, she'd eventually told him to find another Marketing Manager, even offering to return all monies paid since her compassionate leave had begun. Money wasn't something she needed to worry about, not anymore. A natural financier, James had invested wisely. That, and the sale of their house, had made her rich by many people's standards, although she'd rather be dirt poor, living in a tent and feeding off berries if it meant she could be with him again.

"You, living in a tent?" She could hear him laughing at the mere thought of it. "That one time we went camping in the New Forest, do you remember? It was a few years ago now. You hated it: you complained about the spiders, the cold, how far we'd pitched from the shower block, about the shower block itself. Try as I might, I could never persuade you to go again."

"It's a man thing, camping," Jessamin had insisted, confessing afterwards that yes, she did appreciate a little luxury in life; a power shower for one thing, central heating and windows and doors hermetically sealed to keep out incessant insects. "Still, if it meant I could have you back, I'd live under a scrap of tarpaulin, never mind a tent."

Breakfast finished, Jessamin headed to her car – a Land Rover Freelander, bought especially to tackle the Highland terrain. She'd never driven a 4 by 4 before; she'd had a Fiat 500 and James had his Alfa Romeo. The Alfa had been written off in the accident and the Fiat was far from practical as far as Scotland was concerned, so it had to go. She liked her new car; it wasn't too big and it was easy to drive. She also liked how sturdy it was, in the event of… of…

"James, I reckon it'll take another seven hours to get there," Jessamin said, refusing to allow that thought to develop further.

"You'd better get a move on then," he replied and she could just imagine him settling into the passenger seat, folding his arms and looking straight ahead.

Holding that vision in her head, she smiled as she released the handbrake.

It was just after midday when she crossed over the Scottish border, her heart giving a lurch that she'd left one country behind and entered another. The first mistake she made was going through Glasgow rather than trying to skirt around it. The roads, clear until then, became snarled with traffic. An hour and a half later and she'd travelled a mere twenty miles. The motorway continued only briefly after Glasgow, diminishing to two-lane roads that wound through villages such as Dumbarton and Luss – the latter overlooking Loch Lomond, and as hauntingly beautiful as it was reputed to be. Service at the nearby Drover's Inn – one of Scotland's oldest inns – was far more enthusiastic than it had been in the Premier Inn. Jessamin relished the almost musical accent of the sweet young waitress who fetched her sandwich and coffee. It sounded so romantic somehow.

"You and your rose-coloured glasses," she heard James remark, but she was right, the Scots *were* a romantic people – you only had to look at the history books to see that – and fiercely proud, fighting for their country, against all odds on occasion, and winning too. In the Battle of Bannockburn, for instance, in 1313, the English outnumbered the Scots by thousands, but the Scots still proved victorious, refusing to bow down to the sovereignty of Edward II. She was proud to have such blood flowing through her veins; she only wished she knew more about her heritage. Mum had never really spoken about the Scottish side of their family; the picture in the living room was the only nod towards it. As for her Scottish grandfather, he had died when she was seven. Apart from his accent, she remembered an insular man, as remote as the land he came from.

"I don't think he and my mother were ever truly happy together," her mother had confided.

"Why not?" In her youthful naivety, she'd thought marriage equalled automatic bliss.

"I don't really know. It was just something my sister and I sensed. They were polite to each other, mum and dad. It wasn't as if they rowed but there was a definite sadness between them, especially on my mother's part – a sadness that was there I suspect because she could never quite reach him. Sometimes politeness between two people exists to avoid honesty. Honesty is always best. Remember that."

And she had; she and James had always been honest with one another – it was a promise they'd made before getting married. Why then had she accused him of having an affair that night? She didn't know – it was the first time she'd ever done that.

"Babe, forget it," he'd told her so many times since. Or had he? Was it really just her own voice trying to salve her conscience in some way? Trying to make what she'd done – insisting he drive such a long way home when he was exhausted – more bearable? If so, it was despicable. She didn't deserve to forget what she'd done. Her words, her selfish insistence, had resulted in tragedy. She deserved to be in pain, wherever she went.

The rest of the journey was silent. James was quiet too, as

if understanding that nothing he could say right now would make a difference. Only barely did she register the beauty of the countryside that surrounded her – dramatic hills flanking either side of the road and becoming steeper; becoming mountains. Her sat nav was doing a fine job of leading her onwards, and Jessamin trusted blindly in it. For miles and miles, she saw barely any houses, no towns and no garages even, only other motorists, and they were few and far between. It really felt like she was leaving civilisation behind, with no clue as to what she was going to do with herself for the foreseeable future. If she was artistic, she could paint; if she was literary, she could write. Unfortunately, she was neither. Marketing was her trade but what the hell could you market in the arse end of nowhere? No matter: she'd simply eat, drink and sleep – go through the motions just as she had in Brighton – without friends or family cajoling her to do anything more. She'd be at one with nature, with the world around her, and perhaps, with luck, the world beyond her too.

"I knew it," James snapped to attention. "I knew you were going to Scotland to try and connect with me further."

"And you have a problem with that?" she replied, smiling for the first time in three hours.

"No, not at all."

"Are you sure? You don't sound sure."

"It's not that... it's just..."

"What? Come on, James, be honest, we always said we would be."

When silence continued, Jessamin had to prompt him.

"James..."

Eventually he answered.

"I don't want you to be disappointed, that's all."

Chapter Three

AT the last hurdle, the sat nav failed. 'Perform a legal U-turn' was all it had said for the last three miles – the robotic female voice very sure of itself. When Jessamin had given in and done as instructed, it continued to say the same thing! Worried that the machine, in its confusion, might combust, she leant over and switched it off. The owner of the cottage, Mr Fionnlagh Maccaillin, had emailed her with directions and she pulled into the side of the road to re-read them.

She didn't have to go as far as the village apparently; the house was on the outskirts. Peering out of the windscreen, she could hardly believe how dark it was. Beyond the car's headlights, she could make out nothing; it really was as black as coal. How she wished she'd woken earlier and skipped breakfast; made it there in daylight. Already she'd negotiated what appeared to be a mountain pass – the steep climb and then descent suggested so – although the road itself had been wide, well maintained and therefore not too fearsome. On this side of the mountain, however, the night seemed much more ominous. As she had driven onwards, the directions didn't make sense. There was supposed to be a track to the cottage just off the main road to the village but if there was, it was in hiding.

She sighed. "Great, I'm going to end up sleeping in my car at this rate."

"No you're not," James was instantly there to reassure her. "Go into the village. There must be a pub or a shop where you can ask for directions."

Grateful for his advice, she drove on. A sign by the side of the road told her she had indeed reached the village of Glenelk – population 283. There were a few houses dotted round, all detached and all on the left side; some on the hillside overlooking the loch and some nearer to the road.

Where's the pub? Where the hell is it?

Jessamin began to get agitated; the village seemed mainly residential. Soft amber light from behind curtained windows might appear welcoming to some, but it made her – a stranger – feel more lost than ever. At last she spied the village store. Hardly a major commercial enterprise, it was yet another house and, damn it, it was closed! Jessamin contemplated knocking on someone's door then decided against it. The car would be comfortable enough for the next few hours. And even if it wasn't, she'd only have to endure it until dawn when she could see where she'd gone wrong.

"Carry on a bit further," urged James.

She did, none too hopefully. She was beginning to see what Sarah had meant – her mother too. This was beyond bleak. What kind of people could bear it? Little wonder her grandfather had been remote. In a place like this she imagined people to be extensions of the land.

"There's no bloody pub!"

No sooner had the words left her mouth then she saw it – The Stag. On its weathered signboard was a somewhat faded illustration of the creature commonly known as The Monarch of the Glen standing against a sage green background. Jessamin could see the lights were on. It must be open!

With a sigh of relief, she pulled into the car park where

another Land Rover, larger than hers and mud-splattered, was the only other occupant. Crunching across the gravel path, shivering in the night air, she took a deep breath before entering. Despite the lone car, The Stag was not empty. On the contrary, it was really rather lively. There were several groups of people, all men she noticed, of varying ages and builds – some frail and old, some robust and hardy. Without fail, each and every one of them stopped what they were doing to stare at her, and an uncomfortable silence ensued.

"Smile," advised James.

And smile she did. Tentatively at first, widening into an impressive grin; but Jessamin didn't feel like smiling in the least. She felt like turning on her heel and getting the heck out of there; rushing back to the anonymous safety of noisy, neon streets and big impersonal crowds. This was a close-knit community, one she didn't belong to. Then she reminded herself she *did* belong. Her grandfather had been born and brought up near here; some of these people might even be related to her... a startling thought.

"Erm... hello," she said at last.

A man stepped forward – big and burly – his red face suggesting a fondness for liquor.

"Can I help you?"

"Hello," she said again, stepping forward too and holding out her hand. As she did, she took in the faded carpet beneath her feet; the dark veneer of the bar; the scruffy, mismatched assortment of tables and chairs, and the green plaid curtains at two large oak-framed windows. This was a far cry from the modern, chic bars she was used to.

"My name is Jessamin Wade, I'm the new tenant of Skye Croft. I... I can't find it. I was hoping someone might tell me where it is."

"Maccaillin didn't provide you with directions?" the man queried, ignoring her hand.

"Well, yes, he did, but daft as this sounds, I still can't find it."

The man's face, so forbidding before, so suspicious, relaxed slightly. After a few agonising seconds during which Jessamin wondered if she was going to be ejected into the street and barred forevermore from The Stag, the inmates declaring in true *League of Gentlemen* style, 'this is a local pub for local people', the man broke into a grin.

"Pleased to meet you," he said, proffering his hand at last. "I'm Winn Greer, the proprietor. I'm sure one of our fine young men will be only too pleased to escort you to the cottage."

"Oh, Mr Greer, hi." God, she was relieved and so was James. She could hear him chuckling to himself in the recesses of her mind. "There's no need to show me. Like I said, just point me in the right direction and I'll be on my way."

"Call me Winn," the man insisted, putting his arm around her and moving her closer to the bar. "And it's not a problem, not at all. Dougie, fetch a stool for the young lady."

Dougie – the embodiment of a bonny Scots lad if ever there was one, with his blonde curls and bright blue eyes – did as he was told. The occupants of the pub drew closer, introducing themselves one by one – not hostile at all but very friendly.

"I think it's fair to say we don't see many new faces this way," Winn explained. "So please, forgive our initial curiosity. Now, what are you having? Whisky?"

"Whisky? Goodness no! I'm driving."

"Och, you've no need to worry, there's very little in the way of traffic on the roads up here, especially at this time of night," Winn answered jovially.

"No," Jessamin remained firm. "I don't drink and drive."

Winn seemed slightly taken aback by her insistence. "A coke then?"

"That'd be lovely, thank you."

"Do you know Maccaillin?" Dougie asked, with a slight frown.

Jessamin shook her head. "All correspondence between us has been via email."

"The marvels of modern technology," said someone whose name she hadn't caught.

Looking around, she said, "I take it he's not here tonight?"

"Here?" that same someone said, a distinct note of sarcasm in his voice. "He doesn't come in here; he keeps himself to himself does Maccaillin. Since he's been back anyway."

"Why's that?" Jessamin was genuinely interested but no one, it seemed, was telling.

Sipping her drink, she realised how tired she was. All she wanted was to find the cottage, get inside, and close the door.

It was Rory who offered to escort her there – cousin to Dougie apparently, but without the blonde curls; on the contrary, his hair was red and closely cropped. He would accompany her in her Land Rover and then run back when she was safely ensconced.

"That's really inconvenient for you, though," Jessamin protested.

"Not at all," Rory denied. "It's a short run, ten minutes at most."

After saying goodbye to everyone, Jessamin followed Rory outside. He boldly led the way even though it was her car they were walking to. She half expected him to take her keys too and do the driving. Thankfully, he walked round to the passenger door.

Once inside, he turned to her. "Jessamin's an unusual name. Is it a derivative of Jessica?"

"I don't think so," she answered, putting the car into gear and returning to what could only loosely be described as the main road. "My mum chose it. She thought it was pretty as well as unusual. As far as I know it's an old French name, an alternative to Jasmine."

"Are you part French?" Rory enquired, a note of awe in his voice.

Again Jessamin shook her head.

"Sorry to disappoint, but no, I'm part Scottish actually. My grandfather came from here."

"From Glenelk?"

Jessamin thought for a moment.

"Do you know? I'm not entirely sure. But from Lochalsh definitely."

"What was his name?" Rory seemed intrigued.

"Ben Murray."

"Ben Murray?" Rory repeated.

"That's right. Do any Murrays live here still?"

"Not that I know of, and I know pretty much everyone hereabouts. There are several villages in the Lochalsh region though. The Kyle is the largest. Perhaps you'll find information about your family there. Is that why you're here? On a quest?"

"Oh no," Jessamin corrected him, "I just... I wanted to get away from it all for a while and this seemed as good a place as any. The family connection, it's an added interest certainly; it's nice to see where my family came from, but really it's just a coincidence."

"No such thing as coincidence," Rory replied, serious all of a sudden.

Before she could ask him why he thought that, he started pointing. "Skye Croft's up there, make a left turn into the drive. Careful though, it's a sharp left."

After following his instructions, Jessamin pulled into the hard standing before the cottage – able to make it out only because its gleaming white walls were such a contrast to the night.

"Lovely spot you've got yourself here," remarked Rory.

Was it? It was too dark to see.

Climbing out of the car, she let out a cry.

"What's the matter?" Rory was all concern suddenly.

"The key, I never once asked Mr Maccaillin where the house key was."

"The key?" Rory let out a bellow of a laugh. "No one bothers with keys around here. The door will be open."

"Open? But..." she stopped talking and hurried after him instead.

He was right. The door *was* open, leading straight into a low-ceilinged living room.

"You go in and make yourself comfortable. I'll bring your bags in."

"Thank you," replied Jessamin, fumbling for a light switch.

When she turned on the light the room was thrown into view – 'cosy' was indeed an apt description. The small room was furnished with a sofa, an armchair – both with folded tartan blankets on the backrests – and a small pine table with two chairs positioned by the window. There was also an open fireplace with a wicker log basket beside it. Several rugs overlapping each other covered what looked like the original

31

flagstone floor.

Rory, who was taller than her, had to bend slightly before entering the croft.

"Shall I get a fire going?" he asked.

"That's very kind of you, Rory, but not tonight thanks. It's warm enough in here. I might just hit the sack, get sorted in the morning."

"Probably not a bad idea," agreed Rory. "You do look tired, if you don't mind me saying."

She didn't. Smiling, she thanked him for bringing her bags in.

"Will we see you at The Stag anytime soon?" he enquired.

"Oh, well…" she hesitated. "If I'd be welcome?"

He looked perplexed. "Why wouldn't you be?"

"Erm…" How was she going to put this? "I didn't see any other women in there tonight. I just thought…"

"That we still live in the seventeenth century round these parts?"

"No, honestly, erm…" she faltered again. Clearly she'd offended him.

She was relieved when he laughed. "Believe it or not, we're as modern in Scotland as you are in the south. Contrary to what you might think, women are not chained to the kitchen sink whilst their men carouse after a hard day's hunting in the hills. It's much more likely they pursue careers of their own and social lives too – in fact, the girls round here, they're a pretty spirited bunch. They're the ones with the upper hand."

"Oh, that's great." Her shoulders slumped in relief.

"We've even got Wi-Fi. And Sky TV."

"Okay, okay, I get it," she answered, somewhat sheepishly. "By the way, how'd you know I'm from the south?"

"Your accent?" he offered, still distinctly amused.

"Oh yes, of course." She'd never felt so stupid.

"So, will we see you at the pub soon? It's quite the meeting place in the village, along with Maggie's living room on a Thursday evening."

"Maggie?"

"Aye, you'll meet Maggie soon enough."

"Oh right. Yes, I'll come down and introduce myself soon."

"You do that, don't hide away. Isolation, it's not good for the soul. We're social animals, as much as dogs are, as wolves. It's amazing how often we forget that."

After delivering such an unusual farewell, Rory disappeared into the night, breaking into a run almost as soon as he was out the door.

"Well, here we are," said Jessamin, hoping James was listening in. "James?"

"Yeah, I'm here. What are you going to do, explore?"

"You bet. Coming?"

"Try and stop me."

The kitchen was the only other room downstairs. The cabinets – made from some sort of wood – oak she guessed – looked handcrafted. Above the units, the walls had been freshly tiled and on the granite worktop stood the usual implements: a kettle, a toaster, and a knife block. She guessed the flagstone floor would be cold to walk on and resolved to get some slippers. Upstairs, either side of a small bathroom were two equally proportioned bedrooms, both with cast iron beds and both adorned with plump and inviting duvets. They were sparsely furnished, with a wardrobe in one and a chest of drawers in the other. She chose the one positioned directly above the living room. Its simple, plain red curtains and tiny window were identical to those in the other bedroom, but it was the one that was loch facing. Jessamin was also glad to note it was carpeted upstairs; pale grey and soft underfoot.

"Two up, two down, that'd be an apt description I think," said James, wryly.

"It's just me. It's all I need."

"Just you?" James queried.

"Physically I mean," she replied, laughing.

"I suppose I don't take up much space, do I?"

"More's the pity," Jessamin muttered, tiredness beginning to get the better of her.

"You need to rest."

"I know, my eyes, they're closing of their own accord."

"Go and lie down. The morning will soon be here."

"I'm going to do just that," she said, removing her jeans and jumper.

Under the duvet, she imagined James lying beside her, holding her hand, eager to embark on this new adventure with her. After a while she could almost feel the heat emanating from him, warming her to the core.

"James," she said, just before sleep took her. "What do you think Rory meant?"

"Sorry, I'm not with you?"

"You know, when I was talking about my grandfather being from here, I said it was just a coincidence. He replied, 'There's no such thing as coincidence.' What did he mean?"

"Perhaps he subscribes to Einstein's theory."

"Einstein?"

"Yeah you know, coincidence – it's just God's way of remaining anonymous."

Chapter Four

IT was well past his grandfather's suppertime when Fionnlagh Maccaillin returned to Comraich. Rushing in through the front door, he went immediately to the living room where the old man was dozing in his armchair.

"I'm sorry I'm late, Seanair," he said, using the Gaelic term for 'grandfather'. "I was getting Skye Croft ready for the new tenant, she's arriving today. Are you hungry?"

His grandfather opened his eyes with a slowness that pierced Finn's heart. In his youth, Seanair had been such an energetic man, the life force of Comraich. Coming up to his eighty-third year, he was beginning to decline and the house alongside him.

Stan cleared his throat before answering. "Aye, lad, but I'll have something small, a sandwich perhaps, nothing more. I don't want you to go to any bother."

"It's no bother," Finn replied, heading out of the living room and into the kitchen.

The fridge boasted few provisions and Finn cursed under his breath. He should have stocked up on groceries today but instead, after seeing to his grandfather's breakfast and ensuring he was comfortable, he'd headed out into the wilderness. Finn did this often, spending hours losing himself amongst the mountains. At lunchtime, he'd checked on Stan and then gone straight to Skye Croft to provide basic supplies for his tenant when she arrived – tea, coffee, bread and milk. She'd emailed a few days ago to say she didn't expect to be there until late afternoon; the village store was likely to be closed by then.

Once at the cottage, Finn didn't immediately return to Comraich, but lingered in the living room. There was no reason for him to do so – everything at Skye Croft was in perfect order – but he was trying to delay the inevitable. He'd been home for just over eight months and it had been a difficult decision to make – coming back. Despite his grandfather's best efforts and those of his childhood friend, Maggie, his memories of time spent in the village were not happy ones. He'd been away for fifteen years – long enough some might say – but now that time seemed fleeting. If it were not for the fact that his grandmother had been ill and Seanair needed him, he might never have returned.

In his mind, death and Comraich were synonymous. Gran had died here in December, but she was far from the only one. His mother, Kristin, had died there too when he was no more than a year old, followed by his father, some years later. Although Finn had two sisters, they were much older than he was and both had moved as far away as possible as soon as they could. They had families of their own now; their own lives. They hadn't come back for Gran's funeral and nor had Finn insisted. Perhaps to everyone's relief.

Hours had passed at Skye Croft and still he couldn't tear himself away; the cottage seemed to want to hold onto him. How he wished he could stay; never bother again with the outside world and the horrors it held. Peace – that's all he craved, all he'd ever wanted. But he had to get back. Duty called. Duty the army had instilled in him.

Fearing the new tenant would find him still there upon

her arrival, Finn had returned to Comraich; to his grandfather; to a kitchen full of dust-laden cobwebs. What was he going to cook for Seanair? He wasn't concerned for himself but he couldn't let the old man go hungry. Closing the fridge door and rooting around in cupboards, he unearthed a tin of baked beans. Checking it wasn't out of date, he opened it, warmed the contents and spooned it over toast. Placing the plate on a tray with a cup of tea, he retraced his footsteps.

"It's not much, Seanair," Finn apologised. "I'll go shopping tomorrow, get some proper food in."

Stan sat up straight as the tray was put in front of him. "Its fine, lad, I'm grateful for it."

Lad – it was what his grandfather always called him, no matter that he was a grown man now.

"Did you enjoy your walk today?"

Finn nodded although 'enjoy' was not the word he'd use. The walks helped, that's all.

"And the cottage, it's ready, is it?"

"Aye, Seanair, it's comfortable enough."

Whilst his grandfather ate, Finn crossed to the sideboard and poured himself a generous measure of whisky, swirling the contents around the glass tumbler for a few seconds before lifting it to his mouth and draining it. He worried he was drinking too much of late, but it helped to numb him – both physically and mentally. Even so, he'd need to watch it. In no way did he want to resemble another drunk who'd lived at Comraich: his father. But right now, he couldn't help but pour himself another shot.

His grandfather pushed his plate away, the contents only half-eaten.

"Can you not manage anymore?" Finn asked.

Stan shook his head. "That's enough, thanks."

Again, he felt a pang. The old man ate so sparingly. It was as if he were already giving up, which caused mixed emotions in Finn. He didn't want Stan to die – far from it, his grandfather was his only real family – but when he did go, he'd be free of this place and that would bring with it a certain amount of relief.

Stan brought the conversation back round to the new tenant.

"Odd, isn't it, a young lass coming to live in a place like this on her own?"

Returning with another full glass to sit opposite his grandfather, Finn shrugged. "She probably has her reasons."

"I don't doubt it. Look in on her tomorrow though, will you? Make sure she's settled."

Finn assured him he would before leaning forward to stoke the fire.

A companionable silence followed, Finn doing little more than staring at the flames, realising how beautiful they were but also how deadly. The damaged skin on the right side of his body itched, although he refused to lift his hand and scratch – he simply ignored it. When his grandfather spoke again, he flinched; he had thought the old man asleep.

"Ina's son, Dougie, came by today."

"Oh?"

"He was looking for you," Stan answered.

"Me? I don't understand."

"He has a hankering to join the army, wanted your advice."

Finn could feel his hands start to shake.

"Finn... are you okay?"

Quickly, he pulled himself together.

"I'm fine. What did you say?"

"He wants to come back tomorrow."

"Tomorrow?"

"Is that all right, lad?"

He wanted to shout, to yell and to roar. No, it wasn't all right! *Nothing* was all right. But he didn't. Instead, he forced himself to take a deep breath and kept his voice steady.

"Seanair, either you tell him or I will, I've no advice to give."

Chapter Five

GASPING for a cup of tea, Jessamin pulled on the clothes she'd discarded the previous evening and made her way to the kitchen – praying there'd be tea bags as she'd forgotten to pick up any when she'd stopped in Luss. Milk she didn't care about – she could handle her tea black. Lately she preferred it.

As she had suspected, the kitchen flagstones were cold against her bare feet. In fact, the whole house had grown colder overnight; she would have to work out the heating system and get the place warmed up a bit. She'd get a log fire roaring too and relax in front of it with a good book, having brought several with her; a perfect way to while away the hours.

On the kitchen counter, three ceramic jars promised tea, coffee and sugar. Opening the jars she found they were indeed packed to the brim. In the fridge, there was milk too. She flicked the switch on the kettle and whilst waiting for the water to boil, opened and closed various cupboards and drawers. They seemed to be stocked with just about every cooking utensil the heart desired – not that her heart did desire anything cooking-related, but perhaps she would make more of an effort here; make good use of traditional Scottish ingredients such as salmon and venison. She'd probably end up eating a lot better than she had in recent times, by default more than anything. She had a sneaking suspicion Marks & Spencer microwave meals, or any brand of microwave meals for that matter, could not be found readily. She might even put on weight. She'd lost a lot over the last year and a half and it didn't suit her; her face looked drawn at times.

Wondering how long a round trip to the nearest city – Inverness – would take, Jessamin took her tea and went through to the living room, which was still snug, despite sunlight streaming through the curtains. Opening them, the sight greeting her caused her eyes to widen. She expected magnificence but this was something else, something more. Instead of an unruly jumble of rooftops and chimneys, there was wilderness: acres and acres of glorious wilderness. A loch, deep and wide, separated the mainland from Skye; an island that instantly reminded her of a slumbering whale. Above it the sky was blue, with not a cloud in sight. Both land and water dazzled beneath.

After a few moments admiring the scene, she went outside, eager to see what lay behind the house too. It might be bright but it was bitterly cold, causing her to tighten her grip around the hot drink in her hands. A picket fence marked her land, or more accurately the land belonging to the cottage. There was no grass inside it, just gravel and a rotary clothesline. But beyond the fence there was green aplenty; albeit frosted green – with fields, trees and hills in the distance. It was nothing less than idyllic. The air felt pure, much cleaner than she'd ever known it. She closed her eyes and breathed in deeply, relishing how good it felt; listening to the sound of birdsong – the *only* sound. How sweet it was.

Walking back round to the front, she saw there were more houses dotted along the peninsula. They were similar in style to her own, but Skye Croft stood behind them all as though it were the last bastion of civilisation. Deep blue waters lapped at a strip of shore; a beach of sorts in summer, she hoped.

"What do you think, James?" she asked excitedly.

"Good choice, Jess. It's perfect."

She was pleased. It *had* been a good choice.

"At last we made it," Jessamin continued. "James," she said, when there was no reply, "We made it, at last."

"We did," James replied but faintly.

Panic surged within her.

"James," she almost shouted. "You are here, aren't you?"

"Yes, Jess, I'm here."

Oh good, he sounded strong again.

"It's just for a moment, I thought—"

"There's no reason to think anything," he assured her.

"Who you talking to?"

Jessamin started. That wasn't James. She turned rapidly on her heel. Standing before her, on the gravel driveway was a man; a tall man, broad in stature, well built, dressed in khaki trousers, a waxed green jacket and Timberland-style boots. On his right eye was an eye-patch. The other eye, she noticed, was as dark as his hair.

"I'm… no one. I'm speaking to no one." She issued a silent apology to James, but she didn't think the stranger would understand if she explained. "You are?"

The man stepped forward. No, not stepped – he *strode* forward, like a man used to being in charge. "I'm Fionnlagh Maccaillin," he said, offering his hand.

Fionnlagh Maccaillin? Her landlord? Taking his hand, she introduced herself.

"I'm Jessamin Wade, your new tenant. I'm pleased to meet you." Looking around for, but not seeing, a car, she added, "I'm sorry, I didn't hear you arrive."

"I walked."

"You walked?" she repeated. Did nobody drive around here?

He pointed behind him. "I live just over there."

Jessamin looked to where he pointed; to the trees she'd admired earlier, Scots Pine if she wasn't mistaken. Was he a huntsman? Did he live in some sort of shack in there or something?

Before she could enquire, Maccaillin started speaking again.

"I trust you find everything in the cottage to your satisfaction?"

Glancing at the cottage before replying, she said, "Yes, it's nice, very nice."

Under his scrutiny she was suddenly aware of what a sight she must look – no make-up, her clothes rumpled from yesterday, hair unbrushed. One hand reached up almost surreptitiously to tuck a few strands behind her ear.

"And the heating, have you worked it out yet?"

"No," she said, watching as he walked right past her and into the cottage itself, stooping as Rory had done the previous night.

"Please, be my guest," she muttered under her breath, debating whether to point out that although technically it might be his house, she was the one paying rent for it, therefore perhaps he'd like to wait for an invitation before stepping inside.

Following him in, she heard him mutter too as he fiddled with dials on the boiler in the kitchen. For a moment she was able to study him unguarded; his strong jaw line and the width of his shoulders. How long and lean his legs were.

43

"A hunky Highlander," James whispered in her ear, "like the ones you used to dream about."

You're the only one I dream about.

Maccaillin turned to face her.

"There, that should do it. The boiler's a bit temperamental, unfortunately. You shouldn't have any problems with it, but if you do—"

"Head for the pine trees."

"That's right." His smile transformed him. He had looked slightly forbidding before, the eye patch not really helping matters. Eyes were the windows of the soul but with only one eye to look at, it was hard to see what lay within. Smiling, however, he seemed younger. She didn't know his age but she guessed he wasn't much older than her; a few years perhaps, no more.

"Shopping," she said, eager to break the silence that had developed between them. "Where's the best place locally to stock up on groceries?"

"There's a Co-Op in Kyle, just over the Rattan Pass, or you'll have to make do with the village store. Maggie, who runs it, keeps it pretty well stocked."

"The Rattan Pass – is that the mountain I came over last night?"

"Aye, it would be. Have you ever been here before?"

"No," she replied.

"You did well to negotiate it at night then."

"I did think it twisted and turned a bit."

"A bit? It's notorious in these parts – even the locals fear it in winter."

"It's a good job I arrived in spring then."

"It is."

Turning, he started walking towards the door again,

obviously keen to make an exit. Just before the doorway, however, he stopped with his back to her for a few seconds, as though in quiet contemplation whether or not to leave in such an abrupt manner. His better nature winning, he faced her again. Behind him the light had taken on an almost luminous quality, surrounding him in a halo.

"Whatever brings you here, Mrs Wade, I hope you enjoy your stay."

"T…thank you," she stammered.

Maccaillin stared at her as hard as she was staring at him, but whether he found her a vision or a curiosity she couldn't tell.

* * *

"Oh come on, you fancy him just the tiniest bit."

"I do not."

"Yes you do."

"James," Jessamin said at last. "Stop teasing."

"Jess, I'm just having fun, that's all. It's okay to fancy other people, it's natural."

"As long as we don't do anything about it," she finished for him, remembering another of the pacts they'd made.

"But you could now, couldn't you?"

"No, and if you carry on saying that, I'm going to ignore you."

"Okay, okay, I'll back off."

"Good."

Jessamin had decided to walk into the village. She'd had breakfast – toast, butter and more tea – followed by a long, scented bath, and now felt ready to tackle her new surroundings. She supposed it might not look so magnificent in the rain, but on a day like today, with the sun shining, Glenelk was breathtaking. She imagined the frosted hills covered in purple heather in summer, and the loch an exhilarating place to swim in.

"That would be something, wouldn't it, James, to swim over to Skye?"

Keeping to the road, she looked with interest at the various cottages too; each one benefited from plenty of land, something that seemed to be in endless supply up here. They were pretty enough; not grand, more cottage-like in style, and painted in soft shades of cream or white. Brightly coloured doors seemed to be a bit of a trend; hers was pillar-box red, but there were also some that were hot pink, deep purple and burnt orange. They reminded her a little of a Greek village she'd stayed in with James, a year or so after they'd got together, but without the accompanying heat of course.

"That was the holiday you proposed to me, do you remember?"

"I'm not likely to forget, am I?" James replied and she could just imagine his eyes twinkling.

She'd known he was up to something. From the minute they'd arrived on Symi, he'd been acting strangely.

This is it, she'd thought. *He's either going to dump me or ask me to marry him.*

The first few days had gone well; he'd started to relax, although not entirely. From the sun lounger beside her, she could feel him throwing furtive glances at her. Every time she tried to catch his eye, he'd look away. Even making love, he was hesitant – something he'd never been before.

On the fourth day, Jessamin had had enough. They'd just endured a terrible meal at a local taverna. The food had literally been swimming in grease and not of the olive variety. Even the wine had been undrinkable. And as for the atmosphere: it might have been lacking in the restaurant, but between the two of them, it was building – and far from romantically.

"Why'd you keep mucking about with your trouser pocket?" she'd asked, feeling her mood sour by the minute.

"My trouser pocket? I'm not."

"James, I'm sitting opposite you; I can see what you're doing."

"I'm not doing anything like *that*, if that's what you're implying."

"You've been behaving very odd recently."

"No, I haven't."

"Yes, you have."

"No, I—"

"Oh, come on," she had said, beyond exasperation, "let's just go. I need some fresh air. It's not just the food that's awful in this restaurant; the smell is vomit-inducing too."

James had paid the bill and they'd walked along the beach towards home. It wasn't a moonlit beach, as it had been for the last three nights; it had started to rain.

"Perfect," she'd muttered, "just perfect." Not that James had noticed. He was still preoccupied.

Increasingly agitated, she had stopped at their apartment door. It wasn't just any apartment: James had insisted on upgrading to one of the best in the resort, complete with balcony, sea views and private Jacuzzi. Normally she would have loved it – she *had* loved it – but on that moonless night it felt alien to her, as did he. It was no use; she couldn't go on; she wanted to know what his problem was, whatever the consequences.

"James, what's bugging you?"

Despite his skin being several shades darker than normal

47

and his blonde hair brighter, he looked drained all of a sudden; terrified. What of?

"James!" she demanded. "Tell me."

"Well, it's not a case of telling, it's more a case of asking."

"Asking me what?" Her patience had rapidly worn thin.

"To marry me of course! Oh crap, I didn't mean to ask you like that. I've been trying to work out the best time since we got here. Was it on the plane – you know mile high and all that? Or as soon as we got to our apartment? Or on the beach at sunset? I waited for the perfect moment, and now it seems I've chosen the worst."

Although she heard every word he'd said, only two words registered.

"So you *do* want to marry me, after all?"

He'd then started to babble.

"I know we live together already and I know you're younger than me, but I'm sure you're the one I want to be with for the rest of my life. Of course I'll understand—"

"You're sure?"

"I just said I was."

"Absolutely sure?"

"One hundred per cent. Look," and he was off again, "if you have any doubts—"

"I've no doubts."

"Really? You haven't?"

She'd shaken her head.

"So… what are you trying to say?"

"What do you think I'm trying to say?"

"Jess, stop it! This is excruciating. Give me a straight yes or no, please."

"Yes," she'd said, loving the look of surprise and excitement on his face.

"Yes?"

"Yes, yes, yes, YES!"

"YES!" he'd echoed, punching the air in triumph.

Sweeping her off her feet, he'd swung her round. And since then she had barely touched down, not in all the years they'd been together. That rain-soaked moment had been perfect after all.

"Jessamin, hi, it's me. Did you sleep well?"

"Oh, hi, Rory. Yes I did, thanks. Very well."

Lost in memories, she hadn't realised how far she'd walked; straight into the heart of the village, if the village shop represented the heart, that is. She recognised the road from last night. Just slightly further up was The Stag – all in all, about a fifteen-minute walk, or as Rory would have it, a ten-minute run from her door.

"Getting your bearings?" Rory enquired, falling into step beside her.

She tried to guess his age – he was definitely younger than her. No more than mid-twenties, a boy really. Maccaillin, in his mid-thirties, seemed very much a man by comparison.

"I am," she replied, not bothering to point out that she couldn't recall any of the last few minutes of her journey, she'd been so lost in memories. "It's beautiful here."

Rory looked pleased. Pleased *and* relieved. "You're not disappointed then?"

"No," she was genuinely taken aback that he could ask such a thing. "I've seen pictures of Scotland in books and magazines. I've seen the film *Braveheart* about five times," she smiled wryly at her confession. "It's one of my favourites. But books, magazines and films – they can't do a place like this justice. I've never seen anywhere as lovely."

"Have you travelled much?" Rory enquired.

"Abroad, yes," Jessamin replied. "Greece, France, Italy, most of Europe in fact. Further afield, I've been to America, a couple of Caribbean islands, Mauritius."

"But there's nowhere to match this?"

"Nowhere that's as dramatic, no"

They both came to a standstill.

"Maggie's Village Store." Jessamin read out loud the sign above the window. "I remember you mentioning Maggie last night."

"Aye, Maggie's Thursday nights I mentioned – the girls in the village gather round at hers on that night, putting the world to rights or whatever it is they do. I'd love to know; to be a fly on the wall; it'd make for fascinating listening, I'm sure. I expect you'll get an invite soon enough."

He opened the door for her with an exaggerated flourish and she stepped inside. Someone's living room in a former life, the shop had a couple of fridge freezers positioned side by side and numerous shelves stacked with tinned goods. There were also loaves of fresh bread, local eggs and a newspaper rack with what looked a very limited assortment of reading matter. Basic stuff, but enough for one to get by for a few days before heading over the Rattan Pass to the supermarket Maccaillin had mentioned.

Rory introduced her to the lady eyeing her curiously behind the counter.

"Maggie Reid, this is Jessamin... sorry I didn't catch your last name."

"Wade," said Jessamin stepping forward. "Hi, I'm Jessamin Wade."

"She's the new tenant at Skye Croft," Rory explained.

"Skye Croft," Maggie's voice was low and throaty. "Maccaillin's place?"

"That's the one."

To Jessamin, Maggie Reid looked very much a 'salt-of-the-earth' person. There were no airs or graces about her. Her face, weathered as most faces she'd encountered up here were, was free of make-up and might be considered plain, but Jessamin saw warmth in it. Long dark hair restrained in plaits had ample grey threaded throughout, but it wasn't an iron shade; the strands were silver soft, resembling natural highlights. Her frame could only be described as generous but she had a definite waist. There was an enviable hourglass figure beneath it all – enviable because Jessamin's own figure was slim, her chest small and her waist barely defined at all. All her life she'd longed for more of a shape, but then she guessed if she'd had it, she'd want to be lean instead. Such was human nature.

"We don't get many newcomers here," Maggie continued. "We're just that bit too remote for most people's liking. Any particular reason why you decided on Glenelk?"

"A few," Jessamin admitted. "But mostly I'm after peace and quiet."

"An escape?" Maggie astutely pointed out.

"Of sorts," Jessamin mumbled, wondering how far she was going to quiz her.

"Maccaillin, have you met him?"

"Yes, this morning. He seems nice."

Maggie didn't comment further, she just nodded slightly. "What can I help you with?"

"I just need a few basics. Do you mind if I browse?"

"Not at all, I'm glad of your business. Basics are something you'll find here and a few other things besides. For anything more, head over to Kyle; they have a post office, a grocer, a fishmonger, a butcher, a baker, everything you need really. And if that's not enough, the big names in Inverness deliver, even to a place as remote as this. You'll not starve."

"Thanks for the information," Jessamin said, helping herself to a wire basket.

Browsing the shelves, she wasn't really registering what lay in front of her. Instead, she felt awkward, very much aware that she was the stranger in the midst. Rory, who'd been standing patiently by whilst the two women talked, must have sensed this.

"Maggie, your Thursday night gatherings, is there room for one more?"

Jessamin's heart lurched. Surely, he didn't mean her? Please God, he didn't! She hadn't come here to make friends; she'd come here to be alone – alone with James.

She reeled around at the same time as Maggie answered.

"Oh no—" she began.

"Always room for one more."

"Really, I wouldn't want to intrude."

"You're a part of the village now, it's no intrusion."

Too late, Jessamin saw the amused expressions on both Maggie and Rory's faces. Aware of how shocked she looked, she closed her mouth at least.

The smile on Maggie's face made her look almost girlish. Looking more closely, Jessamin realised she was younger than she'd estimated. Maggie Reid was not much older than she was; certainly not in her mid-forties as first surmised.

"Lovey, we don't bite, honestly. You've met the boys, well Rory and Maccaillin; now meet the girls – I think you'll like them."

"I'm sure I will…" Again she faltered, but James gave her strength.

"Go on," he encouraged. "Go to one meeting, it can't

harm. It doesn't have to be a regular thing, not if you don't want it to be."

Today was Tuesday; she had a bit of time to psyche herself up for the meeting, and James was right, it didn't have to become a regular thing. She only had to go the once.

"It's very kind of you to invite me," she said at last. "I'd love to come."

"Grand, that's grand. I'm easily found. My house is to the right of the shop – the one with the yellow door."

"I'm sure I'll find it," said Jessamin, deciding she had enough in her basket and walking to the counter to pay for it. "What time?"

"We gather at seven."

"Seven's perfect. Do I need to bring anything?"

"Just bring yourself. That's more than enough."

Nonetheless, Jessamin grabbed a couple of bottles of white wine off the shelf and bought those too. She'd feel rude turning up at Maggie's house empty-handed.

Before she could load herself up with the bags, Rory sprang forward.

"I'll help you carry those, Jess," he offered.

"I can manage," she protested.

"Rubbish," said Maggie. "Rory's a big strong lad. Let him carry your bags for you."

"Looks like you've got yourself a fan," a voice in her head said.

"James!" she warned him silently.

Jessamin gave in gracefully. "Thanks, Rory, that's very kind of you,"

"Looks like you've got yourself a fan."

Jessamin spun round. Maggie had just repeated James's sentiment exactly – word for word.

The look on her face was hard to make out; she looked innocent enough but there was a slight knowing quality to the smile creasing her features.

"See you Thursday, Jessa*mine*," she continued and Jessamin stared at her.

The way she had said her name... that was just like James too.

Chapter Six

WEDNESDAY did not dawn as brilliantly as Tuesday had. Rather than blue sky, grey clouds hung low in the sky, but Jessamin didn't mind. It was more like the sky in the painting from her childhood and because of that, it felt familiar. Rising from her bed, she noted damp in the air that hadn't been there the day before either. The bedclothes felt slightly wet and her clothes did too – it was as though she were actually in the clouds; the moisture all-pervading.

Grabbing at her dressing gown, she hurried downstairs to turn the heating up. She'd get a log fire going, like last night. It had been very comforting, sitting in front of it with James and a mug of hot tea. Sleep hadn't come as easily as it had done the first night she'd arrived, however; that knowing smile of Maggie's had worried her more than she cared to admit.

"Do you think she knows?" she'd whispered to James in the stillness of the night.

"About me?"

"Yes, about you."

"That you talk to me?"

"Exactly."

"So what if she does?"

"She'll think I'm weird."

"If she does know, she's a little weird herself," James

pointed out.

"I suppose…"

"You really do worry too much, Jess."

He was right; she gave it no more thought and finally, sleep had claimed her.

"Ugh, it's freezing." She was shivering in the hallway now, trying to find the dial for the boiler in order to turn it up. Peering into the darkness of the airing cupboard, she realised it was already on maximum – Maccaillin must have done that yesterday. Confused, she padded over to the nearest radiator. It was stone cold. Heading into the living room, she checked several others and found the same thing. Maccaillin had said the boiler was a bit temperamental; he hadn't said it wouldn't work at all! Last night, she'd been warm enough, though. What had happened to upset it?

Pulling her dressing gown tighter, she resolved to call on Maccaillin rather than phone him. If she were honest, his home, just out of sight and shielded by the trees, intrigued her; images of the Huntsman in *Snow White and the Seven Dwarfs* came to mind – had he worn an eye patch too? Spooky, if he had.

Within half an hour she had showered and dressed – glad she'd invested in sturdy boots and a padded jacket just before leaving for Scotland. Yesterday she'd warmed up whilst walking in the sunshine; today there was no warmth at all.

Jessamin skirted round the picket fence separating the land that belonged to Skye Croft and the land that belonged to… well, the land itself, she supposed, and tramped over the expanse that led to the wilderness beyond. As she drew closer to the trees, the scent of pine was rich in the air. If she had to describe the smell as a colour, she'd choose green, a dark shade. She followed a path of sorts and saw that it led into the trees, which up close didn't seem so densely packed. She also noticed a road, or more accurately, a dirt track to her left – the road that led to Maccaillin's house no doubt. She decided to carry on along the path but to keep the road in sight, so she wouldn't get lost.

She'd only been in amongst the trees a few minutes when she saw a building loom in front of her – a large construction, grey in colour and standing in a clearing. The dirt track she'd kept her eye on ran in front of the house before disappearing into the hills. Approached from the back, the house looked austere; barren. It also looked like quite a pile. If this was Maccaillin's house, he was more than a huntsman.

There was a gravel driveway to the right-hand side of the house and a garden of sorts, but not one that looked particularly well kept or loved. Parked on the driveway was a Land Rover, mud-splattered and roughly the size of a tank.

The front of the house was less forbidding than the back, but only marginally, with a grand entrance framing an ancient oak door; several leaded windows of varying sizes, and even a small turret. A typical Scottish country house, it had a look of neglect about it.

Bracing herself, Jessamin walked up to the front door and yanked on the iron bell pull. Whilst waiting, she scanned the grounds around her for evidence of another house; a smaller house perhaps, one not quite as grand as this, which might be Maccaillin's home. There was nothing; just countryside – *bleak* countryside. After yanking the pull twice more, Jessamin wondered what to do.

"Shall I see if the door's open?" she asked James.

"You mean barge your way in?"

"Well, I need to have my heating sorted out. It's an emergency."

"It's not that much of an emergency. You've got the log fire to tide you over."

"The log fire doesn't touch upstairs though, and that shower I had this morning probably used the last of the hot water. There's no way I can do without hot water."

"Go on then, try the door, but make sure you announce your arrival clearly."

Decisively, Jessamin pushed at the door, needing both hands to tackle its weight. As Rory had said, like all houses in Glenelk, it was unlocked. She pushed further until she was able to step inside. The hallway was impressive, a large square with a solid-looking staircase to one side. Oak-panelled walls rose to picture rail height. Above that they were whitewashed, as was the ceiling, from which was suspended a cast iron chandelier. Stag heads seemed to be a favourite form of decoration; there were several of them – trophies from hunts long gone, she guessed. A grandfather clock struck the hour, startling her. Beside the clock was a table with an earthenware bowl on it. The bowl contained no flowers, which was a shame Jessamin thought; it was gloomy in here; it could do with brightening.

"Hello," she called out, walking across a large plaid rug placed in the centre of the hallway. It was predominantly red but very worn in places. "Is anyone home?"

There was a door to her right and a door to her left; which should she choose? She was just debating when she heard someone answer her.

"Beth? Is that you?"

The voice was old and frail and just as confused as Jessamin's.

"Erm… no it's not Beth. It's Jessamin Wade, the new tenant at Skye Croft Cottage. I'm looking for Mr Maccaillin."

The door to her right opened wider and silhouetted against the interior was a shape; an old man, looking as delicate as his voice had sounded. Quickly she rushed to apologise.

"I'm so sorry to intrude. I hope I didn't alarm you. I think I've got the wrong house."

"You're not Beth."

He sounded so disappointed.

"No, I'm not." Again, she apologised.

When he didn't move, Jessamin moved towards him.

"Are you all right? Can I help you back to your chair?"

Up close she recognised tell-tale signs of grief on the old man's face, the lost look in his red-rimmed eyes; the complete and utter absence of hope. Sympathising wholeheartedly, she reached out to him and placed her hand upon his arm.

"Come and sit down," she said softly. "I'll... I'll sit with you if you like."

"Sit with me? Yes, dear, that would be nice."

Still holding onto his arm, she led the old man back inside the room, her pace slow to match his.

"Is this where you sit?" asked Jessamin, pointing to a tall-backed chair closest to the fire which, she was pleased to see, was glowing brightly in the grate. On the arm of the chair lay a thick tartan blanket. When he sat down, she tucked it over his legs, noting the thinness of them, the thinness of his arms too. The skin seemed to hang on his face.

Quickly she grabbed at a poker and stirred the fire, causing the flames to flicker and dance.

"Are you warm enough?" she asked.

The man nodded. "Your hair, it's pretty. Wavy, like Beth's was. I miss her so."

Jessamin looked around her. The room, although large, had a pleasant, lived-in feel – the grand oak surround of the fireplace very much the focal point. On top of it were several photo frames as well as a collection of ornaments, all rather haphazardly placed. Standing up, she scanned the photos before pointing to a black and white photo of a young woman and a young man standing together just outside the lodge; the man in a suit, the woman in a fitted dress that skimmed her knees, and a matching bolero-style jacket. Her hair was tied back and in her hands she held a modest bunch of flowers.

"Is this Beth?" Jessamin enquired.

The man looked to where she was pointing.

"Yes, that's Beth and I. That was our wedding day."

Jessamin had guessed as much.

"She's very pretty. You make a handsome couple."

"So everyone told us," he replied but he said it more to himself than her.

"Is she…?"

"Dead? Yes, dear. Beth passed a week before Christmas."

Losing someone at any time of year was terrible, but so close to Christmas, a supposed time of joy, made it more poignant somehow. James had died in October; a couple of months before Christmas; not one festive season but two had passed since then. On both occasions she'd tried to sleep the day away and had mostly succeeded.

Brushing thoughts of her own pain aside, Jessamin studied the photo more closely. Although he and Beth were standing together, there was a gap between them. And neither one was smiling. Beth's eyes stared not at the camera but beyond it; somewhere far beyond it seemed. Considering he was still calling out for her, how bereft he looked; he must have loved her very much. If that was the case, why did they look so unhappy on what should have been the happiest day of their lives? Not just her, but him too? As curious as she was, she reminded herself it was none of her business.

She placed the photo back on the mantelpiece, next to one of a dark-haired little boy who also looked forlorn, and asked the old man his name.

"My name? It's Stan. What did you say your name was again?"

"Jessamin Wade."

"The new tenant at Skye Croft?"

"That's right. I'm looking for Mr Maccaillin. I gather I've come to the wrong house."

"Oh no, dear; this is Finn's house too. I'm his grandfather."

Jessamin looked about her. "Is he in? Could I speak to him?"

"He's not in. He's gone on one of those walks of his. He walks for miles, right over the hills, in wind and in rain too; gone for hours at a time. The weather will stop most people, but not him. No telling when he'll be back, I'm afraid. Are you okay? Is it urgent?"

"Oh, I'm fine," she quickly assured him. "It's nothing urgent at all. I have his mobile number. I can always call him later." Noting an empty cup on the table beside him, she asked, "Is there anything I can get you – a cup of tea perhaps? Something to eat?"

"No, thank you. I've not much of an appetite lately."

"Is it just you and Mr Maccaillin that live here?"

"It is," he confirmed. "Used to be such a lively household once, when I was a boy, but it hasn't been for a long time now."

The house did indeed have a lonely atmosphere, as though it were somehow in competition with its isolated location. Jessamin had difficulty ever imagining it as lively, but another quick glance at the photos showed several other family members, not just Stan and Beth and the forlorn little boy, whom she now presumed was Maccaillin. None of the photos looked particularly recent, however. They seemed to be from ages past.

"So, you've been resident for a couple of days," said Stan.

"That's right," answered Jessamin.

"You're accent, it's not Scottish."

"No, I'm from Brighton, the opposite end of the country."

"Ah, the south. I've never been. Better weather I'm told."

"I think so, yes. I've never been to Scotland either, before Monday I mean."

"But something drew you here."

Jessamin started. What a strange thing to say.

"Erm... yes," she replied. "I suppose so."

"I hope you enjoy your stay, dear," his eyelids started to flutter. Clearly she had tired him. "It's a good place to be you know; a place that can heal if you'll let it."

Again his words sent tremors coursing through her. What was it with the Scottish? She'd heard they were a fey race; perhaps it was true. A few seconds later and Stan was snoring, a gentle sound that rumbled around the otherwise silent room. Tucking the blanket tighter around his legs, she decided to head for home. As she'd said to the old man, she could always phone or text Maccaillin; something she'd do as soon as she reached Skye Croft as she was eager to get the problem with the radiators sorted out. Straightening, she glanced at several paintings on the walls before leaving. There was a portrait of a lady, Beth perhaps or an ancestor?

Whoever it was, she was as enigmatic as the *Mona Lisa* with her half smile. There was also a large depiction of a stag, similar in style to the stag on the pub's signboard; the creature standing proudly against a mountainous background, and there were landscapes too; one featuring a waterfall; another very romantic in style, with the ruins of a castle prominent in it; and one of a loch, looking eerily still. Maccaillin and his grandfather clearly loved their art.

Gently closing the living room door, she made her way across the hall again and to the front door. Outside it had started to drizzle and the previously grey clouds were much darker. It was a shame the sky looked so threatening; she would have loved to explore the surrounding landscape. It intrigued her, the way it stretched on and on. *Never mind,* she consoled herself. *There'll be other days.*

She was wet through by the time she arrived back at Skye Croft. The drizzle had turned into serious rain a few minutes after she'd set off. She felt chilled, right through to the bone – a fine time for the heating to go kaput. Opening the door, however, she was surprised to be hit by a blast of heat. Quickly, she walked over to the nearest radiator. It was red hot – not broken at all!

Looking around her, she scratched her head. Why had the heating suddenly burst into life? It was almost as if it had waited for her to leave before kick-starting again. She was grateful Maccaillin wasn't in after all: he'd think she was an idiot, dragging him here on a fool's errand. Heading upstairs to change into dry clothes, she returned to the living room with a book in her hand; a historical novel she'd been meaning to read for a while, about Queen Isabella of France. Although she had once devoured them, she now tended to avoid books where the main theme was romance. They made her feel lonelier than ever.

"Hey," James reminded her as she placed logs onto the fire, "I'm here, remember?"

"Oh, I know. But I miss you, you know, physically. I miss your soap and water smell, the hair on your arms, and how golden they were. That gleam in your eye when you looked at me."

"When I meant business, you mean?"

"When you meant business," she agreed, her laughter tinged with sadness.

"Jess, where you were concerned, I *always* meant business."

"James, don't."

He took mercy on her. "You hold me in your heart, that's what matters."

Sighing, Jessamin changed the subject.

"That old man today, Stan, he's a sweetie, isn't he? He seems lonely though, for Beth I mean."

"He does, but they'll meet again I'm sure."

"I hope so."

She also hoped Maccaillin looked after him properly. Leaving him for hours at a time whilst he embarked on one of his walks suggested otherwise. Anything could happen to him meanwhile. He could easily fall and hurt himself; be left lying cold and alone on the floor – the rugs not doing much to cushion his fall. Perhaps she ought to offer to look in on him from time to time. It wasn't as if she had anything else to do. She had nothing but time, which seemed to stretch in front of her like an endless ribbon. It might be a relief to Maccaillin to have someone to share the caring. Perhaps she'd text him after all; get him over to look at the boiler; if it had stopped working this morning it could easily do so again so it was best to get it checked. And when he was here, she would broach the subject. She felt something flicker inside, the first time she'd felt anything as warm in a long while. It would be nice to be of help; to feel as though she were useful again. And helping Stan might, in some way, help her. In grief, it seemed, she had found a friend.

Chapter Seven

"HI, Maggie. I hope it's still okay for me to come by tonight."

"Jessamin! Of course it is. I'm thrilled you could make it."

Jessamin was ushered down a narrow hallway into what she presumed was Maggie's living room. It was packed with women, about ten in total. Feeling like a specimen in a jam jar, she stood whilst the crowd appraised her. It felt like minutes but could only have been moments. With both hands clutching at a bottle of wine, she wondered if her trembling was obvious.

"Hold," James whispered in her ear, emulating the voice of Mel Gibson as William Wallace in the film *Braveheart*, urging his men to stand firm in the face of attack.

She almost smiled at that, and then she did smile, remembering that was the best way to disarm people. It had worked in the pub and it worked in Maggie's living room. Every single one of the women smiled back.

"So you're Jessamin? Maggie's told us all about you."

"Welcome to Glenelk."

"It's lovely to have you join us."

Someone took the bottle from her hands; someone else thrust a full glass of wine at her. Quickly, she drank, hoping to derive from it some Dutch courage. Another woman stepped forward and guided her to an empty chair, urging her to sit down.

"Girls, girls, girls," Maggie said, her amusement clear. "I know you're all excited by our new arrival, but give her some breathing space – she's looking quite overwhelmed."

The crowd fell back, allowing Jessamin to gulp more of her wine. With horror she noticed she'd already reached the bottom of the glass. Wincing, she looked at Maggie who took the glass and refilled it without so much as a word.

Settling herself down again, Maggie addressed everyone.

"First things first: introductions."

A melange of names was thrown at her: Ailsa, Eileen, Maidie, Shona, Gracie, Ina and Ally were just some she remembered. She might suggest name badges at the next meeting, if she were invited to it, that was.

"And also," Maggie continued, "let me tell you the reason why we meet every Thursday. The boys have the pub; well, mainly they have the pub, but we girls, we want to get away from the men every now and then, so we meet here, every Thursday, to air any gripes we may or may not have with our other halves, and sometimes with each other. In a village this small it doesn't do to hold grievances. They don't just affect one or two people; they tend to affect us all."

Crikey, what was she? Some sort of self-appointed referee?

No sooner had she thought this than Maggie raised an eyebrow at her, as though she'd spoken the words aloud, Jessamin felt like she should issue an apology. Thankfully, Maggie resumed speaking and saved her from doing so; from making a fool of herself.

"Concerning the business of gripes, has anyone got any?"

Several faces looked expectantly around, but in the end all shook their heads.

"Grand," Maggie looked happy about that. "The second

reason we meet…" and here she paused, Jessamin almost holding her breath in anticipation, "is to have a good old gossip. Jessamin, the only strange thing about the women of Glenelk is we look out for each other; other than that, we're as normal as anyone south of the border."

Amen to that, thought Jessamin, raising her glass to clink with the others.

The room suddenly fell into chaos; but a friendly chaos – the chatter of the women almost deafening. Where was Maggie's husband while all this was going on? Was she even married? The living room suggested not. It was predominantly feminine in style with floral wallpaper, knick-knacks on shelves – porcelain cherubs in particular – and soft furnishings in cream.

Some women conversed with each other, but several also crowded around her, Ailsa and Maidie in particular wanting to know what life was like in a place that was as mythological to them as this place was to her. And so she told them, attracting more interest as she explained about the shops, the restaurants, the bars, the nightlife, and the thriving arts and crafts scene in Brighton. She told them about the countryside too, not as spectacular as in Scotland, but the South Downs had a genteel charm. She and James had loved to walk amongst them.

"Who's James?" Gracie (at least she thought it was Gracie) asked. Oh, for those name badges!

"James?" To be honest, Jessamin hadn't even realised she'd spoken his name out loud. "He's my, erm… my husband."

"You're married?" Maidie looked surprised.

"Yes… no… yes…"

"Oh," it was Ally this time, grimacing. "You've split up."

Jessamin shook her head. Split up? Not intentionally.

"He's dead," she admitted.

The word seemed to reverberate. Several pairs of eyes widened, and even those who hadn't been talking directly to her, hushed.

"You don't have to tell us any more," said Maggie, taking Ally's place beside Jessamin.

"No, it's okay. It… it feels good to talk about him to be honest. I haven't really done so since the accident."

"The accident?" Ina prompted.

"Yes, the accident," Jessamin replied. And then, as though the words had been bubbling in her throat all along, biding their time, waiting for release, she told them what had happened.

"Oh my darling."

"You poor thing."

"You're too young to be a widow."

The sentiments kept pouring out but she felt like a fraud for accepting them. As hard as it was on her, it was harder on James; he was the one who'd lost his life.

"Don't worry about me," James whispered in her ear, ever thoughtful.

Maggie reached across and held her hand.

"Thank you for telling us, Jessamin, we feel very privileged. And I think I speak for all of us when I say we'll look after you here."

"Oh, I haven't come for sympathy…" Jessamin started.

"Fair enough," said Maggie. "But we've understanding to give, if you want it."

It seemed as though Maggie could sense she wanted to change the subject.

"You say you've met Fionnlagh Maccaillin – your first impressions please."

There were several sighs but also a couple of groans, most audibly from Maidie, an attractive blonde woman. He was both liked and disliked it seemed.

"He seems very nice," she answered. "He walked over to introduce himself on my first day here; told me to watch out for the boiler because it's temperamental and believe me, it is."

"*He's* temperamental you mean," someone offered, she couldn't quite catch who.

"Ina," Maggie chided. "He's been through a lot, has Fionnlagh."

"Has he?" Jessamin's interest was piqued.

"He has," Maggie replied. "But, as much as we're fond of a gossip, we don't talk about those who'd prefer not to be talked about. And Fionnlagh Maccaillin falls into that category. Nowadays he keeps himself to himself. Something we have to respect."

A few people looked suitably chastised as though they had indeed been gossiping about him. Maidie, she noticed, wasn't one of them; she still looked stern.

"I met his grandfather yesterday," Jessamin continued. "I went to the house to ask Maccaillin to come and check the boiler; it was refusing to fire up, although it seems to have sorted itself out now. He wasn't home but his grandfather was. We sat for a while and talked."

"Stan?" Maggie said. "He's a lovely old man. Devastated he was when he lost Beth."

"Was she younger than him," Jessamin enquired, "or older?"

"The same age," answered Maggie. "I didn't really know her, no one did. She was a bit of a recluse. But Stan, he was always friendly and very down to earth, considering."

"Considering what?" Jessamin hoped it was okay to probe further.

"Considering the wealthy family he comes from – one of the richest in the Highlands; residents of Glenelk since the sixteenth century. He, and by proxy Fionnlagh, own a lot of property hereabouts; land too, although I think a fair portion of it has been sold or leased."

"So Stan's the Laird, is he?" asked Jessamin.

"Stan's never claimed that title, nor has Finn."

Finn? The shortened use of his first name indicated he was more than just an acquaintance of Maggie's. How well did she know him? Jessamin wondered.

Maggie continued speaking. "He's an artist is Stan, and a gifted one at that."

Jessamin could feel her eyes widen. "An artist?"

"Aye, if you've been up to the lodge, surely you noticed the paintings dotted around?"

"Yes." Of course she had. "They were quite grand some of them, big old oil paintings. I presumed they were family heirlooms or something."

"Some of them are I'm sure, but some of them are by him too."

Jessamin felt a little awe-struck. "As you say, he's a very talented man." After a brief pause, she told them about the painting that had inspired her to come here. "It belonged to my mother. It hung in our living room all the while I was growing up. It wasn't a fancy picture, not by any means; not like the ones up at the lodge, but my mother and I, we liked it. It was a loch surrounded by mountains, but not a loch like the one Glenelk overlooks; it was much smaller, and in-land I think. Whether such a place exists or not, I don't know."

"I'm sure it does, even if it's been embellished," Maggie replied. "Most paintings have their roots in truth. You say it's your mother's picture. Does she still have it?"

Jessamin felt almost embarrassed to admit to another death. "Erm… my mother's passed too. She died when I was twenty-five; she had heart problems." Before more sympathies could be heaped upon her, she hurriedly continued, "My father, however, is very well. He remarried and lives in the south of France. I phoned him yesterday to see if he has the picture but he hasn't. I'm going to check with my brother next. Hopefully, I'll have more luck there."

"I hope so too," Maggie said. Her eyes were such a rich shade of brown.

A longing for the picture of her youth surged again within Jessamin. "I don't know," she tried to explain, "there was just something about that picture; it was dream-like, magical."

"Aye," Maggie agreed, "this land, it's a bit like that at times; dream-like I mean, and magical too, especially when the mists close in around us and cut us off entirely. I know I say we're the same as city folk, but sometimes we're not. Despite the mist, it's possible to see further up here, Jess; to feel more. There's too much noise in the modern world; it dulls our perceptions."

"That's another reason why I'm here," Jessamin said softly.

"I know." Maggie's voice was soft too, her insightfulness not alarming Jessamin this time. Rather, she found it comforting.

"Another drink?" It was Ina, clearly deciding the atmosphere needed lifting.

"I'll say so."

"Fill me up."

"One more for the road."

Maggie, whose own glass was full enough, leaned across to Jessamin.

"It'd be nice to get together, just you and me."

"I'd like that," replied Jessamin, meaning it. She hadn't come here to make friends but she liked Maggie; she liked all the girls. It wouldn't harm to get to know them a little more.

"Cheers," said Maggie, winking at her.

"Cheers," Jessamin repeated, sensing James close by, smiling approvingly.

Chapter Eight

MACCAILLIN turned up on Friday morning at nine sharp. Jessamin knew he was coming, but she hadn't expected him to arrive quite so early. Thankfully, she was washed and dressed with her hair brushed and her make-up in place. She'd have been mortified to be caught on the hop again.

She had barely opened the door when he came striding in, his presence filling the room.

"You don't wait, do you?" The words were out of her mouth before she could stop them.

Swinging round to face her, Maccaillin looked truly perplexed.

"Wait for what?"

"To be invited in."

"Invited?" he repeated the word as though it were alien to him.

"Yes, invited," she repeated. "You may own the cottage, Mr Maccaillin, but I'm the one who's renting it, which technically makes it mine. Kindly remember that."

Maccaillin, dressed in much the same garb as he had been on Tuesday when she first met him, did not look impressed by her admonishment.

"Oh," he said, tilting his head to one side, "and the fact that you came barging into my house a few days ago, disturbing my grandfather, I shouldn't mention perhaps? We may not lock our doors around here, but if you knock and there's no reply, the done thing to do is to go away and come back at a mutually convenient time."

Jessamin's mouth fell open. She hadn't expected that.

"I… I wasn't aware I 'disturbed' your grandfather. If I did, I'm sorry."

"Apology accepted. I apologise too. In future, if you call me to come over to sort out any more tenancy issues, I'll wait for a full invitation before stepping over the threshold."

She could feel herself bristling now. This man in front of her may not claim the title of Laird, but he was certainly trying to lord it over her.

"Hopefully there won't be too many issues," she replied crisply.

"Hopefully not." He was just as acerbic.

"The boiler…" she said, biting down on her fury. It wouldn't do to fall out with her landlord, and certainly not in her first week of residence.

Maccaillin looked around him. "It seems warm enough in here. What exactly is the problem?"

"It is warm, *now*. But on Wednesday morning, it was freezing. Despite being turned fully on, there was no heat at all coming from the radiators."

"What did you do to fix it?"

"Me? Nothing. It came on by itself."

"And it's worked ever since."

"Well, yes."

"So, as I said, what's the problem?"

"I… well, there isn't one, I suppose. I was just worried it might happen again."

"When… *if*… it happens again, call me. Until then, I don't see that there's anything I can do."

What an insufferable man! The only insufferable person she'd met in Glenelk so far. Little wonder there'd been groans at Maggie's when his name was mentioned. Groans and sighs actually, his brusque personality may excite some, but not her.

"His grandfather," James whispered in her ear, "that's the main reason you asked to see him, remember? The boiler was just an excuse."

Oh God yes, the artist – Stan, now a frail old man. A frail old man who sat on his own most of the time, she gathered, while his grandson took himself off. She'd like to spend time with Stan, but she wouldn't be able to do so if Maccaillin stood in their way; she needed to make amends.

"Coffee, can I get you some?"

Maccaillin seemed taken aback. He had clearly expected the bun fight to continue.

"And," she added, "I'd like you to look at the boiler anyway."

"Erm... okay."

He was no longer officious. Jessamin sensed an air of vulnerability instead. She preferred it.

"Don't frighten him too much," James joked.

I'll try not to, she silently returned.

As Maccaillin made his way to the hallway, Jessamin asked how he took his coffee.

"Black, please. Strong."

She might have guessed. He didn't look like a man who'd dilute things.

When she returned with the coffee a few minutes later, Maccaillin was staring at the boiler and scratching his head.

"There's nothing wrong with it. Nothing I can see. Hopefully it won't happen again. If you're not satisfied, however,

I'm happy to call a plumber in."

"No, it's fine. If we were heading into winter I might say yes, but summer's just around the corner. There's no urgency."

"And you think summer isn't as brutal as winter on occasion?"

She was aghast. "Surely not?"

"It can be." He was clearly amused by her reaction.

Quickly, she handed over the steaming mug. As he took it, she inhaled. His right hand had suffered significant burns. Up close, the scars were evident.

"Oh," she said, unable to stop herself.

"Oh indeed," he replied, noting her reaction before moving back into the living room.

Jessamin followed, cringing at how tactless she'd been, but also curious to see if he was going to offer any explanation.

"Good coffee," he said, lifting the cup to his mouth. There was to be no explanation then, and why should there be? Again, she was cross with herself.

Jessamin motioned for him to sit down at the table, taking a seat herself to encourage him.

"Tell me about summer in Glenelk," she asked him. "Perhaps I should know what I'm letting myself in for."

Maccaillin did sit down, wincing slightly as he did so. He recovered so quickly though, she wondered if she'd imagined it.

"Sunshine can make even the most barren of places look beautiful, but here, when the landscape is stunning to begin with, summer is glorious. The rain gods, however, do tend to favour the Scots so you have to make the most of warm days when you get them. Forget what you're doing and why you're doing it, and get out there, enjoy every minute."

His words had an almost wistful quality. Intently she listened, appreciating the deep timbre of his voice, his accent. "The cold can bite as early as the end of August. And it doesn't loosen its grip for months, bringing with it ice and snow. The elements are often dangerous; not to be dismissed. We, the people, bow to them... usually."

"Usually?" Jessamin queried.

"There are always some who think they can pit their wits against nature. So many walkers get lost in the mountains. Even in summer you're at risk as the weather can change in a heartbeat. Never go walking in deep country, Mrs Wade; not unless you've let someone know beforehand your route and an estimate of what time you expect to be back."

She was grateful for his concern.

"Call me Jess, please," she insisted. "Do you let people know when you go on one of *your* walks?"

"One of my walks?"

"Yes, the advice you've just given me, do you heed it yourself?"

"I... well, no. But I know these hills. I was born amongst them."

"So, you're the exception to the rule?"

"I'm sorry, I don't understand."

"One of those who doesn't bow to the elements. What happens? Do they bow to you?"

He smiled again and she was glad. She suspected he didn't smile that often.

"I take care, Jess; don't worry."

Taking a deep breath, she broached the subject of Stan.

"Your grandfather, I enjoyed meeting him. What you said earlier, I truly hope I didn't frighten him."

Maccaillin placed his empty coffee cup on the table. Again

she noticed the burns on his hand, how far up his arm did they stretch? Had his eye been damaged at the same time? In the same accident? The elements had got to him after all, it seemed.

"You didn't frighten him," he admitted. "On the contrary, he enjoyed your visit."

"Oh good. I'm so glad." Nervous suddenly, she took a deep breath before continuing. "The thing is, and please say if I'm being inappropriate," she noticed him raise his eyebrow as she said this, "but I wondered if I might visit your grandfather from time to time. We've... we've both lost people dear to us, I thought we might be able to..." and here she faltered – able to what?

"Comfort each other?" Maccaillin offered.

"Yes," she nodded eagerly. "That's it, that's what I meant."

"You think I'm not capable of bringing him comfort?"

"Oh no, I didn't—"

"That I don't know what it's like to lose someone?"

Jessamin held her breath. How insensitive she'd been. Beth had been his grandmother, he must miss her too.

She rushed to apologise but it didn't soften his reply.

"I know well enough what it feels like."

"Of course, I didn't mean to imply... It was, erm..."

"Inappropriate?"

Was he teasing her? She looked closely at him, tried to read his face. The seconds that passed between them were intense, but they did pass.

"I think my grandfather would like you to visit very much."

"Really?" Jessamin felt a rush of excitement. "Oh, I'm so pleased. Check with him of course, I don't want to turn up unannounced again. But if he would like it, that'd be great."

Maccaillin stood abruptly up.

"The old man doesn't go anywhere. He's housebound. Drop by anytime. As you know, the door's never locked."

"I know," she replied, aware that she was blushing. "Erm... I hope you don't mind me asking, but how old is Stan?"

"He's eighty-two."

"He's lived a good long life then." She was impressed.

"A long life, yes." His failure to include the word 'good' was not lost on her.

Unsure how to respond, she remained silent.

"Thanks for the coffee."

Turning, he made for the door. Before leaving, however, he swung round to face her again.

"Thank you," he repeated.

"What for this time?" she asked, smiling.

"For offering to visit my grandfather; he'll appreciate it. *I* appreciate it."

"It's my pleasure," she began but too late. Maccaillin had already left.

Chapter Nine

THE weekend passed peacefully with Jessamin doing nothing more than lazing around, often in pyjamas – especially now she knew Maccaillin wasn't likely to come barging in any time soon; ploughing through her book on Queen Isabella, but not really taking much in, and sleeping. Although she talked to James when awake, in sleep she felt even closer to him; able to touch him, feel him; his lips on hers; his hands stroking her body. She was aware she spent an inordinate amount of time sleeping, but with no one to judge her, what did it matter? It was a relief not to have Sarah chivvying her up; she enjoyed being able to do exactly what she wanted in Glenelk, which of course, was to be with James.

"Has Sarah texted you lately?" asked James.

"She texted me yesterday – asked me when I was coming home – again. She can't believe I've lasted a week already."

"You've impressed me too," James replied.

"I've impressed myself," Jessamin laughed. "Actually, I like it up here. I know this sounds weird, but I feel it's where I should be, for the moment at least."

"In the arse end of nowhere?"

"Stop it," Jessamin chided him. "You'd have loved it here, and you know it."

"I do love it," James countered.

"Stop calling it names then... you and Sarah, you're as

bad as each other."

On Sunday evening her mobile beeped again.

"Oh, Sarah, what is it now?" she muttered, leaving the comfort of the fireside to walk across to the table where the phone was charging.

It wasn't Sarah: it was Maggie.

Hi Jess, would you like to meet tomorrow afternoon? Ally can stand in for me at the shop, so I thought I'd show you the next village along. There's a great coffee shop there, the cake is sublime.

Jessamin had intended to drop in on Stan at some point on Monday morning. Perhaps she still could; an hour or so would be plenty enough time to talk with him. She got the impression he tired quickly. That would leave the afternoon free to spend with Maggie. She'd also love to get started on some sightseeing now that she felt more settled.

That would be great, she texted back. *What time is good for you?*

They settled on two o' clock, and Jessamin felt quite excited about the next day.

"You really do belong," James said as she drifted into sleep.

"Seems like it," she replied.

"You've come home."

She'd sunk too far into the depths of sleep to question those last words, but she was sure it wasn't James who'd uttered them; the voice had been much deeper than his; gruff, like the voice she'd heard back in Brighton, familiar too, but how, she couldn't fathom. In any case, she'd all but forgotten about it by morning, which was thankfully another beautiful day.

Looking at the clock, she saw it was just after seven. She'd get up; have a leisurely bath, a decent breakfast and then walk to the Lodge. It wasn't called the Lodge, where Maccaillin and Stan lived; it had a name, carved in stone above the doorway; a name that began with the letter 'C' but which she couldn't quite recall. It was a Scottish name or Gaelic as the language was called. She'd take more notice today; start calling it by its correct name.

Later that morning, washed, dressed and fed, she paused outside the cottage and took a minute to soak up the beauty of her surroundings: how verdant everything was, how magnificent Skye looked in the distance. Maccaillin had told her the rain gods favoured this part of the world and she didn't doubt it, but she hadn't seen much evidence of it in her first week. Instead, she recalled something else he'd said. *Forget what you're doing and why you're doing it and get out there, enjoy every minute.* And that's what she'd do today – enjoy every minute. As soon as she decided that, the guilt set in.

Immediately James spoke up. "Jess, I *want* you to enjoy yourself."

But whenever James placated her like this, she was never sure if it was him speaking, or herself.

"Does it matter?" James asked her.

"Yes, it bloody matters," she replied, kicking at gravel on the ground.

She didn't deserve a day off from guilt, and no amount of pleading on his (or her own) behalf was going to change that. Yes, she'd go about her day; it wouldn't benefit anyone for her to remain a social pariah, but grief and guilt were what characterised her.

"And don't you forget it," she warned James.

"As if."

She didn't know if it was because he was twelve years older

than her, but James had always indulged her, taken care of her – especially when her mother died – a very rocky time. She'd gone straight from her parents' house to his, wrapped in love all the way. And now – aged thirty-one – she was on her own for the first time ever.

"You're not alone, Jessa*mine*," he whispered in her ear.

She hoped not. She truly did

"You are with me, aren't you?"

"I am."

"And you'll never leave me."

She could hear no reply.

"James," she prompted. Her desperation was not lost on either of them.

"I won't leave you."

The next time Jessamin looked up, the lodge was in front of her – as brooding as it had been the last time, and just as lonely. Remembering the gloom of the hallway, she wished she'd brought some flowers with her. She looked around. Perhaps some wild flowers would do. Her eyes resting on a clump of bluebells, she walked over and picked some, keeping the stems as long as possible.

With them clasped in her hands, she made her way to the front door, pausing to study the word carved in the lintel above: 'Comraich' – what did it mean? She tested the word, rolled it round in her mouth. It was a nice word, its softness belying the hardness of the stone the house was built in.

In a repeat of her last visit, she tugged at the iron bell pull. *Please let there be a reply this time.* She didn't want to barge in, not after what she'd said to Maccaillin and, more to the point, what he'd said to her. She needn't have worried. Someone was at the door, opening it slowly, very slowly, reminding her of the opening of doors in the Hammer Horror films she'd devoured as a kid; there was even the obligatory creaking.

"Stan," she said when his figure was revealed at last, "I hope you don't mind me visiting again." Quickly, she proffered the flowers.

"Ah, bluebells," Stan replied, smiling but not taking them. "The first of the season. They were Beth's favourite, and mine."

Lowering the flowers, she continued, "Can I come in?"

"Of course, dear, away in, away in," and he stepped aside so she could enter.

Quickly, she spied the empty jug on the sideboard.

"Can I get some water for these flowers?"

"Do as you please, lass."

"And whilst I'm in the kitchen, shall I make us some tea?"

"That would be grand. The kitchen," he said, pointing to a door beyond, "is through there."

Grabbing the earthenware jug, she turned again to Stan.

"I… I hope you don't mind me visiting. I asked Mr Maccaillin if it would be okay, and, well, now I suppose I'm asking you."

Stan looked perplexed that she should even think it was a problem. "I don't mind at all."

The old man turned slowly away and made his way back to the living room. Whilst he did, she rushed to the kitchen, filled the jug and positioned the flowers in it. Flicking the switch of the kettle, she returned to the hallway, ignoring the piercing eyes of the stag heads that seemed to follow her every move, and placed the jug in its rightful place. This was not hard to do as the circle where its base had been was dustless compared to the rest of the table. The blue flowers did little to brighten up the hallway; it would need a lot more than that: some bright white paint above the oak panels and better lighting, but it was a start.

In the kitchen, which looked largely ignored and not like the heart of the home at all, Jessamin rummaged around in cupboards to find what she needed and prepared a tray with two mugs, sugar, milk and a teapot. She took it through to the living room where Stan was sitting in his fireside chair.

"Is Mr Maccaillin out?" Jessamin queried.

"Yes, he went out this morning, early."

"Did you build the fire?" she questioned further, noting how impressive it was.

"No, dear, Finn does that before he leaves. I keep it stoked though. I can't do without my fire. Even in summer. It's my bones you see; not enough flesh on them to keep warm."

"Here," said Jessamin, handing him his cup. "This will warm you. Do you take sugar?"

"No, sweetheart, just a little milk."

Jessamin smiled at the term of endearment he'd used.

Settling down in the chair opposite, the chair Maccaillin must occupy whenever he happened to be at home, she felt she should double check. "It's really okay if I visit you from time to time? I'd like to."

There was kindness in Stan's gaze but also sadness. She wondered how far the latter reflected her own. "I'd like that too."

They sipped in silence for a few moments, Jessamin having to discard her jumper, as the heat from the fire was so effective.

"I was speaking to Maggie, who owns the village shop—"

"Yes, I know who Maggie is," Stan interrupted.

Jessamin berated herself. Of course he did. She was the newcomer here.

"She said you're an artist."

"I was," Stan confirmed. "I don't paint anymore." He held up his hands, gnarled and worn. "It's the arthritis, you see."

Jessamin winced. "Does it hurt?"

"Everything hurts when you get to my age."

Hearts especially, Jessamin wanted to say, but didn't. Instead, she gestured to the paintings that hung around her. "Which ones are yours?"

"The one of Beth, the waterfall and the loch."

So the portrait *was* of Beth. Not the Beth in the wedding photo; this Beth looked to be somewhere in her fifties. The one thing the photo and the painting had in common, though, was the distant look in the subject's eyes. Evidently, Stan hadn't seen fit to use artistic licence.

"There are more of my paintings dotted around. I can show you sometime if you like?"

"I'd like that very much. Did you work full-time as an artist?"

"Aye, I did," Stan smiled at the memory. "Sold far and wide; something I could never quite believe."

Jessamin admired his modesty – misplaced modesty because his talent truly was exceptional.

"Do you have a website? I could Google you."

"Och, no, modern technology and me, we're not the best of friends."

She had thought that might be the case. Shrugging, she said, "I was just curious what would happen if I looked up the name Stan Maccaillin, that's all."

Stan raised his head. "Stan Maccaillin, dear? That's not my name."

Jessamin was confused. "But... you and Mr Maccaillin, your grandson..."

"Maccaillin is Finn's name," Stan explained, "but it's not mine. I'm a McCabe."

Jessamin nearly fell off her chair. "You're a McCabe?"

"Why do you look so astounded?"

For a moment she couldn't answer. She had presumed the two men shared surnames; that Maccaillin had been the off-spring of a son. Evidently not, he was their daughter's son.

"I... I think I might have a painting by you," she said at last. "It's a watercolour, of a loch."

Stan looked relieved that it was nothing more serious. "A watercolour? If it's mine, it must have been an early painting. I favoured oils." Reminiscing further, he added, "The lochs always sold well. Have you brought the painting to Scotland with you?"

"No, it's not mine actually; it's my mother's, but she's dead. I think my brother has it."

The need to check became even more pressing. She'd phone Dane as soon as she got home. She'd have plenty of time to do so before Maggie arrived to pick her up. But for now, she could do nothing more than tell him how much she loved that painting.

"The hours I must have spent gazing at it; too many to count I suppose. And now here I am, sitting in front of the artist. Life is strange sometimes."

"Aye, life is certainly that," Stan agreed, a wistful quality to his voice. "I'm glad you liked it though. The loch, is it Loch Hourn, the loch that borders Skye, or is it a smaller loch?"

Jessamin explained to him that it appeared to be inland, framed by nothing but acres of mountains and sky.

Stan nodded in understanding. "The loch I think you're talking about, it's not far from here. I used to spend a lot of time there in my younger days; it was our playground, you see. Me, Beth, Beth's sister and Mally. It's off the beaten track; not many people know about it. Finn spends time there too I think, although usually he prefers the mountains."

Again Jessamin couldn't believe it. "So it does exist? I'd love to see it one day."

"Go there," Stan encouraged. "It's less than an hour's walk. But wait a wee while for the weather to improve; don't venture out on the moor when there's even a hint of rain in the air. Believe me you don't want to get caught, not out there, not on your own."

As impatient as she felt, she agreed. The elements, as Maccaillin had said and now Stan was implying, were fierce, and with them she had no desire to do battle. She had plenty of time to explore at leisure. Instead, she asked him about Beth's sister.

"She had a twin sister, Florence, or Flo as we used to call her. She died though."

"I'm sorry to hear that. Was that recent?"

"No," the sadness in his eyes increased. "It was a long time ago now."

"Oh," Jessamin didn't feel she could probe further and Stan too seemed keen to change the subject.

"Do you have Scottish heritage, lass?"

"Actually I do, on my mother's side, but my family lived all their lives in the south. My parents met in London and then moved to Brighton just before my brother was born."

"I remember you saying this is the first time you've been to Scotland."

"It is, but I'm glad I came, I love it."

"I'm glad too, dear," and his smile seemed heartfelt.

"I'm meeting Maggie this afternoon. We're going for a drive to the next village along."

"Larnside? It's nice, even more remote than this. And beyond it is Amberley, but there's nothing much there; just a few houses."

"And beyond that?"

"The sea."

"Do you… can you go out?"

"I haven't for a long time." Gesturing to the four walls around him, he added, "This is my world now."

"You must miss it, the landscape I mean; the loch especially."

Stan merely nodded in reply. Brightening, he asked her if she'd been across to Skye.

"Not yet, but I intend to very soon."

"Och, it's beautiful is Skye, a place apart. I spent a lot of time there too when I was a boy. The Cuillan Mountains though, as tempting as they are, they're treacherous – keep that in mind. Am Basteir, 'the executioner' is one peak; Sgurr a Ghreadaidh, 'the peak of torment' is another. Names that speak for themselves." As his grandson had done previously, Stan warned her about the perils of venturing into the mountains alone. "But, if it's lively you're after, the main town, Portree, may suit you."

She assured him 'lively' was the last thing on her mind.

"Like Finn then, he prefers his own company. Although he's a man of the Highlands, I worry about him, disappearing like he does. I'm never at ease, not until he returns."

Jessamin bristled. How awful he should cause his grandfather such worry.

"Does Mr Maccaillin run the estate?"

"Aye, he does now, what's left of it. And I'm very grateful

to him. I'm no longer up to the job, haven't been for a long time to be honest; I've let an awful lot slide. Finn's got his work cut out, but he seems happy enough to take on the task. Like I said, I'm grateful to him but I wish he'd come back to Comraich of his own accord, not because he had to."

He had to? Why? Jessamin was intrigued. She didn't have time to ponder it before the old man was talking again. "We're very proud of him."

We? Did he mean himself and Beth? "I'm sure you are," Jessamin replied.

"The trouble is, he's not proud of himself."

She couldn't help it; she had to ask why this time. But just as she was about to, she heard the front door open. She felt a presence – *his* presence – Maccaillin's.

Sure enough, the door to the living room burst open.

"Seanair…" he started and then stopped on sight of Jessamin. "Oh, I'm sorry, I didn't realise you were visiting."

Jessamin jumped to her feet. "Hello, Mr Maccaillin, yes, I thought I'd pop in."

"Very good of you," said Maccaillin, his gaze more intense than the flames that danced in the grate beside her.

Placing her empty cup on the saucer, she grabbed at her jumper and pulled it on.

"I… I'd better be going," she said, as much to Stan as to Maccaillin. "But is it okay if I visit again?"

"Please do," said Stan. "Do you mind if Finn sees you out? It takes so much effort for me to get up from my chair nowadays."

"Of course not," she told him.

"Next time you come, there's no need to knock, come straight in," Stan continued. Jessamin glanced at Maccaillin as he said so, to gauge his reaction. There was none.

"I'll do that."

"And if I'm feeling well enough, I'll show you some more of my paintings."

"I'd like that very much."

Jessamin crossed the divide between them and bent to kiss Stan on both cheeks, noting how paper-thin his skin felt beneath her lips. As she pulled away, he placed one hand on his cheek and let it linger there. Her eyes misted slightly at the gesture.

Maccaillin followed her across the hallway to the front door.

"The bluebells," he said. "I take it you brought those."

"I did," Jessamin felt the need to sound defiant.

"There's no need to bring gifts."

"They're hardly a gift. They're just a bunch of bluebells, picked from close by actually."

She braced herself for his reply. When he murmured his thanks she was surprised. She really thought she was in for a telling-off for picking flowers from his land; for somehow desecrating it. Stan might welcome her as a guest, but she really wasn't sure about Maccaillin. He was a loner, Stan had said as much – this tall, well-built man standing in front of her. He was also something else: an enigma. Stern one minute and then what?

"Less stern?" James offered.

Hoping to encourage his 'less stern' streak, Jessamin told Maccaillin about her pending visit to Larnside with Maggie and how much she was looking forward to it.

"Maggie's taken you under her wing?" he asked. "She does that."

"Does she?" Jessamin matched his question with another. Was he talking from experience?

"She's a good woman," was all the reply she got. "One of the best."

Before he was about to close the door; close her out of the world he and his grandfather inhabited, she pointed to the carving above her.

"Comraich – what does it mean?" She'd meant to ask Stan but had forgotten.

"Sanctuary," Maccaillin replied, the same depth of sadness suddenly as evident in him as it had been in his grandfather, but in his case, she didn't have a clue why. "It means sanctuary."

And with that, the door closed.

Chapter Ten

MAGGIE was sure Jessamin would find Larnside even more breathtaking than she found the village of Glenelk. It was more remote for a start, a true hidden gem; one of those villages untouched by the passing of time. To set foot in it was to set foot in another age entirely; a black and white era, she often thought, despite the jewel-like colours of the hills that surrounded them and the blackened mountains that lined the horizon. The word 'genteel' could have been coined for such a village, or 'sleepy'. But make no mistake, in the depths of winter it was not for the faint-hearted. Cut off from the rest of the world for weeks, sometimes for months at a time, with snowdrifts rising higher and higher, you had to be resourceful; keep your wits about you. But there was no one in Larnside who didn't know that, or who wasn't there by choice.

By contrast, Glenelk seemed like a mecca. It had a pub, a village store and a school at least. Larnside had nothing except houses, and not many of those; a red phone box (which Maggie was sure no one ever used), and a coffee shop: AKA someone's front room.

"Millie Grayson's front room to be precise," Maggie elaborated, as she and Jessamin reached the village and parked the car. "Serving hill-walkers, tourists and, of course, the locals, the finest scones you've ever tasted."

"Scones?" Jessamin licked her lips.

"Oh and coffee and walnut cake too, now *that* you have to try. Believe me, so many times I've tried to copy the recipe, but I've given up. It's easier to come here for a fix instead."

As they walked towards Millie's coffee shop, several fishing boats that lined the loch opposite, bobbed gently up and down, dark waters swaying beneath them.

"So, Larnside's a fishing village, is it?" Jessamin asked.

"Aye, it is. Shell fishing mostly, but there's also a fish farm near the mouth of the loch: it's income for a handful of people at least."

Entering the tearoom, Maggie called out in greeting. With Jessamin following her, she turned right off the hallway into a floral-patterned living room furnished with several tables and chairs. On each table was a pristine white tablecloth with a laced edge, a hand-written menu – Millie's calligraphic skills were also to be envied – and a china bowl packed to the brim with sugar cubes. No sooner had they chosen a table than Millie appeared, fussing over Maggie like a long lost friend, which made Maggie smile. It had only been a fortnight since they'd last seen each other.

"And who's this?" Millie, a woman in her early sixties who looked as comforting as the home-baked goods she produced, turned to greet Jessamin.

Swiftly Maggie introduced them. "Millie, this is Jessamin Wade, Glenelk's newest resident."

Jessamin extended her hand, which was grasped warmly and without hesitation.

"Jessamin – that's unusual. I've heard it before though, I'm sure of it." Millie paused to think awhile before bursting into song. "*What am I supposed to do with a girl like Jessamin?* That's it, that's the song! I can't remember the name of the band but I do remember the lyrics."

"The band was called The Casuals," Jessamin enlightened her. "My mother never said it was where she got my name from, but she used to play the song to me when I was little. She loved it." Jessamin shrugged her shoulders. "I loved it too, I suppose."

The smile on Millie's face was almost beatific as she continued to hum the song's tune for a few moments. "Och, I'll be singing that song all day long now. It's a lovely tune and it's lovely to meet you too. Where are you from, Jessamin?"

"I'm from Brighton, on the south coast."

"It's a long way you've come."

"It is," Jessamin agreed.

"What brings you to Glenelk?" she enquired further.

Maggie wondered if she would tell her and was impressed when she did.

"A picture funnily enough. It belonged to my mother. It was of this region, a loch and the mountains; inland though, not the main loch. It was beautiful."

"I see," Millie said, nodding. "Was your mother keen on Scotland then?"

"My grandfather, her father, was from Scotland," Jessamin answered, which was news to Maggie as well. "He came from the Highlands, from around here somewhere I believe, Lochalsh; but he left as a young man and as far as I know, never came back."

"What was his name?" Maggie asked.

"Ben Murray. I don't suppose either of you have heard of him, it was such a long time ago, but perhaps there are a few Murrays living around here still?"

"Not that I'm aware of," Maggie replied.

"I'm sorry, dear," Millie looked somewhat crestfallen.

"Not at all," Jessamin reassured them. "As nice as it would be to meet them, I'm not really on the look-out for long lost family members. It's an incidental that's all."

"An incidental? It's more than that, Jessamin," Millie insisted.

Clearly worried she'd caused offence, Jessamin started to apologise, but Millie stopped her.

"What I mean is, you're one of us, Jess. You're one of us."

Deciding it was time to get down to the nitty-gritty, Maggie interjected.

"Millie, your fabulous coffee and walnut cake: tell me you've got some?"

Beaming at the compliment, Millie replied, "You're in luck. A slab for you both?"

Maggie looked at Jessamin who nodded in agreement.

"Yes please, and tea or coffee, Jess?"

"Tea, please,"

"The same for me, Millie," Maggie instructed.

Just as they'd finished placing their order, another couple walked in – a man and a woman, clad in hard-core walking gear, brand names prominent on their padded waterproof jackets and with binoculars and cameras hanging around their respective necks. Their mud-plastered hiking boots had been politely left in the porch.

"Och," Millie clapped her hands together in glee. "We've a rush on," she added before scurrying away to greet them.

"A rush?" Clearly Jessamin was bemused.

"For Larnside it is," said Maggie, winking at her. "Actually, I'm doing the village a disservice; it gets very busy here in summer. The hills are sometimes packed to bursting."

"But where does everyone stay? I've seen no hotels this side of the peninsula."

"The majority tend to stay in Kyle or come over from Skye for the day, although Jill – she lives in Amberley – runs a guest house, and there's one here too, in Larnside. And Skye Croft's not the only cottage available for lease; there are several others."

"Holiday cottages you mean?"

"Aye, but let for a week or two, that's as long as most people can bear the isolation."

The couple asked for soup and were disappointed to hear there was none.

Maggie leaned across the table. "That's another thing. Her husband Fergus used to make the soup but he's not so good health-wise. It's just tea and cake on the menu now."

"Shame. If I was coming down off the mountains, it'd be soup I'd want."

"They won't be disappointed for long," she assured Jessamin, "not when they've got one of Millie's specials in front of them."

Changing the subject, she added, "Now come on, I know you've been dying to tell me something ever since I picked you up, what is it?"

Jessamin looked taken aback. "But how do you know?"

"You've been… antsy."

"Antsy?"

"Antsy," Maggie confirmed, smiling.

Needing no further prompting, Jessamin told her all about her mother's painting and Stan being the likely artist, news Maggie did indeed find astonishing.

"And have you phoned your brother to check?"

"Yes, just before we came here. The good news is, he thinks he's got it."

"He thinks?" Maggie asked. "He doesn't know?"

98

Quickly Jessamin explained. "He took quite a lot of stuff when Dad sold up and moved abroad; most of it's in his attic. Apparently it's stuffed to the brim, not just with mum and dad's belongings, but his and his wife's too, so it's not quite the easy task it seems."

"I see." It made sense, sort of. "And Stan, how's he?"

The look of amusement on Jessamin's face disappeared.

"As well as can be expected, I suppose, but he's so lonely, Maggie. There's such an air of sadness around him. I imagine that's since Beth departed."

"You imagine wrong," Maggie replied, aware that Jessamin wore a look of solemnity too. "That air of sadness, it's been there since I was a girl."

"Since you were a girl?" Jessamin questioned.

"Aye, I used to visit a lot. Finn and I, we were best friends."

"Best friends?"

The way Jessamin said it, Maggie was glad their tea hadn't arrived. If she'd been sipping it, she was sure the poor girl would have choked.

"You thought I was older than Finn?"

"No, of course not."

"Jessamin…"

Jessamin looked contrite. "Just a little bit, two or three years, no more."

Maggie hadn't really taken offence. She had been born old; that's what her mother used to tell her, albeit affectionately. Her hair, as if in cahoots with that fact, had greyed prematurely; once it had been raven in colour, a glorious shade. To be fair, it was still thick and it was still strong, something to be grateful for. Explaining further, she said, "We're the same age, Finn and I, thirty-five. We were in the same class all the way through school."

"Is there a school hereabouts?" Jessamin quizzed.

"The primary is at the very start of the village, but it's set back from the main road. You'll notice the signpost for it when you go back over the Pass to Kyle."

"Where's the high school?"

"That's in Kyle itself."

After a moment, Maggie couldn't resist asking, "Was Finn there when you visited?"

"Not initially no; he came in just as I was about to leave."

She couldn't help but note – and not without relief – that Jessamin seemed completely unfazed by him. Instead, she seemed more interested in the house itself, but with Comraich and Finn, one road led to another.

Before she could say anything more, Millie returned to their table, setting down before them a very pretty blue teapot with white spots, two matching cups and saucers and two very generous portions of cake, a walnut perched tantalisingly on the top of each.

"This looks delicious," Jessamin's eyes widened as she said it.

Millie smiled indulgently at her. "I hope you like it. And next time you come, try some of my chocolate and chilli brownies. I've been experimenting with the recipe of late and I think I've got it just right. They've got a kick to them but not too much. The first batch I made, my poor husband needed several pints of water to put out the fire!"

Laughing along with her, Jessamin loaded up her fork and lifted it to her mouth, Maggie waiting just as excitedly as Millie for the verdict.

"Mmm," was all Jessamin could manage, raising her left hand to form an 'o' with her thumb and index finger – an indication of just how divine she thought it was.

Millie beamed whilst Maggie chuckled. For a moment, the grief that clouded Jessamin's eyes receded. Maggie likened that moment to a burst of sunshine on a cloudy day.

As soon as Millie was gone, Maggie started speaking again.

"You wanted to know more about Comraich?"

Jessamin nodded eagerly.

"The house's history, in recent times, isn't a happy one. Finn has two sisters, both married and living elsewhere. One's in America I think, the other somewhere distant too, but where exactly I don't know. His parents had them much earlier than Finn, although to be fair, his mother, Kristin, was still a young girl by today's standards when she had him; twenty-eight I've been told. She died a year after his birth; lost her fight against cancer."

Jessamin was about to take another sip of tea but paused. "She had cancer? That's awful."

"Aye, but her loss might have been easier to bear if Finn had had a protective father. Unfortunately, he didn't; his father was a drunk – whether he was before his wife died I don't know, but certainly he was afterwards. He died too, when Finn was still a boy – cirrhosis of the liver. It was Stan and Beth who raised Finn and I know he was close to Stan."

"That's something at least."

"It is, it is," agreed Maggie. "He was a shy lad was Finn." As she said it, she could feel her voice catch slightly. "I re-member our first day of school; he looked so nervous – the boy from the big house as he was known; so lost. I'd never spoken to him before; his family tended to keep themselves separate. But I spoke to him on that day and he looked grate-ful for it. He latched on to me and I was happy to let him. We became such friends."

She could see Jessamin try to associate the stern, aloof man she knew with the shy schoolboy and fail. Little wonder, Maggie thought; there was a world of difference between them.

"It was in his teens he changed. As we got older, Finn became aware of his looks and his confidence increased, dramatically. Quite the heartthrob he became, quite the heartbreaker. He... he used to exploit his looks, I felt. Girls seemed to fascinate him; it was as though he couldn't quite get enough; he wanted them all – tore through them at a pace. Sometimes we'd argue about it, we argued quite a bit. In short, we grew apart."

Maggie lowered her eyes. It was true, they had grown apart, but nonetheless she still missed him.

"He became angry too, obsessed with the need to spread his wings. He wanted to get out – to experience life. Glenelk and those in it could never hold a man like him."

"He's back now, though," Jessamin pointed out.

"He's back, but whether he'll stay, I couldn't tell you."

"Where was it he went?" Jessamin asked.

"I believe his last post was Afghanistan. He was in the army; the bomb disposal squad to be precise."

Now Jessamin did choke on her tea. "His burns, his eye..."

Maggie nodded. "I assume that's how he sustained those injuries. Something went wrong, although I don't know what. I tried to ask him once but it was short shrift I got."

"The war hero returns..." Jessamin said having taken a few moments to digest this information.

"Indeed, if he was a hero. As I said, no one knows. What I do know is he went away a bold young man and he's come back broken. The curse of Comraich continues."

"The curse?"

"Och, I don't mean it literally," Maggie rushed to explain. "All I mean is it's a house that's seen too much sadness; that's been weighed down by it over the years. It seems like a curse but it's not; in many ways it's just the misfortunes of life. But being there, in his current state of mind, it won't do him any good; it will weigh him down further."

"You're really worried about him, aren't you?"

"Yes, Jess, I am. It... it hurts to see him this way; so closed. Whatever he suffered, it's traumatised him. And Stan, he won't last forever. He's old and he's not in the best of health. Now that Beth's gone, he's playing a waiting game until he's released too, and once Finn's alone at Comraich... well... it's a sanctuary all right, but I'm not sure it's the right kind."

"Since he's been back, have you seen him? I mean properly seen him, to talk to?"

"No," and this was something that caused her even more pain. "He comes into the shop every now and then, we make small talk but that's all. He keeps himself apart as his family once did. I'm amazed you've been allowed access to the lodge, but I'm pleased too."

"It's to see Stan," Jessamin pointed out, "not him."

"Still, your presence at Comraich, it's a good thing," Maggie insisted.

Jessamin still seemed intrigued by his profession, however.

"So he was in the bomb disposal squad, that's incredible. I don't know how people can be so brave, risking their lives constantly. It must make for precarious living."

Maggie leaned forward. "Do you know why I think he opted to join the army?"

Jessamin leaned forward too. "Why?"

"To escape, that was one reason for sure. But also because he wanted to be the exact opposite of his father; a man who, unable to deal with loss, with responsibility, drank himself to death. It's a slow suicide and one that didn't just affect him, but his entire family."

"Was he a violent drunk?" Again, Jessamin's eyes widened.

"Not violent no, but he was neglectful and to some that's just as painful."

"I wouldn't know," Jessamin replied. "I was lucky enough to have a fortunate upbringing – my parents were very attentive – but I can imagine it was hard for Finn certainly, and perhaps one of the reasons why the family kept themselves to themselves?"

"Maybe," Maggie hadn't thought of that, "although Stan was friendly enough. He used to let me watch him paint on occasion when I was a kid. It felt like such a privilege."

Jessamin nodded as though in understanding. After another bite of cake, she asked, "Does Maccaillin drink?"

"I don't think so. No more than you or I. But if he's alone, if his demons won't let go, he might succumb. A liking for liquor sometimes runs in the blood."

Something outside caught Jessamin's eye.

"My God! Did I just see a stag wander by?"

Maggie followed her line of sight. "Aye, you did. You'll get used to such spectacles, believe me. There's more deer than people around here – a whole lot more."

Millie had clearly heard Jessamin's exclamations of wonder and came over to join them once again. The couple, who had also opted for tea and walnut cake, were similarly entranced.

"That's Bogle," Millie explained, "another village resident."

"Is he tame?" Jessamin asked.

SHANI STRUTHERS

"As tame as it's possible for a stag to be. I've sat and enjoyed a slice of cake not two foot from him before. I also offered him some of the said cake, but sadly he declined."

All eyes watched Bogle until he made a left turn and disappeared from sight.

"This place," Jessamin breathed, "it's incredible. I wish we'd visited before."

Her use of the word 'we' was not lost on Maggie.

"Would you like to go for a walk?" Maggie asked, placing her fork neatly on her empty plate.

"I'd love to."

After thanking Millie profusely for her hospitality, Maggie led Jessamin back outside.

"It's so quiet," Jessamin's eyes seemed fixated on the scenery around her.

"You either love it or you hate it. I love it."

"Me too."

Furtively Maggie studied Jessamin's face to see if she meant it. She was glad to see she did.

"So, would you say you've settled in?"

"I would, yes."

"And you'll be along Thursday night as usual?"

"Try and stop me," Jessamin flashed a smile at her, her features, enviably pretty, were even more so because of it. Trying to make it sound as though it were merely an afterthought, she added, "Where does your husband go when everyone comes round? To the pub?"

"I'm not married," Maggie replied. "There's never been anyone who caught my eye."

It was a lie but a white lie. There was no point in revealing who had once caught her eye.

The stretch of shingle they were walking on soon ran out,

105

although the loch continued onwards into the distance. Making her way to a low ridge of wall, Maggie sat down.

"You miss James terribly, don't you?" she said, kicking idly at pebbles.

"Every minute of every day."

"How often do you talk to him?"

The younger woman started visibly at this and Maggie wondered if she'd deny it.

"Erm…" Jessamin faltered, but to her credit only slightly. "I talk to him often."

"And does he reply?"

Again, Jessamin paused. "I like to think so, yes."

"That must be comforting for you."

"Do you think I'm mad?"

For the first time Maggie detected a defensive note. She turned to look fully at Jessamin. "No, Jess, far from it. Just remember to talk to the living too."

"I do. I'm talking to you, aren't I?"

It was an attempt to make light of their conversation, but Maggie ignored it.

"Admitted. But you've come here to escape; to be alone with James. I know he's far from the demon that stalks Finn, but angels and demons alike, they belong to another world; a world you're not a part of – not yet. By all means talk to him as long as there's comfort in it. I've also been known to talk to the dead at times, but keep in mind there might come a time when you have to let him go, and not just for your sake but for his too."

Although Jessamin remained mute, Maggie could hear her silent reply – she had a talent for sometimes being able to read what people were thinking; an intuitive 'gift' her mother had also had, and her mother before her. Sometimes she chose to tune in, other times she didn't. There had been plenty of occasions when she didn't *want* to know what another person was thinking. But right now, she picked up on the words '*I can't*' loud and clear.

"You can," Maggie made sure her voice was gentle but firm. "Let go of him and let go of the guilt. The latter I hope soon, because you don't deserve to suffer the way you do. The former, well, that time will come, but it's not now; Jess, don't look so worried, it's not now."

But Jessamin did look worried – very much so, and her silent assurance to James that she would *never* let him go was not lost on Maggie either.

Chapter Eleven

"HAVE you had lunch today, Stan?"

"I've had a little something, dear, thank you."

"A little what exactly?"

"A cheese sandwich."

"That's not much. You need something to warm you, some soup or something."

"I've not much of an appetite."

Whether Stan had an appetite or not, he needed to eat properly, not just a bit of cheese slammed between two pieces of bread. Jessamin was no cook – James had been the cook – but she was willing to learn and maybe, just maybe, James could help her.

"So you want to make soup?" James asked, distinctly amused.

"*You* used to make soup," Jessamin countered.

"I did, and you used to lap it up."

"Well, now I want Stan to lap it up. He's skin and bone, that man. I swear he's not eating properly. Maccaillin probably isn't either. I'll make them both soup."

"Okay, okay," conceded James. "Onions, potato, carrots and leeks – stock up on all those types of ingredients, as well as some lentils – the red ones – good vegetable bouillon and tinned tomatoes – chopped preferably. You're about to get a master class."

As the weeks passed, Jessamin became very skilled indeed at making soup, and not just of the vegetable and lentil variety; she also made leek and potato, cream of chicken, tomato and basil and lately, butternut squash with a hint of chilli, all of which tasted delicious. The ingredients had been shopped for in Kyle or shipped in from Inverness. She would transfer two flasks of soup over to the lodge, serve one to Stan and leave the other in the kitchen for Maccaillin. She never saw the latter eat it; she barely saw him at all, in fact; just in passing, when he'd throw a 'hello' or a 'goodbye' her way, depending on whether he was coming or going. But when she returned for the second flask, it was always empty.

"Pray God he doesn't just wash it down the sink," she muttered to herself, her apron on, stirring another vat of soup – carrot and coriander this time.

"He's a fool if he does," James commented. "You're getting good at this soup-making lark, you know. Find out about Health & Safety, bottle it and see if Maggie wants to sell it in her shop and Millie for that matter: she said she hasn't got either the time or inclination to make it, so why not do the honours? You were right about those hill walkers; I'd want soup *and* cake."

Jessamin laughed at his suggestion at first but then considered it. A tentative phone call to Millie and she'd secured her first order. Winn Greer was also interested; although he offered a basic selection of sandwiches to walkers during the summer season, he didn't want to get involved in actually cooking for them.

"No," Maggie had said rather dryly when Jessamin had told him of her success with both Millie and Winn, "he prefers to concentrate on serving his first love: alcohol."

Thankfully Jessamin could order all the equipment she

needed off the Internet, the retail outlet she favoured happy to send their wares anywhere in the UK, even the arse end.

"And don't forget to ask over in Kyle. There are plenty of outlets there that might be interested too," James pointed out. "I get the impression they're a pretty supportive community in the Highlands. If one of their own makes it, they'll buy it."

Encouraged by Maggie too, she did just that; amazed at the positive response she received.

"The Highland Soup Queen," Maggie joked.

"All thanks to James," Jessamin replied.

"Don't underestimate your part in it," Maggie countered.

The name Maggie had called her stuck. She designed a logo for the business and had labels made up and sent to Skye Croft. She would write the use-by dates on in marker pen.

Apart from soup-making (copious amounts of it), and visits to see Stan, Jessamin attended every one of Maggie's Thursday night meetings, getting to know the rest of the Glenelk girls. She got on particularly well with Maidie and Ally, who were both slightly older than her and Shona, who was younger. They were funny, sweet and supportive in equal measures. Maggie also insisted that she join the girls on occasional weekend nights at The Stag. Sometimes there'd be a quiz there; sometimes someone would strike up on the guitar and a singsong would ensue, or people would just sit and chat, enjoying the company of friends. Rory's eyes, she noticed, would light up whenever she walked through the door.

"Ah, you set his heart on fire," Shona teased.

"We're just friends," Jessamin assured her, taking pains not to give them or Rory any impression that there could be hope of anything else. "Besides, he's too young for me. He's more your age, isn't he, Shona?"

Shona blushed.

Maccaillin, she noticed, never graced the pub.

"Did he ever?" she asked Maggie.

"When we were younger all of us would meet at the pub, Finn as much as anyone – it's where we hung out; where people would make eyes at each other; where we'd begin the arduous and sometimes not so arduous process of courting. All of us still meet here, older versions of ourselves admitted, but not Finn. Finn hasn't been here since he's been back. And I very much doubt he will. It'll take a miracle to get him through that door."

"There's not many young people here nowadays," Jessamin pointed out, and by young she meant teenagers, as Maggie and her crowd had once been.

"No, that's something that's changed. What teens there are in the village go over to Kyle; they crash at friends' houses or drive, I suppose; I don't know which. And as soon as they're old enough, many of them leave; head for the bright lights of Glasgow or Edinburgh, or some other big city. London too, I'm told, for a fair few of them. The world's a much smaller place now. It's not as daunting as it once was. For kids, the sky's the limit."

We're all running, thought Jessamin listening to her; some of us toward civilisation and some of us as far away as we can get.

The weeks slipped by. Already it was June – something that took Jessamin by surprise: where had most of March, April and May gone? She'd come here for a quieter time, or so she thought, instead she was now building a business (albeit an extremely modest one), and making new friends. There were 283 people allegedly in Glenelk and most of them seemed to want to get to know the newcomer. She'd never been so busy!

"It's good, Jess, to keep busy," James said.

"And why's that? Because you think it takes my mind off you."

"In a way, yes," he confessed.

"Well, it doesn't," she replied somewhat abruptly.

"It's still a good thing," he insisted. "It's better than brooding."

Perhaps, perhaps not – she thought it but didn't say it, not wanting to argue further.

On this particular morning, Glenelk had been graced with pleasant enough weather; the sun wasn't bright but it wasn't raining either – which made a change. In recent weeks it had been very wet – Maccaillin's rain gods in action. Jessamin was just getting ready to go and see Stan when the phone rang.

"Hi, Jess, it's Sarah. How's the soup empire going?"

Jessamin laughed. "I wouldn't call it an empire, Sarah, but, yeah, it's okay. I've got a decent amount of orders so far, and a few more coming in. There's a couple that run a café on Skye who are interested. I'm going over to see them to-morrow."

"And all from the confines of your cottage kitchen, huh?"

"Which is suddenly way too small. I might have to get separate premises at this rate."

"Separate premises? Go you!"

"I'm not quite there yet," Jessamin confessed. "It'd just be nice to have a bit more room that's all – the kitchen at Skye Croft is tiny."

"And soup, aren't you sick of eating it?" Sarah quizzed.

"I must admit I don't tend to anymore." Nowadays she

preferred to stick to solids, although Stan was still very appreciative.

For a while Sarah and Jessamin talked about general matters: how life was in Brighton; Sarah's job at a water board company, which was boring her rigid; the heatwave everyone was beginning to complain about. Jessamin thought again of the rain they'd been having; hopefully the weather would cheer up and some warmth would find its way north.

"Hey, your lease is up in September. Will you be coming home for winter?"

"It's what any sensible sane person would do but…"

"Yeah, I know it; you're neither sensible nor sane."

"Thanks for that," Jessamin replied, laughing again. "At the moment though, I'm okay here and it'd be a shame to move when my soup is in such demand."

"But are *you* in demand? That's what I want to know."

"Sarah…" Jessamin hoped she'd pick up on her warning not to continue down that particular road. Thankfully she did.

"Oh, all right, I just thought, you know: new house, new people, new romance."

"That's never going to happen."

"Never is a long time."

"I'm married, Sarah."

"You're widowed, Jess."

There was a tense silence – a silence lasting only a few moments but which seemed a lot longer. Jessamin was the one who started speaking again. Sarah didn't understand and she couldn't blame her for that. She didn't *want* her to understand.

"You know that picture I was telling you about, the one that belonged to my mum?"

"I remember – the picture that prompted your mad move?"

"The very same. Well, finally Dane got round to checking his attic to see if he'd stashed it in there. I've only had to re- mind him about three times."

"Brothers," groaned Sarah and Jessamin could imagine her rolling her eyes. She had five to contend with. "Why did he put it in the attic?"

"He stashes everything in the attic. Him and his wife, they like the minimal look."

"But not in terms of the attic?"

"No, the attic is stuffed – they're hoarders in denial I think," Jessamin said, laughing.

"Did he have it, then?"

Jessamin couldn't help sighing. "He was sure he'd taken it, but if he had, he can't find it; which only leaves Aunt Lara. Trouble is, she and Uncle Grey are away, touring the Far East. Going whilst they're still young enough to enjoy it, Dane said. I had no idea they were planning to do that. They're gone all summer long."

"Good for her. I want to do that when I've saved enough money: take off – eat my way round the world. First stop, Thailand. You know how much I adore Thai food."

Jessamin did. They had regularly eaten at Thai restaurants in Brighton.

"I do hope she's got Mum's picture though."

"Does it really matter if she hasn't?" Sarah asked.

"Well… I don't know. I'd just hate to think of it as lost or hanging in some stranger's house. Mum and me were fond of it."

"Get Stan to paint you another one," Sarah suggested.

"He doesn't paint any more, and besides, it wouldn't be

the same. That picture… it has sentimental value I suppose. I've just got a hankering to know it's safe."

"And real value, does it have that too?"

Jessamin hadn't really considered how much the picture was worth in monetary terms before. "Maybe, it's an original after all, but as I said, that's not really the point."

"If you say so. Anyway, how is Stan?"

"He's good. I'm off to see him this afternoon."

"And his grandson? Are you getting along any better with him?"

"I don't really see him, so no on that score. I think he likes my soup though. I've also scrubbed the kitchen and now it's gleaming. It was pretty grungy before and the living room looks brighter now. It's amazing what a few strategically placed vases of flowers can do, and a bit of a dust here and there. He hasn't complained about anything I've done so far."

"I should think not, Jess, you're the unpaid help."

"I'm the *grateful* help; I like spending time with Stan. He's a sweet old man." As she said it, Jessamin glanced at the clock on the wall. "Look, I'd better go, Stan's expecting me. He'll be getting hungry."

"You're a saint, you are," Sarah replied. "Speak soon."

"Speak soon," Jessamin repeated, ending the call and shrugging out of her apron at the same time. After filling the usual two canisters with soup, she hurried through the woods to Comraich – *the path well trodden* as she was beginning to think of it.

* * *

"Hello, dear, lovely to see you. What soup have we got

today?"

"Hi, Stan. Carrot and coriander, I hope that's all right."

"I've never tried carrot and coriander before, but if it's made by you, I'm sure I'll love it."

After kissing the old man on both cheeks, her customary greeting, Jessamin went into the kitchen to heat the soup. She'd also baked some bread and was quite pleased with the way it had turned out – soft and light. Tearing off a hunk, she placed it beside the soup bowl on his tray. Next, she tore off a hunk for herself and put the remainder in the bread bin. As the soup warmed through, she looked around the kitchen; at gleaming surfaces and neatly ordered shelves. It was a large kitchen, almost industrial. An idea occurred... *what if?* But quickly she quashed it.

Pouring the soup into Stan's bowl, she carried the tray through to the living room and placed it on the table before him. As he started to spoon the contents into his mouth with shaky hands, she nibbled on her piece of bread.

"This is lovely, dear. I know I say it every time you visit, but I do so look forward to seeing you. You brighten my day."

"And you brighten mine," Jessamin replied, meaning every word.

"How's James?"

"He's fine; proud of my soup-making skills, I can tell you. I don't think he can quite believe the domestic goddess I've turned into. He says there was no evidence of it in the years we were together." Jessamin laughed as she told him this.

As Stan continued to eat, Jessamin asked, "How's Beth?"

Often they'd kick-start their conversations with these two questions. She'd told him quite early on in their friendship that she spoke to James. Stan had confessed he did the same with Beth, 'It's a way of keeping her close', he'd said. It was wonderful not to have to pretend with Stan; not to feel embarrassed or weird. They were two of a kind.

"Beth is as grand as ever. We were reminiscing only last night about one glorious summer we spent together as children. We were eleven; Beth says twelve, but I'm sure I'm right. It was glorious because the sun shone consistently, warming this otherwise cold, cold land. We spent nearly every day by the loch, me, Beth, Flo and Mally."

Jessamin settled back to listen. Stan spoke as much about Flo and Mally as he did about Beth. They seemed to be a unit, the four of them – as inseparable as Maggie had said she and Maccaillin had been as children. She wondered if he'd talk about his daughter, Kristin, too, his only child as she'd since found out; but it was a more distant past he preferred to recall.

"On Skye," he continued, "in the midst of the Cuillan Mountains are the fairy pools. Have you visited them yet?"

Jessamin shook her head.

"Ah, you should, they're glorious. The water is the clearest blue and the sound of water falling – it's like music to the ears. Get Finn to take you there one day. But, as beautiful as they are, they're not as magical as the fairy pools at our loch; our secret loch."

Stan had already explained that Loch Hourn – the one that abutted Skye – was a sea loch. Stan's Loch, as she'd christened it, seemed to have no given name. It was much smaller and land-locked on all sides.

"At our loch, the water is the purest I've ever seen or tasted for that matter – like nectar it is, enlivening you. There are several small pools around it; one has an underwater arch, only tiny but that's where Flo said the fairies hid. Even in winter the pools are beautiful, but in summer the sheen upon them could keep you mesmerised for hours."

Again Jessamin thought how wonderful it must have been to grow up in the great outdoors as Stan and his friends had done. She'd grown up amongst a jumble of crowded streets and had found even the green spaces of Preston Park and Queens Park crowded too. The pebble beach, lined with amusements, also attracted marauding hordes in summer. They would arrive by the trainload and wouldn't leave until the sun had set, sometimes not even then, taking advantage of Brighton's myriad nightlife – its bars, its restaurants, its nightclubs. She longed to visit Stan's Loch –to see for herself the fairy pools he talked of; the expanse of freshwater. It sounded heavenly. Briefly she glanced at her watch. She'd tried to go there before but hadn't got very far. It had been either too cold, too wet, or a horrid mixture of both; the ground slippery beneath her feet – treacherous even. Maybe she'd try again today, now that the rain had stopped.

"Mally suggested we all went for a swim – it was early in the summer, June I think, although it could have been later, I'm not sure. It was daring of us; we knew we weren't allowed; that we'd sworn to our parents we wouldn't swim without adult supervision. But Mally, he could be persuasive, and so we did, stripping down to our underwear and plunging into cool, delicious depths. That was the first time I'd seen Beth without her dress on, and although I was fond of her, I hadn't really thought of her in *that* way before. Afterwards, I couldn't stop thinking of her in that way."

Stan chuckled at the memory.

"Every day we met at the loch during that summer, usually in the afternoon since we tended to spend mornings helping with chores, and every day, without fail, we swam. By the end of the summer I was in love with Beth; a love that never faltered."

It was Jessamin now who smiled at his words.

"Had she fallen in love with you too?"

Stan's face darkened slightly as Jessamin asked this. "Och, no, I was still just Stan to her; just a friend. I was for some years. It was Mally who dominated her thoughts."

"Mally? But he was in love with Flo."

"Aye, I told you that before, didn't I?"

Stan could be forgetful at times, but he'd told her that very thing during one of their conversations. Beth and Flo might have been twins, but it was Mally and Flo who were soul mates. Still, she didn't mind listening again. She loved the pictures he created, not with paint this time but with words.

Stan was nodding his head. "Aye," he repeated. "He was in love with Flo, very much, and Flo was in love with him. Mally was the handsome one you see; he had dark eyes, like a gypsy, a shock of dark hair too. The girls, they love that look, don't they? It's a romantic look, straight out of the story-books. I was the artistic one, sensitive; a bit too much at times. I couldn't compare to Mally. I was also fair and not as strapping a lad."

Having seen pictures of Stan as a young man, Jessamin could only disagree.

"You're too kind, lass, too kind. But Mally, he had some-thing about him; there was none that knew him who'd deny it. Even I was in thrall to him at times. As much as he adored Flo, he enjoyed the attention of Beth. I used to warn him about it, tell him not to encourage her. Playing twins off against each other, that's never a good thing."

"Were they identical twins?" There was a photo of Beth

and Flo as girls in the living room and certainly they looked similar, but the shot was grainy; their faces blurred.

"They were," Stan answered. "But I could always tell the difference."

There were no photos of Flo as an adult. Jessamin had already noticed that. What age had she been when she had died?

"Did the twins fall out because of Mally?" she couldn't resist asking.

"You could say that," Stan replied. He looked tired all of a sudden as if the weight of memories was somehow crushing him. "But that's a story for another day, Jess. Today I want to remember the sunlit days; the days when the four of us could not be parted."

Jessamin could see Stan's eyes closing. His soup was only half-finished.

"Are you tired?" she asked, moving towards him and reaching for his hand.

"I'm always tired, Jess; always wondering when life will give up on me."

"Stan! Don't say that."

Stan's eyes opened – they might have been blue once, a bright colour. Now they'd faded to grey.

"But I want to go," he said gently. "Sitting propped up all day by the fire, being carried to my bed at night, the same thing happening day after day; it's not living. I miss being able to paint; I miss my friends and my family; I miss Beth. I want to be with her again."

She knew exactly what he meant. It was why they'd bonded so quickly.

"I'd miss you if you went and Finn would too. Grant us a little more time."

120

"You're very sweet," Stan's voice was growing faint. "Beth would have liked you."

"Your soup," she asked, "would you like to finish it later?"

"Later would be grand," he managed to reply before his eyelids won the battle.

Within seconds, he was sleeping, intermittent snuffles escaping him.

Jessamin tucked in his blanket and stoked the fire before letting herself out of the living room and making her way to Stan's Loch.

* * *

Stan had given her directions to the loch on a previous visit.

"At the front door, turn right and you'll see a gate. The road continues beyond that, but it's a bumpy road and one that only farmers tend to use. Well, farmers and Finn. Walk along this road; it becomes narrower and narrower – in parts it's hardly a road at all, but stick to it as much as you can. You've another mile or so before the loch comes into view."

There was also another path, running in the opposite direction, winding round the base of a hill before disappearing entirely. That path intrigued her too. It seemed so mysterious, but she'd venture along it another time. Right now, it was the loch she wanted to see.

Zipping up her fleece, Jessamin glanced at the skies and was relieved to see they still looked fairly non-threatening. As she walked, she remembered Maccaillin's warning about never setting off into the countryside without informing someone first, but she wasn't going far, so there'd be no harm in it, surely? Spying a gap between the gate and the fence, she squeezed through it. The wilderness was in front of her – the land peppered only with sheep, either ignoring her or looking curiously at the stranger in their midst. If she dared to get too close, they turned and ran, eager for the distance between them to remain. The continuing path, she was glad to note, was sturdy; a little jagged at the edges and pockmarked here and there. Either side of it the land was covered in wild grass, uneven in texture with mounds and hillocks punctuating it. It was only a few minutes into her journey that Jessamin felt the first burst of rain. She stopped and held out her hand for a moment to check she wasn't imagining the cold wet spots that had started to sprinkle her face. She wasn't. A few more metres and the spots turned into splodges. The clouds seemed to have suddenly dropped too; shrouding entirely the mountainous horizon. With the sun obliterated, she could feel the cold permeating not just her clothes but also her skin, chilling her through to the bone.

"Damn," she cursed under her breath.

Even though she'd been warned, she couldn't quite believe how quickly the weather had turned. There'd been no sign of rain when she'd left Comraich. There was no way she could push through this, not without proper rain gear and thermals. She'd need those and a better sense of location. Visibility was getting poorer by the minute, the second even – she'd lose sight of the path at this rate; stumble onto uneven ground; risk falling. Once again, the rain gods had got the better of her.

"Go back, Jess," she heard James whisper.

Heeding his words as well as Maccaillin's, she called it a day and turned for home.

Chapter Twelve

THE deeper Stan descended into sleep, the more troubled his dreams became. Such happy memories he'd shared with Beth last night and Jessamin this afternoon – he wanted to hold on to those memories and only them; he didn't want to remember what else happened at the loch, many years after they'd first swam in it. So much he seemed to have forgotten in life, but what had happened during another summer, the one when they all turned eighteen, he couldn't forget, although during waking hours he made certain never to acknowledge it. But he was sleeping more lately, and in sleep there was no escape. Perhaps in death there wouldn't be either – in death he'd have dues to pay.

As much as he wanted to be with Beth, his dear, sweet, saddened Beth, atonement frightened him. But could you ruin a man's life and not atone for it? He didn't think so. It went against the grain. There were consequences to actions – always. But whatever he'd done wrong, he'd done something right too: he'd protected Beth. It was what bound them together. Suddenly she'd needed him and he'd liked that, he couldn't deny it. Marriage vows weren't necessary, but nonetheless they had married, on a wet and windy day at the church in Kyle: the happiest day of his life, despite the weather. And she had stuck by him, had Beth, perhaps even grown to love him. She'd loved their daughter Kristin too; had brightened considerably in the years following her birth.

But when Kristin died, she had gone into decline again, severely; said it was her punishment. Kristin's untimely death had hit him too, so very hard, and the children, his grandchildren – how he felt for them; for Kristin's girls; for the son who would never know her or remember how proudly she had gazed upon his tiny face. But he'd had to remain strong; be the rock on which they leant, and refrain from crumbling inside. Kristin's husband had been no good: a vain, self-indulgent and self-pitying man. What his precious daughter had seen in him, he never understood. It was a relief when he died; a relief to them all.

Not wanting to dwell on thoughts of Kristin's husband, his mind returned to Beth.

"Thank you," she had once said to him.

"For what?"

"For loving me."

"I've always loved you."

Ever since the day they first swam in the loch.

Was she scared at the end? Truly, he didn't know. Rather, she seemed pleased to be going.

"To see Flo," she explained, on more than one occasion. It was her twin she pined for above all.

"Wait for me," he'd said.

"Of course. We'll both wait."

And Mally? Would Mally be waiting for him too? Stan knew he was dead; he'd kept tabs on him – easy enough to do when you possessed money to pay for such services. Twenty-four years he'd been dead; twenty-four long years in which to brood, and plan revenge?

Trying to reach the figure that hovered always at the edge of his dreams; refusing despite his pleas, to come closer, he whispered, "I'm sorry, Mally. Forgive me, please."

124

Chapter Thirteen

JESSAMIN had to admit that for a pub located at the arse end of nowhere, it was pretty lively. The entire village had turned out, it seemed, plus people from the surrounding villages. A few residents from Larnside she recognised, including Millie with her husband Fergus, a man supposed to be in ill health but who looked well enough tonight. Rory too was in attendance, making eyes at her. She smiled in return but that's all she did. At the bar, Winn was busy serving drinks, doing a roaring trade no doubt. Local lads, including Dougie the bonny Scotsman she'd met on her first night in the village, were taking it in turns to cover songs from the eighties and nineties on a makeshift stage. Songs by The Proclaimers seemed to be a firm favourite and several people, mainly women, had formed dancing clusters; laughing and singing along.

Sitting in a corner with Maggie, who was tapping her feet in time with the music, Jessamin leant across.

"Guess who might come in tonight?"

"Who?" Maggie enquired, laughing outright as Winn came out from behind the bar to dance a quick jig with Ina.

"Maccaillin."

Immediately Maggie stilled. "What?"

"Maccaillin," Jessamin repeated. "I saw him today; spent the best part of the afternoon with him. I mentioned there was a bit of a shindig going on at the pub tonight and to come along."

"And?" Maggie looked as if she could barely catch her breath.

"And," Jessamin shrugged, "he said he might."

"Are you sure you heard him correctly?"

"Honestly, he did. We... it was nice spending time with him. He took me to Stan's Loch; I didn't even have to ask him, he volunteered. I was quite surprised to tell you the truth; he hasn't been overly friendly since I arrived in Glenelk. But today he seemed different... a little lighter."

"Lighter? Stan's Loch?" Maggie seemed thoroughly confused. Noting Jessamin's empty glass, she said, "I think you need another drink. Pinot Grigio, isn't it? I'll get it and when I come back, I want you to tell me all about your day with Finn, and I mean *all* of it."

Jessamin tried to hide her amusement at Maggie's reaction. "If you're buying, I'm talking."

Maggie returned only minutes later – a glass of wine in one hand and a pint of lager in the other. As the band started on another old favourite – a song by Big Country this time, played enthusiastically to an equally enthusiastic crowd – Jessamin did as Maggie asked.

* * *

Stan had developed a cough and not only that, he sounded wheezy.

"Should I call the doctor?" Jessamin had asked.

"No, it's nothing, dear – I'm prone to coughs and colds, always have been. The damp in the atmosphere, it weakens the lungs. That's my theory anyway."

Surely Maccaillin was concerned; she'd have to ask him – if she could find him. Whenever she visited Stan it was roughly at the same time, just before noon. Just lately, she'd been coming over every day, despite having so much soup to make. The couple that ran the café in Kyleakin on Skye wanted an order; she was doing fairly well now. Not earning enough to make a living, but it wasn't a living she needed to make. It was more something to fill her time. Visiting Stan also made her feel useful – it comforted her like talking to James comforted her; she only hoped she was of some comfort to him too. She always left Comraich by two in the afternoon, sometimes a little earlier, it depended how tired Stan was. During those hours, Maccaillin was never around. Deliberately?

"Even so, I think you need the doctor. Coughs and colds can turn nasty."

Especially when you're old and vulnerable she'd wanted to say, but hadn't. Instead she'd served him his soup – lentil and bacon, his favourite.

"Are you sure you're not sick of my soup?" she checked for the umpteenth time. "I'll make you something else if you are. I could do stew or a pie even."

"Och," Stan shook his head. "Soup is fine. Chewing requires too much energy."

Jessamin explained to Maggie that she'd had to feed Stan the last few spoons of soup. That energy he was talking about, it seemed to be failing at a rapid rate. Wiping his mouth and helping him to a few sips of water afterwards, she left him to his nap. She intended to call Maccaillin later to discuss Stan seeing a doctor, and there was no way she'd take no for an answer.

"As it turns out," she said to Maggie, "I didn't need to call him. As I was on my way out, he came striding in." She tilted her head to one side. "He does that, doesn't he? Stride, I mean."

Maggie smiled fondly. "As an adult perhaps, but as a child, he tended to shuffle."

"Well, today he came striding in and I strode too, right up to him."

"Ah, it's The Highland Soup Queen," Maccaillin had said, referring to the tongue-in-cheek name Jessamin had given her business.

"Mr Maccaillin, I'm glad I bumped into you. I need to speak to you about Stan. It's his chest. He sounds slightly wheezy to me. I think he needs to see a doctor."

Maccaillin seemed to ponder this. "The old man hates doctors but yes, he needs to see one; to be on the safe side."

Jessamin hadn't expected him to agree so readily.

"So I'll leave it to you then?"

"Yes, Mrs Wade. Believe it or not, there are some things you can leave to me. Calling the doctor to come and see my sick grandfather is one of them."

"Oh, I never meant—"

"I'm sure you didn't," Maccaillin interrupted. "Rest assured, I'll do it."

She was the one shuffling then, looking down at her feet in embarrassment.

"Well, I'll be off then. I'm going to try and reach Stan's Loch again today."

"Stan's Loch?"

"The one he used to play by as a child. It's not really called Stan's Loch, but that's how I've come to think of it." She also thought of it as *her* loch, but didn't mention this.

"The one Seanair said you had a picture of?"

"The very same."

"And you've tried to reach it before?"

"I have, but I've never got very far, thanks to the weather."

"Aye, blue skies outside Comraich, they don't mean a thing."

His choice of words sounded cryptic, especially considering what Maggie had told her.

"Anyway," she continued, "I'd best be on my way, whilst the sun's still shining. Let me know what the doctor says."

Although she was already past him, his next words brought her to a halt.

"I could come with you if you want? To Stan's Loch."

If *she* wanted, like he was doing her the favour?

"If *you* want to, you'd be welcome," she replied, turning back to face him.

He looked awkward then – awkward or affronted – she didn't know him well enough to tell. She suspected the former, something that belied his youthful reputation as a Lothario. What was his more adult experience with women, she wondered? Had life in the army left much time for such extra-curricular activities? Certainly, there was no sign he'd been married, the ring finger on his left hand was decidedly bare.

"You've clocked it then?" She could hear James teasing her.

"By accident not by design," she shot back, silently of course. Stan and Maggie might not think she was mad talking to James, but she was certain Maccaillin would.

Softening, she added, "You know what? I'd like it very much if you joined me."

Perhaps it was time to get to know him a little. She liked his grandfather, why not him too?

They set off in companionable silence, closing the door of Comraich behind them and heading for the gate, skirting round it as she'd done previously. Soon nothing but green hills, mountains and clouds lay before them. Oh, and sheep – numerous sheep.

"Who farms the land?" Jessamin asked.

"Our family used to but it's the Adair family who farm it now; they live over in Larnside. Seanair sold quite a bit of our land to them when I was very young; he wanted to concentrate on his art. We only own a few acres now compared to what we once had."

"Seanair." She'd heard him use that term before. "Is that Gaelic for grandfather?"

"It is," he replied. "It's what I've always called him."

"I see. Stan tells me you spend a lot of time walking."

"In the absence of much else to do around here, yes."

"Oh, there's plenty to do around here." There was a slight tease in her voice as she said it. "Read books, explore Skye, visit friends, make soup…"

Jessamin was walking on his left side – his good side. At the mention of soup his face crinkled – a slight dimple appearing in his cheek. A heartthrob in his youth, he could still be considered good-looking despite any injuries he'd sustained.

"How's the soup business going?"

"Pretty good. I sell enough locally to make it worth my while."

"It must be cramped in that kitchen of yours."

"It is, but I manage. There's a second café in Kyle interested in putting in an order, but I think I'll have to decline that. There's only room for so many crock pots at home."

Maccaillin seemed to ponder this but made no reply.

"Do you go this way much?" she asked. "To the loch I mean?"

"Sometimes; more often I go the other way, into the mountains."

"You're a mountain man?" she half-joked.

"I'm used to the mountains, yes."

Here and abroad, she thought. Afghanistan was known for such terrain too.

Changing the subject, she told him about the stag she'd seen in Larnside. The memory of it still enchanted her.

"It was just wandering down the road that runs alongside the loch, as bold as you like. I've never seen one in the flesh before and so close as well. Maggie says I'll get used to the sight; that there are hordes of deer and stag here; they'd take over the land if they weren't culled. Is that something you do? I mean I've seen the stag heads in your hallway and on TV shows where Highlanders gather with guns, ready for the hunt."

As soon as the words left her mouth, she regretted them. Even now, telling Maggie this part of the conversation, she winced. Were guns really something she needed to be talking about with someone fresh out of the army? Or culling for that matter.

Quickly she apologised

"What for?"

Oh dear God, he was going to make her say it.

"For mentioning guns. I… I know you were in the army."

"Seanair tells you a lot."

"Yes." Maggie had told her too, but surely it wasn't a secret.

"And he told me you're a widow."

She stiffened then. Widow – how she hated that word. It

made her sound old; it made her sound alone, abandoned even. She hadn't been abandoned as such. James was still with her, in essence at least. Until Death Us Do Part – not in their case.

"My… my husband has passed, yes."

"And that's why you're here?"

"One of the reasons," she replied, so absorbed in their conversation that she hadn't really noticed the loch until she was just a few feet from it.

Coming to a standstill, she devoured the sight before her. In the afternoon sunlight it didn't look as austere as it did in the picture she remembered. Rather, it looked tranquil; the body of main water glinting lazily, small pools of water rippling around it. The mountains behind it brooded but Jessamin suspected that's what they always did – they towered over everything and they brooded. Just like the man beside her.

"And that," she said, "is another."

"Does the picture do it justice?"

"I think so. As much as a painting can."

"Aye," he said, staring at the scene also, "nothing beats the real thing." After a few moments, he spoke again. "Where's the picture now?"

"I'm hoping my Aunt Lara has it. I've checked with my father and my brother and they haven't, which only leaves her. The trouble is, she's away right now, travelling in the Far East so I can't ask her until she comes back; but fingers crossed that's the case."

"What about your mother?"

"My mother's dead too."

The statement was met with silence.

Breathing in deep, she let out a long sigh. "I really can't

believe I'm here."

"In God's own country."

She looked at him in wonder then. "That's it! That's exactly what this place is!"

In her mind, she asked James what he thought of the view.

"Beautiful," was his wistful reply.

They spent the next half an hour walking around the loch. Jessamin imagined Stan, Beth, Flo and Mally sprawled lazily beside it on a hot summer's day – all four of them on the brink of adolescence. She had not yet asked Stan how Flo had died. Should she ask Maccaillin? No, she didn't want the day tainted with talk of death – she was sure he was sick of it. *She* certainly was.

Feeling the first few spots of rain, they decided to retrace their footsteps.

"I don't think I need to remind you how quickly the weather can change," Maccaillin said.

"You really don't. The last time I tried to come here, it started to rain. Normally, it wouldn't bother me, but this rain was like a shield wall. I couldn't push through it."

"A shield wall," he seemed to contemplate her analogy. "That's a good description. The mist is like that too. Highland rain, highland mist – they're different."

"How so?" she asked. "The mist I mean." The rain she already knew about.

"In a highland mist you can barely see one foot in front of the other. If the rain is like a shield wall, the mist is like castle walls; metres thick in places. You can lose yourself in it – wander seemingly forever. Wherever I've been in the world, I've never seen a mist like it."

He was trying to make it sound treacherous but all he succeeded in doing was romanticising it.

"I wonder when it was that Stan was last here. I should imagine it was a while ago."

"I should think so, I don't know precisely. But yes, I imagine it was a long while ago. He hasn't been able to get out and about for some time now."

"I bet he'd love to see it again."

"Has he said so?"

"Well… no, actually, he hasn't."

"Just as well, he's not up to the journey."

"But there's a road of sorts," she argued, "surely your Land Rover could cope with it."

"There's a road, but it's not a smooth one – he'd get thrown about too much. Besides which even if it's not raining in the village itself, it usually is here. The granite is like some sort of rain magnet. Chances are we wouldn't be able to get up close to it and the view from the track; well it wouldn't be much of a view thanks to the rain. Best he remembers it the way it was."

"It's a shame, though. He talks about this place a lot."

Maccaillin's voice grew curt. "His memories are enough."

They had left Comraich in silence and arrived back the same way. At the entrance to the house he turned to go but she stopped him.

"There's live music at The Stag tonight. I'll be there and Maggie will too. Why don't you come and join us?"

"I'll have to see how Seanair is."

"Of course, but I wasn't thinking for the entire evening; just for one drink. I know Maggie would be pleased to see you." After a moment, she added, "And so would I."

"I might," he said and smiled again. She was glad. When he smiled he didn't look so haunted.

"Regarding the business of soup," he continued, "if the

kitchen at Skye Croft is getting too small, why don't you come and cook here? It would be a shame to turn away potential customers and… well… you're here a lot anyway."

Jessamin couldn't believe her ears.

"Are you sure? I mean, if I did take you up on that, I wouldn't get in your way or anything. And I'd leave the kitchen spick and span at the end of each day."

"I'm sure," he replied. "And please, call me Finn. It's about time."

"Thank you… *Finn*. See you later then?"

"Maybe."

As she turned, he was the one who called out to her.

"Jess?"

Quickly, she turned back.

"Those stag heads?"

"Stag heads? Oh, in the hallway you mean."

"Yes, in the hallway. They're nothing to do with me."

Somehow she'd guessed that.

* * *

"Well, blow me down," Maggie exclaimed. "If he does turn up, that's what you'll be able to do – blow me down with a feather."

"Would it really be that much of a surprise?"

"A surprise? No, lovey, not a surprise. It would be a shock!"

"Or a miracle, like you said before."

"Aye, or a miracle." Looking at her watch she added, "It's already ten o' clock, it's late."

"Not really, last orders won't be called for a while yet."

The minutes ticked away, more drinks were consumed

and the band played on. Rory came over not once but twice and begged Jessamin for a dance, but she declined.

"I've been on my feet all day, I just want to relax now," she explained.

Eventually, Maggie pointed out that Shona, who was currently standing in a corner staring soulfully at Rory, might like to be asked to dance instead. Sighing, he turned away and made his way over to her. Both Jessamin and Maggie were happy to note that after a while his dejected mood lifted; instead he twirled Shona quite happily around the makeshift-carpeted dance floor, both of them laughing.

All the while Jessamin kept a close eye on the door. She noticed Maggie doing so too. Of the two of them, she didn't know who looked the more hopeful.

Chapter Fourteen

FINN pulled in just before the pub, in a hidden and dark spot, somewhere he couldn't be seen. He was used to watching and waiting; he'd done that for many years in the army.

From his vantage point, he could see that The Stag was pretty lively: that was one thing he remembered about these people – they knew how to have a good time. When he was a young man, he'd had a good time right alongside them, but those days were gone. War – constant and often senseless war – tended to subdue the spirit. So did death.

Why had he come tonight? For months he'd managed to keep himself to himself, which was no mean feat in a village this size. Any talk he engaged in – even with Maggie – he kept light and to the point, business dealings included. He'd come tonight because she'd asked him to – Jessamin. Not with any agenda other than friendship on her mind, something plain to see, and which he found refreshing.

Laughter disturbed his thoughts – a couple was walking past. He slid down in his seat but he needn't have worried; they weren't interested in him, only in each other. They were a young couple, probably no more than kids when he'd left the village. He didn't recognise them.

Straightening up, he exhaled. God, he was nervous. More nervous than he had felt in a long time; nervous of his own people, the irony of which was not lost on him. He should leave the darkness, not dwell in it. Go towards the light. But he couldn't move. He could imagine all too well the reception he would get if he dared set foot in there. The music might play on, but people would stop dancing; they would stand and stare instead.

Winn Greer, the proprietor of the pub, would be the first to come forward – the laird of his own territory. He would extend his hand and call him a 'war hero', the way that people always did. He'd insist on a bottle of his finest whisky being opened, and if not a bottle, a barrel,

And then others would come forward, tentatively at first but then more boldly, plucking up the courage to ask him at last about his injuries; wanting to know every gory detail about how he had sustained them. And then more gory details about the conflict he'd witnessed. It amazed him what an appetite for gore people had, as if what they saw on TV or heard on the radio was not quite exciting enough. But those who knew the reality behind those words and those pictures spent all their time trying to forget. There was no excitement involved; nothing in the end but despair; despair that human life could be seen as nothing more than a bargaining tool; that there was nothing more precious about it. Besides which, he was no hero. He would not tolerate being called that.

Part of Finn felt contrite. If he was doing anyone down he was sorry. Greer wasn't a bad man. Finn knew that. He had liked him once, as he'd liked so many of them; but they were like strangers now, or rather he was the stranger amongst them. Still, he should make an effort. He knew the fact that he didn't was the subject of much discussion.

Glenelk – it was such a contrast to where he'd spent the last few years: green and vibrant, as opposed to barren. In October, when he had first arrived, he thought the cold might be the thing to kill him. He'd grown unused to such low temperatures, but had quickly acclimatised, becoming hardy once again. Still, he missed the almost endless sun; the dry heat; his friends; the women – one woman in particular – Suri, a fellow soldier – an African-American with black hair and eyes the exact same colour. He hadn't been in love with her, but he'd liked her sassy nature, a lot, and the sex between them had been amazing; her body lithe and athletic like a panther.

Suri had been devastated at his decision to leave the army.

"We can work this out," she'd said, her voice soft like velvet as she whispered in his ear. "Together, we can put what's happened behind us; we can move on."

But there was no moving on, only moving away – alone. He wouldn't forget her tears at his decision either, and his inability to comfort her.

"Suri," he whispered in the darkness, suddenly craving her forgiveness.

She was still on tour of duty and he hoped she was safe. When he had said goodbye, she insisted there'd be no letters, no correspondence, nothing. Perhaps it was for the best. But still he wondered, hoped and prayed. Every night he did that: he prayed to a God he had never believed in, not just for her, but also for all that remained in the line of fire.

There was more activity at the pub, this time people were spilling out on to the road in front: two young women and a man, the young woman punching one of the men in a playful manner. Despite himself he smiled, remembering when he'd been that young man, making a show of how sore his arm was from the supposed 'blow'.

She was in there, Jessamin; the very antithesis of Suri, but just as mesmerising. That look in her eyes... normally he'd shy away from it. He'd seen too many people look that way – his father, his grandmother, Seanair, himself, it was a haunted look, but in her it didn't repel him. Quite the opposite.

"She's a widow."

Seanair had told him that, and when he repeated the word by the loch on the moor, she had flinched. He understood. He didn't like to be labelled either.

He wondered how long her husband had been dead. Perhaps not long. Grief consumed her still, as did guilt – which surprised him. What had she got to be guilty about? But he wouldn't ask. He didn't want to intrude.

Maggie was in the pub too; they would all be; the village in its entirety, even the old folk, as age was no barrier in a place like this. He should go in, get it over and done with – make an effort – be a part of the community again, at least for however long he stayed.

About to abandon his car, he caught sight of himself in the rear view mirror; even in the darkness his eye patch stood out, blacker than the night. And it was this that stopped him: this permanent reminder of what he had done and why he had hidden away: his eye and the scars that covered half of his torso. He wasn't normal. He didn't even *look* normal. Why pretend otherwise? No, there'd be no rubbing of shoulders tonight with friends old or new; no joking, no laughter, no reprieve from memories that scarred his mind as well as his body, and nor should there be. He shook his head. *Nor should there be.*

Jessamin had asked him to join them and a part of him had been grateful. But he would fail her tonight too – the tally growing.

Firing up the engine, he turned the car around and sped off.

Chapter Fifteen

"STAN, it's okay, it's just a dream."

"Wha… I'm dreaming? Are you sure?"

"Sure I'm sure; it's a dream and it's over. You're okay, you're safe."

Jessamin helped Stan to sit up. Confused, he swung his head from side to side.

"Where am I, dear? Why is there no fire?"

"You're in bed, Stan," Jessamin explained, "not downstairs."

Ill temper quickly replaced confusion.

"Bloody Doctor Buchanan!" Stan burst out with a ferociousness that belied his frailty. "Confine me to bed permanently he would; it's his answer to bloody everything. No answer at all if you ask me, which no one ever does by the way… ask me I mean, as if my opinion doesn't count anymore."

"Stan," Jessamin tried to appease. "I know you'd rather be downstairs by the fire, but Finn and I thought—"

"And damn you and Finn for agreeing with him."

Jessamin tried to suppress a smile. Rather than be offended by Stan's brusque manner she was actually heartened by it. It was good to see the old man's spirit still intact.

"I want to go downstairs," Stan continued.

"You can't, not for another day or so, the doctor said."

"And I said I'm not beholden to what that blasted doctor says. This is my house, I do what I like and I want to go downstairs."

Maccaillin entered the room.

"Seanair, stop giving Jess a hard time. She's only trying to help."

Stan seemed miffed by his grandson's show of support.

"So you two are in cahoots, are you? Deciding between you what's best for me?"

Maccaillin was the one trying not to smirk this time, having to purse his lips together. Jessamin didn't want to risk Stan's wrath further, but she couldn't resist a quick conspiratorial glance at his grandson. The expression on his face matched hers – she and Maccaillin were in cahoots indeed.

Managing to tear her gaze away, Jessamin crossed over to Stan and began smoothing the blankets around him. They were good quality she could tell, although slightly worn in places, just like everything else in the house – including its master.

Stan was clearly still feeling the need to grumble.

"Did no one think to bring me a cup of tea?"

Tea? Of course! What was she thinking? She knew how much the old man loved his cup of tea. "I'll go right now and make you a pot."

"No," Maccaillin held up his hand. "I'll do it. I'll make the tea."

"If you're sure?" she said, caught in his gaze again. His hair had grown slightly longer since she'd been here and it suited him. She imagined the shaved military look would suit him too; his strong features and firm jaw line meant he could carry off such harsh styling, but she liked his hair longer; it softened him. Stan brought her back to the moment.

"Whilst the two of you argue over who makes the tea, I'm dying of thirst. Could one of you please decide and when you've decided, hurry?"

She half-expected Maccaillin to execute a mock salute in response to his grandfather's command – carry on the air of joviality. But he did no such thing. He simply turned and walked away, closing the door gently behind him.

"So," said Jessamin, settling on the chair beside Stan's bed, "what was the dream about?"

"The usual," Stan muttered, not crotchety now; more subdued.

Reaching across to hold his hand, she asked, "Do you want to tell me about it?"

In his eyes the pain of memories was evident.

"It's okay, if you'd rather not, that's fine…"

"No, Jess, I think I'd like to."

The chair made a slight scraping sound as she shifted forward on it.

"The summer of 1945," he began, "it wasn't as glorious as 1944, but we were celebrating for different reasons. Do you know why?"

"The end of the war?" Jessamin offered.

"Aye, lass, it was the end of the war. We'd managed to defeat the Germans at last. The mood in the village was euphoric, even those who didn't understand why: babies, toddlers, young kids, they all seemed to be smiling that summer, despite the incessant rain. Because of the weather, Beth, Flo and Mally came here a lot. We'd spend a lot of time in my room – this very room in fact, wondering if there'd be another war, and if me and Mally would be old enough to join the army when there was."

"There are always wars," Jessamin said, sighing.

"The world's a mad place," Stan concurred. "Even in this far-off stretch of land, there's madness."

"What happened?" Jessamin leant forward as she asked this.

"In the dream or in real life?"

"Both."

"In real life, summers came and summers went; we got older. Flo and Mally started dating. They were sixteen. We always knew they would; that 'something' between them really kicked in during adolescence. During that time, Flo and Beth blossomed into beautiful women. Do you know who Beth reminded me of?"

Jessamin shrugged her shoulders. "Who?"

"A young Marilyn Monroe. Blue eyes, blonde hair, hourglass figure – she was stunning. I used to tell her so, but she'd scoff. She never realised how bonny she was."

"That's *very* Marilyn Monroe. Apparently she didn't believe in herself either."

Stan nodded his head in agreement. "Flo seemed to have so much more confidence. She was definitely the fierier of the two. Beth would often walk in her shadow."

"So they were alike in looks but not in personality?"

"Oh, there were similarities between them; the same sense of humour. Both girls loved books, romance novels primarily – Beth was a real Mills & Boon fan, she'd borrow them from the mobile library and devour them. Their mannerisms were similar too, the way they'd incline their heads to one side when listening to a story; always to the right it was, never to the left. But for me Beth was unique. I saw her as a separate being entirely. She liked that. Mally, on the other hand, he used to say the best thing about the girls was there were two of them to drool over."

Jessamin gasped. "That's very disrespectful!"

Rather than join her in disdain, Stan chuckled. "It is. It is. But that was Mally. He didn't mean anything by it. That was his sense of humour." Straight-faced again, he continued, "I wanted to court Beth; desperately I wanted to. I couldn't think of anything else, not since our first summer by the loch. But the feeling wasn't mutual. I've told you this before, Jess; she had eyes for Mally too."

"It must have been so awkward."

"It was awkward, and it was sad. For so many years the four of us had spent every available minute together, but now Flo and Mally preferred each other's company. It was a natural progression, I realised that, but even so, it hurt. Beth pined. I started to paint. I had that at least. I could lose myself in art, for hours, days, weeks at a time. I'd paint Beth pictures – silly pictures really, of the loch, of her, of the mountains that surrounded us, and I always made sure to bathe them in sunshine."

"Did you ever give her those pictures?" Jessamin enquired.

"Some of them, the better ones," Stan replied, one hand scratching at his collarbone. "It didn't matter anyway. Still she pined, and not just for Mally but for the sister he'd commandeered."

"Did Beth know how you felt about her?"

"Och, lass, I should think the sheep in the fields around knew how I felt about her. I wore my heart on my sleeve."

"But she must have got over Mally. She married you."

"Aye, she did. But by then, I was all she had."

The time had come – she had to ask.

"Stan, Flo's death, is that what the dream was about?"

She noticed Stan swallow hard before replying, grimacing slightly as though it pained him; his throat must still be sore from the cold he'd caught.

"Stan..." she prompted when he didn't reply. "Is that what the dream was about? You were going to tell me, remember?"

At last he nodded. "Yes, that's what the dream is always about. Just like you don't get over losing a twin, or a daughter, you don't get over losing a good friend, and not just one, but two of them."

Jessamin was shocked. "Two good friends? Oh, Stan, I didn't realise. Did Mally die too?"

"No, Jess. Mally didn't die. Mally left."

Chapter Sixteen

BEFORE Stan could tell her how Flo had died or why Mally had left, Maccaillin re-entered the room.

"Sorry I took so long," he apologised. "One of our tenants phoned; a leak in the roof. I've arranged for Rory to go and have a look at it."

"Rory?" Jessamin realised too late how surprised she sounded.

"Aye." Maccaillin looked bemused by her reaction. "He's a bit of an odd-job man, Rory – he can fix roofs, paint and decorate," and then more pointedly, "*mend boilers.*"

Jessamin knew what Rory did; that wasn't what surprised her. What surprised her was Maccaillin having contact with him, or rather having contact with anyone in Glenelk. No man was an island after all, it seemed, no matter how hard they strove to be.

Maccaillin had brought enough cups for all of them, and so they drank tea together, Jessamin taking in the surrounds of Stan's bedroom as she sipped. Another large room – it seemed all the rooms at Comraich were a good size – it was also more feminine in style than the living room, Beth's input no doubt. Floral wallpaper hung below the picture rail and in the far corner stood a double wardrobe in a robust wood, walnut perhaps? A silver-backed comb and brush lay on the dressing table, as well as various bottles – holding cream and scents she presumed; a shrine to Beth. She'd like to take more of a look, to feel closer to the woman she'd just been hearing about. What kind of scent did she like, musky or floral? Somehow she suspected the former. She didn't feel she could snoop too much though; this was Stan's private room – his sanctuary within a sanctuary. She also studied the bed, with its oak headboard and footer. Had Beth died in that bed? If so, how could Stan bear to sleep in it? Or perhaps that was *why* he chose to sleep in it.

Rather than pursue the thought further, she concentrated on the pictures that graced the walls.

"That's one of yours, isn't it?" she said, pointing to a picture of a wild blue-green sea with a rustic whitewashed cottage overlooking it.

"Aye, that's the coastline off Aberdeenshire; a cottage Beth and I went to stay in once when Kristin was wee. I painted that picture to remind us. It was a happy time."

One of the few, Jessamin couldn't help but wonder, remembering Maggie's words. She longed to hear more about Mally and Flo; how what had happened to them affected those they'd left behind, but she felt they'd gone as far as they could today. How much Maccaillin knew of his grandparent's youth she didn't know, and nor would she ask. It was Stan she wanted to hear it from, not him.

"Did you travel much, you and Beth?" she enquired instead.

Stan shook his head.

"I would have liked to have travelled, gone out into the world as Finn here has done. But I had enough of a job to persuade her to go to that cottage; she didn't want to stray too far from her twin; didn't want to stray at all, and I could understand. The bond between them, it was special."

"Where's Flo buried?" Jessamin asked.

"Over in Kyle. Beth's with her now of course. She lies in the plot beside her. I've asked Finn to go over on a couple of occasions just to check it still looks nice, but he assures me it's well tended. I pay for it to be so."

Jessamin glanced at Maccaillin who was staring solemnly into his teacup. Quickly, she returned her attention to Stan.

"So you don't visit the grave?"

"No need," he said, placing his hand over his heart and patting it. "Keeping their graves tidy, that's a mark of respect. But Beth doesn't lie cold in the ground; she lives in me."

Before she could ask any more, Stan started coughing, his body shaking violently.

Maccaillin placed his cup and saucer on the sideboard and stood up, "Seanair, take some water. And then you should rest. I'll be up again in an hour or so to check on you."

"No," the old man protested between bouts of coughing. "I don't want to rest, I rest too much."

"But you need to, you won't get better otherwise," Maccaillin insisted.

Trying to save Stan the pain of speaking further, Jessamin stepped forward.

"I think what he means is, he doesn't want to sleep."

Maccaillin glowered at her – a slightly chilling look, Jessamin felt, not helped by the addition of the eye patch. But rather than shrink from it, she stood her ground. Stan didn't want to sleep and she knew why. Who went willingly into the arms of a nightmare?

As she'd tried to appease Stan earlier, she now tried to appease his grandson.

"It's a lovely day," she gestured towards the window. "Not

cold at all. Why don't I take Stan to sit in the garden for a while? The sun's better than any hot water bottle."

"Take him outside?" Maccaillin looked appalled. "Are you mad? He's not well enough!"

Jessamin bristled. "He doesn't want to sleep right now. Why don't you listen to him?"

"But the doctor—" Maccaillin started.

"The doctor can go to hell," Stan managed, his cough subsiding a little. "And, Jess, that's a wonderful idea. I'd very much like to sit in the garden. I haven't done so in an age." To his grandson, he barked, "My wheelchair!"

Maccaillin clearly felt she was in cahoots with Stan now, and that he was the one excluded. He looked none too pleased at her suggestion or at being ordered about. It took a few moments but at last he acquiesced to the will of the older man, and stormed from the room.

"Good girl," Stan winked at her when they were alone again. "You're a good girl, Jess."

* * *

As soon as the fresh air hit him, Stan fell asleep. Although Jessamin had a batch of soup to make, she decided it could wait a while longer. Instead, she rummaged in a nearby shed for something to sit on, finding underneath the weight of garden tools a blue and cream striped lounger. Liberating it, she brushed mildew off its canvas cover and sniffed. It smelt earthy but not entirely unpleasant. Positioning it beside Stan, she lowered herself onto it, wary that the frame might collapse, but to her relief it held her weight. Content she wasn't going to crash to the floor, she also closed her eyes, enjoying the warm breeze. Soon she was drifting too.

"So you're a good girl, huh? I don't think Maccaillin thinks so."

It was James, with a big grin on his face.

"Maccaillin needs to stop treating his grandfather like a child," Jessamin retaliated. "I'd go mad too if I were confined to bed all day. Anyway, I don't want to talk about him, I want to talk about you. Where've you been? I didn't see you last night."

"You slept deeply, Jess, but I was there."

She could feel her own grin widen.

"Good, I'm glad," she replied, her voice deliberately soft.

Although she could only 'hear' him whilst awake, in sleep his image became more real, sometimes vague, and sometimes distinct. Happily, in this dream, it was the latter; the scenery around them becoming more substantial too. Immediately she recognised where they were – in the garden of the home they'd shared in Brighton. The lilac tree was in full bloom, although it felt more like the height of summer rather than spring, but in dreams things could easily become confused. It also looked grand in scale with green lawns rolling into the distance. In reality, it had been the size of a postage stamp. They were sitting in the shade of the lilac tree, reclining on loungers (sturdy not decrepit ones), reading newspapers and sipping chilled wine. Raising her head to stare at the soft contours of his face, she realised he never glowered; not like Maccaillin.

"You're thinking about him again."

"Who?"

"Maccaillin."

"Only in a negative sense."

"Really?"

"James." Was she frowning in real life or was it only in the dream? "I'm getting fed up with you teasing me about him all the time."

He leaned forward, took her hand and squeezed it; she could actually feel the pressure. "I've always teased you, remember? You're just so damned teaseable."

"Teasable? There's no such word."

"There is now," he insisted.

Still she continued to pout. "I'd really rather you didn't though. It's not funny."

"Okay, okay, no more teasing," he promised.

Jessamin smiled triumphantly. She could always wind James around her little finger; get him to do whatever it was she wanted. At this realisation, her whole body jerked.

"Hey," he said, so in tune with her he had guessed the reason why. "You didn't *make* me drive home that night. I could have said no."

But he never said no, not to her and she knew it – that was where her crime lay. As much as she dwelt on it, however, he refused to. Instead, he asked about Stan.

"You enjoy listening to him, don't you? And his stories of old."

She reclined further into the chair and closed her eyes. "I do."

The sun felt blissfully hot on her face. In the distance, a bee buzzed.

"But are you listening to him, Jess, I mean really listening?"

She was frowning again. What a strange thing to ask, even in a dream.

"Of course I'm listening, why wouldn't I be?"

James seemed to falter. "You haven't found out yet how Flo died."

"He'll tell me in good time. What's the hurry?"

When there was no reply, she said, "James, I think you're the one who's not listening."

Opening her eyes, she turned her head to look at him.

"I am, Jess." His smile was weak. "But I'm tired."

"Tired? You get tired on the other side?"

"Tired," he repeated.

Again there was silence – a silence that stretched far too long. She sat up and peered closer. Something was wrong, very wrong. His face, his gentle, handsome face began to twist and turn, first one way and then the other.

"James..." she said, mystified. She'd never witnessed such a thing before.

Despite her beseeching tone, his face continued to change, as though he were morphing into someone else – someone she didn't recognise – not fully. His hair was much darker than before.

She started to tremble. "James, what's happening? I don't understand."

What had been idyllic was turning into a nightmare.

Receiving no answer, she tried again. "JAMES!"

Finally he opened his mouth to speak but his voice was different too.

"Just find out," he said, and his words, like the beat of a drum, grew louder and louder.

Chapter Seventeen

"HERE, sip this."

Maccaillin handed Jessamin a glass with an amber coloured liquid in it.

"What's this?" she asked.

"It's whisky, get it down you."

"I don't like whisky," she started to complain.

"You don't have to like it, just drink it."

Jessamin did as she was told, wincing initially as the fiery liquid burnt her throat, but after a while relishing the taste of it and how it warmed her from the inside out.

She hadn't had a nightmare in a while. She put this down partly to the sleeping pills she sometimes took, sending her off into dreamless depths; but other than that she was happier here, James had become a part of her everyday life again. That he had changed so dramatically in front of her – become someone else entirely; a dark stranger – had terrified her. Vividly recalling what had happened, she felt the blood drain from her face.

"Take some more whisky. Come on, a big gulp, that's it."

Maccaillin was being very kind but she knew he didn't need this. He had enough on his plate; what with his grandfather's health failing rapidly, he didn't need to be dealing with her grief too. Still, his obvious concern for her was touching. After helping his grandfather to bed, he had returned to her in the living room and hadn't left her side since.

"Stan... he didn't see me upset, did he?" she asked, her voice shaking as much as she was.

"No, you weren't screaming that loudly, I promise."

"Screaming? I was screaming?"

Maccaillin smiled – not an amused smile, it was more kindly than that.

"You were clearly distressed, but don't worry; I wheeled Seanair in whilst he was still asleep and put him back to bed."

That was a relief at least.

"I'm sorry." God, she wished she could control the chattering of her teeth. "I'll be fine in a minute." She stared at the whisky glass. "This stuff is actually helping. I could get to like it." Draining the last of it, she added, "Thanks for looking after me. I'll be gone soon."

"You're going nowhere, not until I'm satisfied you're better. Which right now, I'm not."

As he had no doubt stoked the fire for his grandfather a thousand times, he now stoked it for her. Turning her head towards the window, she noticed the day was still bright – the sun warm although it had left her cold.

"It must be a day for nightmares," she said.

Maccaillin frowned. "Who else had a nightmare?"

"Stan did, earlier on. I woke him from it."

Like you woke me.

Maccaillin poured himself a whisky too then pulled up the chair beside her. It seemed strange sitting beside him and not Stan, but a nice sort of strange she had to admit.

"Nightmares," he said, a sigh escaping him, "they plague us all."

They plagued him too? After active service in the army, she wasn't surprised. She only knew what she saw on the news or read in the papers about the situation in the Middle East, but that was harrowing enough. Living in England, it was possible to feel at least a degree of safety; to distance yourself. Yes, there was always the threat of terrorist attack, but thankfully they were few and far between. But to actually live in a war zone; to experience it as part of your daily reality; to live with endless fear – that must scar you in many ways. She waited a little before speaking to see if Maccaillin was going to say more on the subject of nightmares, but when the seconds turned into a minute it became clear he wasn't going to.

"You didn't show last night," she said instead.

"You noticed."

"Of course."

Instead of looking at the fire, he looked at her.

"Were you disappointed?"

She couldn't tell if he was being serious or not. "Me? No. But I think Maggie was."

"Maggie?" He seemed surprised.

"I thought you were friends."

"We were… we are."

"Close friends."

"Once upon a time."

"She misses you."

"I… does she? I'm not sure that's really the case. I've been gone a long time."

"But you're back now. It might be time to start rebuilding bridges. In my opinion, good friends should last a lifetime."

A shadow crossed his face – annoyance perhaps?

"You seem very concerned with what I should be doing all

of a sudden."

"I'm just pointing out—" she began, but he interrupted her.

"I think I know Maggie better than you do."

"I'm not saying otherwise. I'm just saying she misses you."

Maccaillin turned back towards the fire. Even the amber glow couldn't soften his features. Why was he so defensive? Whatever had happened to him it had nothing to do with Maggie or with anyone in this village, so why shun them? She braced herself for another stinging retort, perhaps he'd ask her to leave; to forget all about setting up her soup business in his kitchen; forget about Stan too. Instead, he asked if she was hungry.

"Hungry?" she repeated.

"Aye, hungry." The look of amusement was back on his face. "As in experiencing or desiring a need for food."

"I know what hungry is," she replied tersely.

"Really? Because you looked totally baffled there for a minute."

"It wasn't that, it was…" she started to defend herself but stopped – his amusement catching. "Yes, a desire for food *is* making itself known in my stomach."

"Good, I'll rustle something up. Anything to silence those neurotransmitters."

"There's some soup in the kitchen…"

"Erm… Jess, do you mind if I make something else? A sandwich perhaps?"

"A sandwich," repeated Jessamin and then she couldn't help it, she burst out laughing. "Yes, of course, a sandwich will be great."

"It's not that I don't like your soup," he said, his hands held up in supplication as he backed out of the room. "I love it, as does everyone around here but—"

"Yeah, yeah, I know. You can have too much of a good thing."

"Exactly," he said, retreating entirely.

Taking advantage of her solitary state, she whispered to James. "Are you here?" Getting no reply, she tried again. "James, are you here?"

"Yes, Jess, I'm here."

She breathed a sigh of relief. His voice was his own again.

"That dream, it was so strange. One minute you were you, the next you were someone else entirely, someone I didn't recognise."

"You've no clue who he was at all?"

"No, I've just said so."

"Look, don't worry about it. It's over now."

"But were you there? Do you know what I'm talking about?"

"Calm down. Don't get agitated again."

"You... he... whoever it was, wanted me to find out about Flo's death."

"Perhaps you should."

"What's the urgency?"

"There's no urgency; just find out when you can."

"I will. I don't want to push Stan that's all, he's so frail."

"Are you talking to yourself again?"

Jessamin jumped. She hadn't noticed Maccaillin re-enter the room.

"I thought you were making sandwiches," she blurted out.

"I am. I just popped back to ask you if you'd prefer cheese or ham."

"Oh right – erm... cheese please."

"And tomato or pickle?"

"Tomato."

"Lettuce?"

"That would be lovely."

"Salt and pepper?"

"Aha."

"And brown or white, we've got both."

At the sight of her raised eyebrows, he raised his hands again. "I tell you what, I'll just go and make the damn sandwich, shall I?"

When he disappeared from view again, she found she actually longed for his presence.

Twenty minutes later they finished their sandwiches. The man had professed he wasn't much of a cook, but he could certainly take two slices of bread, a bit of cheese and some salad, and turn it into something above average.

"There are olives in here," she said, amazed.

"I was often on sandwich duty in the army," he explained.

"In between defusing bombs you mean?"

Again a shadow crossed his face, but it was brief.

"It's good to have another skill," he joked.

Pushing his empty plate aside, Maccaillin slid to the floor to sit with his back against the chair. Every now and then, he leaned forward to coax more flames from the logs. As he did, she stared at his injuries. Not for the first time she wondered how far they extended. Despite the weather being clement of late, he hadn't worn short sleeves.

"You're curious about my burns, aren't you?" he said, catching her looking. "Whether they still hurt?"

Her old friend guilt flared up again. "I'm so sorry—"

"No need to be. I'd be curious too if I were you."

His understanding did nothing to assuage how bad she felt.

"Does it hurt?" she said at last.

"Not as much as the memory, no."

That reply she hadn't expected. "Do you want to talk about it?" She was amazed she could be so bold – with him anyway.

"Do you want to talk about James?"

About the car crash? No she didn't.

"It's okay you know," he said, "if you don't want to. I don't want to either."

Kindred spirits in that respect, she thought wryly.

"Is that why you keep yourself to yourself?" Hopefully it was okay to ask this at least.

"In a way. It's just easier I suppose."

Jessamin nodded. "Are you... were you discharged from service?"

"I was offered a desk job. I'm not a desk man."

"No, I can see that."

James had been a desk man; he hadn't really been into the great outdoors. Maccaillin and him, they were worlds apart – literally. James was into city living, wining and dining in up-scale restaurants. He was into the theatre too. Together they'd seen all the London classics – *Les Miserables, The Mousetrap, The 39 Steps*, the list was endless. Theirs had been a fortunate life, privileged; a life she... they... had perhaps taken for granted.

"And being back, what's it like?"

Maccaillin didn't answer straightaway. Perhaps he didn't want to talk about that either. She was about to apologise again when he started speaking.

"You know I couldn't wait to get away from here. I loved my grandparents, don't get me wrong, but I felt stifled, cut off from the rest of the world. That urge to travel, it's always been in me and the army was as good a way as any to satisfy that urge."

"So you've been all over the world?" *Not just Afghanistan.*

"Pretty much. I was stationed in America for a while. That's where I learnt to make such great sandwiches." His smile chased away any shadows.

"From another army colleague?"

"No actually, from a little old lady called Dorothy who ran a diner we used to visit. 'Go the extra mile', she used to say. 'Cut the bread nice and thick. You army boys need building up.'"

Jessamin hadn't a clue what Dorothy looked like but she imagined her anyway – silvery soft hair neatly curled, and wearing a red apron, mothering all the young men that frequented her establishment – the *heroes.* Taking to Maccaillin in particular: the motherless boy.

"Would you have come back, if… if you hadn't had to?"

Maccaillin looked at her then. "I didn't *have* to come back. There were various places I could have settled. But Gran was ill and I was worried about Seanair; about Comraich falling into disrepair. So I *decided* to come back. At least until… well, until I'm not needed any more."

"And when that time comes, what will you do?"

"I'll leave." After a moment he added, "Jess, why do you look so shocked?"

She really wasn't sure. "Because you said this is God's own country."

"I did. But I don't think it's mine anymore."

"What about Comraich, the house itself?"

"I'd sell it."

"You'd sell it?"

"Aye."

"But it's the family home!"

"That's as maybe, but it's not been a particularly happy family home. Not in my experience anyway."

"Your sisters?"

"Are settled. One's in North America and the other lives on the Isles of Scilly. I have their blessing."

"Beth and Stan loved each other, didn't they?"

Again, Maccaillin paused. "They did but… and I don't actually know how to put this. A darkness existed between them, a secret of some sort. Often I would catch Seanair placating Gran, reassuring her, but about what I don't know. Gran suffered from depression. She lost her twin and her only daughter; she never recovered from either."

"No, of course not," Jessamin all but whispered. "Some losses are too hard to bear."

"Sisters, brothers, husbands, wives, children – I agree," Maccaillin replied, just as sombre as she. "And sometimes people who are little more than strangers."

Jessamin's head jerked upwards. Would he say more? She wanted to know more, not just about him but about the darkness between Beth and Stan; the secret they'd kept from him. It wasn't Comraich that was mysterious, she decided; it was the people who lived within it. She looked about her; at the pictures that graced the walls and the mantelpiece with its photos; Stan's beloved high-backed chair, well worn in places; the rug as faded as every other rug in the house. She had come to know it all so well since she'd been here. How many months was it now? Four months, nearly five – it would be July soon. Not a long time, but time enough to develop a familiarity with it; to develop an affection for Stan.

"And for Maccaillin?" she heard James whisper.

No, James, not for Maccaillin.

But respect for him she certainly had that; not only for how he'd served his country, but also for returning to look after Stan when clearly Glenelk wasn't his favourite place to be. The memories clinging to this house needed exorcising; it needed new life, new memories – a new family entirely. But, thought Jessamin, wouldn't it be better if the old family, the established family, the family that had lived here for generations, broke the mould instead? If Maccaillin could somehow find a way to chase away the lingering darkness and inject it with light? There'd be more justice in that – justice of the poetic kind.

Maccaillin did indeed speak next, but it wasn't to elaborate.

"It's getting late. I should go and check on Seanair."

Jessamin loved the way he said that word – how it rolled off his tongue. She could listen to the Scottish brogue all day. Correction, she *had* been listening to it all day.

"Sure," she said, surprised to see that quite so much time had passed. She'd wander home through the woods. It was still light outside. It wouldn't fade for a while yet.

Starting to rise from her chair, she felt lightheaded again. "Ooh," she said, rubbing at her temple.

Immediately Maccaillin was on his feet, his hand reaching out to steady her – his right hand, his injured hand. His grip firm she noted; not hampered at all.

"Steady, Jess, sit for a while longer. I won't be long upstairs."

"Absolutely not, you focus on Stan. I'll be fine, I've just been sitting for too long, that's all."

"You're still pale."

"Really, I'm fine."

Maccaillin looked to the door then back at her. "I'll drive

you home before heading upstairs," he said decisively.

"I can walk—"

"Jess, save your breath. I'm not taking no for an answer."

She was about to argue further, being used to arguing her point. With James she'd done it all the time, *still* did it. But Maccaillin was not a man to argue with.

"Thanks," she said at last. "I do feel a bit faint."

"Sunstroke perhaps?"

"In Scotland?"

Maccaillin laughed. "Aye, I suppose it is something of a phenomenon. I don't think the sun's ever shone so brightly before."

Oh it has, thought Jessamin, remembering the summer of '44 that Stan so often talked about.

Maccaillin kept his hand on her arm as they made their way through the house, removing it just before she climbed into his car. Settling herself into the passenger seat, she could still feel the heat of his touch. In no time at all, they were outside Skye Croft. After assuring him she could make it inside without further assistance, she thanked him and climbed out, expecting him to drive off straightaway. He didn't, he rolled his window down instead, a contrite expression on his face.

"I'll go and see Maggie."

She smiled. "Promise?"

"Scout's honour."

"You were in the scouts?"

"Actually, no. Just the army."

"That's honourable enough," she replied.

Finally, he put the car into gear.

"Erm… before you go, your grandmother's sister, Flo; how did she die?"

She hadn't meant to ask him, had resolved not to. She still wanted to hear the story in its entirety from Stan, but at the last minute she'd found it impossible to resist. The face in her dreams, the voice – there had been an urgency in them, despite James insisting otherwise. She had to know.

Maccaillin looked thrown by the question, one hand coming up to rub his chin.

"I don't know that much," he confessed. "Stan and Beth didn't like to talk about it."

"But you must know something, surely?"

"Yes, I do," he said, his gaze meeting hers. "I know she fell and hit her head; never regained consciousness. She was brought to Comraich and that's where she died."

"At Comraich?" Jessamin was startled.

"Aye," and his face darkened again, "it's another death the lodge can lay claim to."

Chapter Eighteen

"SHONA, hi, come in. Och, Maidie, lovely to see you. I'm so glad you're feeling better. Summer colds, they're the worst, aren't they? Come in, come away in."

Nibbles were laid out in the living room – crisps, nuts, of which there were several different kinds, and Ina's home-made cheese straws – everyone's favourite. Alongside the nibbles were wine glasses, smaller goblets for the white wine drinkers, and large ones for those who preferred red. Soft drinks were also on offer as well as lager, which Ina and Eileen often mixed with lemonade.

Maggie did a quick head count. "Just Jess to come – she'll be here in a second."

No sooner had she said it than the doorbell rang. "Ah, there she is."

Although she hurried from the room, Maggie had time enough to hear Ina's awe-struck whisper. "Did you see that? She always knows there's someone at the door before the bell's even been rung and not only that, but who it is too. How does she do it?"

Maggie suppressed a smile. *I could tell you, but then I'd have to kill you.*

The gift she'd been born with wasn't something she talked about often. As soon as she was able to understand, her mother had advised her not to make it common knowledge.

"It's up to you, Maggie, and it's nothing to be ashamed of, but in my experience, folk don't like knowing we're especially perceptive. It makes them... uncomfortable."

Maggie had decided it was sound advice and followed it. Not even her closest friends knew about her ability although some, like Ina, suspected.

"Jess, come in. Och, the sun may have been shining today but it's chilly tonight."

Jessamin agreed as she wiped her feet on the doormat. "The clouds are low too; it's misty out there."

"Aye, the mist is never far. I've got the heating turned up. You'll soon be warm."

Maggie took her coat and hung it up neatly beside everybody else's. Thanks to Jessamin's arrival in the village, their Thursday night group now numbered eleven. There were certainly more women in the village who were welcome to come, and some did indeed pop in on occasion, but eleven was the group's core number.

And a fine addition Jessamin was, thought Maggie, going into the kitchen to retrieve the first of the wine bottles from the fridge. She herself would have a lager, not a shandy as some preferred; wine she found too bitter. Jessamin had not only become a token villager, she had set herself up in business. The locals loved her soup, which sold steadily in her shop and in cafés hereabouts, although Maggie had had to ask her to tone down the more creative varieties she'd produced initially. The Co-Op in Kyle might now sell ingredients such as lemongrass and quinoa, but Highlanders were a traditional lot who preferred hearty soups; soups with plenty of vegetables and lentils; soups to fill you after a long cold day that would warm you as effectively as a glass of single malt. Instead of scoffing at her suggestion, Jessamin had taken her advice on-board. And now she had a few regular clients – clients too busy to make fresh soup daily themselves and only too happy to have it supplied. She'd have to hire people if she continued in this way.

And then there was Stan: what a boon Jess must be for him. Every spare minute the girl rushed over to Comraich to see him; to sit and talk; to feed him. Finn must be grateful for her too, although whether he showed it she didn't know. There was a lot Finn kept to himself, his thoughts in particular. He was the hardest of all to read.

The living room was a hubbub of chatter. Ailsa reached up, took the cold wine bottle from her, and started pouring it into the glasses of those she knew wanted it. Maggie sipped at her lager. Although she didn't drink much, she liked the effect of alcohol, primarily because it dulled her perception; her ability to 'catch' thoughts. Just as well, as what was being spoken out loud right now was enough to contend with.

"And how was your date with Rory?" Gracie leaned across to ask Shona.

Suddenly the whole room hushed. Shona, despite appearing vivacious, was shy at heart, at least in romantic matters; she looked mortified to be the centre of attention. Maggie suppressed another smile as she noted the girl's cheeks flame as red as her hair. That was something she and Rory had in common at least – their bright hair.

"Aye, it was all right," she answered, her eyes slowly downcast.

"Just all right?" Gracie, only slightly older than Shona and firmly embroiled in a relationship with Rory's cousin, Dougie, was clearly not impressed by such a response.

Shona shrugged her shoulders.

"His mind didn't seem to be on me that's all."

"Who's it on then?" quizzed Gracie.

"I'm not sure," but as she said it her eyes flickered to Jessamin, who quickly looked away.

Rory had made his fancy for Jessamin clear from the first; but surely he knew he was on a hiding to nothing? Despite being a widow, Jess was very much taken. Besides, Rory wasn't right for her, he was too young for a start... Maggie struggled to think of an apt word: gauche, she supposed. She wondered if Jess would ever start dating again. James had died a while ago now – well over a year and a half – but to Jess he was as real as ever; but not healthily real, obsessively real. If only she'd let him go.

Shona clearly didn't want to continue on the subject of Rory, although she did impart that they had another date lined up. Hopefully, he'd be more attentive towards her on that occasion. Treating herself to a second lager, something she rarely did, Maggie thought it time to spare Shona any more cross-examination. Instead, she diverted the conversation towards Jessamin.

"This soup business of yours, it's doing well. You'll need help soon, won't you? To deliver to the cafés on Skye I mean?"

"Yes," agreed Jessamin, "I don't really want it taking up all my time and it seems to be doing that more and more. I'm glad it's successful but that's not really why I came here."

No, thought Maggie, *you came here to be with James.*

"Maccaillin has said I can work out of Comraich's kitchen though, so that's a bonus."

Oh, had he? This was news to Maggie. Obviously Jess saw him a bit more than she let on for him to make such a generous offer.

Jessamin looked around her. "I was wondering if one or

two of you might like to give me a few hours a week. I'll pay of course, the going rate. Perhaps deliver the soup to Kyle and elsewhere on Skye, help me to make up one or two batches, that sort of thing."

"I'd love to." It was Shona.

"Yes please," added Gracie.

Jessamin looked thrilled. "Oh, thank you, that's such a relief! I'll be set up fully at Comraich by Sunday. Perhaps you could start next week or whenever is convenient for you."

"A cottage industry," said Ailsa. "That's great. There are not many opportunities for employment around here. We tend to scrabble to make ends meet, so every little helps."

Maggie had finished her drink when the doorbell rang again.

Och, who's that? Normally she'd have a fair idea but her mind felt fuzzy round the edges. All eleven were accounted for. She wasn't expecting anyone else. Not unless Moire had decided to leave her lazy, useless excuse for a husband to his beloved TV, as Maggie constantly cajoled her to do. But no, Moire wouldn't leave him, not even for a few hours. She said it was her duty to stay by his side. Silently, Maggie had scoffed. She was scared of him more like; what he'd do to her if she dared to make a bid for independence. There were times in her life when Maggie was very glad she'd never married. She didn't want to be beholden to anyone.

She was about to rise to open the door when Ally offered. "I'll do it, you sit and relax. Heaven knows you do enough for us, Maggie."

Smiling gratefully at her, Maggie joining in a conversation with Ailsa and Maidie instead – there was a Ceilidh band playing in a few weeks in the church hall at Kyle; they were excited about what they were going to wear to it, and who would be there. Considering both of them were married, why they were quite so excited about the latter, Maggie didn't know. Then again, whilst Ailsa was happily married, it was no secret Maidie was less so. Still, she smiled as they chattered, enjoying their lively conversation.

A few minutes later Ally returned.

"Maggie, you have a visitor."

"I have a visitor?" Maggie queried, thinking Moire had decided to visit after all. "Don't you mean *we* have a visitor?"

"No, I don't think I do," Ally replied.

Her mysterious tone threw Maggie; she wasn't used to being kept in the dark. Before she could question further, Ally stepped aside to allow the visitor access into the room. There were gasps and sharp intakes from all around, but not from Maggie. She'd been struck mute. Managing to tear her gaze away to look accusingly at her empty glass, the words *I didn't see that coming* formed in her mind.

"I'm so sorry, I'm obviously interrupting something. I'll come back another time…"

The last time Fionnlagh Maccaillin had stood in her living room had been fifteen years ago. He'd come to say goodbye. The reason: he was leaving Glenelk to join the army. This had been her mother's house then. The older woman had looked at her only daughter, noting how shaken she was by the young man's news. *Just let him go,* she'd said, Maggie the only one able to hear her.

And so she had. What choice did she have? She'd asked him to keep himself safe and to write to her once in a while. He said he would, observing his promise initially with postcards from military bases in the West Country and then further afield, from places considerably more exotic than Plymouth. But gradually, as she knew they would, the postcards dwindled. That he'd sent any in the first place was nothing short of a miracle; a homage to their closeness perhaps as children and early teens. From age fifteen onwards, Finn had been too busy playing the village Casanova to bother much with her. But he broke hearts did Finn, sometimes callously. Certainly she'd been one of his victims, not because he'd ever looked at her with anything like lust in his eyes, but because he hadn't. Had her heart ever mended? She still couldn't say. Perhaps she should have said 'yes' when Lenny McCleod asked her to marry him. Lenny was a good man; he hadn't deserved her treatment of him. Why he should spring to mind right now, she didn't know. Was it because he was the opposite of this man standing in front of her – in all ways? Was it because she'd never given him the chance to help her forget? Would he have been able to? Poor Lenny – she felt guilty for leading him on; for using him, mainly to see what sex was like: no great shakes! She didn't particularly miss it. But he'd seen something in her that Finn hadn't: something that he'd wanted. She recognised the heartbreak in his eyes when she'd refused him; she'd seen it enough in the mirror when she'd studied her own face; her own plain, old-before-its-time face; a face not dissimilar to Lenny's.

She wasn't callous at heart, not like Finn had been; but she'd felt his equal on that day. Lenny had left soon after. He swapped farming the local lochs for working on an offshore oilrig in the Outer Hebrides. His parents, Morag and Artair, never spoke to her again; they blamed her entirely for his departure. What had become of him, she didn't know, but she sincerely hoped he'd found happiness.

Because she hadn't yet replied, the silence in the living room continued: no one dared to speak before Maggie did. This was her house, *her* visitor. When he had stood there aged twenty, he'd had such a cocksure air about him. That had gone completely, in part perhaps because his face was ruined. No, not ruined. He was handsome still; the eye patch didn't detract from his looks. In a strange way, it enhanced them. Vulnerability was appealing, far more than over-confidence. How she wished it wasn't. He looked vulnerable, but also something else – terrified. Once upon a time, standing in a room full of gawping women would have fed his ego; now he looked as if he'd liked to turn tail and run.

'I'll come back another time,' he'd said. Oh no you don't, Finn. Not this time.

Adopting a bright and breezy manner, Maggie pointed to an empty chair. "You're not interrupting anything. Please, sit down."

Out of the corner of her mind she could see a few of the younger girls look at her as if she were mad. Inviting a man to join their Thursday night, strictly women-only get-together? But this wasn't just any man – this was the man who'd got away.

Finn it seemed knew better than to argue.

"Erm… if you're sure."

Immediately his eyes sought Jessamin's, who was smiling encouragingly at him. Was it her idea for him to come visiting? What had she said to persuade him? Maggie could only read minds if she was in close proximity to a person; what transpired when they were out of range she didn't know.

"Where are my manners? Let me introduce you. Some of you know Finn well." She avoided looking at Maidie when she said this. As she was an old flame of his, she knew well enough that Finn wasn't her favourite person in the world. "But there are some amongst you who won't remember him.

He hasn't lived in Glenelk for many years – how many is it, Finn?"

"Fifteen," he duly answered.

Maggie only asked for the benefit of the others; if pushed, she could have numbered the months and days as well as years.

"Aye, fifteen years he's been away," she continued, "a long time. But now he's back. He lives at Comraich with his grandfather Stan. He and I used to be friends."

There were various hellos offered, but only Maidie remained mute. Although some like Shona and Gracie didn't know Finn personally, they knew of him; there wasn't a single person in Glenelk who hadn't wondered about the return of the wounded soldier.

Smiling at each of them, he then concentrated on Maggie.

"I pick my moments, don't I?" he said, shrugging his shoulders in a somewhat forlorn manner, reminding her of the little boy he used to be – so self-effacing.

If there was any lingering awkwardness in the air, his words effectively diffused it. Several women started giggling, behaving in an exaggeratedly girlish manner, for he still made quite an impact did Finn. Only Jessamin, Maidie and Eileen remained cool and collected, but then Eileen was in her sixties and Maggie knew, despite the fact that Eileen had never openly confirmed it, that her preference was for the same gender.

"I don't think anyone minds, Finn," she replied.

"No, of course not," Maidie agreed. "It's nice of you to come and say hello."

Maggie was just thinking how gracious it was of Maidie to say so, when the woman added in a distinctly acerbic manner, "At last."

174

Before Finn had a chance to answer, the others distracted him.

"I'll get you a glass of wine," Ailsa said, springing nimbly to her feet.

Gracie also stood up. "No, no, I'll get you a glass; she'll get you white will Ailsa, but you look like a man who prefers red." She winked at him seductively before scurrying off too.

Only moments later, Gracie returned with a full glass of red, Ailsa pursed-lipped behind her.

"So how are you, Finn? How's Stan?" Maggie asked as Gracie handed the glass over.

"I'm fine but Stan's got a bit of a cough at the moment; a bronchial infection the doctor said. I'm..." and here he looked at Jessamin, "*we're* hoping he'll improve soon."

We? Maggie tried to quash a pang of jealousy.

"If there's anything I can do..." She'd offered before to visit Stan, when Beth had died, but Finn had said there was no need; had been curt about it. Had he been curt initially with Jess? If so she might find comfort in it.

"It's under control." Another dismissal. Just as curt. "So, what's all this? A mothers' meeting?"

"Considering half of us aren't mothers, not exactly, Finn, but we get together every Thursday night, us girls, to put the world to right; and sometimes the village too."

"And men are not allowed?"

"No, they're not."

"I feel privileged."

"You should."

Shona commanded his attention then – asking him what it was like living in the lodge house in the woods. "Surrounded by nothing but trees, I bet it gets spooky at night."

Gracie joined in.

"Being in the army you must have travelled far and wide." Sighing dramatically, she added. "I want to travel one day; get away from here. I hope Dougie gets into the army."

Ina, Dougie's mother, shot her a glance. "And I hope he doesn't," she countered.

With good grace Finn answered each and every question, the room soon becoming cacophonous again as everyone joined in the conversation. Maggie tried not to hang on every word he said but failed – some habits were too hard to break, even fifteen years on. Although Finn had come into the village shop every now and again, it was only ever briefly – to pick up a pint of milk or grab a loaf of bread. Thankfully, she'd heard from Stan beforehand that Finn was coming back, so she'd had fair warning. If he'd walked in as he'd walked into her living room tonight, unexpectedly, she'd have fainted she was sure; hit the deck and probably taken a shelf-load of tins with her.

Growing quieter, she concentrated on watching him instead. The man was warming up – his earlier unease dissipating. He smiled at Ina, apologising to her for not speaking to Dougie, whom he knew was interested in joining the army and who had wanted to speak to him; he laughed with Ally, and to Eileen remarked on how well she was looking. He kept catching Jessamin's eye, and every time he did, she returned his gaze. Again, jealousy flared and with it the same old hurt: she would never be more to him than a friend. Why was it so hard to accept? As the two exchanged another quick glance, Maggie heard the word *Jessamin* form in Finn's mind, and it was imbued with such sweet tenderness; with wonder even. She'd changed him this young woman; in the short time she'd been in Glenelk she'd changed him, and for the better. His presence tonight at her behest proved that.

But could he change her too, or at least her allegiance? The way they were looking at each other, something was happening between them even if they didn't yet realise it.

She felt her heart splinter. It did that so easily, patched up with glue too watered down to be effective. This was her fate, she understood suddenly. Her cruel fate. To watch the only man she had ever loved fall in love with someone else – over and over again.

Chapter Nineteen

"IT'S warm enough to swim in the loch, I'm sure of it."

Shona looked askance at Gracie.

"It's *never* warm enough to swim outdoors in Scotland, Jess."

Jessamin couldn't help it, she laughed at how appalled the pair of them looked at the suggestion she'd just made. With pale, almost translucent skin, they were both also slight of frame – fragile was how they could be described, physically anyway. No wonder they felt the cold.

"Come on," she cajoled, "we've finished work for the day and Stan's been seen to; let's head out to Loch Hourn for a splash about."

"But I haven't got my costume," Gracie complained.

"Gracie," Jessamin replied with her hands on her hips, "we pass both your house and Shona's on the way to the loch, as well as mine. We can just nip in and get them."

After a bit more persuasion both girls caved in and even began to look a little excited.

"I've never swam in the loch before," Gracie confessed.

"Never? Even though you've lived here all your life?"

"It's... I don't know... It's just not something we do. If you want to go swimming you head over to the indoor pool at Kyle. It's not supposed to be an endurance sport, you know."

Quickly the girls wiped down the kitchen surfaces and washed up pots and crocks, drying them thoroughly before putting them away, honouring Jessamin's promise to Maccaillin to keep his kitchen spick and span. Certainly in the time they'd been using it, he hadn't complained. He'd even occasionally come into the kitchen to talk to them, although when he did, Shona and Gracie took to acting like giggling schoolgirls, causing Jessamin to have to suppress a giggle too. Did Maccaillin notice the effect he had on them? And, if so, did his inner Lothario welcome the attention?

A Lothario: it was the second time Jessamin had thought of him like that, but truth to tell, it was only because Maggie had said he'd been that way in his youth. She saw no evidence of it in the man he'd since become. A shy child; Maggie had said that about him too; certainly he'd preferred to keep himself to himself, but lately he was becoming more sociable. The visit to Maggie's Thursday night gathering had kick-started that.

Satisfied that the kitchen could be left until the next day, all three headed for the hallway. Jessamin released her hair from its ponytail. Behind her Shona and Gracie were chatting, their voices enlivening the atmosphere. She knew Stan enjoyed their almost daily presence and she had a sneaking suspicion Maccaillin did too, even if he hadn't come right out and said so.

Thinking of Maccaillin seemed to make him materialise.

"Hi." Shona and Gracie greeted him with unbridled enthusiasm.

"Hello girls," he replied in his thick Scottish brogue. "Hello, Jessamin."

She knew what the girls would say about that when they were out of earshot. "We got 'girls' and you got 'Jessamin'!

Talk about favouritism." James, she imagined, would be nodding in agreement, with one eyebrow arched. She'd have to put him right too.

"Hi Mac... Finn."

She'd done it again, called him MacFinn. Why she stumbled over his name so much she didn't know. This was the third time.

"MacFinn's as good a name as any," Shona said once, after she'd complained to them about it.

"Or perhaps you should call him MacDreamy, you know after that guy in *Grey's Anatomy*? The dishy doctor?" Gracie joined in.

"Finn is just fine," she replied, thinking how much he looked like that particular doctor – tall, dark and handsome – only much better built.

The girls also loved his eye patch.

"It gives him a sort of pirate look," Shona said.

"Hmm, all swashbuckling," Gracie agreed.

They didn't mention his burns although they too must have noticed his hand.

"Where are you off to?" Maccaillin's question drew her back to the present.

"To the loch for a swim; it's a sweltering day."

"A swim? Good idea, the loch will be lovely on a day like today."

"So, you've swum in it then?" Jessamin asked, surprised.

"Aye, when I was younger," replied Maccaillin, "even when it wasn't so sweltering."

"You could come with us if you like," Gracie said.

It was an innocent enough invitation but one that wasn't particularly well thought-out. Surely even Gracie and Shona must have noticed how the man baulked at being asked.

Even though the day was remarkable, he still wore long sleeves; no part of his torso was exposed.

"I... erm... thank you but I've got things to do."

"Are you sure those things can't wait?" Shona wrapped a few wispy strands of red hair around her finger as she asked – a deliberately coy gesture.

"No," he insisted, "but you go ahead and have a good time."

"Aye, aye, captain," said Shona as Gracie giggled.

This time hurt flashed across Maccaillin's face. He wasn't stupid; he knew they were referring to his eye patch. Jessamin felt angry on his behalf.

Before she could butt in, Maccaillin said, "Mrs Campbell, one of my tenants – her boiler..." and without further explanation doubled back until he was out of the front door. By the time they'd reached the gravel drive outside the house, he'd disappeared altogether.

"Shame," sighed Gracie. "A swim with Maccaillin would have been fun."

"Let's just go," said Jessamin, unable to keep her words sounding like a reprimand.

Maccaillin might not have been interested in joining the girls for a swim, but Rory and Dougie certainly were. They'd been basking on the narrow stretch of shingle that rimmed the shoreline, their eyes closed until they heard the girls approaching.

"Gracie!" Dougie stood up to give her a hug. "Have you come to sunbathe?"

"Not to sunbathe, no," Gracie replied, rather proudly. "We've come for a swim."

"A swim? In the loch? I know it's warm but I can assure you, the water won't be."

Rory agreed. "The Atlantic Ocean is freezing!"

Jessamin cringed slightly. Rory had addressed his words solely to her and not to Shona. Trying to give the other girl an opportunity to speak, she remained mute.

When Shona didn't say anything, Jessamin had no choice but to reply. "Well, we're going in and you're welcome to join us… if you've got the nerve."

Dougie pretended offence. "If we've got the nerve? Rory – strip down to your undershorts."

"Wha…?" At least Rory's eyes weren't on her any more. They were on Dougie.

"You heard. We'll not let three young ladies get the better of us. This has nothing to do with nerve; it has everything to do with balls, so it has. Now strip."

Shona and Gracie giggled and Jessamin burst out laughing too, although unlike them, she turned away as the boys began to unbutton trousers and whisk off tee shirts.

Within minutes all five were in the water; not one of them hesitated. They ran straight in, whooping, yelling and cheering each other on, scaring off a bird hovering nearby – an osprey Jessamin thought. James had had a passing interest in bird-watching; whenever they walked in the country he would point out various species to her. She didn't know much on the subject but she did know a bird as magnificent as that.

You would have loved this, James.

"The swimming or the bird-watching?"

Depends.

"On what?"

On whether we're talking about the feathered or the non-feathered variety.

"Jess, you're the only bird I've got eyes for."

She was about to give him a playful telling-off for calling her a 'bird' – he knew she hated that supposed term of endearment – when Rory interrupted her thoughts.

"Jess! Jess! I'll race you to that rock over there," he said, pointing to a sizeable lump of granite sticking out of the water a few metres away.

Oh, for God's sake, Rory, race Shona instead! The way he was acting, it wasn't fair. He was going out with Shona for goodness' sake; they'd been on several dates since their first not-so-great one. His focus should be entirely on her.

"Pretend you haven't heard him," James advised.

Following his instruction, she swam up to Gracie and Dougie. They were a devoted couple at least, with plans to marry, although whether that was before or after Dougie intended to join the army, she didn't know. She tried to imagine him without his blonde curls and couldn't; what a shame he'd have to have them shorn off if he was successful. Earlier, she'd asked Gracie if Dougie had managed to talk to Maccaillin about his plans yet.

"Aye," Gracie had said, "he tried again recently."

"And?"

"He wasn't that forthcoming really; directed him to AFCO in Glasgow; said he'd find out all he needed to know there. We're going next week – making a short holiday of it."

Not that forthcoming? No surprises there.

Meanwhile, Rory, she was glad to note, had taken the hint and returned to Shona's side. The two of them were currently battling it out for supremacy, Shona in the lead by at least an arm's length.

That wasn't the only day they swam in the loch; there were plenty of others throughout July – all five of them gathering together, Jessamin ignoring Rory's longing looks all the while. She'd wear a plain black one-piece as opposed to her bikini; she felt less conspicuous that way, less on show. Maccaillin never joined them, nor did Jessamin expect him to, but the girls often expressed their disappointment about that and one thing was for sure, it wasn't through want of them asking.

Maggie sometimes came to sit on the shore and watch them.

"It's good to see you enjoying yourself," she said to Jessamin one afternoon. "Making the most of the summer. Winter will be here all too soon."

Immediately guilt flared up in Jessamin that she should be enjoying herself, and not only that, but enticing half the village to do so as well.

"Don't feel that way," Maggie warned her, her next words echoing that of Jessamin's best friend, Sarah. "There's no need."

They were easy words to say but not so easy to believe.

"Please don't," James said, referring to her guilt – his voice weary again.

She strove to listen to him, concealing her emotions as best she could. The days at the loch were bliss. She couldn't deny that. As she swam in the refreshing waters – not clear blue like the Caribbean waters she'd swum in with James, but no less beautiful – she thought about others who'd swum in another loch in another age. How young they'd been, with the promise of life still intact; enjoying the moment and those they were sharing it with; imagining the bliss they felt would continue.

She offered to bring Stan to sit alongside Maggie, but he refused.

"I'm not able to, dear, but I'm glad you're having fun. You

deserve to."

In between swimming and making soup, Jessamin sat with Stan in the garden that bordered Comraich; he seemed to enjoy doing that at least, the enduring sunshine making such a pleasant pastime possible. During the rest of July and August, whilst he dozed, she tended to neglected borders, planting flowers she had bought in Kyle: begonias in hot shades of red and orange, petunias and snapdragons. She was no gardener and it all looked a bit haphazard, but Stan seemed to appreciate it. Even Maccaillin threw a compliment or two her way on the occasions he joined them.

"You don't have to do it though, Jess," he said, looking a bit embarrassed. "What you have done, the plants you've brought, at least let me pay you for them."

"Rubbish." She was the one who was embarrassed then. "You let me use your kitchen free of charge, so creating a splash of colour here or there is the least I can do."

"You've certainly done that."

"Sorry?" she replied, not quite understanding.

"Created a splash of colour," he said, colouring himself before hastily retreating.

Stan, who'd been listening, laughed.

"He means you're a breath of fresh air," he explained. "He's just too shy to say it."

"Oh," Jessamin could feel her face becoming hot too.

During their afternoon "sabbaticals", as Jessamin thought of the time she and Stan spent together in the garden, she urged him to tell her more about Mally, Beth and Flo. Through him she was beginning to feel a connection to them; a fondness even. Stan was only too happy to oblige. She hadn't confessed to him that she'd asked Maccaillin how Flo had died. She wanted to, but she was worried he'd feel

185

somehow betrayed; a thought she couldn't bear. Instead she gently probed him on the subject several times, hoping he might tell her himself. Each time she did, he became agitated. "She fell and hit her head," he said, much the same as Maccaillin had. There seemed to be nothing more to it than that. Dismissing the nightmare she'd had, the voice urging her to find out more, she refused to push him further. She listened instead to him relating happier memories.

Mally, he told her that particular afternoon – another one bathed in sunshine – had left school early to help his father farm their land.

"He loved it did Mally, being out in the big wide open; doing something useful with his hands. Education wasn't for him. He loathed sitting still for long."

"How long did you stay in school?" asked Jessamin.

"Until I was sixteen and the girls too. Their parents were strict Methodists; there'd be no way they'd be allowed to leave before a decent time."

"Sixteen's still early by today's standards. I think there's a law in place now that students have to continue with schooling until they're eighteen. I think that's a good thing. Knowledge is important, even if you don't intend to become a high flyer."

Stan nodded. "None of us ever intended to be highflyers, Jess. I never thought I'd be as successful a painter as I was." He sighed. "I guess some things you can't foresee."

"Tell me how you became an artist."

"Och, it's not the most exciting of stories."

"I still want to know," she insisted.

"I started painting from young, and made my ambition to earn a living at it known to my parents, who were thankfully supportive. I also made my intention known to my friends.

Och, Mally used to rib me. 'That's a bit soft, isn't it?' he'd say. 'It's a girl's profession.'" Stan winked at her then. "Highlanders like to appear macho but usually they're as soft as butter underneath. Mally was. And he could paint, could Mally, I taught him."

"You taught him? Even though he ribbed you?"

"He only ribbed me in front of the girls. In private, he asked me to show him the techniques. A talent he had for it too; a raw talent, admittedly, but we all have to start somewhere. Perfection takes practise. Light and shadow interested him in particular, which I used to think was ironic."

"Why?"

"Because that's how I thought of him – as light and shadow. Unfair really, because there's light and shadow in all of us, I realise that now. Beth and Flo were no exception."

"Beth and Flo? How?"

"Flo was the light but Beth... she tended to walk in the shadows." Before Jessamin could ask him to elaborate, he continued onwards. "I enjoyed the time we spent together painting, Mally and I; it reignited our bond. Without anyone to show off to, he relaxed; became the Mally of old. He'd speak about his home life; how he wanted to make something of himself; how much he loved Flo. And he did, he loved Flo; he *adored* her."

"Did you paint here? At Comraich?" asked Jessamin, trying to imagine the contented hours the two friends spent together, and the comradeship between them.

"In bad weather we did. The second living room at the back of the house doubled as my studio, my parents let me have it. As long as I realised that estate management was in my destiny too, they said I could paint in my spare time. I was lucky: my parents had a deep respect for art; they'd travelled to Florence, Rome, Paris, the great art spots of the world."

"I bet you would have loved to travel to those places too?"

"I would have done, but not without Beth."

Such devotion, such selflessness. Jessamin marvelled at it.

"And it didn't matter in the end. Look what I had on my doorstep. There was no need to go abroad to be inspired. Although I utilised the studio a fair amount, more often than not I'd take my easel and my oils and paint outdoors. That's what I preferred doing."

Jessamin hadn't ventured into the second living room since Stan had taken her in there, a few weeks after she'd first arrived. She remembered vividly several canvasses lined up against walls; the smell of paint and linseed oil that lingered in the air; the paintings that hung from hooks – some finished, some works in progress – always to remain that way. Stan's painting days were over. Stan himself had confirmed that. Against the French windows an easel resided, showing where he used to stand, as close to the light as possible.

"Finn has a talent for painting, you know," Stan revealed. "Like I'd done with Mally, I taught him a few techniques when he was younger. Some grand paintings he's done. A few lately too."

"Lately? Since he's been back you mean?"

"Aye, one or two."

She shook her head in surprise. Maccaillin was an artist? That was something she hadn't expected – the hands that could dismantle bombs could also wield a paintbrush. She wondered if he would continue to paint, if not here, wherever else in the world he intended to go; build on his talent as his grandfather had done; perhaps even earn a living from it – a replacement profession.

"The estate, did you manage it alongside painting?"

"In the end no, plans changed."

"In what way?"

"Me and Mally were going to manage it together; that had always been what we had in mind. Not me as the boss – you couldn't be the boss of Mally – as equals."

"But he left, you said he did."

"Aye, he left. My parents got old. My career as an artist took off and so I sold the land. I had to. Art was my first love, not farming." Stan sighed, his faded eyes beginning to cloud. "It would have all been different if Mally had stayed."

"How different?"

"I wouldn't have sold the land."

"And he left because Flo died?"

"Aye, he had to."

His anguish concerned her. "Stan…"

"Och, don't mind me. I'm getting maudlin, that's all."

"Stan, how could you think I'd mind? Of course I don't."

She studied his face. He seemed so tired of late. The cough he'd developed was wearing him down. His entire life seemed etched into the lines of his face – a good life at times, but also painful, like any long life. No one sailed through the years unscathed. She felt bad she'd mentioned Flo's death and Mally's leaving again; there was no need to wallow in sadness, and she said as much.

"You're right, dear. Concentrate on happy times. Why not? We can't go back. We can't change things."

If only…

"And when the sun is shining bright in the sky, it's perhaps easier to do that. But, and I expect you know this as well as I do, it's the dead of night you have to watch out for; when the wind is howling; when the rain pelts relentlessly against your bedroom window; when sleep refuses to indulge you. That's when bad memories tend to rear up; when they demand their fair share of attention too." He shuddered. "The dead of night, it's an accurate description."

Jessamin turned to face the old man fully. "Stan, you're worrying me."

"No, dear, there's no need to worry."

"Despite what I said about concentrating on the good stuff, you can tell me anything, you know that, don't you? Whatever it is... I'm here for you. I'm on your side."

There were tears in his eyes. Quickly, Jessamin reached out a hand to comfort him. He took it, his grip surprisingly firm – desperation lending him strength perhaps? Her breath caught in her throat. What was he going to say? What had upset him so much?

When at last he spoke, his words chilled her.

"The dead of night, Jess. I wish they'd leave me alone."

Chapter Twenty

STAN hadn't said much more after that, but had fallen into melancholy instead – melancholy punctuated only by fits of coughing, the sound even more hacking than usual. Jessamin wheeled him inside, made him a hot drink of lemon and honey and insisted he drank it. Afterwards, he said he wanted to sleep and so she settled him in his chair, glad to note a look of peace on his face as he relaxed.

The next day when she visited, he seemed brighter.

"Did you sleep well?" she queried.

"Very well, thank you. No dreams at all."

As she plumped up the cushion behind him, Stan started speaking again.

"Shona popped in to see me earlier. She seemed very excited about the ceilidh in Kyle. It's soon, isn't it?"

"It is actually. Just a couple of weeks now."

"Are you going?"

Jessamin shook her head.

"I think you should. And Finn too."

Maccaillin at a ceilidh? She couldn't imagine it.

"In fact, I said as much to him before he left this morning. And when I did, he looked the same as you do now."

"Which is?"

"Horrified."

Incredibly, the old man started chuckling to himself, clearly tickled by their respective reactions. After a moment,

Jessamin started laughing too, finding his amusement infectious. Soon they were laughing together, unable to stop, not even when Maccaillin walked in.

"What's so funny?" he asked, puzzled.

"It's just…" spluttered Jessamin.

"Oh dear," managed Stan.

Curiosity drew Shona and Gracie into the living room too.

"I think I know what this is about," Jessamin heard Shona say to Maccaillin.

"Enlighten me, please, because I'd love to know."

"The ceilidh – I was talking about it to Stan earlier. I think they're laughing about going to the ceilidh."

Jessamin enlightened Maccaillin further.

"Stan thinks I should go." After a brief pause, she added, "And you too."

Another burst of laughter escaped her. Why such a suggestion was having this effect, she didn't know and neither did she care, she was enjoying the sudden and unexpected light-heartedness. It was what she needed – Comraich and Stan too. Looking at the old man, she saw tears running down his face.

Maccaillin stepped forward.

"I see. The thought of me at a ceilidh is the cause of all this hilarity."

"It's not that," Jessamin tried to speak again. "It's…" She stopped. There was no use pretending; it *was* that, precisely. "It's me as well though," she added. "It's both of us."

"In that case," Maccaillin continued, very close to her now, less than a couple of feet away, "perhaps we should go together? Give the entire village something to laugh about."

Together? Her and Maccaillin? That stopped her laughing. She felt her face redden and not just her face; heat seemed to rise up from her toes and consume her. He'd well and truly called her bluff.

"Erm... I couldn't possibly. Thanks though..."

Even Stan was quieter now, looking at them with something akin to wonder.

"Are you turning me down?" asked Maccaillin.

"No, not at all."

"So you're saying yes?"

"No... Yes... I... Oh, I don't know." Effortlessly he had tied her in knots.

Shona edged closer too. "Go on, Jess. Say yes, it'll be fun. We're all going."

Gracie joined in. "And no one will laugh at you, I promise."

"No, I know that." Frantically she searched for an excuse. "I don't dance, that's all."

"I don't dance either," Maccaillin responded. "Don't get any ideas on that score."

Jessamin baulked – *don't get any ideas?* The cheek of him! What was he doing asking her to the ceilidh in front of everyone? But if she turned him down she'd make a fool of him, and she didn't want to do that. Neither did she want to go on a date with him.

"It's just an invitation," James assured her, "not necessarily a date. Don't panic."

I'm not panicking. I'm just... confused, that's all.

"Go on," James insisted. "I want you to have a good time."

Even with another man?

"Jess, he hasn't gone down on bended knee and asked you to marry him!"

James was right – it *was* just an invitation and one clearly extended in the spirit of friendship. Looking at Maccaillin, she scanned his face. He seemed serious enough, slightly nervous too and surprised. Had he surprised himself as well as her in asking? Next Jessamin looked at Stan, into his gentle, watery eyes. They were beseeching almost. As for Shona and Gracie, they could barely contain themselves.

At last she spoke. "As long as *you* don't get any ideas, I'd be delighted to go with you."

If he'd called her bluff, she'd called his.

Shona and Gracie rushed forward, almost knocking Maccaillin off his feet.

"Have you got a dress to wear?" Gracie asked. "If not you can borrow one of mine." Sizing her up, she continued, "Yep, I've got several that I think will fit perfectly."

"And your hair," Shona said, reaching out to grab a handful, "we must do something with it. I'm putting mine up. Perhaps you ought to do the same. It'd suit you."

In the face of such girlish enthusiasm, Maccaillin promptly made his excuses and left. Jessamin would like to have done the same but found it impossible to extricate herself. Besides, she was excited too. She'd lied when she said she didn't dance. But the girl who'd once twirled around nightclub floors, a drink in one hand and her eyes closed, lost in the music, seemed to be a girl apart from the one who now stood in the living room of Comraich. Inside though, she could feel who she used to be, stirring. Surely it wouldn't hurt to have a little fun once in a while? James didn't seem to think so. It would be nice to dress up and to have somewhere special to go; or as special as it got in these remote parts. And she *would* dance if someone (besides the non-dancing Maccaillin) asked her, but all the while she'd keep James beside her – living with her, through her – always.

Chapter Twenty-One

DESPITE Gracie's kind offer to lend Jessamin a dress, she had declined. When she moved to Scotland, she'd brought mainly jeans, jumpers and tee shirts, but she had also brought a dress – a black dress. *Not* the dress she'd worn to James funeral – that dress she'd thrown away as soon as the day was over, never wanting to see it again. This was an old favourite; one she'd had for years; a comfort blanket almost. Which is perhaps why it had made it into the suitcase; that and the subconscious female desire to have an LBD in the wardrobe at all times, even if the only thing it did was gather dust. The fact that she now had an opportunity to wear such an item left her feeling quite bemused. She'd imagined it not only gathering dust but disintegrating too.

Taking the dress out of the wardrobe – it looked almost brand new despite its age – she decided to team it with bare legs (the good weather lately meant she had acquired a tan), and a pair of heeled black shoes bought for the occasion in Kyle the previous week.

Fully dressed, she sized herself up in the wardrobe mirror. She'd put on a few pounds lately; it suited her: her face wasn't so gaunt and her arms were less twig-like.

"What do you think, James?" she asked.

"You look like the spectre at the feast."

"James! That's a horrible thing to say."

She could hear him chuckling. "I'm joking with you. You look beautiful as always – but you know I hate black. Why you love it so much is beyond me."

He did hate black. Whenever she dressed up for an evening out with him, she invariably chose black clothing – dresses, trousers, jeans and tops; black all the way.

"You're hiding your light under a bushel," he'd say.

"What do you mean?"

"You should wear bright clothes. Show the world how brilliant you are."

And to be fair, she had tried once or twice; gone out and bought herself a red jacket on one occasion, and a fuchsia top on another. James had been delighted. She, however, felt uncomfortable, as though she were a peacock, parading herself. Quickly she reverted to black.

"My light," she had told James in no uncertain terms, "is going to remain under that bushel. If you like bright colours, wear them yourself."

James had shrugged his shoulders but knew better than to insist.

A horn beeping outside captured her attention. He was here. Maccaillin. Five minutes early.

"He's keen," James remarked.

"Shut up," Jessamin replied.

If she could see him, she'd throw the silk wrap she intended to wear – mid-grey, a token concession to colour at least – at him. Realising this, his laughter echoed around the room.

Shutting the bedroom door, Jessamin made her way downstairs. She had no need of a coat. The evening was warm enough, perhaps the last warm evening of the summer, she thought with slight regret. But she was glad she was making the most of it as she had been instructed, not only by

Maccaillin but by other village residents too.

"You look lovely." Maccaillin had got out of the driving seat and was at the front of the car to greet her.

"Thank you." Silently she cursed that the evening sky wasn't yet dark enough to hide her blush. As he took in the full length of her, he certainly looked appreciative.

He opened the car door for her and she climbed inside. He looked nice too. In fact, his appearance caused her to take an intake of breath – a subtle intake she hoped. She'd only ever seen him in khaki trousers and a waxed jacket, a kind of 'highland uniform'. Tonight, however, he'd turned up in smart black trousers, polished black shoes and a white linen shirt, opened tantalisingly at the neck.

"Tantalisingly?" she could hear James question.

To some I'm sure.

How the unmarried women of Glenelk were going to resist him tonight, Jessamin didn't know.

Putting the car into gear, Maccaillin drove away.

"Are you looking forward to this?" she asked, still unsure if he was.

"I'll endure it," he replied, not giving the game away. "What about you?"

"I'll endure it too," she answered, but light-heartedly.

"That's why I thought we'd go together; give each other a bit of moral support."

"Oh."

The word was out of her mouth before she could stop it. Maccaillin, not one to miss a trick, didn't miss this one either.

Briefly taking his eyes of the road, he glanced at her. "You feel the same way, surely? After all, you did say 'don't get any ideas'."

"Of course I feel the same way." Jessamin tried to keep from sounding anything other than genuine. It was only a moment later she wondered why she had to 'try'.

"Good, let's leave it at that then."

Yes, let's. The urge was to snap back, but she didn't. Instead she held her counsel, some of her earlier excitement waning.

The rest of the journey passed in silence. This man sitting next to her, she couldn't work him out. One minute he was friendly, the next he was brusque. She knew he had suffered; perhaps that was the reason for his defensiveness. To what *extent* he had suffered, though, she didn't know – would he ever tell her? Would they ever be friends? Real friends? Able to confide in one another, comfort each another? Underneath his aloof exterior she detected a man who was kind, generous and brave. He had a dry sense of humour too – her favourite. But would he let her in? Would she let *him* in? '*I mean as friends*,' she silently reiterated, for James's sake. That was all she wanted from Maccaillin – friendship. But she wanted that quite badly.

Twenty minutes later they'd descended the Rattan Pass and entered Kyle. The streets leading towards the Methodist hall were busy with women in dresses and men in kilts – each and every plaid denoting the different clans they belonged to historically. Couples, groups of friends, and individuals, all with smiles on their faces, looked intent on enjoying the night ahead. She was going to have a good time too; she was determined. Glancing at Maccaillin, she noticed he looked pale.

"Hey," she dared to lay her hand on his arm. "Are you okay?"

"I'm fine," he said, pulling into a parking space just

outside the hall.

For a moment or two he sat motionless. Jessamin could almost feel him psyching himself up.

"If you don't want to go in…" she began.

"Nonsense. We're here now. Come on. Let's get it over and done with."

Get it over and done with? Biting back further disappointment, she stepped out of the car. As soon as her feet hit the tarmac, she could hear music – fiddle, flutes and accordions, a whole mixture – the sound loud and ebullient. Excitement flared within her again. In contrast, Maccaillin winced.

He must have noticed her puzzled look because, despite the fact she hadn't commented, he started to explain. "Loud noises, I don't like them."

Of course! She should have taken that into account. He'd been in the army where loud noises were often terrifying noises. Perhaps he'd become sensitised.

"Look, we can go if you want; somewhere quieter; just the two of us."

Maccaillin looked startled that she'd made such an offer. Nonetheless, she thought he might comply. He was dreading the ceilidh – it was so damned obvious – regretting ever saying he'd come. She was about to take charge and steer him back to the car when she heard someone calling to them. It was Shona with Rory in tow, Maggie and Gracie only slightly behind them.

"You look gorgeous, Jess," Shona said, hurrying towards them. After enveloping her in a hug she turned to Maccaillin. "You look grand too, Mr Maccaillin."

"Come on," said Rory, his eyes fixed on Jessamin, "let's go inside; get this party started."

"Oh, we were just thinking—" Jessamin began, but

Maccaillin cut across her.

"Yes, let's go inside." Turning to Maggie, he offered her his arm, which after only a moment's hesitation she took.

Feeling glad that he'd done that – offered his arm to Maggie and not her – Jessamin followed them in. Clearly Maccaillin was going to make the effort after all.

The hall was packed. Colourful bunting was festooned from corner to corner and the band – a five-piece – located at the far end of the hall, were enthusiastically stamping their feet in time to the music. A few people had already formed two lines and were dancing backwards and forwards to each other. Before Jessamin had a chance to take it all in, Rory grabbed her by the hands. "Come on," he urged.

"Oh, I…" But it was no use protesting, he was practically dragging her towards the centre of the hall. She took a brief moment to look back, prompted by concern for Shona. The younger woman did indeed look perturbed, but she also looked resigned. Maccaillin's face, however, had darkened. Was it because of Rory or because he disliked being at the dance in general? And if it was because of the dance, which she strongly suspected, why hadn't he stayed away? He'd managed to stay away from all social gatherings before Jessamin arrived, so why insist they come to this one together? As for Maggie, she simply looked bemused by all that was going on around her

After one breathless dance in which Jessamin was sure she'd got just about every step wrong, not just tripping over her own feet, but Rory's too; falling into him at one point and having to be caught, she pleaded with him to release her. She needed a drink – now.

"I'll buy you a drink," he insisted, rushing off before she could stop him.

Jessamin sighed. This couldn't go on all evening; she had come to the ceilidh with Maccaillin, Rory had come with Shona, and they would have to return to their respective partners at some point soon – very soon she hoped. A few minutes later and her would-be suitor was back; a glass of white wine in hand for her, even though she hadn't said what she wanted.

"Where's Shona's drink?" Jessamin asked.

"Shona?" Rory looked as if he'd forgotten entirely who Shona was.

"Your girlfriend," Jessamin prompted.

"Och, she's not my girlfriend," Rory replied, taking a sip of something dark from his pint glass. "Well, she is, but we're not serious, not serious at all. But you and me, Jess…"

He was stopped from elaborating by Maccaillin materialising at her side.

"Is everything okay, Jess?" Maccaillin asked.

"Everything's fine. Rory was just off to find Shona, weren't you?"

Rory sighed. "Yeah, I suppose," he said before slinking away. Where Shona had gone, Jessamin didn't know; the crowds had absorbed her.

Jessamin turned towards Maccaillin. "Thanks for rescuing me."

"He has quite a thing for you, doesn't he?" Maccaillin still didn't look impressed.

"It's just a schoolboy crush," Jessamin declared.

"A schoolboy?" Maccaillin raised an eyebrow. "He's not much younger than you."

"He's young enough," Jessamin assured him.

Changing the subject, she asked him where Maggie was.

"She spotted the parents of someone she hasn't seen in a

long while, Lenny, I think she said his name was. She went over to have a word with them."

Jessamin craned her neck to see if she could spot Maggie. After a few moments she did. The couple she was talking to, seated on one of the benches that lined the walls, looked to be in their seventies. They didn't seem particularly pleased to see Maggie; their expressions were just as stern as Maccaillin's. As for Maggie, she looked flustered, with her hands raised as though she were pleading her case.

"You haven't got a drink," Jessamin said to Maccaillin, noticing that too.

"I'll get one in a minute. Do you want another?"

"Another? Mr Maccaillin, are you trying to get me drunk?"

"No."

Too late Jessamin realised it was a stupid thing to say. It had been an attempt to lighten the atmosphere between them – the sort of thing friends might say to one another – but she shouldn't have said it to Maccaillin. Not when alcohol had killed his father.

"Mac... Finn, I'm—"

"So you've been persuaded along to the dance, that's a turn up for the books."

Before she'd had a chance to complete her apology, Maidie approached them – or rather she approached Maccaillin.

"Maidie." Instead of looking stern, Maccaillin looked uncertain suddenly. "I didn't really get a chance to speak to you at Maggie's the other night; how are you?"

"Now you ask. It's a bit late don't you think?"

Maidie's tone was nothing less than bitter. Feeling as though she'd somehow become superfluous to requirements, Jessamin took a step back. What was going on? Maidie seemed angry, upset. She also seemed drunk, her red-rimmed eyes unfocussed.

"Good, well I'm glad about that. Jess and I were just going to dance."

Jessamin raised an eyebrow. This was news to her. Maccaillin had already warned her he wouldn't be engaging in such frivolous activities tonight.

"Oh, so it's Jess you've got your eye on now, is it?" Maidie laughed, such a brittle sound. And then she laughed harder. "Your eye on, get it?" she added, pointing to his eye patch.

Although their exchange seemed very private, Jessamin couldn't help but step forward again. "Maidie, I really don't think—"

On hearing her, Maidie whirled round. She was a short woman, no more than five foot, but formidable as the Scots tended to be; her blonde hair, previously restrained in a bun, was beginning to come loose, its tendrils framing her face, but in a haphazard manner rather than charming.

"I like you, Jess," she interrupted, "so I'm going to do you a favour. I'm going to warn you." As she spoke, Jessamin cringed. Her voice was so loud it was attracting attention from several clusters of people standing close by. "Watch Maccaillin. He'll take your heart and he'll trample all over it. He did it to me and he did it to Maggie too. Poor Maggie."

Maggie? What had she got to do with this? Jessamin looked at Maccaillin for clarification but he was staring ahead, anger vying with embarrassment on his face.

Looking back at Maidie, she said, "You've no need to worry about us; we're friends, nothing more."

"Friends?" Maidie spat the word back at her as though it were blasphemous. "Don't be such a fool! He's not capable of being 'just friends' – not with the opposite sex."

"Maidie," Maccaillin's anger was rising, Jessamin could tell. A vein in his neck had started to pulse. "What we had was a long time ago, nearly two decades in fact."

"And you think it's that easy do you, to get over the love of your life?" Sneering at him, she added, "It sums you up, it shows what you know."

"I never led you on—"

"You led *all* the girls on and then you just upped sticks; left me here in this back water."

"You could have left too; there was nothing to stop you."

"On my own?" she screeched. "I wanted to be with you!"

"That wasn't possible."

"Tell me about it," she spat again. "You're a bastard, Finn. That's what you are, a bastard. Why couldn't you have stayed away? Let things be?"

Maidie was sobbing now. She was also staggering – badly. Maccaillin, despite the attack she'd launched on him, reached out a hand to steady her, but she brushed it away, violently. Although the band played on during this exchange, most people were ignoring them, caught up in the spectacle being played out; some whispering, some giggling, and some pointing at him as Maidie had pointed. Maccaillin looked as though he wanted the floor to open up and swallow him. Before Maidie could say anything further, Maggie appeared – a welcome sight.

"What's all this?" she said, reaching out for Maidie and ignoring her initial resistance, forcing her into the circle of her arms. "What's going on here?"

"Why did he have to come back?" Maidie sobbed. "I know you think the same."

"No, Maidie, I don't think the same," Maggie's voice was soothing but firm. "I'm glad Finn's back. Really I am. And

I'm glad he came tonight." Addressing Maccaillin this time, she continued, "It's important you become a part of the community again."

"But he broke your heart," Maidie cried out in protest. "I know he did. Why don't you admit it?"

Colour seemed to drain from Maggie's face at this revelation. Maccaillin too had paled.

"Maggie...?" he said.

Jessamin couldn't believe it. She knew he'd been popular in the village all those years ago, but had he really trodden all over people's feelings like Maidie was insisting?

"Finn, Maidie's drunk," Maggie declared, her manner a little too blasé, Jessamin thought. "Can't you see that? Don't take any notice of what she's saying right now."

Before Maidie could utter another word, Maggie whisked her off, leaving Jessamin and Maccaillin even more exposed to the crowds.

"I need to get out of here," she heard him mutter, not to her, more to himself, but as he turned on his heel, she followed him.

Outside, the air was cool – a welcome contrast to the stifling heat of so many bodies pressed too close together. Maccaillin stopped and took a few mouthfuls as though trying to cleanse himself. Jessamin came to a standstill beside him and did the same.

After a few moments, Maccaillin turned towards her.

"I'm surprised you followed me... that you want to be seen with the devil incarnate."

As shocked as she felt, she didn't want to add to his discomfort.

"What happened between you and Maidie has nothing to do with me."

Nonetheless he tried to defend himself. "I never led her to believe we had a future together, I swear. In a village like this, as soon as you look at a girl you're married to them. That's one of the reasons I left. It's so... suffocating. Nothing ever changes, no matter how many years go by. Everything, *everyone*, stays the same. I couldn't wait to escape."

He looked in actual pain as he was speaking. Again she dared to lay a hand on his arm.

"I believe you," she said.

"You do?" He seemed aghast that she did.

"Yes."

Relief wiped away some of the pain on his face.

"That quiet place you were talking about earlier."

"What about it?" Jessamin asked.

"Let's go there," he said, striding towards the Land Rover and climbing in.

Chapter Twenty-Two

DOWN by the shores of Loch Hourn, the waters rippled gently in the breeze – a breeze that was cool and refreshing, relieving the stickiness of the night. Abutting the loch on the far shore, the Isle of Skye – the giant whale she so often likened it too – still lay in slumber.

Jessamin settled herself down on the pebbled shore. Maccaillin did the same. Night had descended fully now, the sky above them bright with stars. They both stared upwards, marvelling at the myriad constellations; at how clear they were: Orion's Belt, the Plough and Cassiopeia. Eventually, Maccaillin spoke.

"I'm glad that's over."

Jessamin could only agree.

"I'll be the talk of the village for a while."

"Nothing new there, I don't think."

Maccaillin sighed in response and inclined his head towards her. "Can you see why I can't wait to get away?"

"Again, you mean?"

"Again," he confirmed.

Jessamin turned to him. "Don't say that. You'll only go when Stan dies and I don't want him to, not yet."

"Neither do I—" Maccaillin started, but Jessamin was not done.

"And the people here, Maggie, Shona, Rory, all of them,

even Maidie, they're good people at heart – don't be too hard on them."

"I'm not saying they're not good people, I'm saying I don't belong."

"You do belong. You've been away a long time, that's all."

"Maybe."

Jessamin was curious. "Has there ever been a place you felt you did belong?"

Her question seemed to knock him off kilter. Rather than answering straight away, he thought about it. After a short while, he replied. "Not particularly, no."

"So really, here is as good a place as any."

"Perhaps, now that you're here."

At his words, Jessamin felt herself fire up. Was he playing with her as he had played with Maidie and God knows who else during his lifetime? She couldn't stand players. She'd known a few before James and very quickly worked out they were best avoided. The look on her face – an irate look she'd bet – made him sit up straight.

"All I meant, Jess, is that it's more bearable with you here. I wasn't coming on to you or anything." Almost in exasperation, he added, "Like I said, I never led Maidie on, not her or anyone else. I never told her I loved her or gave her the impression I did."

"How long were you with her for?"

"A few months that's all, six or seven."

"And yet she never got over you?"

"She did," protested Maccaillin. "She's married. It's just the drink talking."

Jessamin was not so sure. Sometimes, just sometimes, it was downright impossible to get over the love of your life. And the man Maidie was currently with, what if he'd never lived up to her expectations? What if he'd never even come close?

"And Maggie? What about her?"

"I didn't know about Maggie," he said, his voice low as he answered.

"So, as far as you were concerned you and Maggie were just friends?" She was almost willing him to say yes.

"I... we were close as kids but not so much during teenage years, but that's because hormones were running riot around my body. There were lots of bonny lasses in Glenelk and most of them seemed to like me. I was a teenager for God's sake – I liked the girls right back. I became more interested in them than her, that much I'll admit. But I never did anything wrong, Jess. I only took what was willingly given to me."

"But Maggie, what was wrong with her? Wasn't she bonny enough?"

Again she felt anger towards him. Anger he sensed.

"Don't attack me, Jess, please; not you."

His words and the plea in them brought her up short.

"I wasn't. I'm... I'm interested, that's all."

"In me? I'm flattered."

His comment broke the tension that had been building. She couldn't help but smile. Taking his cue from her, Maccaillin seemed to relax too, his shoulders not so rigid.

"It's not that Maggie wasn't bonny enough," he endeavoured to explain further. "She was, in her own way. But you can't help who you're attracted to, or who you're not."

She couldn't argue with that. "I'm sorry. I didn't mean to pry."

"It's fine. We're friends, aren't we?"

Jessamin turned her head to look at him again. He looked

lost in the darkness, so alone, despite the fact she was sitting beside him. A longing surged within her – to pull him back from whatever brink he teetered on; to keep him safe.

"I hope we're friends." She swallowed as she said it.

She knew so little about him really, but in other ways she felt connected to him. Through Stan, Maccaillin had become a part of her life – a part she'd come to cherish.

"Have you ever been in love before?"

It was a bold question to ask, she knew – a question that was met initially with silence.

"No."

The honesty wrapped up in that one word seemed plaintive.

"I'm sorry," Jessamin said, although why she didn't know.

"Don't be. There's still time, I'm not a lost cause just yet." Again Maccaillin tried to lighten the atmosphere that had become as heavy as the night. "And please, don't hold me accountable for what happened a long time ago. A lot has changed since then. I'm not that person anymore." Almost too quiet to hear, he added, "In some ways, I wish I was."

The heat between them suddenly felt overwhelming.

"Come on," said Jessamin, rising hastily to her feet. "Let's go and cool off."

"Cool off? What do you mean?"

"In the water," she replied, hurrying to the shore's edge.

Maccaillin quickly fell into step beside her.

"What are you suggesting? We go skinny dipping?"

His face at the prospect amused her.

"I'm sure it's nothing you haven't done a thousand times before," she teased.

"Well... I... erm..."

"I'm suggesting we dip our feet in, nothing more."

"Oh." He looked visibly relieved.

Quickly Jessamin removed her shoes, threw them back up the shore and walked into the loch.

"Come on, what are you waiting for? It's lovely and cool."

Maccaillin stood where he was.

"Maccaillin," she called again.

He came closer but remained fully clothed.

"Why do you call me Maccaillin? I've asked you to call me Finn."

Jessamin shrugged. "I don't know. It's just how I think of you. You don't mind, do you?"

He thought for a moment but then shook his head. "No, I don't mind, you can call me what you like." Grinning widely, he added, "As long as it's not 'bastard'."

Jessamin grinned back – the tension there had been, dissolving entirely.

Chapter Twenty-Three

SEPTEMBER arrived and with it the less clement weather. The unexpected heat wave receded, soon to become a distant memory no doubt. Before it got too cold or too wet, however, Maccaillin offered to take Jessamin to the fairy pools on Skye – somewhere she'd been longing to visit ever since Stan had told her about them.

Although it was raining, it wasn't heavy – nothing more than a few spots. And thankfully it was still warm, a light cardigan enough of a barrier against the elements.

"I saw a video on YouTube," Jessamin explained to Maccaillin as they drove over the Skye Bridge, a surprisingly modern structure in such an ancient land. "It was of a lady, Kate Rew her name is; she wrote '*Wild Swim*'. Have you heard of it? It was a bestseller apparently."

"I've heard of wild swimming – we do enough of it up here, or in my case used to – but I haven't heard of Kate Rew," Maccaillin replied.

"Well, there's a video of her swimming in the fairy pools. It looked sublime. I've brought my costume just in case."

"Got a thing for wild swimming, have you?"

"Maybe, I'll know for sure after today." After a moment, she added, "Mind you, this taste I'm developing for all things wild, it's just as well. I haven't found anything tame about Scotland yet – or the people who live here."

He didn't answer just smiled, his gaze fixed firmly ahead.

"Ever heard of Munro bagging?" he asked after a while.

"Yeah, yeah, I have actually, although I don't know what it means exactly. I've always thought it sounds a bit rude, as though we should all feel sorry for poor Munro."

"It's bagging, Jess, not de-bagging. There's no need to feel sorry for anyone."

"Okay, tell me what it is then, I'm curious."

"It refers to any mountain in Scotland more than 3000 foot high and the act of climbing it: I used to do quite a bit of that in my youth, right here in the Cuillins."

"I remember Stan telling me about the names of the mountain peaks on Skye. The Peak of Torment; I remember that one especially."

"Sounds about right. The Cuillins are one of the most formidable Alpine mountain ranges in Britain. But on one of the climbs I did, and it wasn't one of the easy ones either, I was overtaken by an eighty-year-old man."

"Eighty?" She was stunned. "Honestly?"

"Honestly. I was eighteen and about to keel over by the time I got to the top. That man though, he never even broke into a sweat. Put me to shame he did."

Jessamin tried to imagine the young Maccaillin wild swimming; Munro bagging; breaking girls' hearts. Glancing at him sideways, she decided she could imagine all of these – easily.

"I know it's raining slightly, but it's still warm. Are you sure I can't persuade you to swim?"

Maccaillin snorted. "If you want to swim that's fine. Me? I'm happy to sit on a rock and watch."

"Oh, come on," she cajoled, "you've done it before, why not now?"

"Jess, leave it."

Just as she had cringed at the ceilidh when she asked him if he was trying to get her drunk, she cringed again now. She needed to learn to stop pressing his buttons.

"Sorry."

Maccaillin didn't answer so she risked another glance at him, trying to gauge his reaction to her words and subsequent apology. To her relief he didn't look angry. Even so, she couldn't help but wonder again, just how bad were his injuries? So bad that he needed to stay covered, as he had all summer? As well as feeling curious, she felt sorry for him, but he'd hate her for that, she knew.

They were on the island itself now, bypassing the village of Kyleakin on the road that led to the Cuillin Mountains. As they drove, Jessamin's mind returned to Stan.

"Wasn't it good of Maggie to offer to sit with Stan today?" she said, striking up conversation again.

"It was."

"And it was nice of you to have asked her. I know she appreciated it."

"Seanair will too; he was always fond of Maggie."

"Did she visit Stan much when you were away?"

Maccaillin thought for a moment. "Do you know what? I'm not sure. I don't think so, though. Gran didn't like visitors. It's not something she would have encouraged."

Jessamin tried to imagine Stan and Beth alone in that great big house. All the years since Maccaillin's departure, just the two of them in a house which should have brimmed with life, but which had shut its doors on the world instead, incarcerating them.

"You mentioned Beth suffered from depression. I'm guessing her illness was severe?"

"It was. It was crippling. I think she was agoraphobic, although if she was, it was never officially diagnosed. Gran shunned doctors, which, as you know, is Seanair's tendency too. She got worse when my mother died, although I was only a baby then so I wouldn't know what she was like beforehand. It's just what I was told."

"Your mother, her name; can you say it for me?"

If he was taken aback that she'd asked such a thing, she was even more so. She didn't know why she wanted to hear it uttered from his lips, but to her relief, he didn't ask why either. Instead, he answered as though it were the most normal request in the world.

"Kristin. Her name was Kristin."

The way he said it, it sounded like a prayer.

"It's a lovely name."

The ensuing silence was also reverential, the spell broken only when he started speaking again.

"In my teens I don't ever remember Gran stepping outside of Comraich. Sometimes she never left her bedroom and I'm not just talking weeks, Jess, I'm talking months, many, many months. Despite this, despite everything, Seanair remained devoted."

Jessamin shook her head almost in awe. "He's a remarkable man."

"He is. He was Beth's saving grace and he was mine too." He paused and Jessamin wondered if he would continue. After a moment he did. "Without Stan my life would have been unimaginable. He was the one who took care of me. Not my father, not Beth, but him. Every night I prayed he'd be there when I woke up. And every day he was. Without fail."

Although Maccaillin was speaking candidly, his voice was

emotionless, as though he were trying to play down the significance of all that had happened. But his mother dying when he was young, his father dying also a few years later, killed by alcohol and grief; there was no playing down such things.

"What about your sisters, were you close to them?"

"No, they were a fair bit older than me. I barely knew them. By the time I was ten they'd left home. We all did to be fair, just as soon as we were able."

Jessamin remembered Maggie saying so in Millie's tea-room – all the grandchildren, eager to fly, to escape. But one of them had flown back; the question was, for how long? Stan's cough was getting worse; he seemed to become more fragile by the day. She tried to imagine Glenelk without Stan or Maccaillin in it and couldn't. Or rather she didn't want to. It was too painful.

"It's not far now," Maccaillin said. "We should get there before the weather turns."

Jessamin wondered whether by changing the subject he was effectively bringing the topic of his family to a close. A part of her sensed that he was and so she didn't push further. He'd spoken to her of his own accord, with very little prompting at all. She felt flattered that he was comfortable enough with her to do that; that their friendship was deepening.

Staring out of the window, she noticed that the raindrops were fatter than they were before, but she didn't mind. She felt safe and warm in the confines of his car; happily encapsulated.

"This video I was watching," she said as they drew closer to the mountain range, which was black in some areas, as though in silhouette; "it mentioned that the fairy pools were

216

haunted."

Maccaillin didn't miss a beat. "That's right, it's haunted by the spirits of those who drowned at sea. If you see a seal in amongst the pools, you need to keep in mind, it might not be a seal."

"Huh? I don't understand."

"It's a human in seal's clothing." When he heard her laughing, he laughed too. "I'm being serious, Jess. Whenever there's a full moon, the seal sheds its skin and becomes human once again. We're going at the wrong time really. We should come back later, after dark."

"So I'm going to be swimming with humans masquerading as seals?"

"You could well be."

"Now that's what I call wild."

Maccaillin laughed again as he pulled off the road and on to a grass verge. "This is the best place to park. It's not far from here."

Noting that he left the car unlocked, just as he did his house, she fell into step beside him. The rucksack on her back contained a towel and underwear; her black swimming costume she already had on under her clothes. Would she feel self-conscious standing in front of him in next to nothing? She couldn't deny she felt more than slightly worried about it. As it turned out, he was nothing less than gentlemanly when she finally disrobed; turning away from her and not turning back until she was fully submerged. The whole area was glorious: underwater archways, overhead archways, the all-enveloping water crystal clear and deliciously cool – blue in some places, green in others – both such impossible shades. From higher ledges, gentle rivulets fell like tears, white-tipped with foam. Today no other humans were in sight; no humans clad in seal's clothing either, and no fairy folk, the rain putting them off perhaps, but only adding to her enjoyment.

What do you think, James? It's beautiful, isn't it?

"It's lovely, Jess. It's magical."

I wish we'd seen this together. You'd have swum with me.

"I'm seeing it with you now. Let's be content with that."

His choice of words surprised her. Be content – without him? That was never going to happen. Not wanting to listen further, she dived deeper in a bid to feel at one with the elements; to become an integral part of the enchantment that surrounded her.

Dipping and diving, she felt like a seal herself, the water enlivening and calming her in equal measure. How long she swam she didn't know; she could have carried on and on, but the rain was getting heavier. Maccaillin would be getting soaked.

Eventually she emerged, right at the rock where Maccaillin was sitting.

"No seals," she shouted up to him.

"Not yet," he called back. "You want to hang around, see if they make an appearance?"

"No, you look as wet as I do. I'd better get out."

Maccaillin shrugged his shoulders. "Don't worry about me."

But she did worry. The jumper he was wearing was clinging to his frame, highlighting his strength somehow, with muscles that had been carefully concealed before, now very much defined.

Clearing her mind of that thought, Jessamin began to climb out.

"Look away," she instructed. "Although if you could

throw my towel closer before you do, I'd appreciate it."

Maccaillin did as he was told. Quickly drying herself off, she rushed over to where she'd left her rucksack. He, meanwhile, decided to take a walk in the opposite direction whilst she dressed. Just as she was pulling on her jeans and jumper, the clouds, as if only toying with them before, burst open, releasing thick sheets of rain and making her wetter than ever despite her efforts.

Maccaillin returned swiftly to her side. He looked as if he'd jumped in the pools after all.

"Hurry, we need to get back to the car." As he spoke, a raindrop trailed down the length of his nose and fell off the end, causing Jessamin to laugh.

"Come on," he urged, completely unaware of what had just happened. When she didn't respond, he took a step forward before coming to a standstill. "What's the matter?"

Jessamin couldn't stop laughing; she was laughing harder than she'd laughed in the living room with Stan, as hard as she used to cry once upon a time.

"Jess!"

Concern now marked Maccaillin's face. He looked shocked and scared too, clearly petrified that this woman, this strange, strange woman, was going to go into some sort of meltdown before him. Quickly, she rushed to assure him.

"Its fine. I'm fine, honestly. It's just... I've never felt so alive, that's all."

Throwing her head back so the rain could beat upon her face, she had never felt so close either, and not to James, nor to Maccaillin, but to something bigger than either of them; something that was sacred.

It took a while longer to gain control, during which time Maccaillin stared at her, no longer in horror, she was glad to note, but with something akin to amazement.

"I'm sorry," she said eventually.

"Don't be," he said. "I like seeing you laugh."

Like James then, she thought.

"You look like a drowned rat," he pointed out.

"And you don't?"

"Oh, I'm sure a drowned rat looks pretty compared to me. Come on, let's go before we get stranded."

Reluctantly, she started to pick her way through rocks and stones, some of them as slippery as glass. With each step she put between her and the fairy pools, her heart grew heavier; she could imagine no better place to be 'stranded' as he'd put it, than there.

Back at Skye Croft, Jessamin invited Maccaillin in on the excuse of the lease – she'd signed papers agreeing to another six months and needed to give them to him. In truth, they'd shared such a perfect day that she didn't want it to end – not yet.

"I know you're soaking, but I've got some extra large tee-shirts indoors, I wear them to sleep in."

"To sleep in?" he queried, one eyebrow raised.

"Don't look like that: they're clean... honest. I haven't worn either of them recently."

"Oh?" Maccaillin looked even more taken aback.

Deciding it was best not to continue talking about what she did and didn't wear in bed, she hurried inside. "I'll get the fire going. You'll dry off in no time."

Once the flames were roaring, Jessamin went in search of a towel. When she threw it at him, he caught it singlehanded.

"Are you sure you don't want a tee shirt?" she checked.

"No," he replied.

Of course he didn't.

After changing out of her sodden clothes, she made hot chocolate for both of them.

Handing him his mug, he took it gratefully.

"I'm worried," she declared, settling herself down beside him, not on the chair but on the rug.

"What about?"

"You. You're soaking. I've been selfish insisting you come inside."

"Not at all, I need to pick up the lease." Almost shyly he added, "Besides which, I don't want to go home yet either."

"But Stan?"

"I texted Maggie, whilst you were changing. She's still with him; she said she'd stay put until the rain stops. We're fine for a while."

Jessamin felt almost absurdly pleased.

"Please put on one of my tee-shirts," she urged. "I'd feel so much better if you did."

"No," he said again.

"But—"

"Jess," his voice was firm, his expression too. "I'm fine."

Unlike James, he would not bend to her will. Still she tried.

"I don't mind..." she started but then didn't feel brave enough to continue. Would he guess what she was referring to?

Maccaillin hung his head. "I know you don't," he said, understanding her perfectly well.

After taking another sip of the chocolate, she placed it on the table beside him. Taking a deep breath she reached out a hand hoping he wouldn't brush her off. They were friends – he'd said so – and she wanted to know more about him; about what had happened; why he was so distant at times.

Her hand rested on his hand – the burnt hand. He looked startled but he didn't rebuff her. She thought the eye that remained uncovered glistened slightly. Did he ever take his patch off? When he was at home? Wandering around the house? When he went to sleep? He must do: what did it matter what you looked like when you were alone? She wished he'd remove it now; she wanted to see his face in its entirety. He possessed such a handsome face, not damaged at all; not to her.

"Jess," he uttered her name, but couldn't say any more. He sounded choked. Clearly he was struggling. But she had struggled too; was *still* struggling.

"Tell me," she urged. "Finn, tell me what happened.

Chapter Twenty-Four

THE way Jess was looking at him, it was hard to form a sentence, let alone tell her what had happened to him whilst on duty. Not what had happened to him – that he didn't care about – but what had happened to the young man in his care. A young man he'd known for only a few days; who'd been assigned to him; placed under his protection. A young man he'd let down in the worst of ways. Connor haunted him, not just in nightmares but every waking hour. There was never any escape, which was appropriate. He didn't deserve any.

"Finn," she said softly, using his first name again, something she so rarely did.

Words, that's all he had to find. He hadn't spoken about it properly since it happened. Counselling had been offered, had been insisted on, but they couldn't torture words out of him: he wasn't the enemy. He didn't want understanding, he didn't want sympathy, and he didn't want someone telling him 'accidents happen'. He knew perfectly well accidents happened, but they had never happened on his watch. His track record in the army had been exemplary and he was highly respected because of it. He was also, he realised, complacent and it was this that had killed Connor. Those who said, 'It wasn't your fault' – Suri included – he shunned. It *was* his fault – entirely.

Trying not to get lost in thought, he refocused on Jessamin. The light in her green eyes shone brightly despite the loss she'd suffered. That's what she'd done; she'd come to Comraich and she'd brightened it. Not just the house, but Seanair's life also, and his own. He loved his grandfather very much but without Jess visiting as often as she did, and now working from the house, he doubted he'd have been able to bear the atmosphere – it had always been dense; oppressive. He'd never known a woman about the place – a woman *interacting* that is. He would have borne it, of course he would, for Seanair's sake, but when Seanair was no longer here, he wouldn't stay; he *couldn't* stay. The thought of being alone at Comraich was something he found hard to contemplate.

Words – still he strove to find them; to talk about the horror concealed inside.

"Connor was twenty-four, full of life and expectation. The horrors we faced daily hadn't yet tainted him. But they would. They tainted us all. But not yet Connor – he was eager."

Jessamin remained silent but her expression urged him on. Would she hate him when he told her? Would she be unable to forgive him when he couldn't forgive himself? It was a chance he had to take: he wanted their friendship to continue – and he wanted it to do so on an even footing.

"I'm sure you know this already but in Afghanistan, suicide bombers are a constant threat. We know what to look out for – men, women, children, they're all used against us. Planted bombs are an equal danger: regular sweeps of buildings are carried out, several times a day sometimes. We're careful, very. Despite the job we're in, none of us are suicidal; we don't want to be blown to kingdom come."

"But you must have witnessed casualties along the way,

surely?" Jessamin asked. "You've been in the army such a long time."

"Of course," Finn said, nodding gravely. "You can't do a job like ours and not witness casualties, but the unit I was in, we were tight. We... we were good at what we did – an elite team. The morning it happened, we were in a small village in Helmand Province, carrying out another routine sweep – this time in a compound the army was planning to use as a base. We check everywhere, culverts, doorways, walls, the ground itself; anywhere where insurgents might think to plant incendiary devices; you need to be imaginative because *they* certainly are. When we find something, it's about teamwork. We move in, we disarm and we retreat – that's the routine."

Jessamin nodded, seemingly absorbing every word.

"Explosives are primarily intended to wound rather than kill. The reason for that is because wounding a soldier slows down an entire unit while others rush to get him emergency treatment. But some explosions – well, some you're never going to come back from."

When he faltered again, Jessamin took his cup from him.

"I think we need something stronger," she said, rising.

A few minutes later, she was back clutching a bottle of red wine and two glasses. Finn watched as she poured the liquid into two glasses, noting how frail she looked. He'd noticed that at the fairy pools too. He hadn't meant to look at her in her swimsuit, had meant to give her complete privacy, but he'd caught a glimpse even so. How thin she was. It stirred something in him; something stronger, more enduring than lust. He wanted to protect her, but protection, it seemed, was no longer his strong point.

Gratefully, he took the wine from her and downed half its contents; he needed something to bolster his nerves.

"That morning, I went over to one building. Connor, who was a technician, asked me if he could check another, the building next door." He paused and had to swallow hard before continuing. "Jess, it was literally yards away, no more. It had also been recently checked. I honestly didn't think there was any danger. I told him to go ahead; I thought it would be good for his confidence, build it up a bit, but I shouldn't have done. He was in training. I should have kept him by my side."

This time he finished his wine and, without waiting for an invitation, refilled his glass, draining that too. One mistake he'd made, one mistake in fifteen years' service, and someone else had paid for it. Could he go on? Could he tell her? He had to, for his own sake as well.

"Just before Connor walked through the doorway, I had a hunch – a premonition – call it what you will. I just knew he shouldn't walk through that damned doorway; that we'd missed something. The first time ever. I called out but he didn't hear. I started to run. Others around me picked up on my panic and they started running too, shouting his name, following my lead. The racket we were making. He must have heard it; he must have."

Despair overwhelmed him – as fresh today as it was when the incident had happened, less than two years before. Over and over he had relived this; there was no way Connor wouldn't have heard the shouts from fellow soldiers. Why hadn't he stopped to see what all the fuss was about? Why had he kept walking? Not once had he looked back; he hadn't even faltered.

Jessamin's hand was on his again. He crossed his left hand over and placed it on hers; gripped it. He needed the comfort of a fellow human being; *her* comfort if he was honest.

"Somehow he triggered the bomb. I'd closed the gap by then but it was too late. I got blown backwards. I scrambled to my feet and rushed forward again; burst in through the doorway. He had to be alive. He had to be! I didn't feel my skin burning, not at first; nor the shrapnel that had lodged itself in my eye. I didn't feel anything. I only hope to God he didn't either."

He knew a tear had fallen, but he didn't care, just like he hadn't cared when the bomb exploded whether he lived or died; he would rather have died. A part of him had done so anyway, right there in that furnace, alongside Connor; young, enthusiastic, idealistic Connor who wanted nothing more than to defend his country – to make a difference. If hands hadn't stopped him, hadn't pulled him back, he would have continued into the flames and joined the young man, rather than let him go to the other side alone.

"I don't remember much after that," he confessed. "I was out of it for quite a while, in hospital for an age. I left the army shortly afterwards and came home."

Jessamin had finished her wine and discarded the empty glass.

"Your time in the army?" she asked. "Is it over for good?"

"It's over," Finn confirmed. "They wanted me back in the squad, despite my injuries, but I couldn't. Even offered me a desk job, I told you that, didn't I? As though it was some sort of consolation. It wasn't. My mistake had killed a man. I was no longer fit for service – of any sort."

"But, Finn," Jessamin leaned forward, "it wasn't your fault. What happened to Connor, this stupid war that continues to rage on and on, none of it is your fault. You did your best."

Finn shook his head vehemently. "Please don't say it's not

my fault, Jess. I was in charge of Connor. He was in my care. It *was* my fault. His death is on my hands."

Jessamin looked as if she were about to protest further, but then thought better of it.

"I deserve the guilt I carry. It will never leave me. I don't *want* it to leave me. But the guilt you carry, Jess, I don't think it's justified. I understand you're still grieving for your husband, but what I don't understand is why you think you're to blame."

Jessamin withdrew her hand and sat back on her heels. Had she done that because she was angry with him for asking? Was the sharing between them only to be one way?

Finn braced himself; found it difficult to even breathe. The last thing he wanted was to upset her. When she started speaking, her voice soft not furious, he was relieved.

"James rang me to say he was tired; that he wanted to stay in London overnight. There's a hotel round the corner from where he worked, and his firm reserve a number of rooms there because often staff work late – stay over. But I insisted he came home, and I insisted for the most stupid of reasons; because it was Friday night and I wanted to wake up with him on Saturday."

She paused – the only sound to fill the room the ticking clock that stood on the mantelpiece.

"I think you know what happened next. Stan told you," Jessamin continued, sounding remarkably steady. Only her eyes held the key to how distraught she still was. "James crashed his car on the motorway. There was no one else involved. He crashed into the barrier, bounced back off it and over the side of the road into an embankment and some trees." She lifted her head and managed a half smile. "He had an Alfa Romeo, a sports car. He loved that car, but he drove it too fast, always."

He was the one who now wanted to stress that it was no one's fault, but he knew better than that. It didn't matter what anyone said, it made no difference. She hadn't persisted when he asked her to stop saying so; he wouldn't insult her by insisting either.

"I accused him of having an affair, can you believe that? I said that was the reason he wanted to stay over. I knew what I was saying was rubbish, but I'd had a run-in with the manager at work. I wanted to lash out and James was my target." No trace of a smile on her face this time, her expression now matched the devastation in her eyes. "You don't know how many times I've wished I could take those words back; that I'd told him to stay; to come home the next day and tackle the roads refreshed. We'd have had Saturday together and every day thereafter. If only he hadn't listened to me." Inclining her head, she added, "That's the trouble you see; he *always* listened to me."

Finn remembered catching Jessamin talking on a couple of occasions when no one had been around. Was she talking to James? For his part, he knew he talked to Connor, but silently, telling him over and over how sorry he was. He dared to ask the question. Instead of answering, she started crying.

Immediately he was by her side, kneeling beside her, on the floor. His arms went round her, holding her as her body shook; pressing her to him, wishing he could hold her forever. She made no attempt to stop and he was glad; the only relief was in release – no matter how temporary.

Eventually she stilled, but he continued to hold her. He was grateful she didn't seem to mind. The minutes continued to tick. When she drew away, a part of him felt bereft.

"Show me," she said, looking into his face.

For a moment he was confused. What did she mean?

"Take the eye patch off. I want to see your face."

"Jess," he started but her already outstretched hand stopped him from continuing. She was easing the patch gently upwards, removing it completely.

He may as well be naked in front of her, that's how he felt; ashamed too. His looks had attracted plenty of attention; there had been many women in his life, but none that he had loved; none who he felt had ever really seen him, not like this woman could see him. Her gaze penetrated the exterior, saw what was within and – miraculously – didn't recoil.

"Jess," he said again; he breathed the word almost.

Jessamin cupped his face in her hands; held the ruins of it.

"That's better," was her reply.

At that moment he wanted to kiss her; he wanted it more than he'd ever wanted anything. He wanted to lose himself in her; to find sanctuary, real sanctuary, and a relief that was more than just fleeting. He ached to press her lips – soft and full – against his. He imagined what she'd taste like – fresh and exciting like the rain that had so recently drenched them. But he couldn't kiss her. He wouldn't. To do so would be sacrilege. Despite how earnest she was being, how tender, he knew she wouldn't want him to. She belonged to someone else entirely. And with him he couldn't compete.

Chapter Twenty-Five

SINKING into crisp white sheets, sleep welcomed Jessamin, pulling her with insistent fingertips into smoky depths; not frightening as it sometimes was, but comforting; a warm and inviting world – a world she cherished. There were no bright colours, no sounds that were loud enough to grate. All was soft and rounded. In this world, James would often wait for her and tonight he didn't disappoint. She saw him as though through a veil of mist, faint at first but becoming more lucid the closer she drew, his smile in place; not a smile, a grin, his head to one side, his blue eyes twinkling.

"James," she whispered as he took her into his arms and began to kiss her.

Within seconds they were lying on a bed of clouds, the simple shift she'd been wearing rapidly discarded. He was naked too. She could feel him; touch his skin – more real to her than anything – firm, smooth and so wonderfully familiar.

His mouth sought hers, no longer grinning, but insistent, his tongue pushing its way into her mouth and exploring deep within. Her body rose upwards to meet his as though it were something quite apart; something she didn't need to control. Instinctively she knew what to do – how to respond to the man touching her and how to touch him back.

As passion consumed them in equal measure, she cried

out, shattering the silence surrounding them. His breathing too became ragged, each of them wanting to cling to the moment but eager also to move on to the next delight. His hands, his lips, his tongue moved with expert ease the entire length of her body, sending shivers coursing through her – taking her to the brink but not pushing her over – not yet. She could stand it no more. She needed him inside her – the ultimate pleasure.

She pulled him on top and his legs parted hers. One hand reaching down, she guided him in. She was the one smiling now; she had him where he belonged. Jessamin closed her eyes, knowing that in complete darkness she'd be able to feel him more intensely. His movement was slow at first – teasing – but soon he gained momentum, both of them riding yet again to the brink. As their pace increased further, his breath mingling with hers, warm and sweet and so full of life, she inhaled deeply, wanting to devour him, his essence; to consume him whole. Her heart was galloping as beads of sweat broke out on her forehead. What lay beneath them would surely give way soon. She'd be in free-fall, soaring, plummeting and then soaring again.

No longer could she battle against the inevitable; the moment had arrived and it did so with startling ferocity – waves and waves of pleasure forcing every nerve end to pulsate wildly. And the tide was relentless. It surged, again and again, drowning her, overwhelming her, but not in despair this time – in elation. Again she cried out, unable to stop herself; all reason lost.

"Finn!" The word burst from her mouth.

On hearing it, the dream stopped.

* * *

Jessamin watched as the first rays of dawn dissolved the night. Her eyes fixated on a corner of the room, unable to look away. She couldn't think of what had just transpired; the terrible mistake she'd made. She wanted to apologise to James but words refused to form in her mind or her throat. She simply lay in the bed, her legs drawn up beneath her, and let tears chase each other miserably down her cheeks.

How much time passed she didn't know. The room was grey rather than bright indicating that the day outside was not a good one. The pillow beneath her head felt cold and damp. Shifting her gaze at last, Jessamin looked at the clock. It had just edged its way past six – it was early still. She didn't need to be at Comraich for another three hours.

Comraich – the thought of going there, of seeing Maccaillin, was not one she wanted to lie in bed and contemplate any longer. She couldn't think about him again – it felt traitorous even though he was an innocent. He'd played no part in her betrayal. Why had she cried out his name? It had been James who had occupied her mind, her body; who'd always done so. Maccaillin was just a friend.

"Jess." It was James, she knew it, trying to reach her, but for once she wanted to hide. She was too ashamed to speak to him right now, to hear his reassurances.

Sitting up, she swung her legs round the side of the bed, her feet making contact with the carpet. Forcing herself forward she quickly washed and dressed. She had to get out of here; this was his cottage: Maccaillin's. He was everywhere. But where would she go? Not down to the village, she might bump into someone – Maggie maybe – preparing for another day's trading, or Rory out and about on his rounds and looking at her as he always did, with doe-eyed sincerity. She needed to be alone; to think... or not to think which seemed preferable at the moment. Stan's Loch – that's where she would go.

Not bothering to eat or drink, she grabbed her coat from the peg behind the hallway door. As she did she started coughing. Her chest was tight: perhaps she'd caught a chill swimming in the rain the day before. No matter, she'd take some honey and lemon later.

Letting herself out of Skye Croft, she found the day was indeed cold and dull. It was misty too – the clouds so low they were claustrophobic. Zipping up her coat, she pressed forward, towards the path leading to Comraich and beyond, praying Maccaillin would still be asleep and that she wouldn't bump into him. Time had run away from them the previous night; he had left late, well past midnight. Maggie had texted to say that Stan was in bed and sleeping so there was no need to hurry home. Taking advantage of their free time, one bottle of red had led to another, followed by coffee, not one cup but two – drunk at a leisurely pace. After being so candid with each other, conversation had turned to more mundane matters – her soup business, his painting. She expressed a desire to see what he'd created since he'd been home, but he hadn't been keen. So much he still kept hidden.

As she entered the pine trees, their fresh, green smell assailed her. She tilted her face and breathed deeply at the same time as registering a few spots of damp on her face. More rain. Still she pressed on, grimly determined. Her head was beginning to feel muggy, the chill she'd caught taking hold.

Comraich came into view and Jessamin steeled herself. *Please don't let him be up yet.* She wouldn't be able to face Maccaillin. She needed more time to expunge the memory of her dream and if not expunge it, push it to the furthest reaches of her mind.

"Jess." She heard James's voice again.

"No, James, not now," she replied, surprised at how harsh she sounded. "I... I just need to get my head straight, that's all."

James retreated, as she knew he would, ever compliant. A part of her was grateful, but another part of her, a much bigger part, wanted him to be as angry with her as she was with herself; to accuse her of not loving him any more so she could insist that she did. She could then assure him she loved him above everyone and all things, and that she had done since the moment they'd met. That she was his – she was Jessa*mine* – always and forever. But he wanted no such assurances. Why not?

Tears began to pool again and she wiped roughly at them. She cursed James for driving too fast on that long ago October night; cursed Maccaillin for daring to enter her dreams; cursed the entire world. She blamed them all, took back that blame and then heaped it on them again. It was madness but she couldn't stop.

Squeezing through the gap in the gate, she trudged on; the mist was so thick now – like castle walls as Maccaillin had said. She could no longer see the sheep that populated these hills but she could hear them, their distant, disembodied bleating nothing less than eerie.

An image of Maccaillin's arms around her the previous night was vivid in her mind. She pushed it away, but still it lingered. Such comfort she'd found in his arms – solace. But that was *all* she had found. Dreams often took emotions experienced during the day and skewered them; she knew that. The tiniest thing someone said could take on dramatic proportions in sleep; become relevant when in truth it had been *ir*relevant. But Maccaillin comforting her – that was not ir-relevant, and she wouldn't do him a disservice by suggesting it. But it wasn't anything more significant either. That he'd confided in her had touched her. That he'd allowed her to remove his eye patch had touched her too. Emotions had run high between them. She was no fool. She could admit that. But they were emotions that the subconscious had taken and dressed up in fancy clothing.

Jessamin failed to see the cluster of rocks before her. As she'd been in free-fall during her dream she went into free-fall again, her arms flailing either side of her. As knees and palms connected with path and gravel, she welcomed the pain that bit into them; it detracted from the pain in her heart. Turning to sit on her backside, she looked at her hands; they were grazed and bloodied.

"Jess, go back, please." It was James again, pleading with her. But she didn't want to go back. She wanted to reach the loch and felt an uncontrollable urge to do so; wanted to draw comfort from a sight she'd always found comfort in, eager for it to work its magic.

"It's not far now," said Jessamin, rising. "A few more minutes, that's all."

No sooner had she stopped speaking then another cough-ing fit seized her. Should she go back? It would be the sensi-ble thing to do. Not home but to Comraich. Rush into the kitchens, start work, popping out only to check on Stan, to feed him. She glanced at her watch. It was nearing seven thir-ty; too early still. She'd continue onwards.

The mist seemed to be getting heavier. She felt as though she was in another land entirely, a kingdom of clouds. The loch – where was it? Should she turn left now, off the path and towards it? Surely she hadn't overshot the mark? Whilst she was contemplating, she heard voices; people shouting, two or three of them, in the distance, but not too far.

Jessamin stood absolutely still, barely even breathed. Were they in trouble? Tourists perhaps who'd lost their way? What was the best thing to do? Try and reach them or double back, raise the alarm and get help? Maccaillin had warned her about the dangers of hill-walking in the Highlands; how quickly the weather could turn; how easy it was to become disorientated. Perhaps that's what had happened to them.

The shouting stopped. Had she imagined it? Surely walkers wouldn't be out at this hour? She lifted one hand to her temple. Her head throbbed; it felt clammy despite the cold. Thinking it wise to turn back after all, she was stopped in her tracks again. There *was* shouting! She hadn't been mistaken. It was coming from just in front of her – distressed sounds, and most definitely human, not the sound of sheep distorted.

Jessamin called out. "Hello! Who's there? Can I help?"

As she drew nearer she could just make out the loch. It looked stagnant somehow – surreal; not welcoming at all.

"Hello," she tried again. There had been no response the first time.

The shouting ceased. It seemed to be coming in such random bursts. But surely if she could hear them, they'd be able to hear her? If so, why weren't they shouting back? Letting her know their exact whereabouts?

As she continued to move forwards, carefully – the last thing she wanted was to trip again – the silence continued. Perhaps she'd been mistaken. When she'd fallen, she'd only grazed her hands; she hadn't hit her head. She wasn't confused although she did feel slightly dizzy. She decided she would call out once more, wait for a few minutes, then go back, report what she'd heard, and leave it to those more skilled than her to deal with it.

Pleased with her plan, she put it into action. No reply. She waited. Even the sheep quietened down as if they were colluding with her; listening too.

She was about to turn away when a figure on the far shore caught her eye. Squinting, she realised there was not just one figure, there were two and then a third. They were nothing more than shapes in the mist, not looking at her but at each other.

"Hello!" She all but screamed at them this time. Her hands raised, she also started jumping up and down on the spot and waving furiously.

There was no way they wouldn't be able to see her; they weren't that far away. One of the figures appeared to be lying between the other two. Had that person fallen and hurt him or herself? Certainly something was going on. Although they were no longer shouting, they were talking heatedly. She detected a dark, accusatory tone to their exchange that sent shivers racing up her spine. All her screaming had made her throat sore, then the coughing started up again, a loud, retching sound; she was making a racket. But still they refused to acknowledge her. She couldn't cross the loch and the mist was too dense to allow her to circumnavigate it. She'd get herself back to Comraich. Face Maccaillin. He'd know what to do.

Backing away, Jessamin spied a fourth figure looming over the three figures in front of him, staring at them, his hands wide as if in supplication.

"Hello!" she tried one last time.

To her astonishment, the fourth figure lowered his hands and turned towards her, albeit maddeningly slowly. Nonetheless, she was hopeful again, and resumed waving.

"I'm going to go and get help. Stay where you are. I won't be long."

Instead of acknowledging her, the figure continued to stare. Strangely, she could make out nothing about him at all. He was more of an outline than anything else but she had the distinct feeling he was male, anger, shock and confusion rolling off him and towards her. Despite not being able to distinguish his features, she felt his eyes lock on to hers, searching deep, but for what?

Instinctively, she began to back away; glad now they were on the other side of the loch; that they would have trouble reaching her. They would, wouldn't they? Panic flared. What if they were local; if they knew the landscape well; if they rushed as one entity towards her? Suddenly she realised she didn't want to see them, she absolutely didn't!

"Jess, follow me."

It was James! She turned expecting to see him, but there was no one.

"Come on, girl, quickly."

Girl? Since when had he started calling her girl? Blindly, she stumbled forward. The mist had become denser still. Where was the path? It had disappeared? Impossible!

"James, is that you?"

"Take my hand!"

It was an order. James never ordered her. Who was this? She turned around. Had the figures in the mist caught up with her? But there was no one; no one she could see. There were no noises either; all was quiet – too quiet. The silence seemed to be baiting her. She wished she hadn't turned. She had lost her bearings completely. She could see nothing. Certainly not the hand the voice insisted she take. The panic she had felt earlier intensified, dread radiating outwards from her

239

heart.

"Now!" The voice hissed. It was so close; right beside her but still its owner was a mystery.

Another bout of coughing racked her; her chest grew more painful as though stones were bearing down on it. Just as her legs started to buckle, she was pulled forward.

"Wha...?" She was powerless to resist. The grip was so tight there was no hope of throwing him off.

"Who are you?" she screamed. "What do you want? Let me go!"

In reply, she was pulled with even greater force, onwards, further and further until she lost her footing and fell again. As she did, the pressure on her hand released and her already damaged palms as she hit the ground were further damaged.

The path – she was on the path. But which way should she go? She had no idea. To go the wrong way, further into the mountains, would lead to death; of that she was certain.

Scrambling to her feet, she found the figure she'd locked eyes with earlier standing in front of her. Despite it being so much closer, she still couldn't make out any discernible features, although she strained so hard to see she thought her eyes might burst from their sockets. He pointed southwards.

"Go home, Jessamin," he said and without any hesitation, she started running.

Chapter Twenty-Six

JESSAMIN knew she wasn't at the loch any more – she'd gathered that much – but where she was she didn't know. She kept drifting in and out of consciousness, feeling as though a furnace was burning beside her; at other times it was as though the room she was in had no roof or windows. Rather it was suspended in mid-air, allowing cold air to swirl around her; to chill her to the bone. There were faces too, so many of them; some she recognised, others she didn't, but even those she didn't recognise seemed familiar, one man in particular, young and good-looking with a woman by his side. They both had expressions of such concern on their faces; concern and sorrow. Who were they? Maccaillin, Maggie, Shona, Gracie and James; theirs were the faces she took comfort in, particularly James's. Often he would come and sit on her bed, take her hand in his and gently stroke the back of it.

"What's happened, James? Where am I?"

"It's okay, you're safe."

"The loch, the picture, I need it."

"Don't worry about that right now."

"Don't tell me not to worry. Call Aunt Lara. Ask her."

"Jess, I can't—"

"You have to find a way."

At one point, a man with a stethoscope towered over her,

Doctor Buchanan she presumed; so serious he looked, bending closer to listen to her chest and feel the glands around her neck. Maccaillin and Maggie, they looked strained as well. Often they would stand side by side, looking at her with frowns on their faces. She remembered wanting to giggle when they did that, the urge to do so almost insane. But she hadn't giggled. She didn't have the energy. Instead she returned to dreams, weaved in and out of them; hazy, innocuous dreams, the kind you forgot upon waking.

The dream she woke from this morning she could hardly remember either. Sarah had featured, asking, as she always did, when she was coming home; but whatever else had happened in it she couldn't recall – nothing too momentous she suspected. Yawning, she threw her arms wide and stretched. Her head felt clearer, less achy, as did her body. She wanted to sit up and was surprised to find she could do so with relative ease, one arm reaching behind her to shift the pillows into place.

Taking a deep breath, she looked around. As she suspected, this wasn't her room at Skye Croft. It was not humble enough. She was at Comraich, in a bedroom she'd never been in before, but which felt familiar because Comraich was so familiar. Like Stan's room, it was in need of redecoration: the wallpaper with its tiny floral print was faded, significantly in places, where the sunlight hit it, she guessed, but other than that it was cosy enough. It was very much a female room, but which female in particular? One of Maccaillin's sisters perhaps, or maybe it had been his mother's?

The door opened and Maccaillin came striding in.

"Ah, good, you're awake." Crossing over to the curtains, he pulled them open.

"I... yes," Jessamin spluttered. "I'm awake and I'm fine...

I think. I'm not sure how I came to be here though. Did I pass out or something?"

Maccaillin turned to face her. "Pass out? You could say that. Four days ago."

"Wha…?" FOUR DAYS! Surely he was joking. He had to be. This haze she'd been in, there was no way it had lasted that long.

Crossing over to a chair situated beside her bed, he settled himself down.

"You've caused us quite a bit of worry, Jessamin Wade," he continued. "You've been in and out of delirium. At one point, we were going to ship you out to the hospital in Inverness, your temperature soared so high. But between Maggie and me we managed to bring it down. The doctor said you could stay after that, as long as it didn't climb again."

Delirium, soaring temperatures, the hospital at Inverness – was he being serious? She searched his face for signs that he was kidding but she couldn't find any. Rather he looked tired. There were dark circles under his eyes and his skin was not its usual healthy colour. He was also unshaven. It made him look more rugged if such a thing were possible. She thought again about what he'd told her. She'd been ill, she could accept that; but for four days? No way!

Immediately she started to feel agitated.

"The soup—"

"It's okay," Maccaillin leaned forward as though he needed to get closer to reassure her. "Shona and Gracie have seen to everything and Rory's on board with deliveries."

Another thought struck her; one that horrified her. Surreptitiously, she moved her head to one side and sniffed.

"Worried about your personal hygiene?"

"I… well… yes. Oh my God, you didn't, did you?"

A roar of laughter filled the air. "No, I can assure you, Jess, I did not! Maggie did what was necessary in that department."

It was some consolation, but still her face was scarlet. What *had* been necessary in that department?

Not only did Maccaillin lean forward, he scraped his chair forward too; his closeness for some reason unsettling her. Instinctively she reached up to pull at the nape of her nightdress. Nightdress? She looked down. She didn't own a nightdress. It was tee shirts she slept in. But she was dressed in a nightdress: a modest white nightdress; a very large nightdress. It swamped her. Not hers for sure.

"It's Maggie's," Maccaillin said, picking up on her surprise. After a moment, amusement slid from his face. "Jess, what's the last thing you remember?"

"Erm... ooh, I... give me a minute to think."

What she remembered was laughing – at the fairy pools on Skye. Standing with Maccaillin in the rain, getting soaked to the skin and laughing, with him laughing alongside her. What had happened after that? They must have gone home – to Skye Croft or here? She racked her brains: the memories were there but hazy, like picture postcards pinned onto a distant wall. She screwed up her eyes and squinted at them.

"Are you okay?" he asked.

"Yeah, yeah, I'm fine. I'm just thinking."

"And that's what you do when you're thinking, is it?"

"What?"

"Squint?"

Deliberately she ignored him and resumed squinting.

That was it! They'd gone back to Skye Croft after the fairy pools, the pair of them, soaking wet. Warming themselves by the fireside, they'd started to talk. Gradually words

Maccaillin had said came back to her; his mention of a young man called Connor; a village in Afghanistan; a bomb that had exploded, killing Connor and maiming him. He'd told her exactly what had happened; had confided in her. Had she told him more about James? Yes, she thought so. And his eye patch, she'd removed it in an extraordinarily tender moment. This blush on her face – it seemed almost permanent.

The dream she'd had about James – it *was* about James she reminded herself – she remembered that too, and how much it upset her. She'd been angry with herself because of it, and had wanted to clear her head, so she'd taken a walk… but where? Stan's Loch, of course. There, in the mist, the unrelenting mist, she'd seen shapes and heard voices – loud and angry. One voice, one shape in particular had homed in on her, telling her to go home and pointing the way. Not James coming to her aid, but someone else entirely.

As the memories increased in clarity, she cried out. Maccaillin, as worried as he'd looked when she lay in delirium, quickly swapped the chair he'd been sitting in for the side of her bed, occupying the exact same space James tended to favour; his hand the one taking hers and stroking it.

"What is it, Jess? Tell me."

His expression was tender but despite this, she couldn't tell him what she'd seen; he'd think she was mad. Perhaps she *was* mad or en route to madness.

"How did I get here?" she asked, desperate for him to complete the picture.

"You just came running out of the mist. I was outside, about to drive off. I *had* driven off. I was going to Inverness to sort out some lease details with my solicitor about a cottage we own, when I saw you in my rear view mirror. You looked..." he shook his head at the memory, "you looked wretched to be honest – wild-eyed, as if you'd seen a ghost."

Jessamin started at this. How could she tell him that's exactly what she'd seen? A ghost. And not just one, four of them! Quickly, Maccaillin reached out a hand to tuck some hair behind her ear. She started at this too, but if he noticed, he didn't show it.

"Basically, you fell into my arms. You were hot, red-hot; sweat was pouring off you despite the fact it was cold. I got you inside, called Maggie and the doctor, and you've been here ever since."

She'd fallen into his arms? Oh, the embarrassment!

"What did the doctor say was wrong with me?"

"That you'd caught a chill. He was worried it might develop into pneumonia, but the worst was over pretty quickly."

Pneumonia? She remembered waking the morning after swimming in the fairy pools with a sore throat and a cough: a summer chill that had taken a turn for the worse.

"Stan, how is he?"

Maccaillin's face darkened slightly.

"He's no better I'm afraid. His cough's got worse."

"Has the doctor been to see him too?"

"He has." Hesitating slightly, he added, "Jess, I don't think he's going to get better."

"Oh no," She felt tears threaten. "I need to go and see him."

"Hey," as she made to get out of bed, Maccaillin stopped her. "Not so fast, perhaps a bit later on. You've only just come round."

Frustration gnawed at her. She wanted to see Stan. Not only to check on his health but to talk to him. If anyone could make sense of what she'd seen at the loch, he could. But getting past the man-mountain in front of her was going to be hard.

"Jess, he's okay for now, he's comfortable. Concentrate on getting yourself well first."

She couldn't help it. Her tears fell. She'd grown to love Stan over the months she had lived in Glenelk. He was like the grandfather she'd never really known.

Before Maccaillin could comfort her further, Maggie walked in.

"Jess," she said, hurrying over. "You're awake!"

Maccaillin moved away, allowed Maggie to take his place.

"And what's this, you're crying? Oh, lovey, don't cry. You're better now."

Despite her friend's kind words and reassuring hug, Jessamin continued crying. All kinds of feelings were rising up in her; grief for Stan; relief that she was on the mend; guilt for feeling relief – all feelings she wanted to push away but which wouldn't retreat.

"I'll go and make us some tea," Maccaillin offered.

As he hurried from the room, Jessamin pitied him. Between her and Stan, he seemed to be on endless tea duty. She was surprised at how quickly he returned though. She wondered if her tears made him feel awkward and whether tea making was just an excuse to escape her while she did the feminine thing and sobbed. Evidently not.

He handed her a bone china cup with a floral pattern on it. Lifting it to her mouth, she was grateful for the warmth of the liquid as it slid down her throat. Gradually, her tears subsided. As they did, she realised she was hungry, ravenous in fact.

"Are those croissants on that tray?" she said, sniffing.

Again, Maccaillin hurried over but with a plate this time.

She took one bite of the freshly warmed pastry and then another, the food having an almost instant restorative effect. If she had crumbs around her mouth, she didn't care. Polishing off one, she asked for the second and made short work of that too.

Eventually wiping at her mouth with a napkin, she looked at Maccaillin and said, "I need to go home."

* * *

Despite her best intentions, another twenty-four hours passed before Jessamin felt strong enough to get out of bed. After coming to, and speaking with Maggie and Maccaillin, she'd actually slept the rest of the day away; her body still very much in recovery. Maggie helped her to get out of bed eventually and was none too pleased to be doing so.

"You know I think you should stay for a few more days, don't you?"

"I do," conceded Jessamin, "and thank you, Maggie, for everything you've done; how well you've looked after me; but I've imposed enough."

"Nonsense! You haven't imposed at all and it's really Finn you need to thank. He did the lion's share regarding your care. I've been looking after Stan mainly."

Pulling her freshly laundered jumper on, Jessamin paused.

"Finn did the lion's share?" she questioned.

"Yes," Maggie replied, nodding. "I'd have been happy to of course, but he insisted, wouldn't take no for an answer. For the first couple of days, he never left your side." Pointing to the chair beside her bed, she added, "That's where he slept."

"Oh," was all Jessamin could manage, humbled by what Maggie was telling her.

"After your fever had broken and we knew you'd be all right, I insisted he get some sleep in his own bed. He must have only slept in snatches though, because whenever I popped my head round the corner – and I did so at some odd hours of the night I can tell you – he was beside you again, either on the chair or on the side of your bed, stroking your hand."

Jessamin gasped. "Stroking my hand? I thought that was James!"

"I know you did. That's what you kept calling Finn: James. You cried out for him a lot."

"Oh, God."

"No, it was definitely James, I can assure you."

Jessamin smiled, grateful for Maggie's stab at humour.

"So, you stayed at Comraich too?" she tentatively enquired.

"I did, for the first time ever. But if you're going home today, so am I. There's nothing like your own bed."

Again, Jessamin smiled. "You and Finn seem close again."

"We are. Thanks to you."

"Me?" Jessamin was surprised. "What have I got to do with it?"

Maggie stopped helping her and looked at her instead.

"You really don't get it, do you?" she said.

"Get what?"

"What an impact you've had on this village? How important you've become to us. I don't know… I'd say you were meant to be here."

Meant to be here? Could that be true? Sometimes she thought so too.

"Can I pop in to see Stan before I go?"

"You can pop in to see him, but he's sleeping much of the time now. Don't be disappointed if he's not awake."

Stan was indeed asleep when Jessamin entered his room. She walked over to his bed, sat down beside him and held his hand, just as James *and* Maccaillin had held her hand throughout her illness. He had always looked frail, but there was nothing to him right now. She'd need to make him some consommé as soon as her strength returned fully: a clear broth packed with as much goodness as she could squeeze into it. Her mother used to make it for her when she was ill, although to be honest she'd never liked it at the time. Still, it was nutritious, that was what mattered. She'd make that task a priority.

After sitting in silence with him for twenty minutes, Jessamin bent down to kiss Stan on his cheek before leaving the room, shutting the door gently behind her.

Downstairs, Maccaillin and Maggie were in the hallway.

"I'll drive you home," Maggie said but Maccaillin cut across her.

"It's okay, Maggie, I'll do it. You need to get back to the shop."

"If you're sure?" Maggie double-checked.

"I'm sure."

"Thank you." Turning to Jessamin, she explained, "Rory's been holding court whilst I've been here but I know he's got other jobs he needs to attend to."

"Rory's a godsend, isn't he?" Jessamin said, remembering that he was helping Shona and Gracie with soup delivery too.

"He's a good lad and where you're concerned, he'll do anything."

Blushing again, she checked Maccaillin's reaction to Maggie's words but his expression gave away nothing.

Hugging and thanking Maggie, Jessamin followed Maccaillin outside. The car journey home was a silent one, Stan and the loch occupying her mind.

Outside Skye Croft, she stumbled slightly. Immediately, Maccaillin was by her side.

"I wish you weren't so stubborn, that you'd stay longer at Comraich. You're more than welcome."

"You've done enough for me," Jessamin replied, "and I'm very grateful. I'll be fine. It's Stan we need to concentrate on now."

Maccaillin sighed. He couldn't argue with her on that score.

Opening the door to her cottage, she stepped inside. Maccaillin, as soon as he realised she couldn't be persuaded to stay on at Comraich, had come by to turn the heating on and get the fire roaring. The house was warm and welcoming.

"I've changed your bedding too, I hope you don't mind."

How could she mind such kindness?

Crossing over to the sofa, she slumped down onto it, tiredness overcoming her.

"I'll make you a cup of tea," he said, rushing towards the kitchen.

"Again?" she teased.

Maccaillin turned back round. "You don't like my tea?"

"On the contrary, you make a very good cup of tea. For a Scotsman."

"I'm glad you English approve." Laughing, he disappeared from sight.

Alone again, Jessamin thought back to what Maggie had

told her. Maccaillin had done the lion's share of caring for her. He hadn't left her side for forty-eight hours and barely after that. That was beyond the call of duty. How could she ever thank him?

"Oh, James," she said, not really knowing why she felt a sudden surge of despair.

Turning her head, something else caught her eye – a rectangular-shaped package. As Maccaillin re-entered the room, she asked him if he knew anything about it.

"That? Yes, it arrived this morning," he answered, setting a mug down before her.

"Who's it from?"

"Lara."

Jessamin was glad she hadn't yet taken a sip of tea; she would have spluttered it everywhere if she had. She knew she'd mentioned Aunt Lara to him before, but the way he said her name, it was as though he were more familiar with her than he should be. But before she could question him further, he started to explain.

"You kept asking me to get the picture. You said you needed it."

She did remember, but it was James she'd asked.

Immediately, James interjected.

"Jess, how did you expect me to phone Lara? I'm dead, remember?"

Oh come on, I was hardly thinking straight, was I?

The sound of James's laughter receded as Maccaillin started speaking again.

"Jess, are you all right? Are you listening to me?"

"Sorry, I am, I promise. But her number – you don't know it."

"I figured you'd have an address book, so I came here to

check." Almost apologetically he added, "It was easy enough to find, I didn't rummage around too much, I swear."

She waved her hand in dismissal, "No, no, its fine. It's... it's very good of you." Mulling it over, she said, "So Aunt Lara's back from her travels?"

"Aye, about a week or so ago apparently"

Still she was confused.

"How did it get here so quickly?"

"I asked her to send it, special delivery."

"That would have cost her a fortune!"

Maccaillin looked affronted. "I covered all costs, don't worry about that."

"Then I must pay you back," Jessamin struggled to get to her feet.

"Relax," Maccaillin held out his hand. "You don't need to pay me back right now. You don't need to pay me back at all; I was glad to help out."

Jessamin did relax slightly. There was no way she'd allow him to pay for the picture's transportation, but he was right, she didn't have to settle up with him this very minute. Rather, she wanted to see the picture again; she felt desperate to.

"Could you... would you mind unwrapping it?" she asked Maccaillin.

"Not at all."

The package had red 'Fragile' stickers all over it, but even so, she hoped it hadn't been damaged in any way.

Whilst he worked, she remarked on how impressive the postal system was.

"I didn't have it sent via post," Maccaillin casually remarked. "I had it couriered."

Again Jessamin was glad she hadn't yet picked up her tea.

He'd had it couriered? A fortune indeed!

All thoughts of finance were pushed to the back of her mind, however, as the picture was revealed to her. Maccaillin, she couldn't help notice, looked distinctly unimpressed.

"Doesn't look like one of Seanair's paintings," he said. "It must be an early one."

He brought it over to her. Half of her was delighted to see it again after all those years; half of her recoiled.

Nonetheless, she reached out both hands to take it. It used to seem so romantic this picture, unlike anything she'd ever seen before; the landscape at once forbidding and alluring. As she stared at the blues, the greys and the white accents, she shuddered. All her mind could see were the figures standing on the opposite side of the loch; one figure in particular – the figure who had stared back at her. Forbidding was all the picture seemed now.

Chapter Twenty-Seven

IT was several days before Jessamin felt strong enough to return to Comraich. In the meantime, Maggie and Maccaillin were regular visitors, as were Shona and Gracie, eager to show off how well they were running the business in her absence.

"We've even secured a new client," Shona announced proudly. "A cousin of Rory's on Skye runs a small café in Plockton, you know that village made famous by that TV programme years ago – about the Dobson's who bought Duncraig Castle and renovated it; I forget what it was called. Anyway, Plockton is the village Duncraig Castle is in; it's been a busy little village ever since that TV programme; and sometimes Rory's cousin – Gordy – is overrun. If we can ship in soup to him it'll be one less job he has to think about."

Rory too popped in, bringing her chocolates, flowers and magazines.

"Rory, you shouldn't have," Jessamin chided him. "You've been generous enough."

However he insisted it was nothing and continued to bring her small gifts as well as not so small ones. The bunch of flowers he'd brought whilst Maccaillin had been there was really quite impressive, causing the latter to raise an eyebrow. As soon as Maccaillin had left, Jessamin sat Rory down.

"I'm really grateful to you, Rory, for coming to see me when I'm ill; for the flowers and the gifts you've been bringing."

"No, Jess, it's my pleasure. I like spoiling you."

"Rory, Shona's your girlfriend. You should be spoiling her, not me."

Rory shrugged – in that moment he looked like a little boy, not a man in his mid-twenties. "I'm not sure Shona really likes me," he confessed.

"Oh, she likes you," Jessamin replied, nodding her head for extra emphasis.

"Really? She's a bit cold towards me at times."

"She's cold because she thinks you like me."

"But I do."

"No, Rory, you don't."

For the next twenty minutes she explained, in as kindest terms as possible, that she was off limits. She also imparted as much relationship advice as she could muster regarding how to warm Shona up – to make her sizzle in fact – drawing on all the things James had done for her when they first started going out together.

As she talked, she could hear James in the background.

"So, that stunt I pulled with the heart balloons, the limo and the monkey suit, you actually liked? Because you looked pretty pissed off about it at the time."

Jessamin tried not to burst out laughing, not in front of Rory anyway.

I loved what you did with the heart balloons and the limo, but it was the monkey suit I could have done without.

"The monkey suit was genius."

Not when worn in front of my work colleagues, it wasn't.

"I suppose," he conceded.

Instantly she took pity on him.

But, it was a unique way to declare your love. I'll give you that.

Spontaneity, romantic gestures, delivering the unexpected, that's what would win Shona's heart. Rory, she was happy to note, took it all on board and seemed to become full of fire himself, but not before double-checking she was definitely not available.

"I'm definitely not," she told him.

"Is it Maccaillin you're after?"

"I'm after no one."

As he swaggered with renewed vigour down her gravel driveway, she couldn't help but smile. If he put into action even half of what she'd said, Shona was in for a treat.

As for Stan's picture, she kept it propped up against a wall downstairs. Maccaillin offered to fix it to the wall but she refused. She wanted to take it to show Stan, to see if he could remember when he'd painted it; if it had indeed been one of his first creations.

That day was today. She woke up, had coffee and two slices of thick buttered toast and felt more like her old self; no trace of chest pain or muzzy head lingered.

"I wonder what he'll make of it, James," she asked idly.

"The picture? I'm not sure. I must say it is a bit crude. He's supposed to be a brilliant artist. It looks like a child has done this."

"Rubbish," Jessamin disagreed. "It has passion, great passion. It tells you just how much Stan loved the landscape that surrounded him, the loch in particular; how important it was to him. My mother loved it and I do too. This picture is part of my heritage."

"If you say so."

"And you can take that look off your face. Don't think I don't know."

"What look?"

"You're smirking and you know I hate it when you do that."

James chuckled. "Nothing gets past you, does it?"

"Damn right it doesn't. And don't forget it."

After breakfast, Jessamin poured the consommé, made the previous day, into a flask. She took it out to the car and placed it on the passenger seat before returning to get the picture. Once that was safely stowed in the boot, she got in the car and drove off.

The day was grey, the air distinctly chilly. There'd be no more swimming in the loch, not this year. As for where she'd be next year, she didn't know. Perhaps she'd stay, perhaps she wouldn't. If the winter was as harsh as the locals said it was, it might put her off enduring another one.

James was listening in again.

"If we do move, can we move somewhere warmer?"

She was pleased at his use of the word 'we'. The dream she'd had, he didn't seem to blame her for it.

"Where would you like to go?" she asked, pulling on to the dirt track, which would lead into the woods.

"Let me think; the Caribbean again. I liked it there, or Goa. I've always fancied Goa. That's another spiritual place."

"Hmm." Goa did appeal – especially the spiritual aspect.

"What I want is to lie next to you on the beach," James continued, "with you wearing nothing more than a skimpy bikini. No, not even that actually; your top discarded."

"James, stop! You're getting me all hot under the collar. Anyway, you wouldn't be able to lie beside me. You don't like the sun, you go bright red."

"Don't remind me," he said ruefully. "Actually, the sun's not a problem any longer."

"Oh and why's that?"

"Where I am, it can't touch me."

Pulling on to Comraich's gravel driveway and turning the engine off, Jessamin sat back in her seat.

"Where are you exactly?" she asked, wondering why she hadn't asked before.

"I'm… I don't know to be honest. But it's nice enough, Jess, don't worry."

"But you said the sun can't reach you," she said, doing precisely that, worrying. "It's not dark, is it?"

"It's not dark, no, I can see but… it's a strange sort of seeing. It's like looking through a glass tumbler into a room; everything's familiar just slightly distorted."

"Oh, James," she said, wishing she could reach out to him, *really* reach out.

"Don't get upset. I'm perfectly all right. I'm better than all right. I'm happy. But…"

"Yeah?"

"There is one thing."

"What?"

"There's a light, but it's quite far away; it's in the distance."

"A light? Oh, that's good." Jessamin could breathe easier now.

"In a way," James replied.

Again she was perplexed.

"Why only in a way?"

"Because I know that if I go towards it, I'll disappear."

"You'll disappear? But where to?"

"Somewhere far away from you."

* * *

With James's words still ringing in her ears, Jessamin ferried the contents of her car into Comraich. The door was off the latch as always; she could come and go as she pleased, as though she were a part of Comraich too – a fellow occupant.

As she went through to the kitchen, Gracie was the first one to greet her.

"Jess, it's so lovely to see you," she enthused.

Shona hugged her next. "Good to see you back in action, Jess."

Everyone in Glenelk called her Jess, even Maccaillin. No one tended to call her by her full name. She didn't mind – Jessamin was a bit of a mouthful. James was the only one to have lengthened it. That light he was talking about; why would it take him from her?

You won't go towards it, will you, James? You won't leave me?

As Shona and Gracie chatted amiably, Jessamin warmed Stan's soup.

"I'm just going to take this up to Stan, I'll be back soon to help out."

"No need," Gracie said. "We've everything under control. In fact, we're almost finished."

"If you're sure," Jessamin double-checked.

"I'm sure," Gracie insisted. "That picture you brought in by the way," she pointed to the far wall where Jessamin had propped it up. "I wouldn't leave it there. It gets pretty steamy. It'll ruin."

"Oh, it won't be there for long," Jessamin replied. "I'll come down and get it after I've fed Stan. It's him I want to show it to."

Climbing the stairs, Jessamin thought the air in Comraich seemed even more oppressive. But then illness tended to have that effect – her recent illness and Stan's. Only in the kitchen, with Shona and Gracie enlivening it, was the atmosphere different. Pushing open the door to Stan's room, that oppressiveness continued. It was more than illness that was responsible; it was death – lurking in every dark and dusty corner, waiting to strike. There was a smell too; a sharp, clinical odour that would stay with her long after she left him. Before entering fully, she had to stop and collect herself; forcing a brightness into her voice that she didn't feel.

"Stan!" she said, able at last to put one foot in front of the other. "I've missed you."

Stan was sitting up in bed, a blanket round his shoulders and a book lying discarded by his side. He'd been dozing, she was sure of it. According to Maggie, that's all he did lately, as though he already had one foot in another world.

Setting the soup down, she bent to kiss him, hugging him gently as she did.

"It's lovely to see you too, dear." The smile on his face looked more like a grimace. "I'm so glad you're better; we were all so worried you know."

"I'm much better thank you, the tiredness was the hardest thing to shake. I haven't had the energy to do anything. That'll teach me for swimming in fairy pools in the rain."

"Och! That would have nothing to do with it. You caught a chill that's all. A common enough thing up here; the air gets awful damp at times. Plays havoc with the chest."

Motioning to the soup bowl, Jessamin said, "I've made you some soup, some consommé. Let me feed it to you."

"I'll miss your soup," Stan replied.

"Miss it, why?"

"Where I'm going."

"Stan! Please don't speak like that. You're going nowhere, not yet anyway."

"Soon, dear," he said, patting her hand. "Soon I will and you know it."

"No, Stan—" she began but he interrupted her.

"Now, Jess, you're not to hold on to me too."

She was taken aback by his words; struggled to reply. In the end, she concentrated on the soup, spooning it gently into his mouth and taking care to mop any dribbles with a napkin. The food seemed to temporarily revive him and they talked about the weather and her business. When he'd finished, she asked him if he might like to rest awhile. Perhaps showing him the picture could wait another day.

"I'm fine to sit for a while longer, if you are?" he responded.

"Of course," Jessamin said. "I'm only too happy to."

Adjusting the pillows behind him and helping him to a sip of water from a glass by his bedside, she told him about the painting Maccaillin had had couriered up.

"It's here, it's downstairs. Would you like to see it?"

When Stan said that he would, Jessamin left the room, taking the empty bowl with her. She returned only minutes later with the painting in her hands.

"Ta da," she said, walking towards him. "Here it is."

Noting the look of confusion on his face, she peered over the edge of the canvas; she was showing him the blank side.

"Oh, sorry about that." Rectifying her mistake, she quickly turned the picture round and held it triumphantly aloft. "One of your finest, Stan McCabe. In my opinion anyway."

His reaction, she hadn't bargained for.

Quickly she lowered the picture. "Stan, what is it?"

What little colour he'd had drained completely. In contrast, his eyes were bulging, his mouth agape.

"Where... where did you get that?"

"It's my picture, remember? The picture that hung in the living room of my family home."

"Yes, yes, I know that," he sounded impatient now, impatient and something else – angry? Or was it scared? She couldn't tell. "But where did you get it from?"

"Erm... it was my mother's. Well, not my mother's exactly, it was her father's. He died before my grandmother, but when she died, Mum rescued it before house clearance could take it away. It had been kept behind the sofa all the while Mum was growing up, I don't know why. She and Aunt Lara used to sneak peeks at it. Like me, my mum loved it."

As she talked, Stan stared not at her but at the picture his hands clutching the blanket either side of him, his knuckles turning white.

"It was your grandfather's picture?" he said, but not to her, more to himself, as though he was trying to come to terms with that fact. "Jess, your grandfather's name, what was it?"

"His name? It was Murray. Ben Murray."

As his expression of horror intensified, Jessamin stashed the painting against the nearest chair and hurried over to him.

Chapter Twenty-Eight

STAN couldn't believe it. Ben Murray was Jessamin's grand-father?

"But you never said..."

"I know, I'm sorry, I didn't think it significant." Just as Jessamin had rushed over to him, she now rushed to explain. "I'd mentioned it to Maggie and Millie. I'd even told Rory his name I think, when I first arrived here. But no, I never told you. Why? Is it important?"

If only she knew...

All these months he'd been getting to know his dearest friend's granddaughter; growing to love her; to depend on her, and not once had he guessed who she was. But could he be blamed for that? There was no family resemblance, none at all. Mally had been tall, thickset with hair the colour of jet. Jessamin was petite, her brown hair golden rather than dark. And yet there'd been a connection between them when they'd first met and not just because of Beth and James; he'd felt as drawn to her as she had been to him.

"That's... that's not my painting," he said at last.

"Not yours? But, Stan, it's got your name on it." To prove her point, she turned from him, picked the painting back up and showed him the signature scrawled in black.

"Yes, yes, I know it's got my name on it, but it's not mine. That was his joke."

"His joke?" Jessamin repeated. "Whose joke? What are you talking about?"

"Mally's."

"Mally, your teenage friend? I don't understand."

Stan took pity. Jessamin's pretty face was indeed twisted in confusion. Mally's granddaughter, he thought again, shaking his head in wonder. She was standing before him. Drawn back by the very picture her grandfather had painted so long ago. It had to mean something... it had to! Mally had said once there was no such thing as coincidence but Stan had maintained the opposite – the world was built on coincidences. Now, he wasn't so sure. Maybe Mally was right all along. Jessamin had come back for a reason, to breathe life into Comraich, into him, into Finn – to rectify what had been torn asunder so many years before; to build a bridge between the past and the present.

"Sit down," Stan patted the bed beside him. "Sit down and I'll tell you everything."

Jessamin did as she was told.

"Mally is your grandfather."

Hearing Jessamin gasp, Stan reached for her hand.

"His name though..." she started.

"We were all at primary school together, you know that," Stan continued. "Flo, when she was little, she could never say Murray, she called him Ben Mally. Well, Mally kind of stuck, it's what we called him, the three of us. What others began to call him too."

"Oh, I see," but Stan could tell by her eyes that she didn't – not yet.

"And remember I told you also we used to paint together sometimes, me and Mally?"

"Yes," Jessamin replied, nodding.

"The loch, *your* loch, Jess, as well as mine; that was one of Mally's paintings, one of the ones we did together."

"So why's it got your name on it?"

"Mally always insisted I'd be famous one day, he scrawled my name rather than his on it just in case – an early Stan McCabe, selling for thousands. He only meant it tongue-in-cheek, clearly, because he never tried to sell it." Stan breathed deeply. "He kept it, all these years; a reminder of where he came from, of me, of Beth and Flo." Swallowing, he added, "No wonder he kept it behind the sofa. I'm only surprised he kept it at all."

"Stan." Jessamin was almost pleading now.

"I'm getting there, I'm getting there," he assured her. "But first, my throat, it feels so dry, could you pour me a little more water, Jess? Would you mind?"

Without hesitation, Jessamin did as she was asked, setting the tumbler full of clear, cool liquid down in front of him. Lifting it to his mouth, he took several sips. He could really have done with something stronger, a whisky fetched from downstairs to be precise; a Talisker, his favourite, distilled nearby, on the Isle of Skye. But water would have to do.

"We all lost," Stan continued. "Beth lost her sister and I lost my two best friends. But Mally, he lost everything. You didn't know your grandfather well, did you?"

"No, he died when I was seven. My mother would take my brother and I to see my grandparents regularly, I remember that. But it was my grandmother we spent time with. Granddad would always be in his study with the door closed. He'd always been like that, my mum told me, even when she was growing up. He was a gruff man, a loner. I don't think there was much love lost between my grandparents either, not from what Mum said. Something that used to sadden my grandmother a great deal apparently. It wasn't that she didn't love him, on the contrary, she did, but she always felt he was out of reach."

A loner? No, that wasn't the Mally he'd known. Mally didn't like to be alone; it was company he preferred. The four of them spent all their time together. And gruff, he hadn't been that either, he'd been full of life, enthusiastic – until his world crashed down about him. What Mally was, Stan realised, despite the new life he had built for himself in the south; despite marrying and having two daughters, was beyond repair.

"Don't blame your grandfather too much. If you knew why, you'd understand."

"Are you're going to tell me?"

"I am. I'm going to tell you what happened at the loch and why I've never been back to it since. Every picture I painted of it, I painted from memory. I couldn't go back." Stan could feel his eyes blurring but this was not a time for tears; this was a time for truths – at last. Would Beth mind the truth being revealed? Even if she did, he had no choice. He didn't want lies following him to the grave. The record had to be set straight; it was Mally who mattered now, his reputation. He and Beth, they'd made him suffer enough.

Clearing his throat, he continued. "Flo and Mally were a couple, I've told you that many times. Destined to be to-gether from the moment they met. But as you also know, Beth liked Mally too and Mally being who he was, he en-joyed the attention and encouraged it, causing tension be-tween the sisters. I warned him not to do that, but he carried on regardless. A tyke he was, but a tyke with a good heart. He was just young that's all, and the young do stupid things. They don't always understand the consequences." Pausing slightly, he added, "Or rather they understand too late. The day Flo died, she and Mally had argued. Both of them could be volatile, Flo a little more so than Mally, but it was fair to say they both had a temper. They were passionate people you see, the passion of the Highlands instilled in them; the passion of youth too. They were eighteen. We all were."

Stan had to pause again. His voice felt thick in his throat all of a sudden, causing him to cough slightly. "Mally had gone round to see Beth. She worked at the pub sometimes, nothing much, just a few shifts here and there, whatever she could do to earn some spending money. He complained to her about how unreasonable her sister was. Finishing her shift, Beth suggested they take a walk and talk about what had happened where they wouldn't be seen – not an easy thing to do in a village with so many prying eyes. They went where no one else went – to the loch. Meanwhile, Flo had come to see me; distraught she was, crying her eyes out."

"What was the argument about?" asked Jessamin.

"Flo was keen to travel, Mally wasn't. He loved it in Glenelk. He was as much part of it as the mountains, the pine trees and the lochs are a part of it. He was the Monarch of the Glen itself. Flo, she was different. She harboured grand ideas of travelling abroad. Canada appealed to her even though she'd never been there or knew anyone who had. But Mally and I, we were going to manage the Comraich estate together; Mally was content to do just that. That's what they argued about – bitterly. He could see his life set out before him and she could see hers too, but in a different way."

When he faltered, Jessamin prompted him. "Where did you and Flo walk to?"

"I think you can guess where."

"The loch."

"Unfortunately, yes."

This was the hardest part of all to tell – the part he'd never told anybody. "When Flo saw Beth there with Mally, she fell into even more of a rage. I tried to stop her but she hurried over to them, started accusing them of having an affair; screaming at them. Soon Beth was screaming back, telling her sister how lucky she was to have Mally; how she mustn't put her dreams above his. This, as I think you can imagine, only infuriated Flo more. They flew at each other, hands, nails and teeth. They were like two wildcats – impossible to stop. I tried, Mally tried; we shouted at them, tried to reason with them, but there was no reasoning to be had that day. Mally at last managed to get in between the girls. 'Flo,' he was shouting, 'calm down, I'd never betray you, you know that, and if you want to travel, we'll damn well travel.' He tried to reason with her so hard. What happened next I didn't see – truly, Jess, I didn't. Flo fell backwards and hit her head on a rock. Blood. I remember there was so much blood. It was everywhere. It dyed her blonde hair red, the ground beneath her too. I had also fallen, been thrown back, but I crawled forward and held Flo's feet whilst Beth cradled her head. All the fight in both girls had gone."

Jessamin's face, he noticed, was completely white.

"Are you all right?" he asked. "Would you like some water?"

She shook her head. "No. Please, go on."

"Mally stood there, looking down at us. All he kept saying was sorry, over and over again. He was crying. I'd never seen him cry before, not big, strong Mally. Flo's eyes flickered but quickly she lost consciousness. Beth kept apologising too, begging her twin to open her eyes; to just breathe. I asked what had happened – who'd pushed her. 'Him!' screamed

Beth, pointing to Mally. She kept saying it, over and over again, even when help arrived, she said it. But I knew Beth. I'd known her since she was a little girl. I knew when she was lying. If she'd been telling the truth, she would have looked me in the eye. But she didn't. She wasn't telling the truth. She was the one who'd pushed her."

"Did Flo die at the loch?"

"Aye, lass, she did."

"Finn said she died at Comraich."

"She was brought back to Comraich, but it was at the loch she took her last breath."

Jessamin gulped. She looked to be completely in shock.

"Jess, take some water." But as much as he insisted, she refused.

"Stan, what did Mally do? When help came, I mean?"

"Mally took the blame. And I let him. God help me, but I let him."

"Oh, Stan," Jessamin reached out for him. "I... what happened to him?"

"He got taken away by the police and convicted. He served several years for culpable homicide, manslaughter in other words. I never saw him again although I knew that later he got married and had children."

"My grandfather went to prison?" Jessamin's voice was barely above a whisper. "I never knew. Nobody ever said. Surely my mother would have said something?"

"That's if she knew; if his wife even knew. After he was released, Mally moved to London. Perhaps he wanted to live his life there without anyone knowing."

"Yes, that's right; my grandparents did live in London." Her brow creasing, she asked, "But, Stan, how do you know that? Did you keep in touch?"

Stan shook his head. "I hired a private detective, that's how. He fed me information over the years – the last piece of information of course being the day he died."

"Twenty-four years ago," Jessamin's voice was hollow. "When I was seven."

"Aye, a long time ago," Stan agreed.

"But *why* did you hire a private detective?"

Stan shrugged. Would she understand?

"I just wanted to know he was all right. He was my best friend, Jess. I never had another friend like him. I sincerely hoped he'd find peace and perhaps… I don't know… a way to forgive." He paused briefly before adding, "Although the latter I'm not sure about."

Jessamin seemed to ponder this. "He would have hated London."

"I don't doubt it."

Jessamin looked up, something in her eyes almost accusatory.

"How could Beth live with herself, knowing she'd sent an innocent man to prison?"

"She couldn't live with herself, that's the trouble. She was never the same again. The darkness, it plagued her. But, Jess," he said, looking almost pleadingly at her, "it wasn't Beth's fault either, what happened. She didn't mean to do it. She would never have hurt Flo, not intentionally. It was an accident, a horrendous accident – an accident that killed her too really, and Mally by the sounds of it. The pair of them, they only ever lived half-lives after that, which is really no life at all. I tried to tell her it wasn't her fault. I wrote to Mally in prison to tell him it wasn't his either. It was no one's fault; no one's at all."

"Did he write back to you?"

"He did, but just the once. It was a brief letter, perfunctory; he said it was the last thing he could do for Flo, to protect her twin; that Flo would have wanted that."

"But the authorities, couldn't they see it was an accident?"

"When someone is killed, the authorities want justice. Everyone's much happier when blame has been apportioned."

"Did you testify?" she asked.

"I did." And this was what truly haunted him. "I stood in court, I said it was an accident, over and over again, but I didn't say at whose hands the accident occurred."

"What did Mally do, when you were in court I mean?"

"He just looked straight ahead. He never looked at me, not once."

Jessamin had tears running freely down her face now.

"And Beth?"

"Beth was never able to accept what she had done."

Uttering those words, he could hardly bring himself to look at the girl in front of him but he knew he must. With relief and nothing less than amazement, he noticed her accusatory look had gone. Instead, Jessamin's eyes were twin pools of abject sadness.

"What a terrible, terrible situation for all of you," she said. "I wish I'd known though, when Granddad was alive, I wish I'd been... kinder towards him."

"Jess," he rushed to reassure her, "I'm sure you were kind enough."

"But what about Mally's parents? What did they do?"

"They moved away."

"From Glenelk?"

"No, remember I told you they were from Larnside? The scandal made it hard for them to continue living there. I don't know where they went or how much they suffered at their only son being torn from them in such a way. A great deal I should think."

"I should think so too."

"Jessamin, I'm sorry. I'm so, so sorry for allowing your grandfather to take the blame. I just didn't know what else to do. I ruined his life."

"You did what you thought was best at the time," Jessamin reassured him now. "And although I didn't know him well, I'm sure Granddad meant it when he said that it was the last thing he could do for Flo. I'm sure that knowledge gave him the strength to endure."

"I wish I could let him know how sorry I am. I wish I could make him understand that we also suffered – that none of us got away with anything."

Lost in thought, it took Stan a few moments to notice Jessamin staring at him.

"What is it, dear? You look…" How could he describe how she looked? The first word that sprung to mind was 'strange' but it would be rude of him to say so.

"Jess," he prompted.

"At the loch, I saw shadows," she began.

"Shadows – what do you mean?"

"The day I took ill, I was at the loch. I'd had a dream." She hesitated again before continuing. "A disturbing dream and I needed to clear my head before starting work. It was early morning. The clouds were low. I walked to the loch. I felt drawn to it to be honest."

"Go on," Stan encouraged her.

"I heard voices, people shouting at each other. Then I saw them, three figures at first but then four. Two were kneeling on the ground, a figure lying between them. The fourth was looking down at them, his hands spread wide. He then turned and looked at me."

Stan could hardly believe what he was hearing – she had seen figures at the loch? Had heard shouting? "You mean our loch don't you, Jess? Not Loch Hourn?"

"Yes, our loch," Jessamin confirmed. "I panicked and started to backtrack. I quickly became disorientated; something didn't seem right; these weren't people in trouble. They were something else entirely. I tried to run, to get away, but I didn't know which way to run, left or right; it was too misty to make out any sort of landmark that might lead the way. And then the shadow, the figure – the one that had been looking at me – he suddenly appeared by my side, although I couldn't see him; not truly see him, he was just a blur. But I could hear him and I could feel him. He told me to go home, he grabbed hold of my wrist; pulled me forward; he showed me the way." Her eyes growing almost impossibly wide, she leaned forward and said, "Stan, he knew my name!"

"Mally," Stan gripped both her hands. "You saw Mally!"

"I think so, yes. And Flo and Beth and... and you."

Stan withdrew his hands, lifted them to his head, and pulled at the wisps of hair hanging there.

"Take me back, Jess," he begged. "Please, you *have* to take me back."

Chapter Twenty-Nine

"YOU are not taking Stan to the loch, Jess, and that's final."

"But, Maccaillin, he wants to go – he's desperate."

"Oh, so I'm Maccaillin again now, am I?" he said, raising an eyebrow.

Yes he was. No matter what confidences they had shared, right now Finn felt too personal.

"You want to take him back, endanger his life? Because of something you thought you saw; some figment of your imagination, of your fevered mind? Don't be so ridiculous."

Ridiculous? How dare he?

"I didn't say *I* would take him. I hoped *we* might – you and I – together."

"No."

They were standing in the kitchen at Comraich, soup bubbling in cauldrons around them, ready to be bottled, labelled and shipped out. Shona and Gracie were due to start the process in little over half an hour. Jessamin had arrived early with the sole purpose of speaking to Maccaillin about Stan. What the old man had told her yesterday left her reeling. The minute she got home, she'd phoned Aunt Lara – a call she'd intended to make as soon as she felt well enough, and which was already overdue.

"Thank you so much for sending the picture, Aunt Lara, I really appreciate it." What she didn't know that she appreciated was the can of worms that the picture had opened. How could she possibly ask if her grandfather, Aunt

Lara's father, had been in prison? She or her mother had never mentioned it, not once.

"That's perfectly all right," Aunt Lara had replied, the phone line crackling slightly. "The man who called – the artist's grandson – Mr Maccaillin, isn't it? What a lovely voice he has. Do you know for a moment I thought all my dreams had come true; that Sean Connery had finally found me!" She'd ended her sentence on a high burst of laughter.

Jessamin had smiled too even though her aunt couldn't see her. "I'm so glad you took the picture; kept it safe."

"Of course I took it. It was your mum's favourite. I'm only surprised you didn't."

"I took other things."

Aunt Lara quietened. "Yes, darling, the kind of things a daughter should take."

Pausing only briefly, Jessamin said, "I'll send it back."

"Not at all, keep it. I've plenty of other reminders."

But did she want to keep it? That she didn't know.

They talked at length about her aunt and uncle's travels, a conversation Jessamin found fascinating, as they'd visited a number of countries, including Thailand, Vietnam, Laos and Cambodia that she'd wanted to visit with James once upon a time. Afterwards, she decided to come right out and ask the question she needed an answer to.

"Granddad, had he… erm… had he ever been in prison?"

Again Aunt Lara had burst out laughing.

"In prison? Jess, wherever did you get that idea?"

"I… I just wondered. He was always so gruff."

As if being gruff was an imprisonable offence. Thankfully, Aunt Lara was in the mood for humouring her.

"I know he was gruff, darling, but not because he'd been in prison. Dad was the most law-abiding person I've ever known. In that supermarket where he used to work, a lot of the staff used to take some of the food that was past its sell-by date home with them, even though officially they weren't supposed to. They used to go round to the back of the store and stuff their rucksacks full of it. Despite the fact it was an open secret, your granddad never did that; he frowned open-ly upon such practise."

A supermarket? Her grandfather had worked in a super-market when once he could have run a Highland estate? Jes-samin baulked at this, but silently so.

"What did Stan think when he saw the painting again?" Aunt Lara continued.

At this point, Jessamin hesitated. Should she tell her the truth? That it was Lara's father who'd painted it and not Stan? Would there be any point in doing that? Or was igno-rance bliss? Let her believe what Murray had obviously want-ed her to believe.

"He... well, to be honest, he cringed slightly; said it was an early piece. He's got a lot better since."

"I'm sure," Aunt Lara replied. "I'm glad it's with you now, though. Like your mother, you always had such a fondness for that painting. Me? I liked it but I found it quite dark."

Changing the subject, Aunt Lara had been keen to know if she'd met anyone else. *No.* Was she ever moving down south again? *I'm not sure.* The questions she asked were similar to those that Sarah always asked. It seemed neither of them could get a handle on what she'd done; basically buried her-self alive.

It had been, as predicted, a long and exhausting phone call; one of the reasons she'd put it off until she felt better. After finally saying goodbye to Aunt Lara, she had sat staring at the painting, realising what it represented: lost dreams, lost love and lost hope. Except that it was a paradox, because it had been painted at a time when dreams, love and hope had all been within such easy reach. How quickly things can change. She knew that well enough, and so had Ben Murray.

As Stan had apologised to Mally, she now did the same. Closing her eyes, she whispered, "I'm so sorry, Granddad, for your pain; for everything *and* everyone you lost. For a life that didn't turn out the way you wanted it to."

It must have been terrible being torn from a place that Stan said he'd loved so much; that he was such a part of. Not just from Glenelk but from Flo too, his friends and his family. He was only eighteen, for Christ's sake – barely an adult – and he hadn't killed her; he was innocent. They all were. She didn't know how many years of his sentence he'd served, perhaps not all of them. People were often let out early on good behaviour. But did it matter? However many years it had been, each one must have been torture.

She thought back to her experience at the loch. Had it been he who had spoken to her? Her grandfather? Not wanting to frighten her but to help her? Now that she knew the full story, she felt sure what she'd glimpsed that day were events replaying. She was also sure Stan wouldn't rest until he returned to the loch. If Mally was there, he wanted to reach out to him.

This morning, rising early and driving to Comraich, Jessamin was keen to share what she'd learnt with Maccaillin. She felt he had a right to know the secret that had caused so much darkness; that had soaked into Comraich's walls and dragged it down. And he *was* astounded, almost as much as she'd been when Stan had told her.

"Beth pushed Flo? That's how she fell and hit her head?

My poor grandmother, she had that to contend with too."
He then stared at her. "And Mally, I remember Seanair talk-
ing about him from time to time; you're his granddaughter?
That's incredible."

It *was* incredible – there was no other word to describe it.

She then tried to make him realise that Stan was still
haunted by what he'd done; essentially letting Murray lan-
guish in prison for a crime he hadn't committed. In doing
so, she had to explain what she'd seen at the loch.

His reaction she could have anticipated.

"Jess, you were ill. From the sounds of it the chill you
caught had already set in. You were delirious when I found
you, and you may well have been when you were at the loch
too."

"But I wasn't hallucinating, if that's what you're implying.
Yes, I'd started coughing earlier that morning; feeling groggy,
but I wasn't that ill – not then. I know what I saw."

"The mist, it's a strange thing. Sounds carry in it, they can
seem inhuman. Conversely, shapes of boulders and rocks
take on human aspects. I know what I'm talking about. I've
been caught in it enough times. It can be scary, even when
you're used to it, it can fuel the imagination."

"I *saw* my grandfather. He was standing just a few feet
from me. He told me which way to go home. I'd become
disorientated. I could easily have set off in the wrong direction."

If she had, she would have died; Stan agreed with her
about that.

But Maccaillin was having none of it.

"What did you see exactly? His face?"

"No," and for the first time Jessamin felt unsure. "He
was... I don't know, just a shape. But I knew it was him, it

had to be him."

"It wasn't him, Jess."

"But he *knew* my name."

"It wasn't him," Maccaillin repeated, "and you are not taking my grandfather back there on a wild goose chase, you or me. Forget it."

"But—"

"Jess, the ride's a bumpy one. Stan will get thrown about all over the place. He hasn't got the strength to endure that. Don't you realise that by now? And we'd have to park some distance from the loch too, find some way to transport him to the water's edge."

"He has a wheelchair," Jessamin pointed out.

"Not an all-terrain wheelchair. That's what we'd need to get him there, and actually, I doubt there's one in existence that's up to the task."

When she'd insisted further, that was when he'd called her ridiculous. Clamping her lips together lest she said something she might regret, she had stormed out of the kitchen. She thought him insufferable when they'd first met and he was being so again. Effectively he was saying she was a liar – a stupid and hysterical woman, yet she was far from that. Yes, she had fallen ill; she hadn't denied it, collapsing in his arms just outside Comraich. But up until she had started running for home, she'd been perfectly *compos mentis*. That was what he found so hard to believe. Stan believed her though, that was the important thing. And Stan wanted to go back. It was his wish against Maccaillin's, and she knew whose side she was on. She'd take him back, as soon as she was able to. The journey wouldn't kill him, not if she was careful. It was Maccaillin who was being hysterical on that score.

Chapter Thirty

"JESSAMIN, are you okay?"

Maggie was staring at her, a frown on her face. What should she do, lie? No. Lies didn't work, not with Maggie. Unloading a pint of milk, some cereal and a jar of instant coffee onto the shop counter, Jessamin decided to cloak her thoughts instead; to push what she intended to do to the back of her mind and draw a curtain across it. Maccaillin and Maggie were closer now. She didn't want her suspecting something and then informing him.

"I'm fine thanks," Jessamin replied, adopting a wide smile.

"It's just... you don't seem your usual self."

Her bag packed, Jessamin started backing towards the door.

"Really, I'm fine."

"Is Stan okay?" Maggie continued to quiz, preventing her from doing what she wanted to do, which was bolt.

"He's fine too."

"And Finn?"

"As far as I know."

"Is he home today?"

"Erm... no. He's gone to Inverness, I think."

"Inverness? Oh, so Stan's alone? I could come and sit with him if you like. Maidie can look after the shop for a bit or Rory might. I was speaking to Shona earlier today. They're getting on so much better now. He's finally accepted you're out of bounds."

"Good, I'm glad to hear it." She'd never felt so "out of bounds" as Maggie put it; so removed from the world and all that was in it.

"Jess," Maggie asked again, "you didn't say. Shall I come and sit with Stan for a bit?"

"No, no." She could feel herself getting flustered. "I'm going there today,"

"Can't we both go?"

Maggie was persistent – too much. Did she suspect something?

Reminding herself to breathe evenly and to keep smiling, she answered, "Perhaps we can go together tomorrow; play cards with him or something."

"Oh, he loves Gin Rummy, doesn't he?" said Maggie, smiling too.

"He adores it, yes."

"He's competitive though."

"I know." It was a scant answer but the last thing she wanted to do was encourage conversation.

"It's good. It shows he still has a bit of fire in him."

"Hmm." Her responses were getting shorter.

"Are you sure we can't fit a game in today?"

When the bell rang indicating a customer, Jessamin could have whooped for joy. Into the shop walked Eileen, dramatically shaking the rain off her shoulders.

"Brrr, the weather has most certainly turned," the older woman bitterly complained. "This is it. This is all we've got to look forward to. It's winter for us for months to come."

Despite her bleak forecast, Jessamin had to restrain herself from hugging her.

"Hi, Eileen," she said, wondering just how obvious her relief was.

"Jess, hello. How's Stan?"

Giving her the same answer she gave Maggie – that he was fine – Jessamin turned on her heel and hurried out of the shop before any further questioning could ensue – from either of them. As she climbed into her car, James started speaking.

"I really don't think this is a good idea, Jess."

She might be able to hide her thoughts from Maggie, but from James she had no chance.

"Oh, don't you start. It's what Stan wants."

"But Maccaillin has a point. Stan's not up to the journey."

Driving away, her voice was testy as she accused him of being on Maccaillin's side.

"It's not a case of taking sides; it's common sense, that's all."

"It's what Stan wants," Jessamin repeated.

"You've always been stubborn," James replied.

"And you've always been..." Jessamin stopped. What was she going to say? Reckless? Only when driving his car perhaps. Other than that he'd been without fault.

Pulling up outside Skye Croft, she ran to her front door, opened it and, as Eileen had done in Maggie's shop, shook the rain from her shoulders.

"Jess," James continued. "Look at it. This is hardly the weather for venturing out."

"It has to be today. Maccaillin is going to Inverness this morning to stock up on groceries and medicines. It's the only day I can guarantee he'll be out of the way. Otherwise you know what he's like. He comes and goes at whim. I won't be able to keep track of him."

"But it's raining and at the loch, the weather's likely to be ten times worse."

"I'll wrap Stan up well, don't worry. I'll keep the heater in the car blasting too."

"You're making a mistake."

"This is what Stan wants!" she all but bellowed at him. "He's become more and more insistent about it. He feels... I don't know... it will lay some demons to rest – lay Mally to rest, and appease him somehow. Stan hasn't got long left, he's scared." Forcing herself to calm down, she added, "This is what he wants. Why am I the only one who can see that?"

Her outburst met with silence.

"James..." she ventured. "James, you're still here, aren't you?"

"I'm still here," James said after a moment.

"I'm sorry for shouting."

"Don't be."

"Will you come with me?"

"To the moor?"

"Yes."

"Jessamin – Jessa*mine* – I will."

Relief flooding through her once again, she busied herself, gathering everything she was likely to need for the journey: blankets, a flask of hot soup, a bottle of fresh water and two pillows, one for Stan to sit on whilst they were in the car, and one to pop behind his back. She also made sure her phone was fully charged, just in case she got into difficulty.

At lunchtime, Jessamin made her way to Comraich. The rain hadn't stopped but it wasn't pouring any harder she was glad to note. Visibility was also good.

Shona and Gracie had already delivered all the soup orders Jessamin had spent the previous day making and batching so they could get away early. Comraich was empty. Just to be sure – and despite the fact his car wasn't in the driveway – she wandered through the downstairs, calling out Maccaillin's name every now and then, but there was no reply. Instead, silence settled like snowfall on the house; she marvelled at how quickly it did that. It seemed to be some sort of default mode that the house slipped into; only constant injections of chatter and laughter were enough to keep it at bay.

In the living room, she stopped awhile and stared at Stan's empty chair. Would he ever sit there again, enjoying the heat of the fire? With great sadness, she doubted it. He preferred to keep to his room now. That era – so fleeting, for her at least – was over. When Stan went, when Comraich was sold, she hoped a young and lively family would move in; one without so much emotional baggage. Despite paint peeling in corners and dust hanging from light fittings, this was a beautiful house with vast potential. Although she knew well enough that sometimes potential was never realised.

In the kitchen, she marvelled at how clean Shona and Gracie had left it; the stainless steel worktops were sparkling; all the pots on the stove were covered, and in the fridge, all items were labelled clearly in see-through plastic boxes. On the wall, a rota hung, detailing when and where soup was to be delivered. Jessamin smiled to herself. It was a small business she had built, no more than a cottage industry, making barely enough to cover costs, but it had been fun to set up; to experience.

"You're talking as if that's coming to an end too," James pointed out.

Perhaps it was; perhaps everything to do with Glenelk was coming to an end, just as it had done for her grandfather before her. If she went ahead with what she intended to do and Maccaillin found out, there'd be hell to pay. He was a good man, but he had a streak of steel. Life, since childhood, had hardened him. Defy him and he might not forgive her.

Back in the hallway, refusing to look at the stag heads, which seemed to be staring at her as knowingly as Maggie had, she took a deep breath and ascended the stairs, her hand clutching the banister. She would feed Stan first and then she'd wrap him in several layers. She'd attempt to fulfil his wish, but if the going got too rough out there or she suspected he was faltering in any way, she'd turn back. She was willing to take a risk but not a stupid one.

"Amen to that," she heard James mutter.

Pushing Stan's bedroom door open, she was surprised to see him not in his bed, but sitting on the edge of it, fully dressed.

"Stan," she said, hurrying towards him. "Who dressed you?"

"I'm old, dear," he replied, "not incapable. I dressed myself."

Jessamin smiled down at him. "Of course, I'm sorry. I can heat some soup up for you before we go. I've brought fresh consommé or there's lentil and—"

"I'm not hungry, Jess. I just want to get going."

"I really think you should eat first," she persisted, full of doubt suddenly. What if she was making a big mistake? What if something happened to him... to them both... out there? The moors were like a world apart; they could be dangerous. What's more, they hadn't told anyone they were going – they couldn't tell anyone – which made it more dangerous still. She glanced at her watch.

"When did Finn leave for Inverness?"

"A little over an hour ago."

"So we've plenty of time?" She could feel nerves flutter in the pit of her stomach as she asked the question.

"The journey to Inverness takes an hour, he'll be there for two, and then it's another hour to drive back."

It was time enough to take Stan to the loch and back and then tuck him safely up in bed again. Maccaillin need never know. But the rain – was it getting heavier or was it just her imagination? She walked across to the window and peered out. Conditions looked roughly the same as when she'd left the cottage, but the sky, it was darker than before, as though storm clouds were brewing.

"Stan," she said, whirling round to face him, "the rain looks as if it's settled in. Perhaps we oughtn't to go; leave it for another time."

"Jessamin, dear," Stan's voice was patient, as though he was talking to a child. "How much time do you think I've got?"

"But the weather, you haven't eaten…" she could feel herself start to panic.

"Listen to me." Stan beckoned her to come closer. "I don't care about the weather and I'm not hungry. I never am anymore."

"Oh, Stan," Jessamin reached out to him.

"We have nothing to lose by going now. Do you understand what I'm trying to say?"

Of course she did. He was trying to tell her he was going to die anyway and sooner rather than later. In an attempt to stop her tears, Jessamin bit down on her lip.

"Finn will be so cross if he finds out," she whispered.

"Finn doesn't listen to me. You do. And, Jess, you don't know how grateful I am."

Jessamin looked into the old man's eyes – so faded, so tired. She loved him in a way she had never loved her grandfather; as though he was the one who was her own flesh and blood. There was no way she could refuse him. Going back to the loch was what he wanted. What he desired. It was literally his dying wish.

Fingering the lapel of his chequered shirt, she asked, "Do you have a coat, a raincoat I mean?"

Stan nodded towards the wardrobe behind her. "It's in there, along with any hats, scarves and gloves you may want to dress me in if it makes you feel better. But the weather, Jess, I've grown up with it; it doesn't faze me like it does you. It's rain, that's all."

"Just… humour me," she said, straightening.

After wrapping him up sufficiently, she took both his hands in hers and pulled him gently to his feet. Next she linked her arm through his and together they shuffled forwards.

Chapter Thirty-One

THERE was something on Jessamin's mind for certain, but Maggie had the feeling she'd wised up to her. Although she had never come right out regarding her 'gift' – not to Jess, not to anyone – she seemed to have guessed. When Jess had entered the shop earlier, it was as though she'd thrown a barrier up. Her manner was unnatural too. She was surreptitious, furtive, unlike the Jess she knew.

If Eileen hadn't come in, she might have been able to break her barrier down – not mentally but actually; persuade her to confide in her of her own free will. They were friends after all, she and Jessamin. Good friends, she liked to think. As much as she loved Eileen, Maggie couldn't help but curse her now. The woman had kept her for what seemed like an age talking about nothing more scintillating than the weather and her arthritis, preventing her from running after Jessamin and attempting to quiz her further.

After Eileen left the shop, Maggie tried to occupy her time with stocktaking – she had a lot to catch up on. But she couldn't concentrate; couldn't quite shake off the feeling that something momentous was going to happen – momentous but not in a good way.

What was Jess up to? She tried to phone her but the call went straight to answer phone. The next step was to send a text but again she got no reply. She would have closed the shop down temporarily and driven to Skye Croft, but business had taken a sudden upturn: the entire village, it seemed, needed to stock up on essentials of some kind – milk, bread, eggs, pasta and rice. She hadn't been that busy for a long time. It was as though the universe itself was conspiring to keep her occupied.

Should she text Finn? Voice her concern? But what concern? She didn't know exactly. And whatever Jess was up to, there was no way she wanted to get her into trouble. She reminded herself how grateful she was to her: she had been the bridge between herself and Finn. She'd brought him back into her life, Stan too, and Comraich. Not quite in the capacity Maggie had always desired, but where Finn was concerned, being friends with him was better than being without him. Although she sensed he wouldn't stay when Stan eventually passed over; he'd take off again. Certainly he'd hinted as much. She'd have to get used to his absence all over again.

Her mobile lingered at the side of the till. She found herself reaching a hand down and almost caressing it. The feeling she should text Finn grew stronger.

Jess, why wouldn't you look me in the eye earlier when I asked if you were okay?

Maggie racked her brains as to what could possibly be wrong with Jessamin. She'd come into their lives so suddenly; was she planning to leave as quickly – without saying goodbye? If so, why? It didn't make sense. She enjoyed living in Glenelk; had started to make a life there for herself and even started a business; not an easy thing to do in a remote place such as this, but she'd managed it. If she was indeed planning to leave, how would Finn react? He felt for Jess. His devotion to her when she'd been ill had been nothing less than awe-inspiring. You didn't need to read minds to know that he felt for her. What went on between them before Jessamin fell ill she had no idea, nor how much time they'd spent together, but it was a fair amount she'd bet. Feelings like his weren't instant. They tended to grow over time.

Damn! Maggie almost cursed out loud.

Why did it still hurt? Finn would never love her; she knew that, not in the way she'd dreamed of all her life. And, to be fair, he'd never, not once, suggested otherwise. Not with her or Maidie or with any other girl in the village he'd involved himself with as a young man. As for his time abroad, Maggie suspected there'd been a string of girls, but no one particularly special. His feelings for Jess were wrapped in wonder; the emotions she evoked new and exciting for him. He was thirty-five, nearly thirty-six, and never before had someone meant so much.

Jessamin couldn't be on the verge of leaving – it would break Finn's heart if she did, and she didn't want to see him suffer, not in the way that she had suffered. Whatever Jess was up to, he should be alerted. If she was intending to leave, maybe he could persuade her otherwise.

She shook her head. How Jessamin clung to James! She should let him go. As soon as she thought this, she flinched. It was advice she herself would do well to take.

"Damn!" This time she did say it out loud. "You, Maggie Reid, are nothing but a hypocrite."

The phone loomed larger.

Give him a chance. Give *them* a chance.

Snatching it up, she stared at it almost blindly for a few moments and then got to work – typing in the first few letters of Finn's name – his details appearing straightaway.

You need to come back. I'll explain all when you get here. Meet me at Comraich as soon as you can. Maggie.

If she was overreacting, so be it. It was far better to be safe than sorry.

Chapter Thirty-Two

THE journey from bedroom to car was a slow one. Jessamin had to stop several times to allow Stan to catch his breath. Even now, safely ensconced in the car, it was coming in short, sharp bursts.

"Stan…" This time there was a plea in Jessamin's voice. She wanted to take him back inside, stoke the fire, forget this idea that Maccaillin had called 'ridiculous'.

"Just drive, Jess," Stan replied, ending his request with another bout of coughing.

Earlier, before entering Comraich, she'd opened the gate that divided the boundaries of the house from unending countryside; the way was clear for her to drive straight through. The car's heater on full, she pressed her foot to the pedal, driving slowly, aware of every bump, every depression on the track; determined Stan shouldn't be bounced around too much, if at all. In the boot of the car was his wheelchair; that was something she'd done earlier too, even though Stan insisted he wouldn't need it.

As they drove, no faster than walking pace really, the rain got heavier; there was no doubt about it. The windscreen wipers were pressed into action, their blades scraping against the glass, a sound that set her nerves on edge, although normally she never noticed it. They didn't have far to go; a couple of miles, maybe a tiny bit more, down a road which was getting increasingly bumpy, strewn as it was with stones and rocks. Although there had been relatively little mist at the house, that too was increasing in intensity. Fear as well as anxiety flared. Stan might want to meet the ghosts of his past, but she had no desire to – not again.

"Remember what I told you," Stan started speaking, his voice in the silence initially startling her. "It's like a different world out here; it was our world, for the four of us; a place where no one else came; where we could be who we were; who we wanted to be."

"But you've never been back since it happened? You weren't tempted?"

"No, Jess, I was never tempted."

"Despite it being on your doorstep?" Jessamin was amazed.

"Despite it," Stan repeated. "Beth went back sometimes, I'm sure of it, in the early days. Me? When I went walking, I walked the other way."

"But still you painted it?"

"I did. I was never going to forget the place, I couldn't. It was etched on my mind – every blade of grass, every ripple of water, every hill and every mountain top."

Just like it was etched on Jessamin's.

"Do you think he'll be there?" Stan asked.

"Mally?"

"Yes."

"We'll soon find out."

Jessamin peered through the windscreen – visibility was shrinking. No matter, she recognised the immediate land-scape and how the path narrowed. To her, the journey seemed to be passing extraordinarily quickly. She slowed the car down further, but the loch, to her left, soon appeared.

"We're here," she said, pulling over to one side and turning off the engine.

When she was met with silence, she turned to face Stan.

"Are you okay? Would you rather go back?" She was surprised at how much she wanted the answer to be yes, despite how far they'd come.

"Help me out of the car, Jess."

Disappointed, Jessamin did as she was told and rushed round to the passenger side. The rain stung her face, causing her to stop briefly and pull up the hood of her coat.

"Easy," she said, as Stan pressed his old bones into action. "We've got plenty of time, there's no hurry."

Even so, she felt as urgent as Stan did, although what prompted her urgency was quite different. She wanted to be away from here, far away. The mist, which was now surrounding them, felt like the soft folds of a shroud.

James, stay with us. Keep us safe.

But James, she knew, was cross that she'd given in to the old man. He wanted her gone from the moor too.

"I'll get your wheelchair," Jessamin said, wishing the rain would stop, and the mist would lift.

"I can walk from here," Stan insisted. "If you'll help me."

"But, Stan—"

"What use is a wheelchair, Jess?" Stan continued. "The ground is too rough."

Of course it was. Jessamin knew that well enough.

She closed the door behind him. "Hold on to my arm."

He did so, his touch feather-light, like a child's.

"It's not far, just a few steps."

"I know, dear," he said, one hand patting her arm. "I know."

Jessamin couldn't help but smile. If anyone knew where

the loch was, it was Stan.

Pressing forward, she was only glad it wasn't windy. The hat she'd pulled over his head – an old-fashioned tweed hat, with a drop brim – was holding steady, giving him some protection against the elements at least. His coat was tweed too, warm and heavy.

"Mind your step." In front of them, the ground was uneven. It was also saturated although not yet a bog, but it soon would be if this weather continued.

As they walked, Jessamin remained alert: would they hear shouting again, accusations being hurled and the sound of sobbing? Her skin prickled at the thought.

It was quiet, however; *too* quiet. The sooner they were away from here the better – in the mist the loch was not the beautiful place it was in sunlight. It was something else entirely.

"I think I can see the water's edge," said Jessamin. Yes, she could definitely see it, not rippling, but cold and still, hiding the secrets of life and death.

"Stan, don't let go…" she began but to no avail. The old man veered to the right, his gait remarkably steady.

Jessamin brushed rain out of her eyes and endeavoured to keep close to him. Her foot snagged in a pothole, nearly causing her to tumble.

"Stan," she shouted, annoyance vying with fear, "keep close!"

But Stan, it seemed, couldn't hear her – or if he did, he chose to ignore her. As he'd said, this was *his* world, and once again he was lost in it.

"Mally," she heard him cry out, his voice wavering at first but soon gaining in strength. "Mally, are you here?"

Catching up with him, Jessamin too couldn't help asking,

"Granddad?"

There were no voices, no shadows. What she'd seen, perhaps she'd imagined it. Immediately she rebuked herself. She hadn't imagined anything.

"Mally," Stan cried again. "Please. I'm sorry for not speaking out. I'm so, so sorry."

"Hey," Jessamin put her hand on his arm. "You had no choice, remember? You had to protect Beth. Besides which, it was an accident, a cruel, cruel accident, nothing more."

"But Mally," Stan sounded old again, broken, "he paid too high a price, and I let him."

Were those tears running down his face or raindrops?

"Mally understood why; he wouldn't have held that against you."

Stan turned to her and gripped her arms.

"You don't know that, not for sure. Did he… did he ever mention me, Jess?"

No, of course not, she would have told him if he had. As far as she knew, he'd never mentioned anything to do with his past, not to her, not to her mother, not to Aunt Lara.

"I contacted him once, sent him a letter," Stan continued, his words sometimes flowing, sometimes tripping over each other. "I tried to explain."

"I know you did, you told me."

"Did I?"

Alarm bells started to ring in her head. Enough was enough she decided.

"Stan, there's no one here. We need to go home. You're getting drenched."

"Give me one more moment, Jess, just one more." Turning from her again, he shouted, "Mally, Flo, Beth. Please, if you're here, answer me."

There was no doubt he was crying now, his shoulders shaking with the effort.

"Come on. Let's go back to the car."

The Freelander was only a vague shape in the mist. If it got any denser, the car would disappear entirely and she couldn't chance that.

"Stan," she said again with more urgency. "There's no one here, we need to go back."

Stan seemed to listen to her this time. As he turned towards her, there was defeat in his eyes, but then something caught his attention.

"There... over there... who's that?" he whispered.

She didn't want to look but she knew she had to. Despite squinting, she could see nothing.

"Stan, come on."

Trying to force him to turn around, she was surprised at his strength as he shrugged her off.

"It's Mally! I'd recognise him anywhere."

"Stan, there's no one there!"

Stan stepped forward, one hand outstretched.

"For God's sake, you'll fall into the water if you go any further. We have to go back!"

"Mally," he said again, and this time he was smiling. "You came."

Her body beginning to shake, Jessamin dared to lift her eyes, to try to see what he could. Nothing. There was nothing and no one on the other side of the loch.

"We're going back." She wouldn't take no for an answer this time.

As she reached out, movement caught her eye also: the same figure she'd seen last time, seemingly hovering over the loch, walking on water.

"Christ!" she spat. It was coming towards them.

Grabbing for Stan, she pulled him back; too hard, she had to admit. As they fell, she heard a snap. Had it come from her? She flexed her hands and her ankles, but she seemed intact.

"Stan? Are you okay?"

"I…" his voice was faint.

"Stan!" she cried again.

"It's my ankle…" he managed at last, but his voice sounded weaker than ever.

"You've broken your ankle?"

This was beyond horrendous. The shadow coming towards them temporarily forgotten, she rose to her knees beside him.

"I need to get you up. I need to get you back to the car."

"I don't think I can move; the pain, it's too much."

Jessamin looked down at his leg. Nothing seemed obviously wrong – his ankle wasn't lying at an odd angle from the rest of his body, but nonetheless that snap she'd heard, it indicated serious damage.

"Lean on me, I'll try to lift you."

Stan almost laughed at this.

"You won't be able to, dear. I'm too heavy for you."

"I have to get you out of here!" She sounded so shrill.

"Jessamin." Ironically, it was Stan who was trying to calm her. "I'll be okay, don't worry. Have you your phone on you?"

Her phone? Of course! Quickly she retrieved it from her coat pocket.

"Damn it! There's no signal."

She double-checked and triple-checked; she held it up high; she walked several paces to the right and then to the left, but the five circles at the top of the phone remained empty.

"Jess, drive back to the house. Call Finn from there."

"I can't leave you alone!"

"I'm not alone." Again he smiled. "Mally's here. I can see him clearly now."

Mally? Where? She could see no one. The figure she'd glimpsed had gone.

"Stan, you're shivering. You're wet and cold. I can't just leave you here. I can't."

Tears sprang from Jessamin's eyes. Maccaillin was right; she should never have brought him here. She should have just said no. If he died, it would be another death she was responsible for. Cries quickly turned to sobs, but then she bit down hard on them, tasting after a while the metallic tang of blood on her lips. Sobbing was not going to help matters. She had to leave him. She had no choice. She had to start driving back until she got a signal at least: get in touch with Maccaillin, with Maggie, with Rory, with anyone and everyone in the village who could come and help them. Taking off her coat, she wrapped it round him. Under his head she placed her bundled-up scarf.

"I'll be back soon," she whispered, briefly hugging him. "I promise."

To Mally, she shouted, "Look after him, please."

Chapter Thirty-Three

"SHIT, shit, shit!" Jessamin's hands were shaking so much it took several attempts to get the key in the ignition.

"Calm down!" she shouted, her voice bouncing around the car.

"Calm down," James echoed. "Jess, breathe deeply and calm down."

"You're here," she turned to the empty car seat beside her. "Oh, thank God!"

"Of course I'm here. Now come on, breathe in and out, slowly."

She did as he instructed, her hands gradually steadying.

"That's it, that's better," she said, "I think I can drive now. I'm okay."

"Turn the engine over nice and gently and place your foot on the accelerator – again gently. You can do this, Jess, you're in control."

"Yes, yes, I'm in control."

The temptation was to floor the vehicle, tear back down the road at breakneck speed, but James was right, that would be stupid. She'd probably end up leaving the road and getting stuck in a ditch – of no use to anyone. Nice and gently was definitely the way forward. She had to reach Comraich.

The rain was heavy now – not torrential, but who knew when it would become so? Stan couldn't be out in this weather for long; it would be the final straw. It would kill him.

That thought caused her to start shaking again and she almost turned back.

"Just drive," James urged.

"But the blankets I brought..."

"Jess, there isn't time."

Although the journey to the loch had passed at an all-too rapid rate, the return journey seemed to take an age. Despite James's good advice, she needed to go faster; faster still. Almost as though it had a will of its own, her foot pressed down on the pedal, the car readily responding.

"What the...?"

A shape reared up in front of her – big, black and tank-like.

"Brake!" yelled James.

As well as jumping on the brake, she turned the car sideways, only narrowly avoiding a collision.

Her whole body was shaking now, not just her hands. Although the sound was muffled, she heard a car door slam followed swiftly by another.

"Where's Seanair? Is he in there with you?"

That sound wasn't muffled at all. It was loud and clear. It was Maccaillin's voice, and he was striding towards her, such a look of fury on his face.

He yanked the car door open and she almost fell out. Hands caught her but not his; they belonged to Maggie.

"Jessamin, what's happened? " Her manner was so much kinder than Maccaillin's.

"Where's Seanair?" he demanded again.

Swallowing hard, she looked up at him.

"What have you done?" His words flew at her like bullets.

"He's back there," she began, grateful for the comfort of Maggie at least. "At the loch."

"You took him? In this weather? Despite what I said?"

"Finn," Maggie sounded stern. "This isn't the time. We need to go and find him."

"I can show you—" Jessamin began.

"I know the way," Maccaillin growled.

Maggie pulled her along to his car. "Get in," she urged.

Jessamin did so, aware that he would barely be able to tolerate her.

Putting the car in motion, Maccaillin didn't drive anywhere near as cautiously as she had done. Although she cringed, she consoled herself that he knew this road; knew exactly what he was doing. Nobody spoke as he drove, although unspoken words – or more accurately, *accusations* – weighed heavily. How did Maccaillin know she was here? Turning her head slightly, Jessamin looked at Maggie, who was looking right back at her, confusion and disbelief on her face. That was how he knew. Maggie had suspected, earlier on in the shop; her attempt at concealing her intention unsuccessful. Thank God.

The car screeched to a halt.

Reaching for the handle, Jessamin lunged forward. "Stan," she called as she half ran, half stumbled in the direction of the loch. "We're here. Finn and Maggie are with me."

Despite the speed she was going, Maccaillin reached him before she did, bending down beside his grandfather and taking him in his arms.

"Seanair," Jessamin couldn't help but notice how gentle he sounded, in complete contrast with his earlier ferocity. "It's me, it's Finn. Seanair, wake up, you have to wake up."

"Is he unconscious?" Maggie stepped forward, her face

contorted too but with worry.

Unconscious or could he be dead? Jessamin found herself praying fervently it wasn't the latter. When Stan's eyelids fluttered and then opened, she almost fainted with relief.

"Finn, lad, is that you?"

"Careful!" Jessamin shouted. "I think his ankle's broken."

"His ankle?" The glare Maccaillin directed at Jessamin made her shrink back. He looked as if he wanted to kill her.

"It's... we..." she tried to explain, but words failed her.

Maccaillin picked Stan up, cradled him in his arms and started – slowly this time – to retrace his footsteps. Maggie and Jessamin followed him, Jessamin unable to stop from looking back and double-checking that all was quiet behind her. She saw only the mist – like a cloak now – protecting whatever, *whoever*, resided in it.

Laying the old man down on the back seat of the Land Rover, Maccaillin turned to Jessamin. "There's no room for you; you can walk."

"Finn!" It was Maggie now, an angry Maggie. "You cannot leave her to walk; I forbid it."

Maccaillin simply shrugged his shoulders. "Like I said, there's no room."

Choking back shame and despair, Jessamin tried to reassure Maggie. "It's okay, my car's not far, I know the way. Don't worry about me."

"Then I'll walk with you," Maggie declared, throwing another disgusted glance at Maccaillin.

"Aarggh." It was Stan, very clearly in pain now. The shock of what had happened was wearing off, leaving him vulnerable.

"Go with Stan," Jessamin urged, "he needs you. I'll follow on. I'll be okay I promise."

Maggie looked torn.

"If you're coming, Maggie, come now," Maccaillin warned her. "I'm not standing around here waiting for you to make your mind up."

Go, Jessamin thought, sensing Maggie could hear her. Reluctantly she conceded.

"We'll see you back at the house. But hurry, Jessamin, hurry."

For a moment, as the car pulled away, Jessamin couldn't move. She was rooted to the spot. For years she'd loved the loch, had dreamt about seeing it for real. Now she hated it with every fibre of her being. She would never come here again, never. It was not beautiful. It was a place of tragedy, of sorrow and menace. Gradually the feeling in her legs returned and she made for Comraich.

* * *

When Jessamin reached the door, she half expected it to be locked. Maccaillin hadn't wanted her in her car; he wouldn't want her in his house either. Surprisingly it was ajar. Not for one minute, however, did she perceive it as an invitation. Maccaillin had probably rushed in, thinking of nothing more than his grandfather and how he was going to make him comfortable.

In the hallway, the large, dusty hallway with the stag heads she hated so much, she wondered if it was wise to continue upstairs. But she wanted to see Stan. She *needed* to.

Please don't shut me out. Not yet.

On hindsight what she'd done was wrong. But hindsight, as it was so often said, was a wonderful thing. With the benefit of hindsight she would have acted so differently. She wouldn't have quarrelled with James and he wouldn't have rushed home; he'd have stayed safe in London. She would never have come here either, to Glenelk; never have known Stan, Maccaillin, Maggie and Comraich, and a different way to be. Her cosy life in Brighton would have continued, stretching out before her with no need to change anything, because it had been perfect – just perfect. How she wished James was here: her rock, her comfort, her husband. Nothing was right without him, nothing.

"Jess, go upstairs and see Stan." It was James, his voice gentle.

She whirled around. "You are here, aren't you? I mean really here? I'm not imagining it? Please tell me it's not all in my head."

"Go upstairs," he repeated.

Yes. That's what she'd do. She had to, despite Maccaillin, forcing herself all the way up until she reached Stan's bedroom. Pushing open the door, she heard a voice. Maccaillin was on the phone.

"I need you here and I need you now. No, there's no point in driving him straight to the hospital; it's over an hour away. I don't... Doctor Buchanan, please, you have to come."

His words urged her forwards.

"What are you doing here?" Maccaillin held the phone from his mouth on seeing her. "Get out!"

Maggie – her eternal defender – stepped in front of him.

"She has every right to be here. She was only doing what Stan wanted."

He turned on Maggie then. "I told her not to, I told her to leave him be. She's come here and she's... she's ruined everything."

Ruined everything? Is that what he really thought? Shock caused her mouth to drop open. But if she was lost for words, Maggie wasn't.

"Don't you dare, Fionnlagh Maccaillin; she's been a blessing and you know it. She's looked after Stan, she's shared the load, and not only that, she's breathed life into this house when it's been devoid of life for so long. She brought you back to the village when you'd shunned it." Hesitating only briefly, she added, "She also brought you back to me, and for that I'm grateful."

"Maggie," Jessamin was the one to stop her. "I should go."

"You're going nowhere. Stan's the one that matters and he's been asking for you. Go to him."

To her surprise, Maccaillin didn't protest further. Instead, he apologised to the doctor who was still hanging on the line, and continued speaking to him. But, as she padded across the room to Stan she caught his look; he was far from appeased.

The old man had been changed into dry clothes and was awake, but barely.

"Oh, Stan," said Jessamin, flying the last few steps and grabbing hold of his hand. "I'm sorry. I'm so, so sorry." It was an exact repeat of the words Stan had uttered at the loch, to Mally. She, him, Maccaillin… they all had so much to be sorry for.

"Hush, dear, don't fret," his voice was kind, but so weak. "You're not to blame."

His words barely penetrated. She *was* to blame – for everything.

"Your ankle, we need to see to it."

"Never mind about my ankle, it doesn't matter anymore."

"Of course it matters," Jessamin protested. "We have to fix

it."

"Jess," Stan squeezed her hand lightly. "It doesn't matter."

"But…"

Jessamin looked from him to Maggie – beseeching her instead.

"Just comfort him," Maggie said, her voice barely above a whisper.

Next, she dared to look at Maccaillin. He was still angry but he looked stricken too.

Almost throwing the phone down, he walked over to the bed.

"The doctor's coming," he said.

Stan made a tutting sound. "Finn, you and I both know there's no need for a doctor."

"Seanair, you're going to be fine."

"No, lad, I'm not."

Tears started to roll down Jessamin's face. She was powerless to stop them.

"If only you hadn't taken him there." Maccaillin hissed the words at her.

"Stop it!" Stan found the strength to glare at his grandson. "She was doing what I wanted her to do."

Maccaillin looked sheepish suddenly, like a little boy.

"I would have asked you, Finn," Stan continued. "But you wouldn't have listened to me. This girl," he inclined his head towards Jessamin, "she listened to me."

If that was meant to get her back in Maccaillin's good books, it wasn't working.

"Stan," she said instead, "never mind me. Let's concentrate on you."

Maggie stepped forward, a glass of water in her hand. "Would you like some water, Stan?"

Stan nodded, his eyes closing temporarily as he drank the liquid.

Setting the water back down, Maggie crossed over to a lamp beside Stan's bed and switched it on. Jessamin hadn't realised how dark the room had become. For a while there was silence. Stan was breathing evenly, but fighting to keep his eyes open.

Their reverie ended with the doctor's arrival. Crossing the room, he started to examine Stan. Jess, Maggie and Maccaillin moved respectfully to one side whilst he did.

After the doctor had finished, he came over and addressed them in hushed tones. "His ankle is broken but it's the least of his problems. I don't think he can even feel the pain from it, not any more. I'm sorry to have to say this, but you need to prepare yourself for the worst."

Trying to absorb Doctor Buchanan's prognosis, Jessamin could feel the colour drain from her face. Her legs felt hollow as if they would no longer support her. Maggie reached out a hand either to steady her or to comfort. Maccaillin simply stared ahead.

"Jess." It was Stan, hardly any strength in him at all now.

Jessamin bolted forward. "I'm here, Stan," she called.

"Hold my hand."

He stretched out his other hand and called for Maccaillin to come forward too.

"Thank you, Finn, for coming back to look after me when I know you didn't want to. I know this house has never been a happy home for you. I'm sorry."

"Hush," Maccaillin told him, a clear break in his voice. Jessamin wanted so badly to comfort him too. "Don't exhaust yourself by talking. Of course I was going to come back and look after you. There was no question of it. I love you."

Stan only smiled at his words. Next, he turned his attention towards Jessamin.

"And thank you for coming into my life, for understanding me, from the very start. You're a very special girl. Thank you for taking me back to see Mally. Do you know? All these years I thought he was angry with me, but he's not, he's not angry at all. We're going to see the girls soon, together."

"Oh, Stan," was all Jessamin could manage.

"Maggie," Stan called. "Thank you too. I'm glad you and Finn are friends again."

Maggie wasn't crying but she swallowed hard, not once but twice in succession.

Stan coughed. The effort depleted him further. His breathing seemed shallower somehow, more laboured, and a strange noise sounded in his throat, like a rattle.

"Please don't speak, Seanair," Maccaillin implored him. "Save your energy."

Again Stan managed a smile. "For what, lad? For what?"

After a few moments, he motioned for Jess to lean forward. "Don't go," he said. "Stay at Comraich." Wincing slightly, he paused but only briefly. "Look after Finn. He needs looking after and I was never up to the job."

Maccaillin was about to protest but Maggie hushed him.

"Just hold his hand," she instructed.

The rattle in his throat grew louder.

As Stan took his last breath it seemed no one in the room could breathe either. When he was gone, silence like Jessamin had never experienced before, filled the room – every corner, every nook and every cranny. A silence so loud it was deafening.

When at last she breathed out, she dared to glance again in

310

Maccaillin's direction. He wasn't looking at her but his whole body was rigid and not just with pain.

Stan had asked her to look after him. But that was one wish she couldn't fulfil.

Chapter Thirty-Four

AT Jessamin's request, Shona and Gracie removed all her equipment from the kitchen of Comraich. They did so swiftly and without comment. Well, without too much comment.

"Maccaillin came into the hallway just as I was just taking the last of the pots and pans out," Shona informed her. "He didn't say a thing, he just glared at me." Shaking her head, she continued, "Man, he can glare, can't he? Even with one eye."

To that Jessamin could testify.

A week had passed since Stan's death. The funeral was in a few days. The circumstances of his death held up the process slightly, but eventually a verdict of 'natural causes' was recorded – the authorities not as keen to apportion blame as they had been in Flo's case. Maybe it was an age thing – Flo had barely reached eighteen so heads needed to roll, or one head in particular.

Soon after Stan breathed his last, Maccaillin had asked everyone to leave. She, Maggie and the doctor duly did so – Jessamin bending to kiss the old man's cheek once more – flinching slightly at how cold and hard he'd become already. When James died, his father had identified his body; she and his mother were just too distraught. Stan was the first dead body she'd seen and she was glad to note he looked at peace; the skin on his face almost impossibly smooth, all pain, it seemed, erased. Before leaving the room, Maggie tried to hug Maccaillin. He endured her gesture of comfort – but barely.

Outside Comraich, Maggie assured her Maccaillin would come round.

"He doesn't hate you, Jess. Far from it."

He does, she replied, but only in her mind.

"You'll stay for the funeral, won't you?" Maggie called just before Jessamin drove away. She would – but whether she'd attend it would be another matter. She might mark it in her own way instead – alone. After doing that, she'd leave. She knew Shona and Gracie were keen to develop the soup business – market it to a much wider audience – so she'd hand it over. She was done with that too.

Finally alone in the living room of Skye Croft, she cried. She stood in front of the mantelpiece, staring at the whitewashed wall in front of her, and cried for what seemed like eons; water bursting from her eyes and pouring from her nose. Not just rivers, but oceans. She cried and tried to find relief in it when there was none. In her agony, even James couldn't reach her. Exhausted, she eventually moved across to the sofa and lay down, desperate for oblivion to claim her. Thankfully it did, hours and hours of darkness stacking up, one on top of the other and not receding until mid-morning the next day when she woke with a heart that was just as heavy.

Maggie made frequent visits in the days that followed, her concern obvious. The last thing Jessamin wanted, however, was sympathy. She managed only mumbled replies to Maggie's questions.

"Talk to her, Jess," James said. But she ignored him too.

Mally's picture kept catching her eye; kept reminding her of all she'd lost. Echoing the actions of her grandfather all those years ago, she hid it out of sight.

Night after night she lay on the sofa, the fire glowing before her. The flames, such as they were, failed to warm her. She felt chilled to the bone. She barely registered that it was the second anniversary of James's death – but that didn't matter either. Every day since he'd died had been hell. An official marker made no difference. The woodpile was running low, soon there'd be none left at all. Often her body would start shaking, sometimes violently. It wasn't the effects of a fever; her forehead was cool, her mind coherent – too much so. Neither hunger nor thirst bothered her. She just stayed on the sofa, curled up in a tight ball, an attempt to become smaller and smaller still; to disappear. The night before Maggie came back, the fire went out completely, giving the darkness free reign.

Her eyes wide open; Jessamin stared into the hollow of the fireplace. After a while, she reached out a hand.

"Stan," she whispered. "Speak to me."

* * *

When Jessamin woke, she noted it was another grey and drizzly day. The weather hadn't improved since Stan had died – fitting really. Even the skies seemed to be in mourning. Yawning, she heard a knock at the door.

Maggie, she thought, sighing.

Much as she wanted to ignore the knock, she didn't. It wasn't fair to keep her standing in the rain.

"Good morning," Maggie said, her manner determinedly bright. "How are you today?"

"I'm… I'm fine, thank you."

"Good, that's good."

Without invitation, Maggie bustled past her. Immediately, her eyes rested on the two suitcases Jessamin had pulled out the previous day from the cupboard under the stairs. They were left in a prominent position, in the middle of the living room. She'd intended to take them upstairs but hadn't got round to it. That was on the agenda today, along with packing.

"Going somewhere?" Maggie enquired.

"It looks like it." Jessamin couldn't help the insolence in her voice. Anger was beginning to boil in her; it had been for a long time; surging upwards.

"You're leaving Glenelk." It was a statement, not a question.

"Ten out of ten."

"Throwing in the towel, just giving up."

Jessamin bristled. "I'm *not* giving up, Maggie, I've had enough. There's a difference."

"Before or after the funeral?" she enquired further.

"After."

A glimmer of hope replaced the cynicism in Maggie's eyes. "So you're coming to the funeral?"

"No."

Hope snuffed itself out.

"Then why—"

"I want to pay my respects to Stan in my own way. I don't need to attend a formal function to do that."

Maggie looked downright suspicious now.

"In your own way?" she queried.

"That's what I said," Jessamin replied, picking up one of the suitcases and laying it on the dining table.

"But I don't understand. What do you mean, 'your own way'?"

She was like a dog with a bone, thought Jessamin unkindly.

Deciding the only thing she could do was get on with her day, Jessamin crossed over to the table beside the sofa; a table with magazines and books on top. Picking them up, she returned to the suitcase and threw them in. What else? The blanket on the arm of the chair, a gorgeous mohair blanket she'd treated herself to from a shop on Skye not long after she'd arrived; that could go in as well. Maggie shadowed her en route back to the suitcase.

"Jessamin, answer me."

When still she refused, Maggie roared. "JESSAMIN, AN-SWER ME!"

Jessamin stopped in her tracks, the blanket clutched to her chest. Surprising herself, she found the strength to roar back.

"IN MY OWN WAY, NOT YOURS!"

Maggie was the one who looked startled now.

"Oh no, don't tell me... you're not talking to Stan as well?"

Jessamin could feel her cheeks flush.

"Jess..."

"So what if I am?"

"You belong to the living. Not the dead."

"But it's the dead I want!"

The two women stared at each other.

"Okay, okay," said Maggie eventually, as though she were backing down. "Have it your way. Leave. In fact, do you know what? I'll help you pack."

"There's no need..." Jessamin began, but Maggie continued regardless.

She started grabbing things – random things, bowls, ornaments and photo frames – items that belonged to the cottage not Jessamin, and threw them into the suitcase too.

Jessamin looked on in horror.

"Maggie, they're not mine."

Still Maggie grabbed at whatever she could lay her hands on.

"Maggie, don't. Put them back."

When Maggie continued, she tried again to stop her but still got no response.

"MAGGIE, STOP!"

At last, she got through. Maggie whirled round to face her.

"What are you doing?" Jessamin asked, throwing her hands up in the air.

"What am I doing? What are *you* doing, Jess?"

That wasn't the answer she expected.

"I…" she began but couldn't continue.

Seizing her chance, Maggie filled the breach.

"I thought you liked it here."

"I did… I do."

"You seemed happier lately; you'd become part of us. Where do you intend going?"

"Back to Brighton."

"Why?"

"It's my home."

"And what's there for you exactly?"

"I… It's where I come from."

"Answer the damn question."

Jessamin tried again. "I've got friends there."

"You have friends here."

"I've got… I've got…"

But what did she have? With no home, no job, no James, what did she really have back in Brighton? She'd left a life that had carried on quite happily without her.

Watching her hesitate, Maggie seemed to soften.

"Jess, if it's what you really want, to leave, I'll back off. I just don't think it is, that's all."

Maggie was right, she loved it here, in Glenelk; had even thought of staying on. Despite having lived here for a relatively short time, it felt more like home than Brighton did, more real somehow. Jessamin sighed. Who was she kidding? She didn't know what was real any more. She'd long since blurred the boundaries between fantasy and reality.

Maggie stepped forward. "Don't leave," she pleaded. "Finn will come round. He's angry right now, but he can't stay angry forever. Not with you."

"This has nothing to do with Maccaillin." The words burst from her.

"You can't lie to me, Jess."

"Evidently," replied Jessamin, her voice scathing again, she knew.

"Jess, I know you're grieving. I'm grieving, but most of all Finn is grieving. Stan was his grandfather, the only family who meant something to him. Cut him some slack."

She snorted. "Cut him some slack? Like he'd let me."

Maggie continued unperturbed. "He doesn't want you to leave."

"How do you know?" Jessamin challenged.

"You know how I know."

Jessamin hesitated. Should she say it? She was about to but Maggie saved her the trouble.

"I can catch thoughts. It's an inheritance, if you will. Some might say it's a gift. Sometimes it doesn't feel that way though. Sometimes it feels like a curse."

There was a time when Jessamin would have quietly scoffed at what Maggie was saying. She could 'catch thoughts', read people's minds in other words? How ridiculous! But since James had died; since coming to Glenelk; since being called ridiculous herself, she scoffed no more.

"I'd guessed," she said at last.

"I know that too." Maggie was smiling now, warmth flooding her features again.

Jessamin's mind returned to Maccaillin. "He said I've ruined everything."

"He didn't mean it in the way you think."

"How did he mean it?"

"That he was content to leave after Stan passed; to disappear again into the big wide world. You've ruined that plan at least. He may leave but he won't be content."

Jessamin absorbed her words; rolled them round in her mind; tried to make sense of them.

"I can't stay," she said at last. "I don't belong here."

"Glenelk is in your heart, your soul. It's a part of your heritage. You belong, believe me."

"I belong to James."

What Maggie said next left her speechless.

"But James, I think, is ready to let you go."

* * *

Much later, after Maggie had gone, Jessamin sat in darkness again. She wanted to check with James that he wouldn't do such a thing, but somehow she couldn't find the courage.

Chapter Thirty-Five

SHE'D come. He didn't know if she would, but she had, to stand shoulder to shoulder with other mourners on this sad day. The church, set high on a hillside in Kyle – the same church his grandparents were married in – was packed to the hilt. So many had come to bid farewell to Stan McCabe, even those who didn't really know him, just knew *of* him. In this part of the world if one of your own died, that was reason enough to attend the funeral. Those that lived here lived and died together, as they'd done throughout the centuries. That's what he loved about Scotland, although only now he fully realised it.

He, Rory, Dougie and Winn had borne Stan's coffin on their shoulders, carrying him the length and breadth of his final journey – to the alter so mass could be said for him. Each of them wore their clan's tartans. Finn wore the tartan of the Maccaillin's – a dark green plaid interspersed with gold. Ordinarily, he wasn't a church-going man, but today he felt something stirring within him. What it was though, he didn't know. Maybe it was just a desire for heaven to be true; for Stan to be going somewhere better than this; for his life and the sacrifices he'd made, not to be in vain. A talented artist, Stan had been successful. In many ways, however, his success had been limited by his choice not to leave Beth's side and to stay in Glenelk. Finn used to feel frustrated on his behalf, but now he thought he understood. Stan loved Beth, truly loved her. She'd been his world.

The vicar cleared his throat, a hint to the congregation that he was about to start speaking. Quickly Finn took his seat, as did many others, but there were plenty standing, spilling out of the church doors and into the grounds beyond. As mass was said – the holy man's tone suitably solemn – Finn caught sight of Maggie, in the pew across the aisle from him. She leaned forward slightly and smiled at him – a smile that warmed him.

When she'd come to see him the previous night, he'd apologised.

"What for?" she'd asked, staring at him the way she used to – intently.

"I think you know."

"Finn…"

"No, please, listen. I want to apologise, Maggie. I never meant to hurt you. You were my friend, my best friend. I… I never realised you felt the way you did about me."

"Oh, Finn," she had a shine in her eyes which wasn't reproach. "I think you did."

He'd hung his head at that. "There's never any fooling you, is there?"

"You've only just realised?"

"No." He admitted that too. "Another thing, Maggie, I want to say thank you."

"For what?" She'd looked surprised at this.

"For being there for me. It was because of you my childhood was bearable."

She'd reached out to him then and covered his hand with hers.

"When I came back from Afghanistan, I shunned you.

That was unforgivable."

"Finn, *nothing* is beyond forgiveness."

"I'm not sure Maidie thinks so," had been his wry reply.

"Och, never mind Maidie. She's having problems with her husband. They'll sort it out or go their separate ways. What she's going through has nothing to do with you."

After a brief pause, she'd started speaking again. "Now that Stan's gone, will you do what you planned? Will you sell Comraich?"

"I've nothing to stay for," he replied, regretting the words as soon as he'd said them. "Oh, Maggie, I didn't mean—"

"Stop apologising. I know what you mean. If Jess is leaving, so are you."

"This has got nothing to do with Jess."

"That's what she said earlier, about you I mean. The pair of you, I could knock your heads together."

He knew he sounded defensive when he'd asked her why.

"Because the two of you could be happy together if you'd only live in the here and now; if you'd stop clinging to the past. I've never met two people as stubborn."

"I'm not clinging to the past—"

"Yes you are, as much as she is. You're wracked with guilt; she's wracked with guilt; neither of you think you deserve a future, let alone a happy one. I know life has taken from you, Finn, both of you, but now it's trying to give something back. There's a spark when you two are together. I can see it, everyone in the village can, I should think." Shaking her head wearily, she'd added, "You've fought battles all your life, but the one battle that really counts, you're just going to walk away from."

"Maggie, you've got this all wrong," he'd insisted, but she shot him one of her looks – one of her *knowing* looks.

"Don't even bother to deny it. You know I know how you feel about her."

He decided not to protest further. What was the use of pretending, with Maggie anyway? She was right. There'd been countless women in his life; they'd come and they'd gone, and he'd waved them on their way without too much thought – even sweet, brave Suri. But never had he felt the way he'd started to feel for Jessamin. When was the moment he first realised? Was it the first time he'd seen her, swinging round to face him in the grounds of Skye Croft, a startled look on her face? Or was it when she'd reached up and removed his eye patch so tenderly, insisting she wanted to see him – *all* of him? He didn't know. And did it even matter? The fact he felt at all was a miracle. He used to think he couldn't love; that there was something wrong with him. That growing up in a house with such anguish; such sadness, had stunted his emotions. It was thanks to Jessamin he realised he could feel as deeply as any man; he wasn't abnormal – just something of a late-starter. But little good this realisation would do him. His heart might belong to Jessamin, but hers was very much taken.

"You said you were going to see her today. Did you?"

"Yes," Maggie had replied.

"Is she coming to the funeral?"

"I think so."

"And afterwards…"

"She intends to leave."

"Oh." Why he felt so surprised he didn't know. When she had all her equipment removed from Comraich's kitchen, he suspected she was intending to do precisely that. Cornering Shona, she'd said that Jessamin had asked her and Gracie to take over the business. There could only be one reason for that, and Maggie had just confirmed it.

"She thinks I blame her for Stan's death," he'd muttered.

"And do you?"

"No."

"But you were angry with her for what she did – for going against your wishes."

"I was."

"For listening to Stan instead."

"I know."

"You should apologise."

"I know that too."

"Why haven't you?"

He didn't need to say why. This hell he lived in, he deserved it.

"No you don't," she said, letting go of his hand to hug him instead. "No, you don't."

When they finally parted, he'd stepped back.

"What about you?" he asked. Wasn't Maggie as bad as him and as Jessamin? Wasn't she just as embroiled in the past?

"I love you, Finn," she said. "But at last I'm willing to love someone else too."

"Someone else?" he asked, his curiosity piqued.

She'd looked shy then, something Maggie had never been.

"When you went away, I became involved with a man from Larnside; Lenny's his name. He asked me to marry him. I said no. He left and went to work on the oilrigs. At the ceilidh we went to in August, his parents were there. They were cold to me at first – they hold me accountable for him leaving – but gradually they relented. They gave me his address. He's still single, is Lenny, and we've been in touch – a lot."

Despite feeling wretched inside, Finn had smiled at her. Some good news at last.

"If you'd all like to rise for the final hymn…"

The vicar's words shook him out of his reverie; brought him back to the moment, no matter how bleak. Along with everyone else, he rose, glancing behind him only briefly to where he'd noticed Jessamin earlier. She wasn't looking at him; she was looking down, her eyes scanning the hymn sheet. Turning back, he listened to voices rising in a collective swell but didn't join in. He had no heart for singing today or any other day. What was left of it felt like it was breaking further, not just for Connor, but for Stan too, and for the woman he could never have.

Whether he deserved the hell he lived in or not, it looked set to continue.

* * *

The wake was held at Comraich, organised by Maggie and her Thursday night girls. Never before had Finn seen such life in the house. It transformed it – lifted the mood, despite the occasion. As he moved from room to room, stopping to talk to people, a part of him wished they'd never leave. He hated the thought of being alone here tonight.

Could he stay? Not sell after all? He could if Jessamin was staying, but her departure – imminent according to Maggie – would reintroduce the bleakness tenfold.

Where was she? Maggie was right. If there was one thing he had to do, it was apologise. He'd treated her abominably the day Stan died – blamed her entirely. Even when Seanair had made it clear he was grateful to Jessamin, he'd continued to berate her. In some ways, it comforted him – to have someone else to blame. It made a change from always blaming himself. Definitely, he needed to apologise. She knew guilt as much as he did. How dare he load more on her?

The need to see her – to make his peace – became urgent. Where was she?

He scanned the living room, the hallway and the second living room which had been cleared of Stan's paintings, a few of his own too, in order to make way for guests. She was nowhere to be seen.

Despair – such a familiar feeling – washed over him, more intense than ever.

Pull yourself together, man. This is about Seanair, not you.

His stern admonishment did the trick. Whatever he felt, he would feel in private.

In need of a large glass of whisky, he turned around, intending to go back to the living room. That was when he saw her. She was in the hallway; obscured before perhaps by so many people. She was deep in conversation with Ally, who'd been very sweet today, preparing canapés and sandwiches for guests. The relief he felt was enormous.

Should he go up to her right now and interrupt their conversation? He felt as nervous as he'd been as a schoolboy. Did she even want his apology, or did she simply want nothing more to do with him? The latter seemed more likely. Even so, as Maggie said, he had to try. He started to move towards her when the vicar stepped in front of him.

"Funerals," he said, "they're a strange beast. Mournful but at the same time celebratory – we mustn't lose sight of that fact, Finn. Stan lived a very productive life."

Before he even had a chance to reply, the vicar started speaking again, his voice like the drone of a bee on a summer's day, endless. Wishing he could be impolite, but knowing he couldn't be – his grandfather had brought him up to be better than that – Finn stood and listened, being careful not to encourage the man by giving lengthy replies to any of his questions. Nonetheless the conversation ran on and on. It was some time later that the vicar spotted another supposed member of his flock and hurried off, leaving Finn feeling quite exhausted from being talked at so extensively.

Jessamin, the apology. Get it over and done with.

He walked over to where he'd last seen her.

"Hello, Ally, can I just say thank you for everything you've done today. My grandfather would have appreciated it, and I do too."

"Hi, Finn. The pleasure's all mine, believe me."

"I need to have a word with Jessamin actually. Do you know where she is?"

"Jessamin?" Ally said, smiling at him, seductively so he thought; it wasn't just his imagination. "She's gone. But if I can be of any more help, just say."

"Erm… no thanks… really, you've done enough. Did she say where she was going?"

"Back home." The woman's eyelashes fluttered wildly.

"To Skye Croft?"

He was almost glad his question caused Ally to frown. "Actually no, she's going 'home' –you know, to Brighton, where she's from. She said she wanted to make a quiet exit; get a few miles under her belt today. I told her to wait until morning, but she seemed determined." Inclining her head at him, she continued, "I'm surprised you don't know. She said she'd already said goodbye to the people she cared about, and I know you both got on. It's a shame she's leaving. I like Jessamin. I'm going to miss her."

Ally's words hit him like a wrecking ball. The people she cared about she'd already said goodbye to? She'd said nothing to him – not since the day Stan had died.

Making his excuses, he walked away. Jessamin was leaving. She may have even left already. Looking around him, at the house that had only felt like home whenever she was in it, he decided he would leave too at the earliest opportunity. No apologies required.

Chapter Thirty-Six

"JESS, wake up, wake up."

"What? Who's that? What time is it?"

Pulled back from the depths of sleep, Jessamin felt confused; her head was still muggy. How long had she been sleeping? She remembered curling up on the sofa, planning to take a short nap before she hit the road. She had to, she was exhausted; the day's emotion had taken its toll, but still she felt the need to leave. At the funeral today, Maccaillin hadn't even looked at her, not once. Maggie said he wanted her to stay, but she'd seen no evidence of it and wasn't convinced she would in the future either.

Reaching for her mobile, she checked the time. 6.44pm. Impossible! She'd been unconscious for nearly three hours. Sitting bolt upright, she glanced around. Had someone just called her name?

"Jess?"

The hairs on her arms, on the back of her neck, rose simultaneously.

"Who's there? What do you want?"

Panicking slightly, she jerked her head from side to side. She knew it! She should never have followed that great village custom and left her door unlocked. Someone had snuck in here whilst she slept. There was no obvious source, no outline and no shadow to give the intruder flesh. The voice was disembodied. Could it be she was still dreaming?

She heard a sigh, low and soft, followed by more words.

"You are so beautiful."

She wasn't dreaming. There was definitely someone in the room with her!

Her breathing shallow, she leaned over and flicked the switch on the lamp stand, half of her wanting to remain in darkness, the other half knowing she couldn't. With at least part of the room lit, she looked over to the mantelpiece and that's when she saw him.

"James!" she cried out, one hand flying up to her mouth. "You're real!"

"You say that as if you doubted it?"

"No… Yes…" Quickly she corrected herself. "Of course not."

The truth was she'd often wondered if she was kidding herself; making up the conversations they had in her mind; keeping him close – a survival technique. But there was no way she was making this up. James was standing before her, dressed in the clothes he tended to favour at weekends – jeans and a loose shirt, open at the neck. She rubbed at her eyes but they were not deceiving her. She blinked hard, fearful that when she opened them he might disappear. He didn't.

In wonder, she half rose from the sofa.

"Can I touch you?" she breathed.

The smile on his face faltered.

"No, Jess. It's best you stay where you are."

She couldn't help it. She was fiercely disappointed. She wanted to run to him, wrap her arms around him, feel his arms around her too – strong and solid, not wispy and insubstantial. If she could do that, she wouldn't let him go – not this time – she'd hold on forevermore. If he disappeared, no problem; she'd disappear right with him.

Refusing to let disappointment take hold; reminding herself how lucky she was to be able to see him – actually *see* him – she whispered, "You've come back."

Again James faltered.

"I have, Jess, but it's to say goodbye."

Despair, so much greater than disappointment, washed over her. She tried to process his words and failed. She tried again and the same thing happened.

"I don't understand," she confessed at last.

"Jess," he replied, his manner, as always, patient. "I've stayed for as long as I can. I can't stay any longer. I have to go. Deep down, I've known that and so have you."

Despite his instructions, Jessamin rose fully from the sofa, but she didn't walk towards him; she feared if she did she might disturb whatever magic had brought him here tonight, and that the illusion of him might waver like ripples in an ocean before dispersing entirely.

Shaking her head, the only word she could utter was "No" – over and over again.

"Jessamin, stop that and look at me. We've so little time."

Time? What was he talking about? They had nothing but time, they had an eternity.

"You can't go," she said at last.

"I have to."

"Fine, if that's the case, I'm coming with you."

His expression grew serious. "Don't say that."

"Why not? Why should I live without you? I can't."

"On the contrary, you've done very well without me. You've built a life for yourself."

"It's no life," she protested. "Not without you in it."

331

"It's a good life, Jess, and it could be a great one if only you'd let it."

"I don't want it," she continued defiantly.

"Okay, okay," he said at last. "So what do you intend to do?"

"Whatever it takes."

"Kill yourself?"

She jolted at his brutal choice of words, but remained defiant.

"If needs be."

"Even if you did, you wouldn't be able to follow me."

Again she was confused. "Why?"

"Because my path is my own. Let me walk it."

Her mouth fell open. It wasn't just his words that shocked her; it was how he sounded too: tired, beaten almost. It was a miracle she could see him, nothing less than a miracle. It was what she'd wanted; what she'd wished so hard for, day after day, night after night. What she had come here for. But now the miracle was turning sour.

Daring to move closer to him, only an inch or so, no more than that; using every ounce of strength she possessed not to throw herself forward, she scanned his face instead. The lines around his eyes were deeply etched; the grooves between nose and mouth pronounced. In death, he should remain forever young. But he wasn't truly dead, was he? She hadn't let him be.

"I don't want you to go." It was all she could think to say.

James Wade – for so many years she had loved him. From the moment she first saw him in a bar in Brighton. He'd been standing in a group with his friends and she'd been standing in a group with hers. Nonetheless, their eyes met across a crowded room, his friends, her friends disappearing, leaving them the only two in existence, the only two that mattered. Often they had laughed about it; how their romance kick-started on a cliché. She'd envisaged a lifetime with him – growing old together; ribbing each other about the signs of ageing, middle-aged spread perhaps, the grey in their hair increasing – laughing about it because it didn't matter. Not when someone loved you.

She closed her eyes. "If only I hadn't—"

Immediately he stopped her.

"Jess, don't you realise, that sometimes, just sometimes, there's no one to blame?"

Her eyes snapped open. Yes, that was something she *had* come to realise lately. She was also coming to realise something else. Her grief, it anchored him.

"But if you leave, how will I go on?"

It was a genuine question. She truly didn't know.

"You're not alone, Jess."

Then how come she felt it despite James standing in front of her? Despite…?

"Go to him."

"I belong to you."

"It's time to move on."

"Never."

Her refusal weighted him further. She could see his shoulders slump; his head fall forward slightly. The despair that she was feeling was too heavy a load for him to carry.

"James," she said, frightened.

He looked up. His eyes seemed to implore her.

"Jess, you might not realise, but you've been letting go too."

"I have not!"

"We haven't been speaking as much of late."

"We have. I'll speak more. I'm sorry,"

"Jess, I want you to start again. Try and understand, I *need* you to."

Maggie's words beside the loch at Larnside came back to her unprompted. *'Let him go... not just for your sake, but for his too.'*

"But where will you go? What will you do?"

"Don't worry about me."

Anger flared. "Don't tell me not to worry!"

In contrast, he smiled.

"Fiery as well as stubborn, I've always loved that about you."

"James!"

"That light I was telling you about?"

"Yes, I remember."

"That's where I'm going."

"But what is it?"

"It's home."

Home? But his home was with her, surely? It had been for twelve years now – not an insignificant amount of time. It was meant to have been for so much longer until... until... Panic seized her and its grip was iron. She couldn't let him go. She wasn't that selfless.

"I belong to you," she repeated, almost spitting the words at him.

"A part of you, not all of you."

"Yes. All of me!"

"Not anymore."

What he was saying was a travesty. Surely he didn't believe it either.

"Say my name," she challenged. "Go on say it."

"Jessamin."

"No. You know what I mean. Say it."

When still he didn't reply, she shouted. "SAY IT!"

"Jessa*mine*." In contrast, he whispered.

"That's right," she yelled, punching the air triumphantly. "That's what you used to call me. Jessa*mine*. I'm yours, re-member, *yours*."

"Jess, you *were* mine, and I was yours – we belonged to each other, but only for a moment in time. That's all we had. That's all *anyone* ever has."

She could feel her breath catch in her throat and her chest start to heave.

"So, I can't go with you? I can't be yours again? You can't be mine? Is that what you're saying? There's no way to bridge this… this intolerable gap between us?"

"That is what I'm saying." Incredibly, he was smiling again. "But, Jess, come on; the time we had, we made the most of it, didn't we? Every moment was perfect."

At his words, she struggled to maintain control; almost broke down, tried to collect herself and struggled again. She had to find a way to make him stay.

"You said you wouldn't leave me. You promised."

"If I don't leave, you won't live again."

"That's not true!"

"It is. You still have your life to live and I, well… I have somewhere else I need to be. I'm getting weaker. No, don't turn away. Look at me. Admit it."

He was not as solid as before; he was fading. Still she clutched at straws.

"But we came here to be closer."

"That was your idea, not mine."

She shook her head in denial. "I heard you! When I found Skye Croft on the Internet, you said, *'That's it, that's the one.*'"

"That wasn't me."

"Who was it then?"

"You know who it was."

She stopped short. "Mally?"

"Mally," he confirmed. "And Jess, the voice that welcomed you here on your first night, do you remember?"

She did – it was a voice she'd dismissed because she didn't recognise it.

"That was Mally too."

"But why…"

"I'm not the only one looking out for you it seems."

She looked around her, half in fear, half in hope.

"Is he… is he here?"

"Not any longer."

"Where's he gone?"

"He's gone home, with Stan, with Beth and Flo. They've all gone home."

"Home? To the light?"

"To the light."

"So that's it. He's left me and now you're going to leave me too. Both of you; you're just going to float off into the bloody ether and desert me?"

In answer, he repeated his words from earlier. "You're not alone,"

"I am alone!" she protested. She wanted to scream the words at him. Scream them over and over again and never stop screaming.

"Go to him."

"Go to who?" She felt like tearing at her hair. "Why do you keep saying that?"

"Because you want to."

"I don't!"

"And I want you to."

Jessamin was incredulous. "You *want* me to?"

"Yes. Because that's how much I love you – enough to let you go."

"If you loved me you'd stay." Even to her own ears she sounded like a petulant child.

"You know I can't."

No, what he wanted was for her to reciprocate.

"I'm... I..." Coherent words refused to come.

"Jess, Maccaillin is worthy of you. I've watched him. He's a good man."

She flinched at his name. "He doesn't want me."

"He does, Jess. He needs you, and that's why I'm going."

She almost hated Maccaillin in that instant.

Almost.

"If you'd... If we'd... I never would have..."

He didn't need her to explain further. "I know. I know you wouldn't have."

"That dream..."

"Has nothing to do with anything."

He was the one who stepped forward now.

"Jess, the only way you're ever going to heal is to love again."

Love again? Risk losing everything – again?

She didn't need to say those words out loud to be heard.

"You never lose, not when you love. Love is eternal. It's what makes us who we are."

She couldn't argue with that. Because of James she'd blossomed. Throughout the years they were together he had lent her strength, substance and purpose. All the things she had already but which he'd magnified. And she'd done the same for him. Now he was asking her to give him one more thing – his freedom. Still she faltered.

"Jess," he continued, "you've got the biggest heart. There's plenty of room for two."

Absorbing his words, she took a few moments to breathe, inhaling deeply and then exhaling. Eventually she plucked up the courage to ask.

"Will I still be able to talk to you?"

"You can talk to me as much as you like. And I'll listen. But you're going to have to trust me on that. You won't be able to hear me. Not where I'm going, it's too far away."

She didn't doubt it. He'd be light years from her – across vast oceans of time and space, in another realm entirely.

She braced herself for one more question.

"When I go home—"

He interrupted her. "A long time from now."

She nodded slowly. "When I go home, a long time from now, will you be the one to meet me? Not my parents, not Maccaillin, but you?"

"I will, I promise."

That was some consolation at least.

"So, Jess, will you do it? Will you say goodbye?"

She bit down hard on her lip. "I don't have much choice, do I?"

"No." A savage word, but it was one he did his best to soften. "Goodbye, Jessamin. Live long and live hard. And don't be afraid. There's really no need."

At his words, her chest constricted. She was Jessa*mine* no more.

"I love you, James."

"I love you too."

Before he faded entirely, she called out again.

"Wait! Let me touch you, just one more time."

Complying, he held up his hand, his palm open and facing towards her. Jessamin did the same, matching her fingers one by one to his, trying to string the moment out, to get him to stay for as long as possible, even though she now accepted he couldn't.

She was touching thin air, nothing more.

"Goodbye," she whispered.

All that lay in front of her was the mantelpiece and the wall. He was gone – gone as if he'd never been there and there was nothing tangible left behind to prove otherwise. Unable to keep standing, she hunkered down on the floor, wrapped her arms tightly around herself and stayed that way for some time. Many might but she didn't doubt what she'd seen; what she'd heard. James had left her. But he left her with one thing – his blessing.

Maccaillin's name formed in her mind. *I've watched him,'* James had said. *'He's a good man. He's worthy of you.'* James wanted her to go to him. But should she? She didn't need a man to live. This past year had taught her well enough she could stand on her own two feet. But, if you wanted someone, did that make a difference? Jessamin thought it might. Did she want Maccaillin? Yes. She could no longer deny it.

Standing up straight, Jessamin wiped at her eyes and her nose.

She checked the time again. All mourners had probably left Comraich by now. Maccaillin should be alone. Or rather he *shouldn't* be alone, not tonight. She'd go to him; she'd freshen up first but then she'd go to him. See if James was right.

* * *

339

Dressed in jeans and a jumper, Jessamin pulled on her boots, grabbed her jacket and left Skye Croft behind her. The night was cold and it was black, but it was soothing also.

Instead of driving, she decided to walk to Comraich, heading across the field that led to the pine trees, the lack of light creating no hindrance. She could walk this path blindfolded if need be. She knew every step, every rock and every tree that lined the way. She heard a noise in bushes to one side of her; saw the silver glint of wild eyes – some kind of animal curious as to why a human was out and about at this hour. Jessamin smiled. She felt part of the animal's world, the world around her and the world beyond – connected once again.

Within minutes, Comraich was in front of her. From the rear windows no lights glowed. Perhaps Maccaillin was in the living room. For a moment she hesitated. Did he still hold her responsible for Stan's death? There was only one way to find out.

At the front of the house there were no lights either. Jessamin frowned. She'd already noticed his car on the driveway, indicating his presence. Was he sitting in the darkness? If so, she understood. She'd done it enough times.

The night seemed to amplify the crunch of gravel beneath her feet. At the door, she paused and looked up at the words hewn not roughly but carefully, meaningfully even, out of stone – Comraich – *Sanctuary*. She found herself hoping with all her heart it was true.

Tentatively she tested the door. It was open. She'd got used to letting herself in during her time here, but now she thought it appropriate to announce her presence first rather than sneak up on him. Tugging at the bell pull, she waited patiently but the door remained steadfastly shut. Taking a deep breath, she turned the handle.

Inside, she reached for the light switch.

"Finn," she called. "Are you here?"

No reply.

She'd try the living room first. That too was empty and very tidy with no sign that scores of people had inhabited it earlier. For a moment, she stared at Stan's worn chair, remembering the first time she'd met the old man. She had pushed her way in unbidden then as well, calling out Maccaillin's name, determined he should come and tend to the boiler at Skye Croft – a boiler that strangely enough had started working perfectly in her absence and had never faltered since. It wasn't Maccaillin who'd greeted her then, it was Stan, calling out a name too – Beth's. James said he'd been reunited with her and she hoped it was the happy, carefree Beth of his youth; that in death old wounds had healed.

Jessamin tried the kitchen next. Plates from the wake were washed and neatly stacked but not yet put away. The second living room was empty too; trestle tables that had previously held plates of food bereft of even a tablecloth. Exiting each room, she left the lights on – a deliberate gesture: it was time for the house to abandon its customary gloom.

She stood for a moment at the bottom of the staircase and then dared to venture up. Perhaps he'd gone to bed already. On the landing, she thought she heard voices – a soft, low hum interspersed with light laughter. Maccaillin and... and someone else? She listened carefully. The voices became murmurs, died down, rose up again. Had she made a terrible mistake in coming here? Was someone else busy consoling him? Maidie?

Despite the temptation to turn and run, she refrained. Tonight was about closure.

At the door to his bedroom, she knocked. There was only silence; no gasp of surprise from within; no one calling 'Who's there?' in a startled manner. Heartened, she pushed the door open and peered inside. There were no shapes on the bed either. When light filled the room, she looked around. It was the first time she'd seen where Maccaillin slept. It was a large room dominated by a king-sized bed and otherwise containing only a wardrobe and a chest of drawers. No frills at all, it was typically masculine with an air of loneliness clinging to it as it did to all the rooms. Despite this, all she could think was: *It's empty; he's not in bed with anyone.* She realised she was breathing easier again; before entering she'd barely dared to breathe at all. Crossing the landing, she checked Stan's room. Again it was empty like every other bedroom, including the one she had lain in whilst ill. Where was he?

Returning downstairs, she heard a whisper. *Who* was that? She'd checked the house thoroughly; there was no one there. Perplexed, she stood again and listened. As she did, she realised. The voices – they had nothing to do with the here and now – they were echoes from another lifetime. Ghost voices she supposed. But instead of frightening her, they made her smile. They were soothing too.

What should she do? Should she leave and go back to Skye Croft? Try again in the morning. Perhaps Maccaillin had gone to Maggie's. It was too late to head out of Glenelk tonight; to even attempt to negotiate the Rattan Pass, although she'd driven it at night once before, on the day she'd first arrived. But it wasn't the thought of the Rattan Pass that stopped her. Rather, the realisation that she didn't want to leave Maccaillin or Comraich. She loved this house – a house that no one had loved for so long. To earlier generations it had been the equivalent of a tomb, encasing them. To her it was history – *her* history and Maccaillin's; belonging to both of them. A history they could re-write.

Deciding she would wait for him, she re-entered the living room. The fire, kept burning throughout the day, was dying down until only embers glowed in the grate. Drawing from a pile of logs stacked beside it, she threw two onto the fire and set light to some paper, also stacked close by, so they'd catch. When the flames reared up, she backed into Stan's chair.

"Oh, Stan," she whispered, one hand running over the arm – the material so thin in places. "I'm going to miss you."

Her mind walked through all the rooms above again, imagining four best friends spending long rain-soaked afternoons in Stan's bedroom; talking together, laughing, but not only that – falling in love. She thought how young they'd been, Stan, Flo, Beth and her grandfather – how innocent. Looking forward to life and the promise it held.

But as much as she mourned Stan, she was happy for him. He died knowing Mally had forgiven him; was waiting for him – Mally and the rest of his friends. He was, at last, where he wanted to be; with *whom* he wanted to be. She closed her eyes again – it was as if the exhaustion of the day, the past weeks, months and years, was catching up with her. The faces of those who'd passed accompanied her into sleep and with them, the knowledge that you never 'lost' anyone. Not even when you let them go.

Chapter Thirty-Seven

"JESS, wake up, wake up."

"James?"

There was a brief moment of silence before a reply.

"It's just me I'm afraid."

Whatever she had seen on Maccaillin's face – initially hope, Jessamin was sure of it, swiftly changed. Instead, disappointment marked him; disappointment mixed in with something else, something she recognised only too well: anger. He was still so full of it.

"Maccaillin... *Finn*... I must have fallen asleep again."

She didn't bother to check how long for this time. It didn't matter. All that mattered was that she had woken, really woken, in a new place, a new life. She felt re-born.

As he started to back away from her, she sat up – struggling slightly as she'd slumped so far down. He was no longer in the Highland regalia he'd worn earlier; he was wearing once again his 'uniform' – khaki trousers and a similar coloured shirt – a man of the mountains, tall and rugged, blending perfectly with his surroundings. She watched as he turned his back on her, as one hand reached towards an impressive selection of whisky bottles kept on the sideboard. Selecting a bottle, he poured a large measure into a tumbler and downed it in one. Immediately after, he repeated this action. How much of that stuff had he drunk today? Were they his first or had he had several before? His father had been an alcoholic but she'd seen no sign of that illness in Maccaillin. To her knowledge, he was a moderate drinker, no more. But living in a place like this – especially all alone – it was enough to drive even the most devout member of the Temperance Society to drink. This house needed life; it needed laughter or it was the kind of house that turned on you.

"Where did you go?" she asked, trying to kick-start conversation.

"Just out – for a walk."

"To the loch?"

"No. Not the loch." After a brief pause, he poured another shot of whisky. "Why are you here?"

"To see you of course."

He seemed surprised.

"So I warrant a goodbye do I?"

Jessamin lowered her eyes briefly. It was true. She *had* been going to leave without saying goodbye to him. It was James who'd stopped her.

"About Stan," she ventured. "I'm so sorry…"

"This has nothing to do with Stan, leave him out of it."

As silence rained down on them, as heavy as any moorland squall, he drank yet another hefty measure of whisky. At this rate, he'd finish the bottle.

"Finn," she said, rising. "Leave the whisky alone."

At her words, he whirled round.

"Leave the whisky alone?" He almost spat the words at her. "Who do you think you are, coming into my house and issuing orders? I'll drink as much as I damn well like."

To prove his point, he discarded his glass, grabbed the bottle by the neck and guzzled at it.

"I… I didn't mean…." She was shocked. The venom in his voice was like a blow to the face.

He took a step towards her, two steps.

"You didn't mean what?" he asked.

At the same time, she stepped backwards – a part of her thinking that what they were doing, it was like some kind of strange and twisted dance.

"I came here to talk, I thought—"

"But that's just it," he said, refusing to give her a chance to elaborate. "You don't think do you – about how you make a man feel? About how you've made me feel? You don't think about anything except yourself… yourself and… and a dead man."

A dead man? He was referring to James. She had to explain.

"I saw him tonight—"

"You see him every night, Jess."

Damn, why wouldn't he let her speak? She could try and shout him down but she wasn't sure if she'd be able to. He seemed unstoppable – not just a man – but also a force of nature. Rendered mute again, she could only listen as he continued to throw words at her.

"You see him every day. You talk to him. I've heard you, on several occasions. You talk to him as if he's actually in the room with you, as if he's standing right beside you." Shaking his head as though in disgust, he added, "And I thought *I* was mad."

Mad?

"I am not mad! There is nothing wrong with talking to James, it comforted me, it's what got me through. But tonight, I did see him, I honestly did. It was incredible. A miracle! He came to see me, at Skye Croft." She faltered. Oh

God, she did sound mad. Something Maccaillin seized upon.

"See what I mean?" he cast the bottle aside as though it contained poison rather than nectar. Only she seemed to notice the thud as it hit the ground. "You walk, you talk with the dead, and now... well, now they appear to you and not just James, but your grandfather too, over at the loch. Why you bother with the living, I don't know. You've no need of them. The irony is, it's the living you *don't* see."

"That's not true." Her time with the dead was done. She wanted to live again.

"It *is* true, Jess. Your grandfather's dead. James is dead. And do you know what? You might as well be dead too."

She stared at him in disbelief. How could he say such a thing, be so cruel? He had seen how alive she was, at the fairy pools. She'd never felt so alive. The anger of lost hope – she thought she was done with it, but it came rolling back with a vengeance.

Backing away, she wanted to hurt him as he had hurt her, but how? She scrabbled around in her brain; tried to seize on something, anything, to wound him.

"You... you bastard!" she screamed at last.

It was the one thing he'd asked her not to call him; the only weapon she possessed – not the sharp instrument she'd hoped for, rather it was blunt, pitiful even.

Not waiting to gauge his reaction, she turned towards the door. If he wasn't going to listen to her, she'd leave. Come back when he was calmer, or not come back at all.

The door – where the hell was it? Even though she'd tried to suppress them, the tears in her eyes were blinding. Managing to locate it, she ran towards it and out into the hallway. As disorientated as she had been on the moor, she turned her head wildly from side to side trying to spy her quarry – the front door this time and subsequent escape. Through a blur she saw it and picked up pace, all the while thinking how ill-named this house was. Sanctuary? That was the last thing it offered.

Before she'd even registered him, Maccaillin was beside her, in front of her, blocking her exit, shouting at her.

"Jess, don't! Please."

"Get out of my way!"

Despite the fact he was so much bigger than she was, she felt she could throw him aside if she had to. In desperation, she tried and proved herself wrong. Instead his hands came up and grabbed her shoulders; forced her to stand still, his face mere inches from hers.

She could only continue to attack him with words.

"James *did* come and see me tonight and the reason he did was to say goodbye. He told me..." she faltered but only for a second. "He told me to go to you; he said that you were a good man. A man he thought I wanted; that I thought I wanted too. But I don't want you. If I'm beyond reach, so are you; but more than that, Maccaillin, you're beyond redemption."

His grip on her slackened.

"You thought you wanted me?" He looked stunned by her revelation.

"Yes. But I don't want your anger, or your despair. I don't want you waking up beside me night after night in a cold sweat, consumed with guilt. What happened to Connor, it *wasn't* your fault any more than what happened to James was mine. I know you don't like people saying that, but it's the truth. My grandfather, Stan and Beth, they made me realise that mistakes happen, but they're not premeditated, they're not meant. That's the difference, Finn – the big difference –

none of us *intended* for tragedy to happen."

"Jess, I—"

But she was far from done.

"If I'm going to try and let go of my guilt, if I'm going to make an attempt, so must you. That's the only way we're ever going to make it work."

"Make what work?" he asked tentatively.

"You and me."

Like the shift that had occurred in her, she witnessed the same happen in him. Anger seemed to flee, despair also. Hope returned; a glimmer at first, but growing stronger.

"When I came back, when I saw you, in Seanair's chair, sleeping, I thought…"

"You thought what?"

He continued as if she hadn't spoken. "But then you woke up and you called for James instead." He had to pause, take a deep breath. "I don't know, I saw red I suppose. I was angry, jealous; I don't think I've ever been jealous before. I'm so, so sorry."

She could see what a new emotion it was for him. He seemed bewildered by it.

"And what happened, with Connor; I will, Jess. I'll try and live with it."

"Yes, Finn, *live* with it. Don't let it destroy you. Even the dead don't want that." She reached out a hand and touched his face. "Feeling hollow inside, there's nothing worse."

"I don't," his voice was barely above a whisper. "Not any-more."

His hand – the damaged hand – reached up to touch her face also.

"Take off the damned eye patch," she said. This was how she'd test him.

"Jess…"

"When you're with me you don't need to wear it. Take it off."

She wasn't about to be resisted and he seemed to sense this. He did as he was told, holding it in his hands for a second, almost clinging to it, before letting it drop to the floor.

"And your shirt, take it off too."

"My shirt?" At this request he looked horrified.

"Yes."

"Here? Now? In the hallway?"

"Right here, right now. Your scars, I want to see them."

"But—"

"If it helps, I'll go first."

To prove she was serious she crossed her arms over her body and began to lift her jumper.

"No." His hand shot out to stop her. "I'll do it. Just tell me why."

"It's the final barrier between us. I want it gone."

Although still reluctant, his fingers did start to work at his buttons, but they were slow, clumsy even. Impatient, she began to help him, soon taking over entirely. Once all buttons were undone, she drew his shirt apart and exposed what he'd always tried so hard to conceal.

The bomb blast had affected the entire right side of his torso. The skin there was covered in a pattern of scars – crisscrossed, some raised, still livid looking, and others flat with an unnatural sheen to them. Without the slightest hesitance, she reached out and touched them; ran her hands the entire length and breadth of them.

When he spoke, his voice was thick with emotion. "My scars, I hate them."

"Why?" Deliberately she asked the question.

After a brief pause he revealed why. "They remind me that I failed."

She grew fierce again. "They remind *me* how brave you are. How hard you tried to save Connor, how you risked your own life in order to do just that. I love them. I love *you*."

The shift completed.

"Stay with me, Jess," he spoke urgently as though he still felt he needed to persuade her. "Live with me, here, at Comraich. Help me make it a good place to be again."

"Break the curse you mean?"

Her words brought him up short.

"It's something Maggie said," she explained.

As understanding dawned, he nodded in agreement.

"Break the curse," he said, leaning in to kiss her.

Chapter Thirty-Eight

JESSAMIN had been warned winter could be brutal in the Highlands and it was a warning that had not been issued idly. It *was* brutal. Snow, ice and temperatures falling well below minus ensured that most people kept to their houses, with what heating they had fully utilised.

Not that she was complaining.

"So," Finn said, taking a blanket from the sofa behind them and wrapping it around her bare shoulders as they sat in front of the fire glowing in the living room; the fire that they'd so recently made love by, "you're not growing bored of life in Glenelk?"

She turned her head slightly. "Bored? Chance would be a fine thing. You keep me busy enough."

"I could keep you busier still," he whispered.

"I don't doubt it," she replied, almost purring. "But we need to get some sleep. We've got an early start tomorrow."

"An early start? Why, it's Sunday, where are we going?"

"For a walk."

"A walk?" he repeated. "Where to?"

"The loch."

"In this weather? No way."

"Yes, way," she insisted. "The snow's deep but if we keep to the path we'll be okay. I want to try anyway."

Finn shifted her slightly so he could look into her eyes.

"And your reason is?"

As she stared back into the face she'd come to adore, seeing beyond what lay on the surface to the deep waters below, waters that she'd helped to calm, she smiled.

"I'll tell you tomorrow," she said, reaching up a hand to pull him closer.

* * *

The next morning she was relieved to see bright sunlight streaming into the room.

"Come on," she said, en route to the shower, "get your thermals on."

In the bed, Finn groaned.

"Really? Can't we just stay here," he said, patting the empty space beside him in what he clearly hoped was a tantalising manner.

In answer, Jessamin grabbed a long-sleeved vest from the chest of drawers and threw it onto the covers. She then made a swift exit before he could change her mind.

Less than half an hour later, they were standing outside Comraich, breathing in the cold, crisp air.

"You know I think you're mad, don't you?" Finn said, pulling him to her.

"You have told me once or twice," she replied, playfully elbowing him away.

"Once or twice? I could have sworn it was more."

Grabbing his hand, she pulled him forward.

"Come on, let's try and get to the loch and back before it starts snowing again."

"And my reward for agreeing to this will be?"

"Another fireside session," she said, laughing outright.

As they'd done months ago at the onset of summer, they walked in companionable silence. The difference now was that they were hand in hand. The other difference was they were in love. Finn had confessed that he was even then, from the minute he'd first seen her, in fact; but she hadn't been, she'd loved James. Now she loved them both.

The going was tough, the snow deep; a foot in places, two feet in others. On the surrounding hills it would be so much more. She knew he'd rather turn back, but she was determined. So different the landscape looked when it was covered in white: it was much softer. For once, the mountains in the distance didn't look brooding; they looked like noble, majestic guardians, protecting the land they presided over. Sheep no longer grazed on the hills as they'd been herded into shelter, protected.

"Are you okay, not too cold?" Finn asked, protective also.

"I'm fine," she assured him. Yes, it was cold and certainly the snow made walking an arduous task, but it wasn't far now and the sun was still very much in evidence.

Rather than waste precious energy talking, they concentrated on what they could see of the path, keeping their heads down – enduring, but in her case at least, happily so.

As the loch came into sight, relief coursed through her.

"It's still there," she said, exhaling heavily.

Finn looked bemused. "Of course it's still there. Lochs don't just disappear."

"No, I know that," she said, feigning annoyance. Even so, she had wanted to check.

Lonely. That's what the loch looked, but in the circumstances, that was a good thing. Instinctively she knew that no figures would surround it again – no *ghostly* figures that was, not even in the mists. It was lonely and it was alone and it would stay that way until children of another age, hers and Finn's perhaps, discovered it again and made it theirs. Finn came up to stand behind her, wrapping his arms around her as he'd done last night in front of the fire.

"What are you're thinking?" he asked. His breath felt warm against her skin and she relished it.

"I'm thinking I'm glad we came today."

"Tell me why."

"Because Stan never came back, not after what happened, not until his very last day. But I did. I came back, even though I said I never would; even though I hated it at one time. I came back and nothing, not the snow, the ice or the past, stopped me."

He turned her round to face him.

"Another curse broken?"

Jessamin considered his words.

"Yes, that's it, Finn, that's it exactly."

"I thought so," he said, holding her tight.

They stayed that way for several moments. She wanted to stay longer but his arms, strong though they were, weren't enough of a barrier against the cold. The sky, no longer blue, looked threatening – more snow was on its way.

Stepping back slightly, she looked up at him. "Let's go home."

"Aye, home," he repeated just as intently.

As they left the loch behind, she couldn't resist a lingering glance back. *I'll see you soon,* she promised, but right now it was sanctuary she wanted, and their lives within it.

THE END

Also by the author

Eve: A Christmas Ghost Story
(Psychic Surveys Prequel)

What do you do when a whole town is haunted?

In 1899, in the North Yorkshire market town of Thorpe Morton, a tragedy occurred; 59 people died at the market hall whilst celebrating Christmas Eve, many of them children. One hundred years on and the spirits of the deceased are restless still, 'haunting' the community, refusing to let them forget.

In 1999, psychic investigators Theo Lawson and Ness Patterson are called in to help, sensing immediately on arrival how weighed down the town is. Quickly they discover there's no safe haven. The past taints everything.

Hurtling towards the anniversary as well as a new millennium, their aim is to move the spirits on, to cleanse the atmosphere so everyone – the living and the dead – can start again. But the spirits prove resistant and soon Theo and Ness are caught up in battle, fighting against something that knows their deepest fears and can twist them in the most dangerous of ways.

They'll need all their courage to succeed and the help of a little girl too – a spirit who didn't die at the hall, who shouldn't even be there...

Psychic Surveys Book One:
The Haunting of Highdown Hall

"Good morning, Psychic Surveys. How can I help?"

The latest in a long line of psychically-gifted females, Ruby Davis can see through the veil that separates this world and the next, helping grounded souls to move towards the light - or 'home' as Ruby calls it. Not just a job for Ruby, it's a crusade and one she wants to bring to the High Street. Psychic Surveys is born.

Based in Lewes, East Sussex, Ruby and her team of freelance psychics have been kept busy of late. Specialising in domestic cases, their solid reputation is spreading - it's not just the dead that can rest in peace but the living too. All is threatened when Ruby receives a call from the irate new owner of Highdown Hall. Film star Cynthia Hart is still in residence, despite having died in 1958.

Winter deepens and so does the mystery surrounding Cynthia. She insists the devil is blocking her path to the light long after Psychic Surveys have 'disproved' it. Investigating her apparently unblemished background, Ruby is pulled further and further into Cynthia's world and the darkness that now inhabits it.

For the first time in her career, Ruby's deepest beliefs are challenged. Does evil truly exist? And if so, is it the most relentless force of all?

Psychic Surveys Book Two:
Rise to Me

"This isn't a ghost we're dealing with. If only it were that simple…"

Eighteen years ago, when psychic Ruby Davis was a child, her mother – also a psychic – suffered a nervous breakdown. Ruby was never told why. "It won't help you to know," the only answer ever given. Fast forward to the present and Ruby is earning a living from her gift, running a high street consultancy – Psychic Surveys – specialising in domestic spiritual clearance.

Boasting a strong track record, business is booming. Dealing with spirits has become routine but there is more to the paranormal than even Ruby can imagine. Someone – something – stalks her, terrifying but also strangely familiar. Hiding in the shadows, it is fast becoming bolder and the only way to fight it is for the past to be revealed – no matter what the danger.

When you can see the light, you can see the darkness too.

And sometimes the darkness can see you.

Psychic Surveys Book Three:
44 Gilmore Street

"We all have to face our demons at some point."

Psychic Surveys – specialists in domestic spiritual clearance – have never been busier. Although exhausted, Ruby is pleased. Her track record as well as her down-to-earth, no-nonsense approach inspires faith in the haunted, who willingly call on her high street consultancy when the supernatural takes hold.

But that's all about to change.

Two cases prove trying: 44 Gilmore Street, home to a particularly violent spirit, and the reincarnation case of Elisha Grey. When Gilmore Street attracts press attention, matters quickly deteriorate. Dubbed the 'New Enfield', the 'Ghost of Gilmore Street' inflames public imagination, but as Ruby and the team fail repeatedly to evict the entity, faith in them wavers.

Dealing with negative press, the strangeness surrounding Elisha, and a spirit that's becoming increasingly territorial, Ruby's at breaking point. So much is pushing her towards the abyss, not least her own past. It seems some demons just won't let go...

Psychic Surveys Book Four:
Old Cross Cottage

It's not wise to linger at the crossroads...

In a quiet Dorset Village, Old Cross Cottage has stood for centuries, overlooking the place where four roads meet. Marred by tragedy, it's had a series of residents, none of whom have stayed for long. Pink and pretty, with a thatched roof, it should be an ideal retreat, but as new owners Rachel and Mark Bell discover, it's anything but.

Ruby Davis hasn't quite told her partner the truth. She's promised Cash a holiday in the country but she's also promised the Bells that she'll investigate the unrest that haunts this ancient dwelling. Hoping to combine work and pleasure, she soon realises this is a far more complex case than she had ever imagined.

As events take a sinister turn, lives are in jeopardy. If the terrible secrets of Old Cross Cottage are ever to be unearthed, an entire village must dig up its past.

Blakemort:
A Psychic Surveys Companion Novel
(Book One)

"That house, that damned house. Will it ever stop haunting me?"

After her parents' divorce, five-year old Corinna Greer moves into Blakemort with her mother and brother. Set on the edge of the village of Whitesmith, the only thing attractive about it is the rent. A 'sensitive', Corinna is aware from the start that something is wrong with the house. Very wrong.

Christmas is coming but at Blakemort that's not something to get excited about. A house that sits and broods, that calculates and considers, it's then that it lashes out - the attacks endured over five years becoming worse. There are also the spirits, some willing residents, others not. Amongst them a boy, a beautiful, spiteful boy...

Who are they? What do they want? And is Corinna right when she suspects it's not just the dead the house traps but the living too?

Thirteen:
A Psychic Surveys Companion Novel
(Book Two)

Don't leave me alone in the dark...

In **1977**, Minch Point Lighthouse on Skye's most westerly tip was suddenly abandoned by the keeper and his family – no reason ever found. In the decade that followed, it became a haunt for teenagers on the hunt for thrills. Playing Thirteen Ghost Stories, they'd light thirteen candles, blowing one out after every story told until only the darkness remained.

In **1987**, following her success working on a case with Sussex Police, twenty-five year old psychic, Ness Patterson, is asked to investigate recent happenings at the lighthouse. Local teen, Ally Dunn, has suffered a breakdown following time spent there and is refusing to speak to anyone. Arriving at her destination on a stormy night, Ness gets a terrifying insight into what the girl experienced.

The case growing ever more sinister, Ness realises: some games should never be played.

This Haunted World Book One: The Venetian

Welcome to the asylum...

2015

Their troubled past behind them, married couple, Rob and Louise, visit Venice for the first time together, looking forward to a relaxing weekend. Not just a romantic destination, it's also the 'most haunted city in the world' and soon, Louise finds herself the focus of an entity she can't quite get to grips with – a 'veiled lady' who stalks her.

1938

After marrying young Venetian doctor, Enrico Sanuto, Charlotte moves from England to Venice, full of hope for the future. Home though is not in the city; it's on Poveglia, in the Venetian lagoon, where she is set to work in an asylum, tending to those that society shuns. As the true horror of her surroundings reveals itself, hope turns to dust.

From the labyrinthine alleys of Venice to the twisting, turning corridors of Poveglia, their fates intertwine. Vengeance only waits for so long...

This Haunted World Book Two:
The Eleventh Floor

A snowstorm, a highway, a lonely hotel…

Devastated by the deaths of her parents and disillusioned with life, Caroline Daynes is in America trying to connect with their memory. Travelling to her mother's hometown of Williamsfield in Pennsylvania, she is caught in a snowstorm and forced to stop at The Egress hotel – somewhere she'd planned to visit as her parents honeymooned there.

From the moment she sets foot inside the lobby and meets the surly receptionist, she realises this is a hotel like no other. Charming and unique, it seems lost in time with a whole cast of compelling characters sheltering behind closed doors.

As the storm deepens, so does the mystery of The Egress. Who are these people she's stranded with and what secrets do they hide? In a situation that's becoming increasingly nightmarish, is it possible to find solace?

A note from the author

If you'd like to, please subscribe to my newsletter to keep up-to-date with book releases, competitions and special offers http://eepurl.com/beoHLv or connect via my Facebook page – https://www.facebook.com/shani.struthers/ and Twitter – https://twitter.com/shani_struthers. Either way it'd be good to hear from you!

www.shanistruthers.com

Printed in June 2021
by Rotomail Italia S.p.A., Vignate (MI) - Italy